Selena felt like

All of her secrets

"So that's it?" he asked. "We kiss after all these years of friendship, and you're fine."

"Knox," she said, "you don't want me to be anything but fine. Believe me. It's better for the two of us if we just move on like nothing happened. I don't think either of us needs this right now." *Or ever.*

She wanted to hide. But she knew that if she did hide, it would only let him know how close he was delving into things she didn't want him anywhere near. Things she didn't want anyone near.

"Yeah," he said. "I guess so."

"You don't want to talk about our feelings, do you?" she asked, knowing that she sounded testy.

"Absolutely not. I've had enough feelings for a lifetime."

"I'm right there with you. I don't have any interest in messing up a good friendship over a little bit of sex."

Knox walked past her, moving back into the shop. Then he paused. "I agree with you, Selena, except for one thing. With me, there wouldn't be anything little about the sex."

Maisey Yates is a *New York Times* bestselling author of over one hundred romance novels. Whether she's writing strong, hardworking cowboys, dissolute princes or multigenerational family stories, she loves getting lost in fictional worlds. An avid knitter with a dangerous yarn addiction and an aversion to housework, Maisey lives with her husband and three kids in rural Oregon. Check out her website, maiseyyates.com, or find her on Facebook.

Melissa Senate has written many novels for Harlequin and other publishers, including her debut, *See Jane Date*, which was made into a TV movie. She also wrote seven books for Harlequin Special Edition under the pen name Meg Maxwell. Her novels have been published in over twenty-five countries. Melissa lives on the coast of Maine with her son; their rescue shepherd mix, Flash; and a lap cat named Cleo. For more information, please visit her website, melissasenate.com.

THE RANCHER'S BABY

NEW YORK TIMES BESTSELLING AUTHOR
MAISEY YATES

BESTSELLING AUTHOR COLLECTION

 Harlequin®
BESTSELLING
AUTHOR
COLLECTION

Recycling programs
for this product may
not exist in your area.

ISBN-13: 978-1-335-46949-6

The Rancher's Baby
First published in 2017. This edition published in 2025.
Copyright © 2017 by Harlequin Enterprises ULC
Special thanks and acknowledgment are given to Maisey Yates
for her contribution to the Texas Cattleman's Club: The Impostor
miniseries.

One Night with the Maverick
First published in 2022. This edition published in 2025.
Copyright © 2022 by Harlequin Enterprises ULC
Special thanks and acknowledgment are given to Melissa Senate
for her contribution to the Montana Mavericks: Brothers &
Broncos miniseries.

 Harlequin Enterprises ULC
22 Adelaide St. West, 41st Floor
Toronto, Ontario M5H 4E3, Canada
www.Harlequin.com

Printed in U.S.A.

CONTENTS

Also by Maisey Yates

The Carsons of Lone Rock

Rancher's Forgotten Rival
Best Man Rancher
One Night Rancher
Rancher's Snowed-In Reunion
A Forever Kind of Rancher

Gold Valley Vineyards

Rancher's Wild Secret
Claiming the Rancher's Heir
The Rancher's Wager
Rancher's Christmas Storm

Copper Ridge

Take Me, Cowboy
Hold Me, Cowboy
Seduce Me, Cowboy
Claim Me, Cowboy
Want Me, Cowboy
Need Me, Cowboy

Visit the Author Profile page
at Harlequin.com for more titles!

THE RANCHER'S BABY

Maisey Yates

CHAPTER ONE

My fake ex-husband died at sea and all I got was this stupid letter.

That was Selena Jacobs's very dark thought as she stood in the oppressive funeral home clutching said letter so tightly she was wearing a thumbprint into the envelope.

She supposed that her initial thought wasn't true—strictly speaking. The letter proclaimed she was the heir to Will's vast estate.

It was just that there were four other women at the funeral who had been promised the exact same thing. And Selena couldn't fathom why Will would have made her the beneficiary of anything, except maybe that hideous bearskin rug he'd gotten from his grandfather that he'd had in his dorm at school. The one she'd hated because the sightless glass eyes had creeped her out.

Yeah, that she would have believed Will had left her.

His entire estate, not so much.

But then, she was still having trouble believing Will was dead. It seemed impossible. He had always been so…so *much*. Of everything. So much energy. So much light. So much of a pain in the ass sometimes. It seemed impossible that a solemn little urn could contain everything Will Sanders had been. And yet there it was.

Though she supposed that Will wasn't entirely contained in the urn. Will, and the general fallout of his life—good and bad—was contained here in this room.

There were…well, there were a lot of women standing around looking bereft, each one of them holding letters identical to hers. Their feelings on the contents of the letters were different than hers. They must be. They didn't all run multimillion-dollar corporations.

Selena's muted reaction to her supposed inheritance was in some part due to the fact that she doubted the authenticity of the letter. But the other part was because she simply didn't need the money. Not at this point in her life.

These other women…

Well, she didn't really know. One of them was holding a chubby toddler, her expression blank. There was another in a sedate dress that flowed gently over what looked to be a burgeoning baby bump. Will had been too charming for his own good, it seemed.

Selena shuddered.

She didn't know the nature of those women's relationships to Will, but she had her suspicions. And the very idea of being left in a similar situation made her skin crawl.

There were reasons she kept men at arm's length. The vulnerability of being left pregnant was one of them. A very compelling one.

As for the other reasons? Well, every woman in this room was a living, breathing affirmation of Selena's life choices.

Heartbroken wives, ex-wives and baby mamas.

Selena might technically be an ex-wife, but she wasn't one in the traditional sense. And she wasn't heartbroken. She was hurt. She was grieving. And she was full of regret. She wished more than anything that she and Will had patched up their friendship.

But, of course, she had imagined that there was plenty of time to revive a friendship they'd left behind in college.

There hadn't been plenty of time. Will didn't have any more time.

Grief clutched at her heart and she swallowed hard, turning away from the urn to face the entry door at the back of the room.

The next visitor to walk in made her already battered heart jolt with shocked recognition.

Knox McCoy.

She really hadn't expected him to come. He had been pretty scarce for the past couple of years, and she honestly couldn't blame him. When he had texted her the other day, he'd said he wouldn't be attending the funeral, and he hadn't needed to say why.

She suspected he hadn't been to one since the one for his daughter, Eleanor.

She tried to quell the nerves fluttering in her stomach as Knox walked deeper into the room, his gray eyes locking with hers. She had known the man for more than a decade. She had made her decisions regarding him, and he...

Well, he had never felt the way about her that she did about him.

He looked as gorgeous as ever. His broad shoulders, chest and trim waist outlined perfectly in the gray custom-made suit with matching charcoal tie. His brown hair was pushed back off his forehead, longer than he used to keep it. He was also sporting a beard, which was not typical of him. He had deep grooves between his dark brows, lines worn into his handsome face by the pain of the past few years.

She wanted to go to him. She wanted to press her thumb right there at those worry lines and smooth them out. Just the thought of touching him made her feel restless. Hot.

And really, really, she needed not to be having a full-blown Knox episode at her ex-husband's funeral.

Regardless of the real nature of her relationship with Will, her reaction to Knox was inappropriate. Beyond inappropriate.

"How are you doing?" he asked, his expression full of concern.

When he made that face his eyebrows locked together and the grooves deepened.

"Oh, I've been better," she said honestly.

A lopsided smile curved the corner of his mouth upward and he reached out, his thumb brushing over her cheek. His skin was rough, his hands those of a rancher. A working man. His wealth came from the chain of upscale grocery stores he owned, but his passion was in working the land at his ranch in Wyoming.

Her gaze met his, and the blank sadness she saw in his eyes made her stomach feel hollow.

She wondered if the ranch still held his passion. She wondered if anything did anymore.

"Me, too," he said, his voice rough.

"Will is such an inconsiderate ass," she said, her voice trembling. "Leave it to him to go and die like this."

"Yeah," Knox agreed. "His timing is pretty terrible. Plus, you know he just wanted the attention."

She laughed, and as the laugh escaped her lips, a tear slid down her cheek.

She'd met Knox at Harvard. From completely different backgrounds—his small-town Texan childhood worlds away from her high-society East Coast life—they had bonded quickly. And then... Then her grandfather had died, which had ripped her heart square out of her chest. He had been the only person in her family who had ever loved her. Who had ever instilled hope in her for the future.

And with his death had come the trust fund. A trust fund she could only access when she was twenty-five. Or married.

The idea of asking Knox to marry her had been... Well, it had been unthinkable. For a whole host of reasons. She hadn't wanted to get married, not for real. And her feelings for Knox had been real. Or at least, she had known perfectly well they were on the verge of being real, and she'd needed desperately for them to stay manageable. For him to stay a friend.

Then their friend Will had seen her crying one afternoon and she'd explained everything. He had offered himself as her solution. She hadn't been in a position to say no.

Control of her money had provided freedom from her father. It had given her the ability to complete her education on her own terms. It had also ended up ruining her friendship with Will. In the meantime, Knox had met someone else. Someone he eventually married.

She blinked, bringing herself firmly back to the present. There was no point thinking about all of that. She didn't. Not often. Her friendship with Knox had survived college, and they had remained close in spite of the fact that they were both busy with their respective careers.

It was Will. Whenever Will was added to the mix she couldn't help but think of those years. Of that one stupid, reckless decision that had ended up doing a lot of damage in the end.

For some reason, she suddenly felt hollow and weak. She wobbled slightly, and Knox reached toward her as if he would touch her again. She wasn't sure that would be as fortifying as he thought it might be.

But then the doors to the funeral home opened again and she looked up at the same time Knox looked over his shoulder.

And the world stopped.

Because the person who walked through the door was the person who was meant to be in that urn.

It was Will Sanders, and he was very much alive.

Then the world really did start to spin, and Selena didn't know how to stand upright in it.

That was how she found herself crashing to the floor, and then everything was dark.

FUCKING WILL. OF course he wasn't actually dead.

That was Knox's prevailing thought as he dropped to his knees, wrapping his arm around Selena and pulling her into his lap.

No one was paying attention to one passed-out woman, because they were a hell of a lot more concerned with the walking corpse who had just appeared at his own funeral.

It was clear Will was just as shocked as everyone else.

Except for maybe Selena.

Had she loved the bastard that much? It had been more than ten years since Will and Selena had been married, and Selena rarely talked about Will, but Knox supposed he should know as well as anyone that sometimes not talking about something indicated you thought about it a whole hell of a lot.

That it mattered much more than the things that rolled off your tongue with routine frequency.

As he watched the entire room erupt in shock, Knox was filled with one dark thought.

At the last funeral he had attended he would have given everything he owned for the little body in the casket to come walking into the room. Would've given anything to wake up and find it all a nightmare.

He would have even traded places with his daughter. Would have buried himself six feet down if it would have meant Eleanor would come back.

But of course that hadn't happened. He was living a fucking soap opera at the wrong damned moment.

He looked down at Selena's gray face and cupped her cheek, patting it slightly, doing his best to revive her. He didn't know what you were supposed to do when a woman fainted. And God knew caregiving was not his strong suit.

His ex-wife would be the first to testify to that.

Selena's skin felt clammy, a light sweat beading on her brow. He wasn't used to seeing his tough-as-nails friend anything but self-assured. Even when things were terrible, she usually did what she had done only a few moments ago. She made a joke. She stood strong.

When Eleanor had died Selena had stood with him until he couldn't stand, and then she had sat with him. She had been there for him through all of that.

Apparently, ex-husbands returning from the beyond were her breaking point.

"Come on, Selena," he murmured, brushing some of her black hair out of her face. "You can wake up now. You've done a damn decent job of stealing his thunder. Anything else is just showing off at this point."

Her sooty eyelashes fluttered, and her eyes opened, her whiskey-colored gaze foggy. "What happened?"

He looked around the room, at the commotion stirring around them. "It seems Will has come back from the dead."

CHAPTER TWO

WILL WASN'T DEAD.

Selena kept playing that thought over and over in her mind as Knox drove them down the highway.

She wasn't entirely clear on what had happened to her car, or why Knox was driving her. Or what she was going to do with her car later. She had been too consumed with putting one foot in front of the other while Knox led her from the funeral home, safely ensconced her in his rental car and began to take them... Well, she didn't know where.

She slid her hand around the back of her neck, beneath her hair, her skin damp and hot against her palm. She felt awful. She felt... Well, like she had passed out on the floor of a funeral home.

"Where are we going?" she asked.

"To your place."

"You don't know where I live," she mumbled, her lips numb.

"I do."

"No, you don't, Knox. I've moved since the last time you came to visit."

"I looked you up."

Knox hadn't come back to Royal since his divorce. She couldn't blame him. There was a lot of bad wrapped up in Royal for him. Seeing as this was where he'd lived with his family most of the year when he'd been married.

"I'm not listed." She attempted to make the words sound crisp.

"You know me better than that, honey," he said, that slow Texas drawl winding itself through her veins and turning her blood into fire. "I don't need a phone book to find someone."

"Obviously, Knox. No one has used a phone book since 2004. But I meant it's not like you can just look up my address on the internet."

"Figure of speech, Selena. Also, I have connections. Resources."

She made a disgusted sound and pressed her forehead against the window. It wasn't cold enough.

"You sent me a Christmas card," he said, his tone maddeningly steady. "I added your address to my contacts."

"Well," she said. "Damn my manners. Apparently they've made me traceable."

"Not very stealthy."

"*And* you're rude," she said, ignoring him. "Because you did not send me a Christmas card back."

"I had my secretary send you something."

"What did she send me?" Selena asked.

"It was either a gold watch or a glass owl figurine," he said.

"What did she do, send you links to two different things, and then you said choose either one?"

"Yes."

"That doesn't count as a present, Knox. And it certainly doesn't equal my very personal Christmas card."

"You didn't have an assistant send the card?" he asked, sounding incredulous.

"I did not. I addressed it myself, painstakingly by hand while I was eating a TV dinner."

"A TV dinner?" he asked, chuckling. "That doesn't jibe with your healthy-lifestyle persona."

"It was a frozen dinner from Green Fair Pantry," she said pointedly, mentioning the organic fair-trade grocery store chain Knox owned. "If those aren't healthy, then you have some explaining to do yourself."

She was starting to feel a little bit more human, but along with that feeling came a dawning realization of the enormity of everything that had just happened.

"Will is alive," she said, just to confirm.

"It looks that way," Knox said, tightening his hold on the steering wheel. She did her best not to watch the way the muscles in his forearms shifted, did her best to ignore just how large his hands looked, how large *he* looked in this car that was clearly too small for him. One that he would never have driven in his real life.

Knox was much more of a pickup truck kind of man, no matter how much money he made. Little luxury vehicles were not his thing.

"I guess I don't get his bearskin rug, then," she said absently.

"What?"

"Don't you remember that appalling thing he used to have in his dorm room?"

Knox shot her a look out of the corner of his eye. "Not really. Hey, are you okay?"

"I am… I don't know. I mean, I guess I'm better than I was when I thought he was ashes in a jar." She cleared her throat. "I'm sorry. Are you okay, Knox? I realize this is probably the first—"

"I don't want to talk about that," he said, cutting her off. "We don't need to. I'm fine."

She didn't think he was. Her throat tightened, feeling scratchy. "Okay. Anyway, I'm fine, too. My relationship with Will... You know."

Except he didn't. Nobody did. Everyone *thought* they did, but everyone was wrong. Unless, of course, Will had ever talked to anyone about the truth of their marriage, but somehow she doubted it.

"How long had it been since you two had spoken?" Knox asked.

"A long damn time. I don't believe all the things Rich said to me before the divorce. Not anymore. He was toxic."

As little as she tried to think about her short, convenient marriage to Will and what had resulted after, she tried to think about Will's friend Rich Lowell even less. Though she had heard through that reliable Royal grapevine that he and Will had remained friends. It made her wonder why Rich wasn't here.

Rich had been part of their group of friends, though he had always been somewhat on the periphery, and he had been...strange, as far as Selena was concerned. He had liked Will, so much that it had been concerning. And when Will had married Selena, Rich's interest had wandered onto her.

He had never done anything terribly inappropriate, but the increased attention from him had made her uneasy.

But then... Well, he had been in their apartment one night when she'd gotten home from class. He'd pro-

duced evidence that Will was after her trust fund—
the trust fund that had led to their marriage in the first
place. And she needed that money. She needed it so she
would never be at her father's mercy again. The trust
fund had been everything to her, and Will had said he
was marrying her just to help her. She'd trusted him.

Rich had been full of some weird, intense energy
Selena hadn't been able to place at the time. Now that
she had some distance and a more adult understanding, she felt like maybe Rich had been attracted to her.
But more than a simple attraction…he'd been obsessed
with Will. It almost seemed, in hindsight, as if he'd
been attracted to her *because* he thought Will had her.

And what Rich had said that night… Well, it had
just been a lot easier to believe than Will's claim that
he wanted to help her because they were friends. Trust
had never been easy for her. Will was kind, and that
was something she'd wanted. Not because she was attracted to him, but because she had genuinely wanted
him to be a real friend. After a life of being thoroughly
mistreated by her father, hoping for true friendship
was scary.

Selena had spent most of her childhood bracing herself for the punch. Whether emotional or physical. It
was much easier to believe she was being tricked than
to believe Will was everything he appeared to be.

She and Will had fought. And then they had barely
limped to the finish line of the marriage. They'd waited
until the money was in her account, and then they'd
divorced.

And their friendship had never been the same.

She had never apologized to him. Grief and regret

stabbed her before she remembered—Will wasn't actually dead.

That means you can apologize to him. It means you can fix your friendship.

She needed to. The woman she was now would never have jumped to a conclusion like that, at least not without trying to get to the bottom of it.

But back then, Selena had been half-feral. Honed into a sharp, mean creature from years of being in survival mode.

The way Knox had stuck by her all these years, the kind of friendship he had demonstrated... It had been a huge part of her learning to trust. Learning to believe men could actually be good.

Her ability to trust hadn't changed her stance on love and marriage. And she fought against any encroaching thoughts that conflicted with that stance.

It didn't really matter that Knox sometimes made her think differently about love and marriage. He had married someone else. And she had married someone else. She had married someone else first, in point of fact. It was just that...

It didn't matter.

"I know this dredges up a lot of ancient history," Knox said, turning the car off the highway and onto the narrow two-lane road that would take them out to her new cabin. Now that she had the freedom to work remotely most of the time—her skin-care company was so successful she'd hired other people to do the parts that consumed too much time—she had decided to get outside city limits.

Had decided it was time for her to actually make herself a home, instead of living in a holding pattern.

Existing solely to build her empire, to increase her net worth.

Nothing had ever felt like home until this place. Everything after college had just been temporary. Before that, it had been a war zone.

This cabin was her refuge. And it was *hers*.

Nestled in the woods, surrounded by sweetgrass and trees, and a river running next to her front porch.

Of course, it wasn't quite as grand as Knox's spread in Jackson Hole, but then, very few places were.

Besides, grandness wasn't the point. This cabin wasn't for show. Wasn't to impress anyone else. It was just to make her happy. And few things in her life had existed for that reason up to this point.

Having achieved some happiness made her long for other things, though. Things she was mostly inured against—like wanting someone to share her life with.

She gritted her teeth, looking resolutely away from Knox as that thought invaded her brain.

"Which is now a little bit annoying," she pointed out. "He's not even dead, and I had to go through all that grief, plus, you know…"

"Thinking about your marriage?"

She snapped her mouth shut, debating how to respond. It was true enough. She had been thinking a lot about her marriage. Not that it had been an actual, physical marriage. More like roommates with official paperwork. "Yes," she said finally.

"Divorce is hell," he said, his voice turning to gravel. "Believe me. I know."

Guilt twisted her stomach. He thought they shared this common bond. The loss of a marriage. In reality, their situations weren't even close to being the same.

"Will and I were only married for a year," she commented. "It's not really the same as you and Cassandra. The two of you were together for twelve years and…"

"I told you, I don't want to talk about it."

Blessedly, distraction came in the form of the left turn that took them off the paved road and onto the gravel road that took them to her cabin.

"Why don't you get this paved?" he asked.

"I like it," she said.

"Why?"

That was a complicated question, with a complicated answer. But he was her friend and she was glad to be off the topic of marriages, so she figured she would take a stab at it. "Because it's nothing like the driveway that we had when I was growing up. Which was smooth and paved and circular, and led up to the most ridiculous brick monstrosity."

"So this is like inverse nostalgia?"

"Yes."

He lifted a shoulder. "I understand that better than you might think."

He pulled up to the front of the cabin and she stayed resolutely in her seat until he rounded to her side and opened the door for her. Then she blinked, looking up into the sun, at the way his broad shoulders blotted it out. "What about my car?" she asked.

"I'm going to have someone bring it. Don't worry."

"I could go get it," she said.

"I have a feeling it's best if you lie low for a little bit."

"Why would I do that?"

"Well," he said. "Your ex-husband just came back from the dead, and both of you cause quite a bit of media interest. You were named as beneficiary of his estate along with four other women, and that's a lot of money."

"But Will isn't dead, and I don't care about his money. I have my own."

"Very few people are going to believe that, Selena," Knox said, his tone grave. "Most people don't acknowledge the concept of having enough money. They only understand wanting more."

"What are you saying? That I'm...in danger?"

"I don't know. But we don't know what's going on with Will, and you were brought into this. You're a target, for all we know. Someone is in an urn, and you have a letter that brought you here."

"You're jumping to conclusions, Knox."

"Maybe," he said, "but I swear to God, Selena, I'd rather have you safe than end up in an urn. That, I couldn't deal with."

She looked at the deep intensity in his expression. "I'll be safe."

"You need to lie low for a while."

"What does that mean? What am I supposed to do?"

Knox shrugged, the casual gesture at odds with the steely determination in his gray eyes. "I figured I would keep you company."

CHAPTER THREE

SELENA LOOKED LESS than thrilled by the prospect of sticking close to home while the situation with Will got sorted out.

Knox didn't particularly care whether or not Selena was thrilled. He wanted her safe. As far as he was concerned, this was some shady shit, and until it was resolved, he didn't want any of it getting near her.

All of it was weird. The five women who had been presented with nearly identical letters telling them that they had inherited Will's estate, and then Will not actually being dead. The fact that someone else had been living Will's life.

Maybe none of it would touch Selena. But there was nothing half so pressing in Knox's life as his best friend's safety.

His business did not require him to micromanage it. That was the perk of making billions, as far as he was concerned. You didn't have to be in an office all the damned time if it didn't suit you.

Plus, it was all…pointless.

He shook off the hollow feeling of his chest caving in on itself and turned his focus back to Selena.

"I don't need you to stay here with me," she said, all but scampering across the lawn and to her porch.

"I need to stay here with you," he returned. He was

more than happy to make it about him. Because he knew she wouldn't be able to resist. She was worried about him. She didn't need to be. But she was. And if he played into that, then she would give him whatever he wanted.

"But it's a waste of your time," she pointed out, digging in her purse for her keys, pulling them out and jamming one of them in the lock.

"Maybe," he said. "But I swear to God, Selena, if I have to go to a funeral with a big picture of *you* up at the front of the room…"

"No one has threatened me," she said, turning the key and pushing the door open.

"And I'd rather not wait and see if someone does."

"You're being hypervigilant," she returned.

"Yes," he said. "I am." He gritted his teeth. "Some things you can't control, Selena. Some bad stuff you can't stop. But I'm not going to decide everything is fine here and risk losing you just because I went home earlier than I should have."

She looked up at him, the stubborn light in her eyes fading. "Okay. If you need to do this, that's fine."

Selena walked into the front entrance of the cabin and threw her purse down on an entryway table. Typical Selena. There was a hook right above the table, but she didn't hang the purse up. No. That extra step would be considered a waste of time in her estimation. Never mind that her disorganization often meant she spent extra time looking for things.

He looked around the spacious, bright room. It was clean. Surprisingly so.

"This place is… It's nice. Spotless."

"I have a housekeeper," she said, turning to face

him, crossing her arms beneath her breasts and offering up a lopsided smile.

For a moment, just a moment, his eyes dipped down to examine those breasts. His gut tightened and he resolutely turned his focus back to her eyes. Selena was a woman. He had known that for a long time. But she wasn't a woman whose breasts concerned him. She never had been.

When they had met in college he had thought she was beautiful, sure. A man would have to be blind not to see that. But she had also been brittle. Skittish and damaged. And it had taken work on his part to forge a friendship with her.

Once he had become her friend, he had never wanted to do anything to compromise that bond. And if he had been a little jealous of Will Sanders somehow convincing her that marriage was worth the risk, Knox had never indulged that jealousy.

Then Will had hurt her, devastated her, divorced her. And after that, Selena had made her feelings about relationships pretty clear. Anyway, at that point, he had been serious about Cassandra, and then they had gotten married.

His friendship with Selena outlasted both of their marriages, and had proved that the decision he'd made back in college, to not examine her breasts, had been a solid one.

One he was going to hold to.

"Well, thank God for the housekeeper," he said, his tone dry. "Living all the way out here by yourself, if you didn't have someone taking care of you you'd be liable to die beneath a pile of your own clothes."

She huffed. "You don't know me, Knox."

"Oh, honey," he said, "I do."

A long, slow moment stretched between them and her olive skin was suddenly suffused with color. It probably wasn't nice of him to tease her about her propensity toward messiness. "Well," she said, her tone stiff. "I do have a guest room. And I suppose it would be unkind of me to send you packing back to Wyoming on your first night here in Royal."

"Downright mean," he said, schooling his expression into one of pure innocence. As much as he could manage.

It occurred to him then that the two of them hadn't really spent much time together in the past couple of years. And they hadn't spent time alone together in the past decade. He had been married to another woman, and even though his friendship with Selena had been platonic, and Cassandra had never expressed any jealousy toward her, it would have been stretching things a bit for him to spend the night at her place with no one else around.

"Well," she said, tossing her glossy black hair over her shoulder. "I am a little mean."

"Are you?"

She smiled broadly, the expression somewhere between a grin and a snarl. "It has been said."

"By who?" he asked, feeling instantly protective of her. She had always brought that out in him. Even though now it felt like a joke, that he could feel protective of anyone. He hadn't managed to protect the most important people in his life.

"I wasn't thinking of a particular incident," she responded, wandering toward the kitchen, kicking her shoes off as she went, leaving them right where she stepped out of them, like fuchsia afterthoughts.

"Did Will say you were mean?"

She turned to face him, cocking one dark brow. "Will didn't have strong feelings for me one way or the other, Knox. Certainly not in the time since the divorce." She began to bustle around the kitchen, and he leaned against the island, placing his hand on the high-gloss marble countertop, watching as she worked with efficiency, getting mugs and heating water. She was making tea, and she wasn't even asking him if he wanted any. She would simply present him with some. And he wouldn't drink it, because he didn't like tea.

A pretty familiar routine for the two of them.

"He put you pretty firmly off of marriage," Knox pointed out, "so I would say he's also not completely blameless."

"You're not supposed to speak ill of the dead. Or the undead, in Will's case."

He drummed his fingers on the counter. "You know, that does present an interesting question."

"What question is that?"

"Who died?" he asked.

"What do you mean?"

"There were ashes in that urn. Obviously they weren't Will's. But if he's not dead, then who is?"

Selena frowned. "Maybe no one's dead. Maybe it's ashes from a campfire."

"Why would someone go to all that trouble? Why would somebody go to that much trouble to fake Will's death? Or to fake anyone's death? Again, I think this has something to do with those letters. With all of the women in his life being made beneficiaries of his estate. And this is why I'm not leaving you here by yourself."

"Because you're a high-handed, difficult, surly, obnoxious…"

"Are you finished?"

"Just a second," she said, taking her kettle off the stove and pouring hot water into two of the mugs on the counter. "Irritating, overbearing…"

"Wealthy, handsome, incredibly generous."

"Yes, it's true," she said. "But I prefer beautiful to handsome. I mean, I assume you were offering up descriptions of me."

She shoved a mug in his direction, smiling brilliantly. He did not tell her he didn't want any. He did not remind her that he had told her at least fifteen times over the years that he did not drink tea. Instead, he curled his fingers around the mug and pulled it close, knowing she wouldn't realize he wasn't having any.

It was just one of her charming quirks. The fact that she could be totally oblivious to what was happening around her. Cast-off shoes in the middle of her floor were symptoms of it. It wasn't that Selena was an airhead; she was incredibly insightful, actually. It was just that her head seemed to continually be full of thoughts about what was next. Sometimes, all that thinking made it hard to keep her rooted in the present.

She rested her elbows on the counter, then placed her chin in her palms, looking suddenly much younger than she had only a moment ago. Reminding him of the girl he had known in college.

And along with that memory came an old urge. To reach out, to brush her hair out of her face, to trace the line of her lower lip with the edge of his thumb.

To take a chance with all of her spiky indignation and press his mouth against hers.

Instead, he lifted his mug to his lips and took a long drink, the hot water and bitterly acidic tea burning his throat as he swallowed.

He really, really didn't like tea.

"You know," she said, tapping the side of her mug, straightening. "I do have a few projects you could work on around here. If you're going to stay with me."

"You're putting me to work?"

"Yes. If you're going to stay with me, you need to earn your keep."

"I'm earning my keep by guarding you."

"From a threat you don't even know exists."

"I know a few things," he said, holding up his hand and counting off each thing with his fingers. "I know someone is dead. I know you are mysteriously named as a beneficiary of a lot of money, as are a bunch of other women."

"And one assumes that we are no longer going to inherit any money since Will isn't dead."

"But someone wanted us all to think that he was. Hell, maybe somebody wanted him to be dead."

"Are you a private detective now? The high-end health-food grocery-chain business not working out for you?"

"It's working out for me very well, actually. Which you know. And don't change the subject."

A smile tugged at the corner of her mouth.

He was genuinely concerned about her well-being; he wasn't making that up. But there was something else, too. Something holding him here. Or maybe it was just something keeping him from going back to

Wyoming. He had avoided Royal, and Texas altogether, since his divorce. Had avoided going anywhere that reminded him of his former life. He'd owned the ranch in Jackson Hole for over a decade, but he, Cassandra and Eleanor hadn't spent as much time there as they had here.

Still, for some reason, now that he was back, the idea of returning to that gigantic ranch house in Wyoming to rattle around all by himself didn't seem appealing.

There was a reason he had gotten married. A reason he and Cassandra had started a family. It was what he had wanted. An answer to his lifetime of loneliness. To the deficit he had grown up with. He had wanted everything. A wife, children, money. All of those things that would keep him from feeling like he had back then.

But he had learned the hard way that children could be taken from you. That marriages crumbled. And that money didn't mean a damn thing in the end.

If he'd had a choice, if the universe would have asked him, he would have given up the money first.

Of course, he hadn't realized that until it was too late.

Not that there was any fixing it. Not that there had been a choice. Cancer didn't care if you were a billionaire.

It didn't care if a little girl was your entire world.

Now all he had was a big empty house. One that currently had an invitation to a charity event on the fridge. An invitation he just couldn't deal with right now.

He looked back up at Selena. Yeah, staying here for a few days was definitely more appealing than heading straight back to Jackson Hole.

"Okay," he said. "What projects did you have in mind?"

HE NEVER SAID he didn't like tea.

That was Selena's first thought when she got up the next morning and set about making coffee for Knox and herself. Selena found it singularly odd that he never refused the tea. She served it to him sometimes just to see if he would. But he never did. He just sat there holding it. Which was funny, because Knox was not a passive man. Far from it.

In fact, in college, he had been her role model for that reason. He was authoritative. He asked for what he wanted. He went for what he wanted. And Selena had wanted to remake herself in his mold. She'd found him endlessly fascinating.

Though she had to admit, as she bustled around the kitchen, he was just as fascinating now. But now she had a much firmer grasp on what she wanted. On what was possible.

She had felt a little weird about him staying with her at first, which was old baggage creeping in. Old feelings. That crush she'd had on him in college that had never had a hope in hell of going anywhere. Not because she thought it was impossible for him to desire her, but because she knew there was no future in it. And she needed Knox as a friend much more than she needed him as a…well…the alternative.

But then last night, as they had been standing in the kitchen, she had looked at him. Really looked at him. Those lines between his brows were so deep, and his eyes were so incredibly…changed. Physically, she supposed he kind of looked the same, and yet he didn't. He was reduced. And it was a terrible thing to see a man like him reduced. But she couldn't blame him.

What happened with Eleanor had been such a shock. Such a horrible, hideous shock.

One day, she had been a normal, healthy toddler, and then she had been lethargic. Right after that came the cancer diagnosis, and in only a couple of months she was gone.

The entire situation had been surreal and heart-breaking. For her. And Eleanor wasn't even her child. But her friend's pain had been so real, so raw... She had no idea how he had coped with it, and now she could see that he hadn't really. That he still was try-ing to cope.

He hadn't come back to Texas since Eleanor's death, and she had seen him only a couple of times. At the funeral. And then when she had come to Jackson Hole in the summer for a visit. Otherwise...it had all been texts and emails and quick phone conversations.

But now that he was back in Texas, he seemed to need to stay for a little while, and she was happy for him to think it was for her. Happy to be the scapegoat so he could work through whatever emotional thing he needed to work through. Knox, in the past, would have been enraged at the assessment that he needed to work through anything emotionally. He was such a stoic guy, always had been.

But she knew he wouldn't even pretend there wasn't lingering damage from the loss of his little girl. Selena had watched him break apart completely at Eleanor's funeral. They had never talked about it again. She didn't think they ever would. But then, she supposed they didn't need to. They had shared the experience. That moment when he couldn't be strong anymore. When there was no child to be strong for, and when his wife had been off with her family, and there had simply been no reason for him to remain standing upright. Selena had been there for that moment.

If all the years of friendship hadn't bonded them, that moment would have done it all on its own.

Just thinking of it made her chest ache, and she shook off the feeling, going over to the coffee maker to pour herself a cup.

She wondered if Knox was still sleeping. He was going to be mad if he missed prime caffeination time.

She wandered out of the kitchen and into the living room just as the door to the guest bedroom opened and Knox walked out, pulling his T-shirt over his head—but not quickly enough. She caught a flash of muscled, tanned skin and…chest hair. Oh, the chest hair. Why was that compelling enough to stop her in her tracks? She didn't even have a moment to question it. She was too caught up. Too beset by the sight.

Genuinely. She was completely immobilized by the sight of her best friend's muscles.

It wasn't like she had never seen Knox shirtless before. But it had been a long time. And the last time, he had most definitely been married.

Not that she had forgotten he was hot when he was married to Cassandra. It was just that…he had been a married man. And that meant something to Selena. Because it meant something to him.

It had been a barrier, an insurmountable one, even bigger than that whole long-term friendship thing. And now it wasn't there. It just wasn't. He was walking out of the guest bedroom looking sleep rumpled and entirely too lickable. And there was just…nothing stopping them from doing what men and women did.

She'd had a million excuses for *not* doing that. For a long time. She didn't want to risk entanglements, didn't want to compromise her focus. Didn't want to risk pregnancy. Didn't have time for a relationship.

But she was in a place where those things were less of a concern. This house was symbolic of that change in her life. She was making a home. And making a home made her want to fill it. With art, with warmth, with knickknacks that spoke to her. With people.

She wondered, then. What it would be like to actually live with a man? To have one in her life? In her home? In her bed?

And just like that she was fantasizing about Knox in her bed. That body she had caught a glimpse of relaxing beneath her emerald green bedspread, his hands clasped behind his head, a satisfied smile on his face...

She sucked in a sharp breath and tried to get a hold of herself. "Coffee is ready," she said, grinning broadly, not feeling the grin at all.

"Good," he said, his voice rough from sleep.

It struck her then, just what an intimate thing that was. To hear someone's voice after they had been sleeping.

"Right this...way," she said, awkwardly beating a path into the kitchen, turning away from him quickly enough that she sloshed coffee over the edge of her cup.

"You have food for breakfast?" he asked, that voice persistently gravelly and interesting, and much less like her familiar friend's than she would like it to be. She needed some kind of familiarity to latch on to, something to blot out the vision of his muscles. But he wasn't giving her anything.

Jerk.

"No," she said, keeping her voice cheery. "I have coffee and spite for breakfast."

"Well, that's not going to work for me."

"I'm not sure what to tell you," she said, flinging open one of her cabinets and revealing her collection of cereal and biscotti. "Of course I have food for breakfast."

"Bacon? Eggs?"

"Do I look like a diner to you?" she asked.

"Not you personally. But I was hoping that your house might have more diner-like qualities."

"No," she said, opening up the fridge and rummaging around. "Well, what do you know? I *do* have eggs. And bacon. I get a delivery of groceries every week. From a certain grocery store."

He smiled, a lopsided grin that did something to her stomach. Something she was going to ignore and call hunger, because they were talking about bacon, and being hungry for bacon was much more palatable than being hungry for your best friend.

"I'll cook," he said.

"Oh no," she said, getting the package of bacon out of the fridge and handing it to Knox before bending back down and grabbing the carton of eggs and placing that in his other hand. "You don't have to cook."

"Why do I get the feeling that I really do have to cook?"

She shrugged. "It depends on whether you want bacon and eggs."

"Do you not know how to cook?"

"I know how to cook," she said. "But the odds of me actually cooking when I only have half of a cup of coffee in my system are basically none. Usually,

I prefer to have sweets for breakfast. Hence, biscotti and breakfast cereals. However, I will sometimes eat bacon and eggs for dinner. Or I will eat bacon and eggs for breakfast if a handsome man fixes them for me."

He lifted a brow. "Oh, I see. So you have this in your fridge for when a man spends the night."

"Obviously. Since a man did just spend the night." Her face flushed. She knew exactly what he was imagining. And really, he had no idea.

That was not why she had the bacon and eggs. She had the bacon and eggs because sometimes she liked an easy dinner. But she didn't really mind if Knox thought she had more of a love life than she actually did.

Of course, now they were thinking about that kind of thing at the same time. Which was…weird. And possibly responsible for the strange electric current arcing between them.

"I'll cook," he said, breaking that arc and moving to the stove, getting out pans and bowls, cracking eggs with an efficiency she admired.

"Do you have an assignment list for me?" he asked, picking up the bowl and whisking the eggs inside.

Why was that sexy? What was happening? His broad shoulders and chest, those intensely muscled forearms, somehow seeming all the more masculine when he was scrambling eggs, of all things.

There was something about the very domestic action, and she couldn't figure out what it was. Maybe it was the contrast between masculinity and domesticity. Or maybe it was just because there had never been a man in her kitchen making breakfast.

She tried to look blasé, as though men made her breakfast every other weekend. After debauchery. Lots and lots of debauchery. She had a feeling she wasn't quite managing blasé, so she just took a sip of her coffee and stared at the white star that hung on her back wall, her homage to the Lone Star State. And currently, her salvation.

"Assignment list," she said, slamming her hands down on the countertop, breaking her reverie. She owed that star a thank-you for restoring her sanity. She'd just needed a moment of not looking at Knox. "Well, I want new hardware on those cabinets. The people who lived here before me had a few things that weren't really to my taste. That is one of them. Also, there are some things in an outbuilding the previous inhabitants left, and I want them moved out. Oh, and I want to get rid of the ceiling fan in the living room."

"I hope you're planning on paying me for this," he said, dumping the eggs into the pan, a sizzling sound filling the room.

"Nope," she said, lifting her coffee mug to her lips.

Knox finished cooking, and somehow Selena managed not to swoon. So, that was good.

They didn't bother to go into her dining room. Instead they sat at the tall chairs around the island, and Selena looked down at her breakfast resolutely.

"Are you okay?"

"What?" She looked up, her eyes clashing with Knox's. "You keep asking me that."

"Because you keep acting like you might not be."

"Are you okay?"

"I'm alive," he responded. "As to being okay…that's not really part of my five-year plan."

"What's your five-year plan?"

"Not drink myself into a stupor. Keep my business

running, because at some point I probably will be glad I still have it. That's about it."

"Well," she said softly, "you can add replacing my kitchen hardware to your five-year plan. But I would prefer it be on this side of it, rather than the back end."

He laughed, and she found that incredibly gratifying. Without thinking, she reached out and brushed her fingertips against his cheek, against his beard. She drew back quickly, wishing the impression of that touch would fade away. It didn't.

"Yes?" he asked.

"Are you keeping the beard?"

"It's not really a fashion statement. It's more evidence of personal neglect."

"Well, you haven't neglected your whole body," she said, thinking of that earlier flash of muscle. She immediately regretted her words. She regretted them more than she did touching his beard. And beard-touching was pretty damned inappropriate between friends. At least, she was pretty certain it was.

He lifted a brow and took a bite of bacon. "Elaborate."

"I'm just saying. You're in good shape, Knox. I noticed."

"Okay," he said slowly, setting the bacon down. His gray eyes were cool as they assessed her, but for some reason she felt heat pooling in her stomach.

Settle down.

Her body did not listen. It kept on being hot. And that heat bled into her cheeks. So she knew she was blushing brilliant rose for Knox's amusement.

"I'm just used to complimenting the men who make

me breakfast," she said, doing her best to keep her voice deadpan.

"I see."

"So."

"So," he responded. "There's nothing to do other than work," he said. "Lifting hay bales, fixing fences, basically throwing heavy things around on the ranch. Then going back into the house and working out in the gym. It's all I do."

Well, that explained a few things. "I imagine you could carve out about five minutes to shave."

"Would you prefer that I did?"

"I don't have an opinion on your facial hair."

"You seem to have an opinion on my facial hair."

"I really don't. I had observations about your facial hair, but that's an entirely different thing."

"Somehow, I don't think it is."

"Well, you're entitled to your opinion. About my opinion on your facial hair. Or my lack of one. But that doesn't make it fact."

He shook his head. "You know, if I had you visiting in Jackson Hole I probably wouldn't work out so excessively. Your chatter would keep me busy."

"Hey," she said. "I don't chatter. I'm making conversation." Except, it sounded a whole lot like chatter, even to herself.

"Okay."

She made a coughing sound and stood up, taking her mostly empty plate to the sink and then making her way back toward the living room, stepping over her discarded high heels from yesterday. She heard the sound of Knox's bare feet on the floor behind her. And suddenly, the fact that he had bare feet seemed intimate.

You really have been a virgin for too long.

She grimaced, even as she chastised herself. She hated that word. She hated even thinking it. It implied a kind of innocence she didn't possess. Also, it felt young. She was not particularly young. She had just been busy. Busy, and resolutely opposed to relationships.

Still, the whole virginity thing had the terrible side effect of making rusty morning voices and bare feet seem intimate.

She looked up and out the window and saw her car in the driveway. "Hey," she said. "How did that happen?"

"I told you I was going to take care of it. Ye of little faith."

"Apparently, Knox, you can't even take care of your beard, so why would I think you would take care of my car so efficiently?"

"Correction," he said. "I don't bother to make time to shave my beard. Why? Because I don't *have* to. Because I'm not beholden to anyone anymore."

Those words were hollow, even though he spoke them in a light tone. And no matter how he would try and spin it, he didn't feel it was a positive thing. It seemed desperately sad that nobody in his life cared whether or not he had a beard.

"I like it," she said finally.

She did. He was hot without one, too. He had one of those square Hollywood jaws and a perfectly proportioned chin. And if asked prior to seeing him with the beard, she would have said facial hair would have been like hiding his light under a bushel.

But in reality, the beard just made him look…more masculine. Untamed. Rugged. Sexy.

Yes. Sexy.

She cleared her throat. "Anyway," she said. "I won't talk about it anymore."

Suddenly, she realized Knox was standing much closer to her than she'd been aware of until a moment ago. She could smell some kind of masculine body wash and clean, male skin. And she could feel the heat radiating from his body. If she reached out, she wouldn't even have to stretch her arm out to press her palm against his chest. Or to touch his beard again, which she had already established was completely inappropriate, but she was thinking about it anyway.

"You like it?" he asked, his voice getting rougher, even more than it had been this morning when he had first woken up.

"I… Yes?"

"You're not sure?"

"No," she said, taking a step toward him, her feet acting entirely on their own and without permission from her brain. "No, I'm sure. I like it."

She felt weightless, breathless. She felt a little bit like leaning toward him and seeing what might happen if she closed that space between them. Seeing how that beard might feel if it was pressed against her cheek, what it might feel like if his mouth was pressed against hers…

She was insane. She was officially insane. She was checking out her friend. Her grieving friend who needed her to be supportive and not lecherous.

She shook her head and took a step back. "Thank you," she said. Instead of kissing him. Instead of doing anything crazy. "For making sure the car got back to me. Really, thank you for catching me when I passed out yesterday. I think I'm still...you know."

"No," he said, crossing his muscular arms over his broad chest. "I'm not sure that I do know."

Freaking Knox. Not helping her out at all. "I think I'm still a little bit spacey," she said.

"Understandable. Hey, direct me to your hardware, and I'll get started on that."

Okay, maybe he was going to help her out. She was going to take that lifeline with both hands. "I can do that," she said, and she rushed to oblige him.

CHAPTER FOUR

KNOX WAS ALMOST completely finished replacing the hardware in Selena's kitchen when the phone in his pocket vibrated. He frowned, the number coming up one he didn't recognize.

He answered it and lifted it to his ear. "Knox McCoy," he said.

"Hi there, Knox" came the sound of an older woman's voice on the other end of the line. She had a thick East Texas drawl and a steel thread winding through the greeting that indicated she wasn't one to waste a word or spare a feeling. "I'm Cora Lee. Will's stepmother. I'm not sure if he's ever mentioned me."

"Will and I haven't been close for the past decade or so," he said honestly. Really, the falling-out between Will and Selena had profoundly affected his friendship with the other man.

In divorces, friends chose sides. And his side had always clearly been Selena's.

"Still," Cora Lee said, "there's nothing like coming back from the dead to patch up old relationships. And, on that subject, I would like to have a small get-together to celebrate Will's return, just for those of us who were at the service. You can imagine that we're all thrilled."

If she was thrilled, Knox wouldn't have been able to tell by her tone of voice. She was more resolute. Determined. And he had a feeling that refusing her would be a lot like saying no to a drill sergeant.

"It will be kind of like a funeral, only celebrating that he's not dead. And you'll be invited. He said he wanted you to come."

"He did?"

"Not in so many words, but I feel like it is what he wants." And Knox had a feeling it wouldn't matter if Will did want it or not. Cora Lee was going to do exactly what she thought was best. "And he wants that ex-wife of his to come, too. He says you two are close."

"Which ex-wife?" He had gotten the distinct impression that there was more than one former Mrs. Sanders floating around.

"The one you're close to," Cora Lee responded, her voice deadpan.

Reluctantly, Knox decided he liked Will's stepmother. "Well, I'll let her know. She went to the funeral, so I imagine she'll want to go to this." He wasn't sure he particularly wanted to, but if Selena was going, then he would accompany her. He was honestly concerned that the other women who had been named beneficiaries, or whoever was responsible for sending the letter, might take advantage of a situation like this.

"Good. I'll put you both down on the guest list, and I'll send details along shortly. You have to come, because I wrote your names down and there will be too much brisket if you don't."

And with that, she hung up the phone. He looked down at the screen for a moment, and then Selena came in, her footsteps soft on the hardwood floor.

He looked up and his stomach tightened. Her long black hair was wet, as though she'd gotten out of the

shower, and he suddenly became very aware of the fact
that her gray T-shirt was clinging to her curves a little
bit more than it might if her skin wasn't damp. Which
put him in mind to think about the fact that her skin
was damp, which meant it had been uncovered only a
few moments before.

What the hell was wrong with him? He was thinking like a horny teenager. Yeah, it had been a few years
since he'd had sex, but frankly, he hadn't wanted to.
His libido had been hibernating, along with his desire
to do basic things like shave his beard.

But somehow it seemed to be stirring to life again,
and it was happening at a very inappropriate time, with
an inappropriate person.

The good thing was that it must be happening around
Selena because she was the only woman in proximity,
and it was about time he started to feel again. The bad
thing was... Selena was the only woman in proximity.

"Who was that on the phone?" she asked, running
her fingers through her hair.

"Will's stepmother. She wants us to go to a non-
funeral for him in a few days."

"Oh."

She was frowning, a small crinkle appearing on her
otherwise smooth forehead.

"Something wrong?"

"No. It's a good thing. I'm glad to be asked. I mean, I
was thinking, when I assumed he was dead, that it was
so sad he and I had never...that we had never found a
way to fix our friendship."

"You want to do that?" He was surprised.

"It seems silly to stay mad at somebody over something that happened so long ago. Something I know neither of us would change."

"The marriage?"

She laughed. "The divorce. I don't regret the divorce, so there's really no point in being upset about it. Or avoiding him forever because of it. I mean, obviously there was conflict surrounding it." She looked away, a strange, tight expression on her face. "But if neither of us would go back and change the outcome, I don't see why we can't let it go. I would like to let it go. It was terrible, thinking he was dead and knowing we had never reconciled."

Knox pressed his hand to his chest and rubbed the spot over his heart. It twinged a little. But that was nothing new. It did that sometimes. At first, he had thought he was having a heart attack. But then, in the beginning, it had been much worse. Suffocating, deep, sharp pain.

Something that took his breath away.

No one had ever told him that grief hurt. That it was a physical pain. That the depression that lingered on after would hurt all the way down to your bones. That sometimes you would wake up in the middle of the night and not be able to breathe.

Those were the kinds of things people didn't tell you. But then, there was no guidebook for loss like he had experienced. Actually, there was. There were tons of books about it. But there had been no reason in hell for him to go out and buy one. Not before it had happened, and then when Eleanor had gotten sick, he hadn't wanted to do doomsday preparation for the loss he still didn't want to believe was inevitable.

Afterward…

He was in the shit whether he wanted to be or not. So he didn't see the point of trying to figure out a way to navigate more elegantly through it. Shit was shit. There was no dressing it up.

There was just doing your best to put one foot in front of the other and walk on through.

But he had walked through it alone, and in the end that had been too much for him and Cassandra. But he hadn't known how to do it with another person. Hadn't really wanted to.

Hadn't known how he was supposed to look at the mother of his dead child and offer her comfort, tell her that everything was going to be okay, that *anything* was going to be okay.

But now they had disentangled themselves from each other, and still this thing Selena was talking about, this desire for reconciliation, just didn't resonate with him. He didn't want to talk to Cassandra. It was why they were divorced.

"It's not the same thing," she said, her voice suddenly taking on that soft, careful quality that appeared in people's tones when they were dancing around the subject of his loss. "Mine and Will's relationship. It's not the same as yours and Cassandra's. It's not the same as your divorce. Will and I were married for a year. We were young, we were selfish and we were stupid. The two of you… You built a life together. And then you lost it. You went through hell. It's just not the same thing. So don't think I'm lecturing you subtly on how you should call her or something."

"I didn't think that."

"You did a little. Or you were making yourself feel

guilty about it, and that isn't fair. You don't deserve that."

She was looking at him with a sweet, freshly scrubbed openness that made his stomach go tight. Made him want to lift up his coffee mug and throw it down onto the tile, just to make the feeling stop. Made him want to grab hold of her face, hold her steady and kiss her mouth. So she would shut up. So she would stop being so understanding. So she would stop looking at him and seeing him. Seeing inside of him.

That thought, hot and destructive, made his veins feel full of fire rather than blood. And he wasn't sure anymore what his motivation actually was. To get her to stop, or to just exorcise the strange demon that seemed to have possessed him at some point between the moment he had held her in his arms on the floor of the funeral home and when they had come back here.

He had his life torn apart once, and he wasn't in a hurry to tear up the good that was left. At least, that was what he would have said, but this destructive urge had overtaken him. And his primary thought was to either break something or grab hold of her.

He needed to do more manual labor. Obviously.

"I'm not sure you're in a great position to speak about what I do and don't deserve," he said, the words coming out harder than he'd intended.

"Except you're here at my house because you want to protect me, and you just replaced all my cabinet hardware, and it looks amazing. So I guess I would say you deserve pretty good things, since you're obviously a pretty good guy."

"Cabinet hardware isn't exactly a ringing endorsement on character," he said.

He needed to get some distance between them, because he was being a dick. It was uncalled-for. Selena wasn't responsible for his baggage. Not for making him feel better about it, not for carrying any of the weight.

"What about the work you need done outside?" he asked.

"Sorting through the shed. But we're going to need a truck for that."

"Do you have one?"

"I actually do. But I don't drive it very much."

"Why do you have a truck?"

"Extravagance?"

He didn't believe her, since Selena didn't do much for the sake of extravagance. If she had wanted to do something extravagant, he knew she could've gotten herself a big McMansion in town. Some eyesore at the end of a cul-de-sac. God knew she made enough money with that skin-care line of hers. But instead she had buried herself out here in the boonies, gotten herself this little cabin that wouldn't be extravagant by anyone's standard.

"To try and make friends," she said. "It's really helpful when you have something for people to use when they move. You'd be surprised how popular it makes you."

"Honey, this is Texas. I don't think there are enough people around without a pickup for that to be true."

"You'd be surprised," she said. "And my best friend hasn't been back to Texas in so long that I had to resort to making new friends any way I could."

Now she was making him feel guilty. As if he didn't already feel guilty about the illicit thoughts he'd just had about her.

"Well, you're probably better off," he said, keeping his tone light, brushing past her and heading out the front door.

To his chagrin, she followed him, scampering like a woodland creature out onto the porch behind him. "I don't know about that."

"Do you have the keys to the truck?"

"I can grab them," she said.

For some reason, he had a feeling she was stalling, and he couldn't figure out why. "Can I have them?"

"How about I go with you?"

"Don't you have other things to do? As you reminded me yesterday, you have your own money, and therefore don't need Will's estate, because you're a multimillionaire. Not from nothing, though. You actually run a giant business."

"We both do. And yet here we are. I can afford to take some time off to visit with you, Knox."

That made him feel like an ass. Because he was trying to put some distance between them.

All you do is put distance between yourself and people these days.

Well, he could do without that cutting observation from his own damn self.

"Fine." He didn't mean to grunt the word, but he did, and Selena pretended to ignore it as she went back in the house, reappearing a minute later with keys dangling from her fingertips.

She was grinning, to compensate for his scowl, he had a feeling.

"I will direct you to the truck," she said, keeping that grin sparkly and very much in place.

"You made it sound like you had an old pickup truck

lying around," he said when they approached the shiny red and very new vehicle parked out back.

"I told you I bought it partly for extravagance. I couldn't resist."

Unlike himself, Selena had actually grown up with money, but he had always gotten the feeling her father had kept a tight leash on her. So whatever cash had been at her disposal hadn't really been hers; her life hadn't really been hers.

In contrast, he had grown up with nothing.

No support. No parent who had even bothered to try and be controlling, because they hadn't cared enough.

All in all, it was tough to say which of them had had it worse.

"Just because?"

"Because I do what I want," she said, confirming his earlier thought.

"Yes, you certainly do," he said.

She always had. From going to school, starting her own business, marrying Will when it had seemed like such a crazy thing to do. They had still been at Harvard at the time, and he hadn't seen the damned point in rushing anything.

But she had been determined. And when Selena Jacobs was determined, there was no stopping her.

"I'll drive," she said.

He reached out and snatched the keys from her hand. "I'll drive."

"It's my truck," she protested.

He paused, leaning down toward her, ignoring the tightening feeling in his stomach. And lower. "And I'm the man, baby."

She laughed in his face. He deserved it, he had to admit. But he was still fucking driving.

"That does not mean you get to drive."

"In this case it does," he said, jerking open the passenger-side door and holding it for her.

She gave him the evil eye, but got into the truck, sitting primly and waiting for him to close the door.

He rounded to the driver's side and got in, looking down at the cup holders, both of which contained two partly finished smoothies of indeterminate age. "Really?" he asked, looking down at the cups.

"I have a housekeeper," she said. "Not a truck keeper."

He grunted. "Now, where am I going?"

"You should have let me drive," she said, leaning toward him. And suddenly, it felt like high school. Being in the cab of the truck with a girl who made it difficult to breathe, knowing what he wanted to do next and knowing that he probably couldn't.

Except back then, he would have done the ill-advised thing. The dick-motivated thing. Because back then he didn't think too far ahead.

Well, except for two things. Getting the grades he needed for a scholarship to Harvard and getting laid.

Those things were a lot more compatible than people might realize. And the bad-boy facade made it easy to hide the fact that he was on a specific academic track. Which had been good, in his estimation. Because if he had failed and ended up pumping gas, no one would have been the wiser. No one would have known that he'd had a different dream. That he'd wanted anything at all beyond the small Texas town he had grown up in.

Fortunately, Harvard had worked out.

He had become a success, as far as everyone was concerned.

He wondered how they talked about him in Royal now. Probably a cautionary tale. Evidence of the fact that at the end of the day not even money could protect you from the harsh realities of life.

That you bled and hurt and died like everyone else.

All in all, it wasn't exactly the legend he had hoped to create for himself.

After Eleanor's funeral, someone had told him that you couldn't have everything. He had punched that person in the face.

"Just head that way," she said, waving her hand, clearly not too bothered with being specific in her directions.

He drove across the flat, bumpy property until he saw a shed in the distance, a small building that clearly predated the house by the river. He wondered if it had been the original home.

"Is this it?" he asked.

"If I were driving, you wouldn't have to ask."

"You are a prickly little cuss," he said, pulling up to the outbuilding and putting the truck in Park.

"It's good for the pores," she said, sniffing.

"So it's not all your magic Clarity skin care?"

"That works, too, but you know, a healthy lifestyle complements all skin-care regimens," she said, sounding arch. Then she smiled broadly, all white teeth and golden skin, looking every inch the savvy spokeswoman that she was.

"Question," he said as they got out of the truck.

"Possible answer," she quipped as the two of them walked to the shed.

"Why skin-care products? Is that your passion?"

"Why organic food?" she shot back.

"That's an easy answer," he returned. "That mom-and-pop place I used to go to for deli food when I had a late-night study session was doing crazy business. And it didn't make any sense to me why. When they wanted to retire, I ended up talking to the owner about the business. And how good food, health food, was an expanding market. I mean, I didn't care that it was healthy—I was in my early twenties. I just liked the macaroni and cheese. I didn't care that it was from a locally sourced dairy. So when the opportunity came to buy the shop, I took it. It was a risky business, and I knew it. It could have gone either way. But it ended up growing. And growing. And before I knew it, I owned a chain of grocery stores. And it became a billion-dollar industry. All because I liked the macaroni and cheese."

They got out of the truck, slamming the doors in tandem. He looked around at the scenery. He could see why Selena had bought the place. It was quiet. Remote, like his ranch in Wyoming. There was something to be said for that. For being able to go off grid. For being able to get some quiet.

"Now you," he said, prompting her.

She wrinkled her nose, twisting her lips to one side. "I guess it's similar for me. I knew I wanted a business that was mine. I knew I wanted to do something that was under my control. And I did a lot of research about profit margins and low overhead start-up. You know I got a business degree, and I also took all of that chemistry. Just as a minor. The two things are compatible. Skin care and chemistry. And like you said, natural organic products were on the upswing."

"So you're not particularly passionate about skin care."

She lifted a shoulder. "I find that you can easily become passionate about a great many different things. I love having my own money. I love controlling my life. I really like the fact that what I do empowers women in some regard. Skin care is not a necessity, but it's nice. When you feel good about yourself, I think you can do more with your life. Mostly, my passion is in the success." She smiled. "I feel like you can relate to that."

He wasn't sure. Things had changed for him so dramatically over the past few years. "Once you make a certain amount of money, though," he said, flinging the doors to the shed open, "it really is just more money."

"More security," she said. "All of this has to go." She waved a hand around as if it was a magic wand that might make the items disappear.

He looked down at her and smiled. She was such an imperious little thing. Sometimes he could definitely tell she had come from a wealthy family, a privileged background. She gave an order, and she expected to be followed. Or maybe that was just Selena.

"Not necessarily," he said, the words coming out a lot more heavily than he'd intended as he picked up what he thought might be part of an old rocking chair.

"I'm sorry" came Selena's muted reply. "I wasn't thinking when I said that."

"I wasn't thinking of the past either," he said. "It's just that money doesn't let you control the whole world, Selena. That's a fact."

"Well, my father sure thinks it does. And he thought he could use it to control me." She cleared her throat. "That was why... It was why I had to marry Will."

Those words hit him square in the chest, almost like one of the large stacks had fallen square on him. "What do you mean you had to marry him?"

"I just… My grandfather died my freshman year. Do you remember that?"

"Of course I remember that. You were distraught."

She sucked in a deep breath. "He was the only person who ever believed in me, Knox. He was the only person who acted like I could do something. Be something. I loved him. So much. He was also definitely an antique. And there was a trust fund. A trust fund that was set aside for me, but I couldn't access it until I was twenty-five, which was when he figured I would be an adult. Really."

"Twenty-five? That seems…"

"Or I could have gotten married." She looked up at him then, her eyes full of meaning. "Which is what I did."

Her meaning hit him with the force of a slap. He was in shock. And the way he responded to that feeling was by getting mad. He growled and walked out of the shed, heading toward the pickup and flinging the piece of chair into the truck bed. Then he stalked back inside and picked up something else, didn't matter particularly to him what it was. "So you had to marry him because you needed the money?" he asked finally, his heart pounding so hard he was sure it would gallop out of his chest.

All this time he'd thought she'd fallen in love with Will. And that had truly put her off-limits, even after the marriage ended. She had chosen another man when Knox was right there. There wasn't a stronger way to telegraph disinterest.

Their friendship had been too important, way too important, to act on any attraction on his end. Particularly when she'd made it clear how she felt when she'd married Will.

Except she hadn't loved Will. Hadn't wanted him.

"Yes," she said. "I remember that you thought it was crazy when we got married. When we didn't just live together. Well, that was why."

"You didn't tell me," he said, his tone fierce and a hell of a lot angrier than he'd intended it to be. "I'm supposed to be your best friend, Selena, and you didn't tell me what was happening?"

"You had your own stuff, Knox. You were dealing with school. And you were on a scholarship to be there. I didn't want to do anything that would interfere with your grades. And that included bringing you into my drama."

"I was your best friend," he reiterated. "I've always taken your drama. That's how it works. How the hell could you underestimate me like that?" He shook his head. "No wonder the two of you got divorced. You married because of a trust fund."

"I don't want to rehash the past with you," she snarled, picking up a bicycle tire and stomping out of the shed. "It doesn't matter. It doesn't matter what happened between me and Will. Not now. The marriage ended, end of story. It was definitely a bad idea. Don't you think I know that? We divorced. It completely ruined our friendship."

"Why?"

"Are you and Cassandra friends?" she asked.

"No," he said. "But as you have pointed out several times, my marriage to Cassandra was not the same as your marriage to Will. So let's not pretend now. Why did it ruin your friendship with Will?"

She bristled visibly. "Because of Rich Lowell."

"That guy who used to follow Will around? The tool with the massive crush on you?"

"That tool only got interested in me when he thought Will was. And after we married he said some things to me... They didn't seem completely far-fetched. He asked me why Will would suddenly want me when... when he didn't before. He implied Will only wanted my money. Of course, Rich didn't know the details of the trust fund, he only knew I came from a wealthy family, but he made me question... Why would Will agree to marry me only to help me get my trust fund? It was so hard for me to believe he was doing it because he was my friend. That he was doing it because he cared about me. I couldn't imagine anyone doing that.

"When you grow up the way I did... When you have to walk on eggshells around your father, you kind of fold in on yourself. And you focus on surviving. That was what I did. I became this creature who only knew how to scrabble forward. I was selfish, and I couldn't imagine anyone *not* being selfish. So when Rich asked me those questions...it just seemed more likely that Will wanted something from me than that he actually wanted to help me. I got mad at Will. I told him I didn't want anything to do with him. That if he thought he was getting any of my money he was completely insane." She laughed, the sound watery. "You know, that's why it was extra hilarious that he left me that inheritance. I mean, I guess he didn't. Because he wasn't dead. Because he didn't even really write the letter."

Knox had some sympathy for her. He truly did. Because he could remember Selena as she had been. It had been so hard for her to trust. So difficult for her to believe anyone wanted anything for her that wasn't a benefit to themselves.

For a kid from the wrong side of the tracks, knowing Selena had been somewhat eye-opening. He'd discovered that people who lived on the other side of the poverty line still had problems. They could be half-feral. They could be insecure. They could have real, serious life-and-death problems. He had always imagined that if he had money he could buy off all of life's bullshit. Meeting Selena had been his first realization that wasn't the case.

But even with the sympathy he felt, there was anger. So much damned anger. Because he hadn't deserved to be lied to for the better part of the last decade. She had never told him any of the truth, and he couldn't quite stomach that.

The nature of her relationship with Will had always been a secret from him.

He whirled around to face her and she squeaked, taking three steps backward, her shoulder blades butting against the side of the shed.

"You lied to me," he said.

"Well," she shot back, her acerbic tone reminding him of the past. "I didn't realize all of my baggage affected your daily life to this degree, Knox."

"You know it doesn't," he said.

"So why are you acting like it does? Why are you acting like it matters at all? It doesn't. It's ancient history. If I'm not upset about it anymore, then why are you?"

"Obviously, you and Will are upset about it, or the two of you would still speak to each other."

"The rift in our friendship has nothing to do with our divorce. It has everything to do with the fact that I accused him of being a gold digger." She sighed heavily. "You can imagine he was not thrilled with that. He pointed out that he didn't need money, of course. And I said being from rich parents didn't mean you didn't need money. I was exhibit A."

"I understand why that would bother him, but he couldn't forgive you for that? Will was not the kind of guy who took himself that seriously back then, and I can't imagine he's changed all that much in the years since."

She grimaced. "I never asked him to."

"You never asked him to forgive you?" he asked, incredulous. "Even though you accused him of something when he was trying to help you?"

She made a sound that was halfway between a growl and a squeak. "It doesn't matter."

"Then why are you so defensive about it?"

"Why are you acting like this? You're pissed because I didn't talk to you?"

"Because you didn't trust me," he said, moving nearer to her.

She shrank back slightly, turning her head. And her reaction just about sent him over the edge. He knew she'd had a rough past, but that was a long time ago. And he was not her father. He didn't use physical threats to intimidate women, and he had damn sure never done it to her.

He had been nothing but careful with her. And she had lied to him all these years about her feelings for

Will. She hadn't trusted Knox back then. And she was acting like he might do something to hurt her now, when he was here because he wanted to make sure that she was safe and protected.

He reached out, gripping her chin with his thumb and forefinger, forcing her to look up at him. "Don't act like that," he said, his voice hard. "Don't look at me like I'm a damn stranger."

She tilted her chin up, her expression defiant. And then the wind picked up and he caught that sweet smell that spoke *Selena* to him. Lavender and the Texas breeze, and why the hell that should affect him, he didn't know. But it did.

"Then don't act like a stranger," she said.

His blood reached the boiling point then, and before he knew what he was doing, he had leaned in closer, his nose scant inches from hers. "I'm not acting like one," he said, his voice rough. "But I'm about to."

She had never really wanted Will. She had never chosen Will over Knox.

That changed things.

And then he closed the distance between them and pressed his lips to hers.

CHAPTER FIVE

Knox was kissing her.

She was sure she was dreaming. Except it was nothing like one of her typical dreams. In those fantasies—which she had always been quite ashamed of—they were always having some nice moment, and then he would capture her lips gently with his before pulling her into his warm, comforting embrace.

In those fantasies, he always looked at her with his lovely gray eyes, and they would soften with warmth and affection before he would lean in.

In this reality, his gray eyes had been hard. He had not been smiling at her. And his lips were... This was not a sweet foray over the line of friendship. No. This was some kind of barbarous conquering of her mouth by his.

This was an invasion. And there were no questions being asked. He was still holding her chin, the impression of his thumb digging into her skin as he tugged down and opened her mouth wide, angling his head and dipping his tongue deep. Sliding it against hers. And she wanted to pull away. She wanted to be angry. Wanted to be indignant.

Because he was angry at her, and he'd been yelling at her. And she was angry at him. He had no right to question her when he had no real idea of what she had lived through. No real idea of what she'd been trying to escape.

Not when he had no idea that the reason she hadn't told him the truth wasn't because she didn't trust him, but because she didn't trust herself. Because what she had really wanted to do, even back then, was ask *Knox* to marry her. But she had known, deep down inside, that with him, a marriage could never be fake. That with him, she would always want everything. And his friendship was so special, she had never wanted to risk it.

Her feelings for him had always been big. Somehow, she had known instinctively that if she made him her husband it would be easy for him to become everything. As painful as it had been, as suspicious and horrible as she'd behaved with Will over their friendship...

Giving in to wanting Knox, to having him...that would have destroyed the girl she'd been.

So she'd kept a distance between them. She'd done what she'd had to do to guard her heart and their friendship. And now he was demolishing all of that good work. That restraint she had shown, that diligence she had practiced all these years.

She was furious. Something more than furious. Something deeper. Something that compelled her to do what she decided to do next.

She shifted, grabbing fistfuls of his shirt, and angled her head, tasting him.

Because it wasn't fair that he was the one who had done this. When she was the one who had spent so long behaving. When she was the one who had worked so hard to protect what they had—to protect herself.

He had no regard for her. No regard for her work.

And he had to be punished for that.

She nipped his lower lip and he growled, pressing his hard chest against her breasts as he pinned her to the side of the shed. He gathered her hands, easily wrapping one of his hands around both her wrists, holding them together and drawing her arms up over her head against the wall.

Bastard.

He was trying to take control of this. Trying to take control of her.

No. He was the one who was ruining things. He was the one ruining *them*. She hadn't gotten the chance to do it. She had been good. She had done her best. And now he wanted all the control?

No. Absolutely not.

She bit him again. This time her teeth scraped hard across his lower lip, and he growled louder, pressing her harder against the wall.

His teeth ran across the bottom of her lip. He nipped her. And somehow, the anger drained out of her.

There was something primal about having her best friend's tongue in her mouth. She had to simply surrender. That was all. Beginning and end.

A wave of emotion washed over her, a wave of need. The entire ocean she had been holding back for more than a decade.

Knox. It had always been Knox that she wanted. Always.

She had messed up everything when she married Will. *Everything.* And when they had divorced it had been too late. Knox had been with Cassandra. And their relationship had been real and serious.

That still bothered her. He had found something real with someone else. She never had.

It would never be the same. Because she had never... She had never loved anyone but him.

And he had loved someone else.

That internal admission hurt. More than that, it made her heart feel like it could shatter into a million pieces with each beat.

But then it just beat harder, faster as Knox shifted, curving his arm around her waist and drawing her against him. She could feel his hardness. Could feel the insistent press of him against her hip that told her this kiss wasn't about teaching her a lesson. Wasn't about anger.

Yes, it had started with anger. But now it was just need. Deep, carnal need between two people who knew each other. Two people who knew exactly what each had been through. There were no explanations required between her and Knox.

That isn't true. There are no explanations required on his end. But I haven't been honest with him. And he knows it. It's why he's angry.

She squeezed her eyes shut and ignored that internal admonishment, parting her lips and kissing Knox deeper, harder.

She was ready for this. Ready to let him undo her jeans, push them down her thighs and take her virginity right there against the side of the shed.

And there was a phrase she had never imagined herself thinking.

Her virginity. Oh, *damn it*. That would be a whole other conversation.

But then suddenly, the conversation became irrelevant, because Knox wrenched his mouth away from hers and wheeled back, his lips set in a grim line, those gray eyes harder than she could ever remember seeing them.

"What?" she asked, breathing heavily, trying to act as though her world hadn't just been tilted on its axis.

"What the hell?"

"You kissed me, Knox. You got mad at me and you kissed me. I'm sure there's some kind of Freudian horror that explains that kind of behavior, but I don't know it."

"You bit me," he pointed out.

"And you pinned my wrists against the wall." She gritted her teeth and turned away from him, hoping to hide the mounting color in her cheeks. Hoping he wouldn't know just how affected she had been by the whole thing. She was dying. Her heart was about to claw its way out of her mouth, her stomach was turning itself over, and she was so wet between her thighs she didn't think she would ever live down the embarrassment if he found out.

"I didn't realize," he said.

"That you pinned my hands?"

"That *that* was there."

"What? Attraction?" She tried to laugh. "You're a hot guy, Knox. And I'm not immune to that. I mean, maybe I'm not up to your usual standards..."

"What usual standards?" he asked. "I was married for ten years, Selena. I had one standard. The person I made vows to. I haven't been with anyone since."

"Oh," she said. "So I guess that explains it." Her stomach twisted in disappointment, then did a free fall down to her toes. "You are super hard up."

"I was angry," he said.

"Awesome," she said, planting her hands on her hips. "Angry and hard up apparently translates into kissing women you didn't know you were attracted to!"

"I knew I was attracted to you," he said. "But I don't dwell on it."

She paused for a moment, tilting her head to the side. "You…knew you were attracted to me."

"Yes. I have been. Since college. But there's never been any point in exploring that attraction, Selena. You were not in a space to take that on when we first met."

She knew what he was saying was true. She had been attracted to him from the moment they'd met, too, but she'd also built a big wall around herself for a reason.

"I wanted to focus on school," she said, the words sounding lame.

"Until Will and a trust fund came into play?"

"Whatever. You didn't make a move on me. And then our friendship became the thing. And…our friendship is still the thing." No point spilling her guts about what a sad, insecure person she was.

"Yes," he said.

"That's good. I can have sex with any guy," she said, waving her hand as if she had simply hundreds of men to choose from to satisfy her appetites. "You're my only best friend. You've known me for so long and let's just not… Let's not make it weird."

"I just think…"

"You haven't had sex in a while—I get it," she said. Which was pretty damned laughable since she hadn't ᵗ˙₋ᵉx ever and he was the one who had jumped on her.

"I'd like to think there was more to it than that," he said. "Because there's more to us than that."

She lifted a shoulder. "Fine. Whatever. I'm not that bothered by it. It was just a kiss. Nothing I can't handle."

She was dying inside. Her head was spinning and she was sure she was close to passing out. She would be damned if she would betray all those feelings to him.

She felt like her top layer had been scraped back, like she was dangerously close to being exposed. All of her secrets. All of herself.

She cared about Knox, she really did, but she kept certain things to herself. And he was poking at them.

"So that's it?" he asked. "We kiss after all these years of friendship and you're fine."

"Would you rather I light myself on fire and jump into the river screaming?"

"No," he said closely, "and that's an awfully specific response."

"Knox," she said, "you don't want me to be anything but fine. Believe me. It's better for the two of us if we just move on like nothing happened. I don't think either of us needs this right now."

Or ever.

She wanted to hide. But she knew that if she did hide, it would only let him know how closely he'd delved into things she didn't want him anywhere near. Things she didn't want anyone near.

"Yeah," he said. "I guess so."

"You don't want to talk about our feelings, do you?" she asked, knowing she sounded testy.

"Absolutely not. I've had enough feelings for a lifetime."

"I'm right there with you. I don't have any interest in messing up a good friendship over a little bit of sex."

Knox walked past her, moving back into the shed. Then he paused, kicking his head back out of the doorway. "I agree with you, Selena, except for one little thing. With me, there wouldn't be anything little about the sex."

KNOX WASN'T SURE what had driven him to make that parting comment to Selena after they had kissed against the shed wall. But she had been acting strange and skittish around him ever since.

Not that he could blame her. He had no idea what in hell he'd been thinking.

Except that even though he was angry at her, she also looked soft, and tempting, and delicious. Finding out she had violated his trust, that there were things about her he didn't know, made him feel like their friendship was not quite what he had imagined it was. And in light of that realization, it had been difficult for him to figure out why he shouldn't just kiss her.

Asshole reasoning, maybe, but it had all made perfect sense in the moment. In the moment when he had brought his lips down on hers.

Yeah, it had all made perfect sense then.

The next few days had been incredibly tense, in a way that things never usually were between them. But he could at least appreciate the tension as a distraction from his real life. It was strange, staying with Selena like this in close quarters—that kiss notwithstanding.

ause it reminded him a lot of their Harvard days.

 like he'd been blind to how gorgeous she was

then. But he'd made a decision about how to treat their friendship, due in large part to Will.

In many ways that decision had made things simple. Though the kiss was complicated, it was nothing compared to loss or divorce or any of the other things he had been through since.

But now they had that party for Will, and they had to actually go be in public together. And she had to try and act like she was at ease with him rather than looking at him like he might bite her again.

Though *she* had started the biting.

Knox buttoned up his dark blue shirt and tried not to think overly hard about all the biting. And the fact that it had surprised him in a not-unpleasant way.

Damn. He really *did* need to find a woman.

But every time he thought about doing that he just felt tired. He didn't want to cruise bars. He didn't want to find strangers to hook up with.

If he was that desperate for an orgasm he could use his right hand.

He had been in love with Cassandra, once upon a time. Though it was hard to remember the good times. Not because they had faded into memory, but because they hurt.

They also ruined the idea of anonymous sex for him.

He was over that. Done with it. He knew what sex could be like when you *knew* someone. When you had a connection with them. He didn't have any interest in going back to the alternative.

He knew a lot of guys who would kill to be in his position. Away from the commitments of marriage. Knox just didn't see the appeal.

He had never found it monotonous to be with the

same person. He had thought it offered far more than it took. To know somebody well enough that you could be confident they were asking for what they wanted. To just know what they wanted at a certain point.

He'd been with his wife for over a decade. The only woman for all that time. It had never seemed a chore to him.

The idea of hooking up—that seemed like a chore.

But damn, he needed to get laid. He was fantasizing about getting bitten by his best friend, so obviously something had to change.

That was the funny thing. Because while he remembered and appreciated the married sex he'd had with Cassandra, he didn't specifically fantasize about *her*. Possibly because she was bound up in something too painful for him to fully relive.

He and Cassandra were over. Done. Everything in him was done with what they'd had.

But he still found himself in the midst of a sex paradox.

He gritted his teeth, walked out of the bedroom he was occupying at Selena's and stopped still.

She was standing in the middle of the living room wearing a bright red dress that conformed to her glorious figure. Her long black hair was styled in loose waves around her shoulders, and she had a flower pinned on the side, part of her hair swept back off her face. She looked beautiful, and effortless, which he knew wasn't the case.

She had spent a good while affecting that look, but she did a damned good impression of someone who hadn't tried at all.

He wanted to kiss the crimson lip color right off

her mouth. Wanted to pull her into his arms and relive the other day.

And he knew he couldn't. Knew he couldn't touch her again, and he couldn't look like he was standing there thinking about it, because they had to get to that party. And he had to manage to get there in one piece, without Selena chewing him up and spitting him out because he was acting like an ass.

He reached over and grabbed his black cowboy hat off the shelf by the door. "I'm ready," he said, positioning it on his head. "Are you?"

"You're wearing jeans," she said.

He lifted a brow. "I'm a cowboy, honey. We wear jeans to parties. Plus, it's Texas."

"I'm wearing *heels*," she said, sticking out one dainty foot and showing off the red stilettos and matching toenail polish on her feet. As if he hadn't already taken stock of that already, with great interest. "The least you could have done was throw on a pair of dress pants."

"I have cowboy boots on," he returned. Then he stuck his arm out, offering it to her. "You go with me as is or you go by yourself, babe. Up to you."

She sighed, an exasperated sound, and reached out, taking hold of his arm before moving to the front door with him. This was the first time she had touched him since the kiss. And damn it all if he didn't feel a hard shock of pleasure at the delicate contact of her hand against his arm, even though it was through fabric.

Selena, for her part, seemed unaffected. Or at least, she was doing a good impersonation of someone who was.

"I'll drive," she said, producing her keys and moving to her little red car before he could protest. He had a feeling he would hate butting up against Selena's temper right about now even more than he hated letting someone else drive, so he didn't fight her on it.

"You can drive in those shoes?" he asked when Selena turned the car out onto the highway.

She waved a hand. "You know, Ginger Rogers did everything Fred Astaire did backward and in heels. I can drive a car in stilettos, Knox," she said, her tone crisp and dry like a good Chardonnay.

He would like very much to take a sip of her.

"Good to know," he said.

"You're not impressed with my logic," she said, sounding petulant.

"The fox-trot isn't driving, so no."

"Don't worry, Knox." Her tone was the verbal equivalent of a pat on the head. "I'll get us there safely. You can be my navigator."

He grumbled. "Great."

"The Chekov to my Kirk."

"Come on," he said. "I'm Shatner. Everyone knows that."

She laughed. "No one knows that. Because it isn't true."

"Clearly I'm the captain of the starship *Enterprise*, Selena."

"O Captain! my Captain! I'm the one driving."

"Technically, as you are the one in red, I would be very concerned by the metaphor."

"This is going into serious nerd territory, Knox." She chuckled. "Do you remember we used to stay up all night with the old *Star Trek*, eating ice cream until we were sick when we were supposed to be having study group?"

"We studied," he said. "We all took it pretty seriously."

"Yeah," she said. "But at a certain point there was just no more retaining information, and we ended up vegging."

"Our college stories are pretty tame compared to some."

"Yeah," she said. "But I don't think you and I ever wanted to compromise our good standing at the university by smoking a lot of weed. We had to get out there and make our own futures. Away from our families."

"True," he returned.

"Which is why we are the successful ones. That's why we're the ones who have done so well."

He felt like he was falling into that great divide again. He wasn't sure what those words meant anymore. Hadn't been for some time. "I guess so."

Tough to think that he had spent all that time working like he had. Through school, and in business, only to reach existential crisis point by thirty-two. It was surprising. And a damn shame.

"Well," she said. "I think anyone who ever doubted us has been proved wrong. How about that?"

He shook his head, watching the familiar scenery fly by. It was so strange to be back here in Royal. He'd met Cassandra in Royal when visiting Will, and he'd decided he'd move there after college to be closer to her. They'd started their life here, their family.

He took it all in. The great green rolling hills and the strange twisty trees. So different from the mountainous terrain in Wyoming. So different from the jagged peaks that surrounded his ranch, which he'd always kept even during the time he'd lived in Royal. The ranch made him feel like he was closed in. Protected. In another place. In another world. Rather than back here where time seemed too harsh and real.

"True enough."

At least he had found a way to talk to Selena again. At least, they'd had a moment of connecting. A moment where the weirdness of the kiss hadn't been the only thing between them. They had a history. She'd known him as a college kid, out of step with the privileged people he was surrounded by, determined to use that opportunity to make something of himself. She'd known him as a newlywed, a new father, a grieving man. A newly single man.

Selena was one of the most important people in his life.

"I know you think you're the captain," she said softly. "Just like I know you don't like tea."

A jolt went down his spine. "What?"

"You don't like tea."

"I...know. I didn't think you knew. You serve it to me all the time."

"And you never say anything."

"My mama would have slapped me upside the head," he said.

He didn't talk about her much, and for good reason, really. WillaMae McCoy was a hard, brittle woman who had definite ideas about right and wrong, until it came to the men she shacked up with and the bottle of liquor she liked best to dull the heartache of losing them.

"Really?" Selena asked.

"Yes. She was big on 'Yes, ma'am,' 'No, ma'am.' Good posture and holding the door open for a lady. And I certainly wouldn't have been allowed to turn down a cup of tea."

"Even if you didn't like it?"

He lifted a shoulder. "Manners."

"Well. Don't do that with me. You can always tell me."

Finally, they arrived at Will's family ranch, the place decked out for a big party. The lights were all on inside the house and he could make out a faint glow coming from behind the place.

And just as he had told Selena, most of the men were in jeans and button-up shirts, wearing white or black cowboy hats. It was Texas. There was no call to put on a tie. Though some of the men wore bolos.

"You okay?" he asked. Because lost in all the strangeness of the past few days, lost in the revelation that Will and Selena had married for reasons other than love, had been the fact that Will was her ex-husband. And it was possible that—even though they had actually gotten married for the trust fund—she was still hurt by the entire thing.

She hadn't said she wasn't, and she had spent all these years avoiding Will. Seeing as she'd gone to his funeral, she'd imagined she'd missed the chance to ever connect with him again.

But look how that had turned out.

"I'm fine," she said, forcing a smile. "It's a good thing," she said. "Getting to see Will. I'm glad that I got this chance."

"All right," he said.

Without thinking, he rounded to her side of the car

and opened the door for her, taking her hand and helping her out of the vehicle.

Then they walked into the party together. He placed his hand low on her back as he guided her through the front door of the massive ranch house. She whipped around to look at him, her eyes wide.

He removed his hand from her back. He hadn't even thought about it, how possessive a move it was. He had just done it. Because it had felt reasonable and right at the time.

He could tell by the expression on her face that it had actually been neither.

He stuffed his hand in his pocket.

The housekeeper greeted them and then ushered them out into the yard, where Cora Lee was waiting, greeting them with open arms and kisses on both cheeks.

When she pulled away, Knox had that sense again that she was the kind of woman you didn't want to cross. Sweet as pie, but there might be a razor blade buried in the filling.

Or at least, if there needed to be one, there would be.

"So good of you to come," she drawled.

"Of course," Selena said. "I'm just thrilled that Will is okay."

"So are we all, sugar," she said.

They moved back through the party and Selena shivered. He fought the urge to put his arm around her again. Obviously, she wasn't having that. Clearly, she was not open to him touching her. In spite of the fact that they had been friends for years.

It was that kiss.

And as he stood there, conscious of the newfound

boundaries drawn in their relationship, he asked himself if he regretted that kiss.

No, sir. He sure as hell did not.

Because it had woken up some things inside of him he hadn't thought would ever wake up again.

And those thoughts put his mind back at the place it had been while he was getting ready for the party. He wasn't sure how he was going to move forward.

But maybe the desire for anonymous sex would come next.

He damn sure hoped so. Because relationships... Marriage. None of that was ever happening again.

And that, he realized, standing there in this crowded, loud Texas party with country music blaring over the speakers, was the real tragedy.

He had reached the point that so many people idealized. He had crawled out of the gutter, bloodied his knuckles getting there. He'd found love. He'd gotten married. He'd had a child.

And it had all come crashing down around him.

He knew what it looked like to achieve those things, and he knew what it looked like standing on the other side of losing them.

They were nothing but heartbreak and rubble.

He didn't want them again. He just couldn't do it.

He took a step away from Selena. He was not going to touch her again. That much was certain.

CHAPTER SIX

Selena felt Knox's withdrawal.

Although he had taken only a slight step to the side, she could sense that something had changed.

His eyes were distant. And he looked a lot more like the sad, wounded man she had first seen after his daughter's funeral than he looked like the friend she'd reminisced with in the car about their nerdy college life.

She started to say something, but he spotted someone they both knew from college and gave her a cursory hand gesture before walking away.

She felt deflated.

She knew she was acting a bit twitchy. But damn, Knox looked handsome in that outfit. In those jeans that hugged his muscular thighs and ass. And that hard place between those muscular thighs that she had felt pressed up against her body just the other day.

The cowboy hat. Oh, the cowboy hat always made her swoon. Cowboys weren't her type. If they were, she would have her pick. She lived in Texas.

No, sadly *Knox* was her type. And that had always been her tragedy.

She was brooding, and pretty darned openly, too, when her friend Scarlett McKittrick spotted her from across the lawn and headed her way. Scarlett being

Scarlett, she *bounded* across the lawn, her eyes sparkling with determination in the dim light. She was like a caffeinated pixie, which was generally what Selena liked about her, but also part of why she'd been avoiding Scarlett since Knox had come to town. She didn't want her friend to grill her on why he was hanging around, or to start asking questions about what was happening between them. She'd end up telling Scarlett everything and confessing she wanted Knox. She just didn't want to have that conversation.

It made her feel a little guilty since Scarlett's adoption of her son had just been finalized and she knew Scarlett might feel like the baby was why Selena wasn't hanging around as much. But that wasn't the reason. She and Scarlett had been friends for years, even though the bond wasn't as intense as the one Selena shared with Knox, which was unsurprising, since Selena didn't secretly harbor fantasies about making out with Scarlett.

"Hi," Selena said, trying to sound bright.

"Hi, yourself," Scarlett said, her eyes assessing Selena in her overly perceptive manner. "I have escaped by myself for the evening, so I'm feeling good." She ran her hand through her short hair and grinned. "Thanks for asking."

"Sorry," Selena said. "I'm a terrible friend."

Scarlett waved a hand. "Yeah. A bit. But I'll live. What's happening with you and Knox?" The subject change nearly gave Selena whiplash.

"Nothing," Selena said, lying through her teeth.

"He seems… I mean, I haven't seen him *since*."

"I know," Selena said. "He's made himself scarce."

Scarlett bumped her with an elbow. "So have you recently."

"I'm sorry. I've been dealing with all the stuff with Will. And Knox came to stay at my house after the funeral that wasn't and he hasn't exactly left."

Scarlett's eyebrows shot up. "Really?"

"Yes," she said. "Don't go thinking weird ideas about it. There's nothing weird."

"If you say so. But he looked… He doesn't look good, Selena."

She took a deep breath of the warm night air, catching hints of whiskey and wildflowers, mingling with smoke from a campfire. "I know. He's not the same. But how could he be?"

"Yeah. I guess if he was, you'd be forced to think he was pretty callous. Or in denial."

Selena shook her head. "Well, I can say he's not in denial. He's pretty firmly rooted in reality."

Except for that kiss. That kiss had been a moment outside of reality. And it had been glorious.

"Anyway," Selena said, "he's feeling paranoid because of everything with Will. I mean, *someone* faked Will's death. And *someone* wanted me and everyone else at that memorial service. It's weird. And it is nice to have Knox here just in case anything goes down."

"Yeah. I questioned the wisdom of having a party tonight, even though the only people Cora Lee invited were those of us at the service when Will walked in. But also, it's Texas, and at least eight percent of the people here have a sidearm, so anyone who tried to cause trouble would end up on the wrong side of a shoot-out."

"No kidding."

"Hey," Scarlett said, obviously ready for a new topic. "When are you guys coming out to Paradise Farms? Or if you'd rather do something different, the ranch next door to mine is doing a thing where you can go glamping."

Selena blinked. "I'm sorry—what?"

"You know—" Scarlett waved her hand around "—*glamorous camping.*"

"I don't know anything about that. Mostly because I don't know anything about camping, Scarlett. As you well know."

"It's not like regular camping. Yes, you ride horses, and go on one of the long trails that takes two full days to complete, and there's an overnight checkpoint. But the food that's included is amazing and the tent that's set up is a really, really nice tent, luxurious even."

"I... I don't know." The idea of being alone with Knox on an abandoned trail, riding horses, sleeping under the stars—or under the canvas top of a very nice tent—all seemed a little bit...fraught. And by fraught, she meant it turned her on, which was probably a very bad thing considering their situation.

"Well, think about it. It'd be a great way to take a break from all the drama here in town. The invitation is open. Because it's new, the schedule is really vacant. And I know they'd be happy to have testimonials from both of you. You can come out to Paradise Farms and use my horses. Right now, people are bringing their own to ride the trail."

Selena tried to smile and not look like she was pondering Knox and close quarters too hard. "I'll think about it."

"Do that." Scarlett grinned. "And text me. I'm dying

at home buried under diapers and things. Babies are a lot of work."

"Okay. I promise."

Scarlett shifted. "Okay. Well, do text me. And…if anything…comes up. If you need to talk about *anything*. Please remember that you can call me."

"I will. Promise."

That left Selena standing alone as Scarlett went off to talk to someone else. She tapped her fingers together, and a passing waiter thrust a jar of what she assumed was moonshine into her empty hands.

She leaned forward, sniffing gingerly, then drew her head back, wrinkling her nose.

"I'm surprised you came."

She turned to see Will Sanders, her ex-husband—sort of. They hadn't spoken in so long it was weird to have him here next to her, talking to her. And it also made the years feel like they had melted away. Like there had been no fight. No stupid marriage. No accusations. Like greed and money—her greed—had never come between them.

"Yeah," she said, "fancy meeting you here. Especially since I thought you were dead."

"I would've thought you were pretty psyched about my demise, gingersnap."

"I've never understood that nickname. I'm not a redhead."

He winked, but it was different somehow than it had been. "No, but you're spicy with a bit of bite."

"Right. I guess I bit you a time or two." But not the way she'd bitten Knox. Not the way Knox thought she might have bitten Will. Her mind was terminally in a gutter right now.

"Yeah. But that's water under the bridge. A lot is thrown into perspective when you've been through what I have." She examined him for the first time. The hard line of his jaw, the slightly sharper glint to his eyes. He was not the same man he'd been. That much was certain. She could make out faint scarring on his face and wondered how much surgery he'd had to have to get himself put back together. She'd heard someone mention that Will had been in a boating accident in Mexico and left for dead. He'd been recovering and trying to make his way home all this time.

She wondered if there was anything that could put his soul back together.

"I'm sorry," she said. "And that was so easy to say it makes me seriously question why I didn't do it earlier."

"I know why you didn't do it earlier. Because you were angry. Because you were scared. It's fine, Selena. I'm not the kind of guy you need in your life anyway."

"Oh, I know," she said. "But it would be nice to be on speaking terms with you."

"I'm sorry if I hurt you," he said.

"You did not hurt me," she said, making a scoffing sound.

"I thought that was why you got so angry at me. Because you were in love with me."

In spite of herself, in spite of the absurdity of the situation, Selena let out a crack of laughter. "Will Sanders, you thought I was in love with you?"

"Yes."

"You are so full of it!" she all but exploded. And for some reason, she felt lighter than she had in days. Weeks. *Years*. "I was not in love with you."

"You asked me to marry you to help you get your trust fund. And then you got mad at me…"

"Because I thought our friendship was too good to be true, Will. I didn't have it the easiest growing up. I didn't have people in my life I could trust. I trusted you. And when Rich planted that seed of doubt…"

Everything in Will's body went hard like granite. Right down to his expression and the line of his mouth. "Right. Well. Rich has a lot to answer for."

"I just…" She tapped the side of the jar. "I wanted so badly to believe that what we had was real friendship. I guess maybe that wasn't super common for you with women, but it meant something to me."

"So—" he frowned "—you weren't in love with me?"

She laughed. "No."

"Then why did you ask me to marry you? You could have just as easily asked Knox. Did I win a coin toss?"

Unbidden, her gaze drifted across the expanse of lawn, and her eyes found Knox. Effortlessly. Easily. Her eyes always went right to him.

"I see," he said, far too perceptive. Old Will would never have been so perceptive. "Well, this does make a few things clearer."

"I'm sorry I was such a terrible friend," she said. "I'm sorry I let my issues drive us apart. And I'm sorry I listened to Rich when you had never given me a reason to mistrust you. You would make a horrible gold digger, Will, and I see that now."

"Yeah, well, nothing like dying and coming back to life to make people think better of you," he commented. "Of course…the thing with my life at the moment is I can't have it back."

"What?"

"Someone has been living it for me, Selena. I didn't write you that letter. I didn't write letters to anyone."

"Will…" She stared at him, at the changes in his face. "What happened, Will?"

"Not talking about that yet," he said, his voice tight. "I don't know what's actually going on and until then… until then I'm just keeping watch on everything."

Silence settled between them, and Selena swallowed hard and nodded. "Well…well, I'm glad you're okay. And I'm really glad you're not dead."

Suddenly he smiled, and she thought she saw a glimpse of the Will she'd once known. "You know, when this is over I think I'm going to start a line of greeting cards. The Awkwardly Interrupted Funeral line. *So glad you're not dead. Hey, you rose from the grave and it's not even Easter.*"

"That sounds great," she responded, laughing.

Well, at least one relationship in her life wasn't a total mess.

"I have to make the rounds. As a reanimated corpse, I'm extremely popular." He stuffed his hands in his pockets and winked again. It seemed a little try hard at that point, but she could understand.

Will's life couldn't be totally normal at the moment, all things considered.

"Great," she said, a smile tugging at her lips.

She wrapped her arms around herself and looked at who was attending the party. She caught sight of Will's stepbrother Jesse Navarro, who was always a dark and sullen presence. Selena didn't know him personally, but she knew of him. She had moved to Royal after college, lured by Will's tales of it as some sort of promised land.

And it always had been for her. She'd found a sense of home here. Part of that was because at first she'd had Knox, since she and Will hadn't been on speaking terms. But even after Knox had left...

The town was special to her. Even if she was a late-comer.

She had seen Jesse at events before. Even without being a member of the Texas Cattleman's Club, it was impossible to move in the moneyed circles in Royal and not have some clue about who the people were in your age bracket.

She also saw the woman who'd had the child at Will's funeral. And she wondered if that was Will's baby. Wondered if she knew the truth about anyone.

Because the fact remained that if Will was the one responsible for all that heartbreak she'd been standing in the middle of at the funeral, as much as she might like him, he had a lot to answer for. A lot to atone for, now that he was back.

Suddenly, Jesse's gaze landed on that woman, and his eyes sizzled with heat.

Selena felt like she had to look away, like she was witnessing an intimate moment.

When she looked back, whatever connection she thought she'd spotted seemed to be gone. And the woman hadn't seemed to notice at all.

She looked around again, trying to get a visual on Knox, and saw that he was gone. Then she saw a figure standing just outside the lights on the lawn, holding a bottle of beer. She knew that was him. She knew him by silhouette. That wasn't problematic at all.

She ditched the moonshine in the jar and reached for a bottle of her own beer, walking gingerly across the grass in her heels, making her way to where he was standing.

"Hi," she said.

He didn't jump. Didn't turn. As if he had already sensed her. That thought made the back of her neck prickle. Was he as aware of her as she was of him?

"Hi," he returned, lifting his bottle of beer to his lips. He took a long, slow pull. And she was grateful for the shroud of darkness. Because had it not been so dark, she would've watched the way his lips curved around the bottle, would have watched the way his Adam's apple moved as he swallowed the liquid.

And her whole body would have burned up. A lot like it was doing now, just imagining such things.

"I talked to Will," she said.

"Did you?" he asked, the words laden with a bite.

"I think we made amends, for what that's worth. It was something that needed to happen. There's a lot of stuff in my past, and I'm all bound up in it. No matter how successful I get, no matter how far I move forward, it's just there."

He lifted a shoulder. "I can relate to that."

Except she knew he was talking about something a lot more grave, and she felt instantly guilty.

"Why aren't you at the party? Don't you want to talk to Will?"

"I decided I wasn't really in a party mood once everything got going."

"All right." She wrapped her arms around herself to keep from wrapping her arms around him. "Do you want to leave?"

"That's fine. If you're having fun."

"I'm not sure I would call laying a ghost to rest fun. Just potentially necessary."

"Right."

Then she did reach out and touch him. Her fingertips brushed his shoulder, and she felt the contact down to her stomach, making it clench tight. "Knox."

His name was a whisper, a plea. But she didn't know what for. For normalcy? For an explosion?

His muscles tensed beneath her touch, and she felt like her stomach had been scooped out. Felt like she had been left hollow and wanting, aching for something that only he could give her.

She remembered what it felt like when his mouth pressed against hers. Finally, after all that time. She had kissed other men. Half-hearted attempts at finding a way she could be attracted to somebody who wasn't her best friend. It had never worked. It had never excited her.

This kiss haunted her dreams. It haunted her now.

She wanted to kiss him. She wanted to give him comfort. In any way she could. And they were out here in the darkness on the edge of this party. Where Will Sanders had come back from the dead and everything was just freaking crazy.

So she decided to be crazy, too. She slid her hand upward to his neck, curving her fingers around his nape. And then she brought herself around to the front of him, placing her palm on his chest, directly over his heart, where it was raging hard and fast.

"Selena," he said, a word of warning. A warning she wasn't going to heed.

She stretched up on her tiptoes—because she was

still too short to just kiss him, even in these heels—and a rush of pleasure flooded her, a rush of relief, the moment their mouths met.

She was lost in it. In the torrent of desire that overtook her completely as his scent, his flavor, flooded her senses.

It was *everything*. It was everything she remembered and more. Kissing him was like nothing else. It was like every fantasy colliding into one brilliant blinding firework.

Oh, how she wanted him. How she wanted this. She wrapped her arms around his neck, still clutching the bottle of beer tightly, and then he dropped his bottle, grabbing hold of her hips with both hands and tugging her heat against his muscular body. She could feel his arousal pressing against her stomach, and she wanted... she wanted to ride it.

She wanted to ride *him*.

"Please," she whispered.

She didn't know what she was begging for, only that if she didn't get it she would die.

He moved one hand down to her side, then down her lower hip around to the back of her knee. Then he lifted her leg and drew it up over his hip, opening her to that blunt masculine part of him.

She gasped and tilted her hips forward, groaning when a shot of pleasure worked its way through her body. She tilted forward, riding the wave of pleasure. Allowing herself to get caught up in this. In the rapturous glory of his mouth on hers, of his hard, incredible masculinity.

She would let him take her here, she realized. Let him strip her naked on the edges of this party and lay her down in the damp grass. Sweep her panties to the side and thrust inside of her, even though she'd never let another man do it before. She wasn't afraid. Not even remotely.

This was Knox McCoy and she trusted him with all that she was. Trusted him with her body.

I don't trust him. There's so much I haven't told him.

But if she told him everything, then he wouldn't look at her the same. What if he saw the same abused girl she always saw when she looked in the mirror, rather than the confident businesswoman she had become?

She couldn't stand for that to happen. She truly couldn't.

So maybe if there was this first. Maybe they could both find something in it. Something they needed.

He drew away from her, suddenly, sharply, his chest heaving with effort. She wished she could see his face. Wished she could read his expression. Then he slowly released his hold on her thigh, and she slid an inch or so down his body. Not the most elegant dismount, that was for sure. She was grateful for the darkness, because he couldn't see the fierce blush in her cheeks, couldn't get an accurate read on the full horror moving through her at the moment.

"I'm not sorry," she said, pulling her dress back into place.

"Did I ask you to be?" he bit out, his words hard.

"No," she said, "but you stopped."

"I stopped because I was close to fucking you right here at a party. Is that what you want?"

"I…" She was dizzy. She couldn't believe she was

standing here listening to her friend say those words, directed at her. "That's a complicated question, Knox."

"No." He shook his head. "It's really not. Either you want to get fucked on the ground at a party by your best friend or you don't."

She looked away, feeling self-conscious even though she knew he couldn't see her expression. "Maybe not… on the ground…at a *party*."

"Selena," he said, gripping her chin, leaning forward and gazing at her with his dark, blazing eyes. "I can't give you anything. I can't give you anything other than sex."

"I didn't ask you for anything," she said, her voice small.

"We're friends. And that means I care about you. But I'm never, ever getting married again."

"It's kind of a long leap from fucking in the grass to a marriage proposal, don't you think, Knox?" she asked, self-protection making her snarky, because she needed something to put distance between them.

"I just meant this doesn't end anywhere but sex, baby. And I need our friendship. I haven't had a lot of bright spots in my life lately, and I hate to lose the one I have."

"But you want me," she said, not feeling at all awkward about laying that out there. Because he did. And she knew it.

"That doesn't mean having."

And then he just walked away. Walked away like they were in the middle of having a conversation. Like her heart wasn't still pounding so hard it was likely to go straight through her chest. Like she wasn't wet and aching for satisfaction that he had denied her, yet again.

And that was when she made a decision. She was going to have Knox McCoy. Because there was no going back now. They wanted each other. And she had been holding on to all those feelings for him for so long that she knew a couple of things for certain. They weren't going away, and no man could take his place as it was.

She had known a lot of girls in college who had thought they needed to get certain guys out of their systems, which had always seemed to her a fancy way to excuse having sex when you wanted it, even though you knew it was a really bad idea and the guy was never going to call. It had always ended in sadness, as far as she had seen.

But Knox had been in her system for so long, and there was no other way he was getting out of it. She knew that. This wasn't a guy she had met in class a few weeks ago, a guy she had exchanged numbers with at a party.

She had known Knox for the better part of her adult life and she wasn't just going to wake up one morning and not want him.

So maybe this was the way forward.

She pulled her phone out, still not ready to go back to the party, to go back into the lights where people might see her emotional state. Where they might be able to read what had just happened. And she texted Scarlett.

So, about that glamping.

CHAPTER SEVEN

KNOX HAD STUCK it out at the party just to be a stubborn cuss. By the time he and Selena got back in the car and started to drive to the ranch, he expected her to unleash hell on him.

Instead, she didn't. Instead, she was silent the entire way, and he didn't like that. He didn't like it at all. He'd enough of hard, sad silences. He preferred to be screamed at, frankly. But Selena didn't seem to be in the mood to give him what he wanted.

And he said nothing.

Then when they pulled in the driveway and finally got out, heading into the house, she spoke. "We're going glamping tomorrow," she said, her expression neutral, but vaguely mischievous.

"What?"

"Scarlett suggested it. We're going on a trail ride. And we are staying overnight in a luxury tent."

"I was going to head back to Jackson Hole," he said, lying, because he had no plans to do that at all. And for the first time, he questioned why.

He didn't like that all these interactions with Selena forced him to do things like ponder his motivations.

"I don't care. Change your ticket. You're rich as God, Knox. It's not like it's a problem."

"No," he said slowly.

"You're coming glamping with me, because you're still not okay, I'm clearly not okay, and we need to do something to get back on track. We are not leaving our friendship here. You are not going off to Wyoming for however the hell long and not seeing me. Because it's going to turn into not seeing me for months, for years, as we avoid all the weirdness that has sprung up between us."

Oh, he was personally all right with avoiding the weirdness. But obviously, she wasn't.

"Okay," he found himself agreeing, and he couldn't quite fathom why.

"It'll be fun," she said, grinning at him, all teeth. And it made him damn suspicious.

"I'm not overly familiar with fun," he said, purposefully making his tone grave.

"Well," she said, "this will be."

He had his doubts, but he also knew Selena Jacobs on a mission was not a creature to be trifled with. And not one easily derailed.

So they would go on a trail ride. They would go camping.

Once upon a time he'd liked to ride, he'd liked to camp. Why the hell not?

Maybe she was right. Maybe it would remind him of some of the things he used to like.

Although, privately, he feared that it would go much the same way as the party had gone. That all it would do was reinforce the fact that he couldn't enjoy things the way he used to. That he had nothing left to look forward to in his life.

Because he couldn't think of a single dream he

hadn't achieved. Then two of them he lost. And one of them just didn't mean a thing without the others.

And he had no idea where the hell you went from there.

Camping, it seemed.

He shook his head and followed Selena into the house.

BY THE TIME they were saddled up and ready to ride, Selena was starting to have some doubts. But not enough to turn back.

They were given a map and detailed instructions on how the trail ride would work, and then she and Knox were sent off into the Texas wilderness together. Alone, except for each other.

And the condoms Selena had stuck in her bag.

Because this was a seduction mission more than it was anything else, and she was completely ready to go there.

Well, except for the nerves. And the doubts. There were those. But that was all virgin stuff.

Oh, and the fact that she was going to see her best friend's penis.

The thought made her simultaneously want to giggle and squeeze her thighs together to quell the ache there.

Her cheeks heated as she realized the rhythm of the horse's gait did a little something for it. Her face flamed, her whole body getting warm.

Knox McCoy had turned her into a sex-crazed pervert. And they hadn't even had sex yet.

He might not want to have sex with me.

Yes, that was the risk. She might get Knox alone in a tent, around a romantic campfire, and she might strip herself completely naked and get denied. It was possible. It was not a possibility she was hoping for. But it might happen. The idea did not thrill her.

But there was no great achievement without great risk. And anyway, if there was one thing she had kind of learned from this whole experience with Will's death-that-was-not-actually-a-death, it was that time was finite.

She had stood at Will's funeral and had regretted leaving things bad between them. She didn't want to regret Knox.

Somewhere in the back of her mind she knew that if this ruined her friendship with Knox she was going to regret that. She was going to regret it a whole hell of a lot. But at least she wouldn't wonder. Right now, it seemed worth the risk.

Maybe on the other side it wouldn't. But she wasn't on the other side yet.

She squared her shoulders and they continued to ride down the trail.

It was beautiful. The land was sparse, filled with scrub brush and twisty, gnarled trees that were green in defiance to their surroundings. She had been told that the trail would wind toward some water, and that it would get shadier and greener there, which was why it was good to do this leg early in the morning, before the sun rose high in the sky and the heat and humidity started to get oppressive.

But the view around her wasn't her primary reason for being here, anyway. It was him. It was Knox.

"So," she said, "it's nice out."

"Yeah," he responded, taciturn like he had been last night.

It was funny, how she had gone from the one being all angry about the kiss to him being all angry. What a delight.

She hoped that banging him was slightly more delightful.

The thought made her nerves twitch.

"So, how many hours is it to camp?" he asked.

"About six," she said.

"That seems a little bit crazy," he responded.

"I know," she said, and then she frowned. Because she hadn't really considered that. The fact that she was going to launch a full-out seduction after having been on the back of a horse all day. Honestly, there was a sweat situation that might be problematic. Not that she minded if he was sweaty. She was all okay with that. It was pheromones or something. She had always liked the way Knox smelled when he'd been sweating. After he had gone for a run in college and he would come back to hang at her dorm for a while, steal some food off her and her roommate. He had walked by her, and her stomach would go into a free fall.

It was so funny, how she had buried that reaction down deep, and how it was all coming up now. Bringing itself into the light, really.

She had been in full denial of her feelings for him for so long. While she had definitely known they were there, she didn't focus on them. But now she was admitting everything to herself. That she was a sucker for the way he smelled. That his voice skimmed over her skin like a touch. That in so many ways she had been waiting for him. Waiting for this. And that excuses about how busy she was, how important the company was, were not really the reasons why she didn't date.

It was because no man was Knox, and never would be.

As she made idle chatter for the rest of the ride, she fought against cloying terror. She was headed toward what was her undeniable destiny and almost certain heartbreak.

But she'd come too far to turn back now. She simply couldn't.

Eventually, they did come to that river, and they found themselves beneath the canopy of trees as the sun rose high in the sky. They arrived at camp before the sun began to set, a glorious, serene tent out in the middle of nowhere right next to the river.

There were Texas bluebells in the grass that surrounded it. A little oasis just for them. There was a firepit, places to sit. It really was the most civilized camping she had ever seen.

"I am going to jump in the river," Knox said. He got off the horse and stripped his shirt off over his head.

And she froze. Just absolutely froze as the shirt's fabric slowly rolled up over his torso and revealed his body.

Lord, what a body.

"What?" he asked.

Well, great. She'd been caught staring openly. At her friend's half-naked body. Talk about telegraphing her seduction plans.

"Nothing." She blinked. "I'll go... We can get the horses settled and then I'll get my swimsuit."

But her gaze was fully fixed on his broad, bare chest. On all those fantastic, perfect muscles. Which she had felt through his shirt a time or two in the past few days. But now... Seeing it like that, dusted with just the right amount of pale hair, glistening with sweat... She wanted to lick him.

She imagined the rules of friendship generally prevented that. But she was fully violating those anyway, so she was just going to embrace the feeling.

"Come on," he said, nodding once. "Let's get the horses into the corral."

She went through the motions of leading the horses into the gated area and making sure there was fresh water in the trough, but really, she was just watching Knox.

The way the sun glinted on his golden hair and highlighted the scruff on his face—she wanted so badly to run her fingers over it. The way the muscles in his forearms went taut as he removed the horses' bridles and saddles...

He bent down low, setting about cleaning their hooves, his body putting on a glorious play of strength and sculpted masculinity that took her breath away.

He was such a familiar sight. But in context with desire, with what she wanted to have happen later, he was like a stranger. And that both thrilled and excited her.

When they finished taking care of the animals, he straightened, and she was momentarily struck dumb again by his beauty. It was a wonder she'd ever managed to get to know the guy. His looks were a serious barrier to her ability to form cogent thoughts and words that were more than noises.

"Why don't you go on in and get your suit?" he asked, handing her her pack.

His fingers brushed against hers and she felt the

touch like a bolt of lightning. All the way through her body.

Selena scurried into the tent, barely able to take in the glory of it. There was an actual bed inside, seating, a woodstove, all surrounded by beautifully draped canvas. The bed was covered in furs and other soft, sumptuous things. It was the perfect place to make love to a man you had been fantasizing about all of your life.

And when darkness fell, she was going to do just that.

The corners of her lips turned upward when she realized there was only one bed in the place. And she wondered if Scarlett was matchmaking. If Selena had been that damned transparent. She changed quickly into a black bikini, ignoring the moment of wishing it covered more of her body, and headed outside.

She was gratified when Knox's expression took on that similar "hit with a shovel" quality she had been pretty sure her own had possessed a few moments ago when he had stripped off his shirt.

"Nice suit," he said.

He was wearing a pair of swim shorts that she wondered if he'd been wearing beneath everything else the whole time. Or if he had just quickly gotten naked outside.

And then she thought way too long and hard about that.

"Thank you," she said.

The shorts rode low, revealing every sculpted line just above that part of him that was still a mystery to her. She was doing her best not to look like a guppy spit out onto the shore. Gaping and gasping. She had a feeling she was only semi-successful.

"There's only one bed," she commented. "I didn't realize that."

As if that mattered. She was planning to seduce him anyway.

"Oh," he said. "Well, I can sleep on the floor."

"Let's worry about that later," she said, because she hoped that both of them would be completely all right with the fact that there was only one bed just a little bit later.

They went down toward the river, and in spite of the heat, when she stuck her toe in the slow-moving water, she shuddered slightly.

"Oh, come on," he said. "It's not that cold."

As if to demonstrate all of his masculine bravado, he went straight into the water, wading in up to his hips and then lying flat on his stomach and paddling out toward the center of the wide body of water.

She took a deep breath and followed suit, screeching as the water made contact with the tender skin on her stomach. "It is cold," she shouted at him.

"You're a baby," he responded, turning over onto his back and paddling away from her.

"I am not a baby," she said. She swam toward him and then splashed at him. He laughed, reaching out and grabbing her wrist, drawing her against him. She didn't know what the intent had been. Maybe to stop her from splashing him, but suddenly, her legs were all tangled up with his and her breasts were pressed against his bare chest. The wet swimsuit fabric did absolutely nothing to provide a barrier between them. Her nipples were hard, sensitive, partly from the chill of the water and partly just from him. From her desire for him.

"Knox," she said. "If you don't like it, tell me. I don't want to be tea."

"You're not tea," he said.

"Good. I'd hate for you to sleep with me because of good manners. A girl wants to be wanted."

And something in his eyes changed. His jaw was tight, the lines by his mouth drawn, deep. And she could see the struggle there. The fight.

"I don't need forever," she said. Her seduction plan had just gone out the window. This electricity between them was sparking right now. And she was going to make the most of it. She was going to take it. "I just need you. For a little while. I've wanted you... Always. I have. This isn't new for me. And it's not going away." She raised her hands, trusting him, trusting his strong, steady hold to keep her afloat. She traced those deep lines on either side of his lips with her thumbs, stroking him. Touching him the way she had always dreamed about touching him. Freely, without holding back.

That was the sad thing. She felt a whole hell of a lot for him, and yet she'd always, always held it back, held back a part of herself.

She was tired of that. And she was surrounded by reminders of why it was wrong. Time wasn't infinite. She'd thought she'd missed a chance to apologize to Will.

She wasn't going to miss this chance.

"You want this?" he asked, his voice rough. "You want me right now? Let me tell you, Selena, all I can give you is selfish. I haven't had sex in two years. A little bit more, maybe. Because it's not like there was a whole lot going on during the divorce. During the grief. And I... I don't have any control left in me. I wanted to do the right thing. I wanted to be honest with you about what I could and couldn't give you, but if you keep offering it to me…"

"If I keep offering it to you then you need to trust me." She met his gaze and held it. Tried to ignore her breathlessness, her nerves. "I'm your friend. I've been your friend for a long time. Haven't I always taken what you've given to me? Haven't we always been there for each other? That's what this is. I want to be there for you. And I want this, too. This isn't pity sex, Knox. I want it. I want you. I think you want me. So let's… Let's just trust that we'll find our way. Because we are friends. We've been through hell together. It wasn't my hell, Knox, but I walked alongside you. Trust me. Trust me to keep walking with you."

She was on the verge of tears, emotion clogging her throat, and crying wasn't what she wanted. It wasn't what this was supposed to be. It was supposed to be physical, and it was becoming emotional. But too late she realized, as she clung to him while he treaded water for them both, with Knox it was never going to be anything but emotional. Because they cared for each other.

And emotion was never going to stay outside of the sex. It was never going to be sex in one column and friendship in the other. They were bringing sex into a friendship. And that was big and scary, and not something she could turn away from.

"Trust me," she said, a final plea before he closed the distance between them.

CHAPTER EIGHT

KNOX HAD KNOWN he was lost the moment she had come out of the tent wearing that bikini. He hadn't even given himself a chance. When he had grabbed hold of her in the water... It hadn't been to stop her from splashing him. It had simply been because he couldn't stand to not touch her anymore. He had to do it. He'd had to bring her against his body. Because he couldn't stand to not have his hands on her.

And as he held her he had the fleeting concern that this was going to be the most selfish sex on the face of the planet, and he was going to treat his best friend to it. She didn't deserve that. She deserved more. She deserved better. But he didn't have control. Not anymore.

He was a man stripped of everything. Life had simply stolen every fucking thing from him in the last two years. He couldn't fight this. Not with what he had left.

He just wanted. And he was so tired of wanting. There were so many things he couldn't have. He could not have Eleanor back, no matter how much he wanted her.

He couldn't fight death. No matter how he wanted to. How he wished that there was a sword he could have picked up so he could do battle with death. Instead, he'd had to stand by helplessly, not able to do a damn thing. For a man who had never accepted the limits of life, losing to death with such resounding finality had been incomprehensible.

But he could have this. He could have Selena.

He didn't have to fight it, and he damn sure wasn't going to. Not anymore.

So he kissed her. He kissed her like he was drowning in this river and she was the air. He kissed her like there wasn't going to be anything after it. Because for all he knew, there wouldn't be. Life was a bitch. A cruel, evil bitch who took as much as she gave, so he was going to take something of his own.

Maybe anger at the world wasn't the way to approach a seduction. Maybe it wasn't the way to engage with his best friend, but he couldn't help himself. Couldn't do anything but lean into it. Lean into her. When she parted her lips and slid her tongue against his, he forgot to keep kicking, and they sank slightly beneath the water, the surface slipping past their shoulders. "We need to get out of here," he said, paddling them both toward the shore.

"There's that bed," she said softly, stroking her hand over his face, over his shoulders, the slide of skin against skin slick from the water.

He looked into her dark eyes to get a read on what she was thinking. "Did you plan this?"

"No," she said, looking very much like the picture of pristine innocence. In a black bikini that looked like sin.

"You didn't." Her eyes sparked with a little bit of heat, and a lot of the stubbornness he thought was cute about Selena at the best of times. It was cuter now, considering he was holding her nearly naked curves.

"Well." Her smile turned impish. "I didn't know

there would be one bed. But I did know that I wanted you. And I figured this was as good a way as any to go about having you."

"Minx," he said, kissing her again. Kissing her until they were both breathless, out there in the bleached Texas sun.

Then he swept her up and carried her back toward that tent.

He didn't bother to dry either of them off when he deposited her on the plush bed at the far side of the canvas wall. He stood there, looking at every delicious inch of her. Those full breasts, barely contained by the swimsuit top, her small waist and firm stomach. Those hips. Wide and delicious, and her thighs, which were full and lovely. Shaped like a delicious pear he definitely wanted to take a bite out of.

He pushed his wet shorts down his thighs, careful with his straining arousal. And it was gratifying to watch her mouth drop open, to watch her eyes go wide.

She squeezed her thighs together, drawing one leg up slightly, biting her lip.

"See something you like?" he asked.

She nodded. "Yeah," she said. And it was rare for Selena to not have a snarky comment follow.

"Do you want this?" he asked.

"Yes," she said, the word breathless. "I want it so much." She rolled to her side, her wet hair falling over her shoulder, her eyes wide. "Don't change your mind."

He glanced down at his extremely prominent erection. "Oh, I'm not in a position to change my mind. Or to do much of anything with my mind at the moment, especially thinking."

She settled back into the blankets, looking satisfied with that statement. "I'm okay with that."

He got onto the bed, moving over her, kissing her again, reaching behind her neck and undoing the tie on her bikini top in one fluid motion. Then he did the other one, taking the wet cups away from her breasts.

His breath caught in his throat as he looked at her. At that glorious, golden skin, her tight, honey-colored nipples.

He leaned forward, flicking the tip of one sensitive bud with his tongue, gratified when she gasped and arched against him. He sucked her deep into his mouth, lost completely in his own desire. His need to feast on her, to gorge himself on her beauty.

He wasn't thinking about anything in the past. Wasn't thinking about anything but this. But her. There was no room for anything but desire inside of him. There was nothing else at all.

He smoothed his hands down her narrow waist to those full hips, gripped her bikini bottoms and tugged them down her legs. And he groaned when he saw that dark thatch of curls at the apex of her thighs. He kissed her stomach, all the way down low to that tender skin beneath her belly button. Then he forced her legs apart, his cock pulsing, his stomach muscles getting impossibly tight as he looked at his friend like this for the first time. He felt her try to close her legs, try to move away from him.

He wasn't going to let her get away with that.

She might have orchestrated this little camping trip. Might have thought she could conduct a seduction. And he was seduced; there was no doubt about that. But she wasn't in charge. Not now. Hell no.

He leaned forward, breathing in the scent of her. Musk and female and everything he craved. His mouth watered, and he leaned forward, sliding his tongue over her slick flesh, flicking that sweet little clit with the tip of his tongue. She gasped, her hips bucking off the bed, simultaneously moving toward him and away from him. He held her fast, grabbing hold of both hips, drawing her roughly against his mouth where he could have his fill and maintain control of the movements.

She tried to twist and ride beneath him, but he held her fast, pleasuring her with his lips and his tongue, pressing his fingers deep inside of her until she cried out, until her internal muscles pulsed around him.

"Knox," she said, his name thin and shaky on her lips, her entire body boneless. And that satisfied him. Because it had been a long damn time since he'd had a woman, and there was a deep satisfaction to making her come that he couldn't even describe.

He could do that to her body. This need, this skill existed inside of him, and the desire to practice it was there. He'd left that need boxed up inside of him for years. In a stack in the corner of his soul. Anything that wasn't work, anything that wasn't breathing.

Right now, this felt like breathing. And he didn't simply feel alive. He felt like Knox.

He wanted to do it again. Again and again. He wanted to make her scream his name. But she was reaching for him, urging him up her body, urging him to kiss her again. Who was he to deny her?

He was going to give her everything.

Everything he had.

He settled between her thighs, kissing her deeply. He wanted this to last longer. Wanted to go on. But he just didn't possess the control. He needed to be inside of her. And he needed it now. He could only take so much satisfaction from her orgasm without desperately needing his own.

He pressed the head of his cock to the entrance of her body, found her wet and ready for him. Then he slid himself upward, drawing his length over those slick folds, teasing her a little before moving back to her entrance and thrusting in hard.

Then he froze as she tensed beneath him. As she let out a cry that had nothing at all to do with pleasure.

Somehow, Selena was a virgin.

SELENA TRIED *SO* hard not to be a baby when the sharp, tearing pain moved through her. He had just made her feel so good. And really, she wanted this. She wanted him. But the invasion of his body into hers hurt and she hadn't been able to keep back the cry of shock when he had entered her.

Screaming in pain was probably not the best move on her part. A pretty surefire way to kill the mood. Knox froze, looking down at her with anger written all over his handsome face.

She felt him start to move away from her, felt his muscles tense as he prepared to pull back. So he could stop touching her. So he could run out into the desert in the late afternoon and take his chances with the sun and snakes rather than with her. But she didn't want him to go.

So she clung to him, desperation probably leaving marks behind on his skin, digging her nails into his shoulders and kissing him fiercely, rocking her hips against his, ignoring the pain. She didn't want him to stop. It was too late anyway. Her virginity was gone. The hard part, the scary part, was over.

She didn't want to stop. Not now.

He tried to pull away again but she moved her hands down, clapping them over his muscular ass and holding him to her. She shook her head, her lips still fused to his.

He said nothing. Then he just continued on, slowly withdrawing from her body before thrusting back inside. He shuddered, lowering his head, his forehead pressed to hers. And she recognized the moment where whatever reservations he'd had were washed away by his own tide of need.

She'd had an orgasm already; he had not.

"Yes," she whispered as he began to move inside of her. As he began to establish a steady, luxurious rhythm that erased the pain she had felt only a moment before.

She wrapped her legs around his narrow hips, urging him on, chasing the pleasure she had felt before. And it began to build, low and deep inside of her, a band of tension that increased in intensity, drawing her closer to a second release. But this one seemed to come from somewhere deeper.

This time, when she shattered, it was just as he did, as his muscles tensed and his body shuddered, as his own orgasm washed through her, his thick, heavy cock pulsing as he spilled himself into her.

And when it was over, they lay there gasping, and she knew she was never going to be the same again. That there was no getting anyone out of her system. That her need for him would never change.

But along with that realization came a deep sense

of peace. One that she was sure would vanish. But for now, she clung to it. For now, she clung to it and him, because reality would hit soon enough.

And she was in no hurry.

Because she had a feeling as soon as the afterglow receded there would be questions. She had a feeling there were in fact going to be quite a few follow-up questions. And what she really hadn't thought through in this moment was that there were going to be a lot of questions about Will.

She closed her eyes. Of course, she had already alluded to the fact that their marriage wasn't everything it seemed. So maybe Knox wouldn't be completely shocked. Maybe.

Well, even if he was—maybe that wasn't the end of the world. Maybe it was time to share the truth with him. She had closed him off. And now... Now he had been inside her body. So maybe that time was over. Maybe she just needed to go for it.

There was only one way to find out.

"Yes," she said, finding courage from deep inside that she hadn't realized existed. "I was a virgin."

He swore and moved away from her. She looked over at him just in time to see him scrubbing his hands over his face in what one might be forgiven for assuming was despair.

She folded her hands and rested them on her bare stomach, staring up at the canvas ceiling. "I assume you have queries."

"Yes," he responded. "I have several."

"Well," she said. "My marriage to Will wasn't real. I mean, we were never in a relationship."

"Never?" He treated her to a long hard look.

"No," she said. "We were never in a relationship at all. It was purely to help me get the trust-fund money."

"Why didn't you come to me? You could have picked either of your friends to help you out with this and you asked him?"

Panic fluttered in her breast and she took a deep breath, trying to tap it down. She wasn't going to tell him that she hadn't asked because she couldn't face the possibility that living with him wouldn't have felt fake to her. She wasn't going to bring up her feelings at all. "I just... Look what happened with my friendship with Will afterward. Don't tell me I was wrong in trying to protect our friendship from problems like that. Choosing Will seemed necessary. Marrying him seemed like the only thing I could do to make sure that you and I were going to be okay. You were always more important to me, Knox. I just didn't..."

"That's bullshit, Selena," he said. "I know it is. Give me a straight answer."

"Why?" she asked. "I don't want to give you a straight answer. Because there is no good answer."

"I want the truth."

"Fine," she said. "I was afraid we would end up like this." She swept her arm up and down, indicating their nudity. "I didn't worry about that with Will. Not at all. It was just never like that between us. I never had those feelings for him."

"You had them for me."

"Yes," she said. "That's kind of obvious, considering we are lying here naked."

"But even back then?" he asked.

He'd already confessed to being attracted to her, but

she hadn't handed out a similar confession. For her it felt so raw. So deep.

"I wanted you. But I knew I wasn't in a position to have you. I thought maybe someday... And then...marrying Will was a bad choice, Knox. And it's one I've never been particularly interested in interrogating. It ruined a lot of things."

"About the time you got divorced I was with Cassandra."

"Yes," she said. "In a lot of ways, I was grateful for that. Because it helped us preserve our friendship. I don't regret that neither of us made a move. I feel like it was actually better. I feel like if it had happened when we were young, we wouldn't have been able to...process this. We wouldn't have been able to separate the attraction from the friendship."

"And you think we can now?"

"I think we're both tired," she said, obviously. "I think we're both fatigued after spending a long time denying what we wanted. It's a pattern. In both of our lives. I'm not going to pretend to compare my struggle to yours. I'm really not. But...why fight this? We both wanted it. And for the first time, we're in a place where we can both take it. It was always wrong, and maybe in the future it will be wrong again. Maybe it will just naturally fade away."

"Is that what you really believe?"

"Yes," she said. "I do. I believe this is something we can work out. This is something we can have."

"But... Hell, Selena," he said. "You've really never been with another guy?"

"No. I was really busy. I was really busy growing the company and..."

"Yeah, usually that's the kind of thing people say when they miss a lot of coffee dates. Not when they just kind of forgot to have sex ever."

Now this, she could not be honest about. She was not going to have a discussion with him about how no man had ever seemed to measure up to him in her mind.

Because that was beyond sad.

"It really wasn't something that mattered to me. And then... Over the past few weeks with you..." She cleared her throat. "I'm attracted to you. I always have been. But it's not something I dwell on. I mean, you were married to somebody else. You had another life. And I always respected that. I did. What you had with Cassandra... I would never have dreamed of encroaching on it. I care about you like a friend, and I kind of want to tear your clothes off and bite you like a crazed lioness, and those two things are separate. But there was never any crazed lioness fantasies while you were married." That was a little lie. There was the occasional fantasy, but she had known she could never act on it.

He paused for a moment, then placed his hand on her. "So your attraction went dormant?"

"Yes," she said. "Your marriage was the winter of our attraction. It hibernated."

"Your libido hibernated," he said, his tone bland.

"Yeah," she said. "And my burrow was work. Work and friends and establishing my life in Royal." She let out a heavy sigh. "I never wanted to get married and have a family," she admitted. "My father was... You know he was difficult. And it's..." She knew it was time to share everything. They were naked, after all. They were naked and he had just taken her virginity, and there really were very few secrets left between them. But the last one was hers. She was holding it. She had to give it up.

"My father used to beat us. He was violent. His temper was unpredictable. We walked like there was broken glass under our feet all the time. Doing the very best we could not to bring that temper up. It was terrible. Terrifying. I will never, ever submit myself to that kind of thing again."

"So is that why you avoided relationships?"

"I would say that's why they weren't a priority. I'm not sure that I avoided them. I just didn't pursue them."

"You're being difficult."

"Yeah, well," she said. "I reserve the right to be difficult. I *can* be difficult now. That's the beauty of life on your own terms."

"And you think that's the key to happiness?" he asked, brushing his knuckles idly over her hip. It was a question void of judgment, but it made her chest feel weird all the same. Mostly because she'd never thought of it in those terms.

"It's a luxury. One that I appreciate. That's why I was so desperate to marry Will," she said. "Because I needed that money. Because I needed to be able to control my life. Because if I couldn't, then I was always going to be under my father's thumb."

"He *hit* you?" he asked.

"Yes," she said. "All the time. For anything. For attitude, disrespect. For not complying with his wishes when he wanted us to. We didn't have any control. We had to be the perfect family. His perfect wife. His perfect daughter. He didn't want me to go to college. He didn't want me to have any kind of autonomy at all. My grandfather is the one who helped me enroll in

Harvard. But then he died. And I knew I wasn't going to find any more support. I wasn't going to have the resources for college. I was going to have to go back home, Knox, and I couldn't face that. I didn't want to need my father again. Ever. And I needed to get my hands on that trust fund in order to make that happen. In order to protect myself. To protect my mother. After I got it, I moved her out of the house. I installed her somewhere he couldn't get to her. I did everything I could do with my money to make sure we were never beholden to him again."

He shifted, tightening his hold on her. "I didn't know it was that bad." His words were like ground glass, sharp and gritty, and it gratified her to know that Knox was holding her tight with murder on his mind, because he couldn't stand the thought of her being hurt.

She was right to trust him.

"We all have our own struggles," she said, working to keep her tone casual. "I never wanted anyone to look at me like I was broken. Like I needed to be treated gently. I've always felt strong. Growing up that way, I had to be. But I protect what I have. I protect what's mine.

"You can see how our relationship, love, all of that never figured into my plans. I could never see myself submitting to a man controlling my life. To anyone controlling my life. To love controlling my life. Because that was my experience. It took so much for my mother to leave because she loved him, not just because she was afraid of him. Because part of her wanted to make it work. Wanted to find the man she had once known. The one who had made her fall for him in the first place. No matter how much I tried to tell her that man never existed, it was difficult for her to accept."

Selena took a deep breath before continuing, "She refused to press charges in the end. She used to cry. And say that I ruined her life by breaking up the marriage. By sending her to live in Manhattan, far away from him, and safely ensconced in an apartment there. She would think about going back to him, and it was only her fear that kept her away. She skips therapy all the time, no matter how many appointments I set up. I just… I never wanted to be that creature. Ever."

Knox grabbed hold of her chin, met her gaze. "You never could be."

She reached up, curled her fingers over his wrist and held his arm steady. "Any of us can be. At least, that's what I think. One step in the wrong direction and you're on that path, and at some point you're too many steps in, and you can't imagine going back. I've never thought I was above anything. I've never thought I was too good, too smart… Because that's not it. That's not what does it. We can all get bound up in it."

He looked genuinely stricken by that. "I never thought of it like that," he admitted.

"I know. It's human nature to want to believe people are at fault for their own bad situations. And oftentimes they are complicit. But I don't think it was a fundamental personality flaw that made my mother stay with my father. It was fear of change. A fear of losing what she had. Because what if she ended up with less?"

"But she stayed in a house with a man who hit her daughter. You might be able to excuse that, Selena, but I don't think I can."

She looked away from him. "Sometimes I have a

hard time with that. I won't lie to you. I can't have a relationship with my father. He's not a good man. He hurt me. He hurt my mother. He was made of rage that had nothing to do with us. I'm convinced it had everything to do with some kind of anger at himself. But whatever it was, it's nothing I want touching my life. So yes. I feel like I could be angry at her. Maybe I would even be justified. Because you're right. She did stay. Her fear was bigger than her desire to take action to get us out. In the end, my fear of living in that hell forever is what made me take action. And I just… We are out. And I don't have the energy for anger anymore. I want to have at least one relationship with one family member that isn't toxic. I want to heal what I can."

"That's pretty damned big of you," he said.

She laughed, lifting her shoulder. "Sure, but then, I also don't want to have a romantic relationship, so I'm emotionally scarred in other ways."

"I can appreciate that."

Silence fell over them and she allowed herself to fully take in the moment. The fact that she was lying there, skin to skin with her best friend. With the man she had fantasized about all of her life. She had told him everything. She had finally laid bare all the secrets she had been so scared to roll out. But on the heels of sharing everything came the revelation she had been working on avoiding. The real reason she had been afraid of confiding in him all this time.

It wasn't just that she cared for him. It wasn't just that she was attracted to him. She was in love with Knox McCoy, and she always had been. In love with a man she could never allow herself to have, because she had sworn that she would never get involved in those kinds of relationships.

And she was such a fool. Because she had been in love with him from the moment he had first walked into her life. She had thought she could keep him as a friend, and ignore the bigger feelings, the deeper feelings, but that was a lie. There was no avoiding it. There never had been.

But she didn't tell him that. She had let out all her other secrets and replaced them with another. One that she hoped he would never discover.

Because as horrifying as it was to admit to herself that she was in love with him, it would be even worse to have him know and have him reject her.

So she laid her head on his chest and focused on the rhythm of his heartbeat, on the way his skin felt beneath hers.

It wasn't love. But for now, maybe it was enough.

CHAPTER NINE

THEY FINISHED OUT the trail ride the next day in relative silence. Knox was saddle sore, because it had been a while since he had ridden a horse. And it had been a while since he had ridden a woman. But he and Selena had definitely indulged themselves the entire night. He still wasn't sure what to make of any of it. Of the fact that he'd made love to his best friend, of the fact that she had been a virgin.

Yeah, he didn't even the hell know. But things weren't terribly awkward, which was a miracle in and of itself.

When they arrived back at Paradise Farms he noticed that Selena was pretty cagey with Scarlett as they deposited the horses and thanked her for the generous loan.

"She knew, didn't she?" Selena asked when they got back into the car and headed down the highway.

"Do you think so?"

"Well, I wonder, because she obviously knew the tent only had one bed."

He chuckled. "So you think she was trying to set you up?"

"I think she was trying to set *you* up," she said. "She thought you seemed sad."

"I am," he responded, his tone dry. The answer more

revealing than he'd intended it to be. He had meant to make the comment kind of light, but it was difficult for him to keep it light these days.

"I'm sorry," she said.

"Don't apologize," he said. "There's no damned reason to. You didn't do anything. Nobody did."

"I'm not apologizing, not really. I'm just sorry that life is so messed up."

He huffed out a laugh. "You and me both. I'm not sure what you're supposed to do with a bunch of broken pieces," he said, the words torn from him. "When they're all you have left. When you had this full, complete life and then suddenly it's just gone. I don't know what the hell you're supposed to do with that."

"I don't either," she commented. "I really don't. I guess you try to make a new life, new things. Out of the broken bits."

"I don't think I have the desire or the energy," he said.

"What's the alternative?" she asked, her voice hushed. "I'm not trying to be flippant. I'm asking a serious question. If you don't rebuild, what do you do? Just sit there in the rubble? Because I think you deserve a hell of a lot more than that."

"What's the point? Everything you do, everything you are, can be taken from you." He didn't know what had gotten him into such a dire place. He'd just had sex for the first time in years and now suddenly they were talking about the fragility of life. "All these things you make your identity out of. Husband. Father. Billionaire. They're just things. They get taken from you, and then what? It's like you said about your mother last night. You lose sight of who you are, and then you're

just afraid of what will be left. Once you lose those titles that defined you then...then there's just nothing.
That's how it feels. Like I'm standing on a hell of a lot
of nothing. Somehow I'm not in a free fall...but I don't
trust this will last. I don't trust that the whole world
won't just fall apart again."

They turned up the dirt road onto her property and
didn't speak until they were inside the house again.
Then finally she turned to him, her dark eyes full of
compassion. He didn't like that. The compassion. Because it was so damned close to pity.

"I don't know what to say," she said, when they got
into the house. She looked at him with luminous eyes,
and he could read her sincerity. Her sadness.

He didn't want either.

He reached out, grabbing hold of her wrist and
wrapping his arm around her waist, crushing her to
his body, because he couldn't think of anything else
to do. He needed something to hold on to, and she was
there, like she had always been. In the middle of that
horrible breakdown that he'd had at Eleanor's funeral,
she'd been there. And she was here now. There was a
yawning, horrific ache inside of him, and she was the
only thing he could think of that would fill it.

"I used to be a husband," he said, his voice rough.
"I used to be a father. And now I'm just a man with a
hole inside, and I don't know what the hell I'm going
to do to fix it. I don't even know if I want to fix it. I
don't know who I am."

"I do," she said softly. She lifted the hand that was
currently free and brushed her fingertips against the
side of his face, tracing the line of his jaw. "You're a

man, Knox. A man that I want. For now...can that be enough? Can you just be that for me?"

Everything inside of him roared an enthusiastic hell yes. He could be that. He could do that. It was actually the one damn thing he knew in that moment. That he could be Selena's lover. That he could satisfy them both. He didn't know what the hell was going on in the rest of the world, but he knew what could happen here, in her bedroom.

And so he picked her up, holding her close to his chest as he carried her to the back of the house and deposited her on her bed. He stripped them both of their clothes, leaving the lights on so he could drink his fill of her beautiful body. He was about to do to her what he had done last night, to force her legs open and taste her as deeply as he wanted to. But she sat up on the bed, moving to the edge and pressing her hands to the center of his bare chest.

"Let me," she whispered. She pressed a kiss to his pectoral muscle, right next to his nipple. "Let me show you. Let me show you how much I want you."

He tensed, his entire body drawn tight like a bow. She continued an exploration down his torso, down his stomach, and lower still until she reached his cock. She curved her fingers around him, leaning forward and flicking her tongue over the head. His breath caught sharply, his entire body freezing.

"I've never done this either," she said. He looked down at her and saw that she was making eye contact with him, her expression impish. "If you were wondering."

Of course he had wondered, because he was a man, and damned possessive even if he shouldn't be. And the fact that she was doing this for him, only for him, and had never done it for anyone else was far too pleasing a revelation by half.

She braced herself on his thighs and took him deeper into her mouth, arching her back and sticking her ass in the air. He pressed his palm down between her shoulder blades and tried to keep himself from falling over as she continued to pleasure him with her lips and her tongue. It was a hell of a thing, accepting pleasure like this. He hadn't fully realized what he'd been doing to himself all this time. Punishing himself. Taking everything away that he possibly could.

Sex. Leisure time. All of it.

He hadn't allowed himself to enjoy a damned meal since his daughter's funeral. It was all hurry up and then get back to work. Leave work and then exercise. Work the ranch. It was only during this past week while he'd been here with Selena that he had begun to get in touch with some of the things he had left behind. Things like the company of people he cared about. Like going to an event and seeing people you knew. Like how much he enjoyed the touch of a woman. And he didn't know what he felt about all these revelations—the knowledge that he'd been punishing himself and the fact that he had started letting go of that punishment this week.

Piece by piece.

He felt a sharp pang of guilt join with the overriding sense of pleasure she was pouring onto him with all that sweet, lavish attention from her mouth.

Need was roaring through him now, and it was almost impossible for him to keep himself in check. He knew he needed to, but part of him didn't want to. Part of him just wanted to surrender to this completely, surrender to her completely.

But no, she deserved better than this.

In the end, she deserved better than him, but he was too weak to turn her away.

He didn't have the power. And that was what it always damn well came down to.

That when it came to the important things, he didn't have the strength to make an impact.

But he could make it good for her. And he would take that.

"Not like this," he said, his voice rough.

He grabbed hold of her arms and pulled her up his body, claiming her mouth in a searing kiss, his heart pounding hard, his breath coming in fierce gasps. Then he laid her down on the bed, hooked her leg up over his hip and thrust into her deep and hard, taking her until they were both breathless, until they were both completely caught up and consumed in their release.

When it was over they lay together. Just a man and a woman. Who had wanted each other. Who had needed each other, and who had taken steps to act on that need.

It was simple. Peaceful. He let his mind go blank and just rested. Listened to her breathe in and out. Focused on the feel of her silken skin beneath his touch. The way her hair spread over his chest in a glossy wave.

It didn't last long.

Didn't take long before he remembered who he was. Who they were. Before he had to face the fact that even though he felt like he might have been washed clean by what happened between them, he was still the same. Deep down, he was still the same.

Selena curled more tightly against him and he

wrapped his arm around her, relishing the feel of her warmth, of her feminine softness, of her weight against him. Those words, those thoughts, triggered terror inside him. So he pushed it away.

"Are you going to stay away forever again?" she asked, her tone sleepy.

"What do you mean?"

"I mean, this is the first time you've been back to Royal since…well, you know since what. You've been in Wyoming. I had to chase you down over there to even see you."

"I know," he said.

"Is that what we are going to do? Are you going to leave and put distance between yourself and Texas again?"

And between himself and her. That part was unspoken, but he sensed it was there. And that it was a very real concern.

"It's hard to be here," he said. Finally. "The life Cassandra and I made together was here. It was a good life. It's one that I could have lived till the end. This beautiful house… Our beautiful family. It was good. It really was. I made it. I had all the things you think you want when you picture reaching that perfect position in your life. Then it crashed into a wall." He shook his head. "Nobody likes to go back to the scene of an accident. And that's what it feels like to me."

"I can't even imagine," she said, her voice muffled. She buried her face against his bare shoulder and he curled his hand around the back of her head, holding her. It was strange, to touch her like this, so casually. As if it all hadn't changed between them just last night. Because touching her like this felt natural. It felt right.

"Grief is a hell of a thing, though," he said. "It doesn't really matter where you are. It doesn't really care. It's in a smell, a strange moment that for some reason takes you backward in time. It's seeing a little girl that's the same age as Ellie would've been now. Or a little girl the same age she was when she died. Just seeing people walking together. Couples walking through life. It's freezing in the grocery store because you've picked up a box of crackers."

He tried to laugh, but it was hard. "We carry these crackers in the store. You know, graham crackers. Organic, obviously. And they were her favorite." He cleared his throat but it did nothing to ease the pressure in his chest. "I can't walk by that damn shelf, Selena." The words were broken, tearing through him, leaving him bloody and ragged inside. "Because I remember the way she used to wipe her mouth on my shirt and leave a trail behind. She would just...ruin all these really nice shirts. It was frustrating, and I think it annoyed me, even though I never got mad at her. Because she was just a baby. Just a little girl." It was surreal. Lying there, talking about this. Like he was watching someone else do it. But if it was another man's life, it wouldn't have hurt so much. "I'd give anything—my damned life—to wash graham cracker out of a shirt again."

He felt wetness on his shoulder and he realized she was crying, and then he realized there was an answering wetness on his own cheeks. "I didn't need to stay away from Texas to protect myself. There's no shielding yourself from something like this. I can lose my shit over a fucking cracker."

She buried her face in his chest. "I wish I could fix

it," she said. "And those are the most frustrating words I've ever said. Because they don't give you anything. And they don't fix anything."

"Between the two of us I think we have a lot of broken pieces," he said, clearing his throat.

"I guess so."

"I won't stay away this time," he said, moving his hand up and down her bare curves, down her waist, over her hip. "I don't think I could." He was quiet for a long time. "I haven't told anyone that story." She didn't have to ask which one. "I just kept all this stuff to myself."

And he knew it was why his marriage had ended, or at least it was part of the reason why. Because he'd gone inside of himself, and Cassandra had retreated into herself. And neither one of them had known how to find their way back to each other, and they hadn't had the energy—or the desire, really—to even begin to try.

"Thank you for telling me," she said. "Thank you."

"You said you felt like you hadn't done anything. But you have. You did. You gave me this. This memory. This moment. The first thing I've really enjoyed in years. That's not nothing."

"What are friends for?" She smiled, and then she kissed his lips.

And after that, they didn't speak anymore.

CHAPTER TEN

KNOX SPENT THE next week at Selena's house, and he didn't really question what he was doing. Yes, he had an inkling that he was avoiding his real life. That he was avoiding dealing with the charity event that his ex had organized, that he was avoiding the reality of life in general, but he didn't much want to focus on any of that.

The mystery surrounding Will's return hadn't been solved, but there had been no more fake letters and no attempts by anyone to contact Selena. Knox was leaving all of that to the investigators and Will's family.

Instead, he wanted to focus on this newfound layer of his relationship with Selena. Wanted to focus on enjoying the way things felt again. Sex. Food. He and Selena were enjoying a lot of both.

And he was still helping her sort out her property. Slowly, though, because he really wasn't in a hurry to finish. He was working out in the shed, while Selena took care of some business things in the house, when his phone rang.

It was from a number he didn't recognize, so he picked it up just in case it was a business call. "Hello?"

"Knox," the voice on the other end said.

Cassandra. The impact hit him like a punch to the stomach. And his initial response was rage. Absolute rage that she was intruding on this peaceful moment in his life. On this new thing that was happening with him.

He didn't want to hear her voice. Not while he was standing here in Selena's shed, mounting a new shelf so she had adequate storage.

"I don't know this number," he said.

"I got a new phone," she responded, her voice tenuous.

"Why did you call?"

And he felt like an ass for being impatient with her. For being such a jerk, because it wasn't like she had ever done anything to him. They had never really done anything to each other, and that had been the problem in the end.

"You never responded to the invitation for the Ellie's House fundraiser," she said.

"Did I need to? I wrote a check."

"I want you there," she said. "Ellie's House is really important to me. It's the only thing that makes me feel like what I went through—what we went through—wasn't completely pointless and cruel. I want this to be important to you. I want you to be there. To lend your connections. Your appearance matters."

"Don't say it like that," he said. "Don't say it like the charity isn't important to me. Like *she's* not important to me."

There was a long pause on the other end. "I didn't mean it like that. I really didn't. I did not call to have a fight with you, I swear."

He shifted, looking out the door of the shed at the field and trees off in the distance. The leaves blowing in the breeze, the sun shining down on it all. Like the world wasn't really a dark and terrible place. Like he wasn't being torn to shreds every time he took a breath. "We didn't fight while we were married. What's the point in fighting now?"

That produced another long silence. "There isn't one." Cassandra took a breath. "It would mean a lot to me if you could come. And I need to tell you something. Something that… I don't know how to say. I don't know…where to begin."

His chest tightened. "What?"

"Knox… I… I'm getting married."

He had not expected that. Neither had he expected the accompanying feeling of being slapped across the face with a two-by-four. "What?"

"I met someone." Something in her voice changed. Softened. Warmed. Happiness, he realized. He hadn't heard it in her voice in a long time. Certainly not when talking to him. "I didn't expect it. I wasn't looking for it. I didn't even want it. But he's… He makes me happy. And I didn't think I could be happy again. I have purpose with Ellie's House, and… I really want you to come. And I want you to see him. To meet him."

"I'm sorry—why the hell would I want to meet your fiancé, Cassandra?" he asked. He could feel his old life slipping away. Moving into the distance.

Or maybe she was moving on and life was going past him.

"You don't love me," she said. "You're not *in* love with me, anyway."

That wasn't even close to being part of the visceral, negative reaction to her announcement. That much he knew. He didn't want Cassandra. He'd had her, they'd had each other, and they hadn't tried to fix things.

There was something else. Something he couldn't pinpoint. But it wasn't about wanting her back.

"No," he said.

"But we still care about each other, don't we? We were together for ten years. It's such a long time. Our whole twenties. It was you and me. We went through something… You're the only other person on earth who will ever know how I feel. You're the only person who experienced the same losses as me. You'll always matter to me for that reason. I just need you there. I need this closure. Please come."

Those words hit him hard. And somehow, he found that he didn't have the strength to turn her down. "Okay."

"Bring somebody," she said. "I mean it. Find a date. Find…something. We deserve to be happy."

After that, they got off the phone, and he struggled with his feelings about what she'd said. Because at the end of the day, he wasn't entirely sure he deserved to be happy.

He stumbled out of the shed and went into the house. Selena was sitting in there, her dark hair piled up on top of her head in a messy bun. She was holding a pen in her mouth and staring down at her laptop.

She was so damned beautiful he could barely breathe. "Hey," he said.

She looked up and she smiled at him, and it felt like the sun coming out from behind the clouds. Which, for a man who had spent the past two years in darkness, was a pretty big thing.

"Do you want to come to a charity thing with me?"

"Sure," she said, giving him a strange look.

"It's Cassandra's thing," he said.

"Oh," Selena said, her expression cautious. "For Ellie's House?"

He frowned. "You know about that?"

She bit her lip. "About the foundation, yes. I wasn't invited to any charity event. But I sent some money in a while back."

He cleared his throat and shoved his hands into his pockets. "Well, she told me to bring a date."

The corners of her lips turned upward, just slightly. "Then I'm happy to fulfill that role."

"Great," he said, trying to force a smile.

It was only later that he questioned the decision. He realized he was committing to bringing Selena to a public function, as his date. Which had less to do with how it might look—he didn't care, and anyway, it was well established that they were friends—but that he was bringing her along as a plus-one to his grief. That he was basically submitting himself to showing it all to the public.

But it was too late now. He'd already agreed. He'd already asked her to come with him. He was just going to have to get a handle on himself. To get some of his control back.

Because everything was moving in a direction he wasn't sure he liked. All that was left to do was try and keep a handle on himself.

KNOX ACTED STRANGE for the next week. Which was not helped at all by the fact that Selena was starting to feel a little bit strange herself.

She was trying not to dwell on it. Was trying not to dwell on anything other than the good feelings Knox created in her. Who knew how long all this would last?

She didn't want to waste any time being upset or worried. Didn't want to waste time being hypersensitive to his moods or to her own.

There was way too much good happening. And she knew it was temporary. So she planned to just pull herself together and enjoy.

She tried to shake off her lethargy as she looked in the mirror and finished putting her makeup on. She was just so tired. She didn't know if it was because of the lack of sleep since Knox had moved in, or what. Stress, maybe, from the upcoming event for Ellie's House.

Because as much as she knew that he wasn't making a statement by bringing her, it still felt momentous that he'd asked her to come with him. He would probably be annoyed with her for thinking that. But she was coming to an event with his ex-wife and his ex-wife's fiancé. An event for a charity his ex-wife had created for the daughter they had lost.

He could have easily gone by himself. And Selena had a feeling that a few months ago that was exactly what he would have opted to do. Since he had been doing things on his own for the past couple of years.

The fact that he'd reached out to her was probably why he was acting weird. The intensity of the whole situation. She really couldn't blame him.

She checked her reflection in the mirror and had a momentary feeling of uncertainty. And then a flash of jealousy followed closely by a bite of guilt.

She had to wonder if he might compare her to his tall, blonde ex, who was more willowy than she was curvy. And Selena wouldn't really be able to blame him if he did. She and Cassandra were so different. The idea of standing next to Cassandra and playing a game of compare and contrast had been making her feel ill.

Of course, that wasn't what was going to happen. And Cassandra had always been very nice to her.

It'd been strange when she and Knox had gotten divorced, because Selena had genuinely liked her. As much as you could like the woman who had ended up with the man of your dreams, *obviously*.

But as Selena had recused herself from having those kinds of dreams, she'd never really been angry with Cassandra. Knox being married had always been both a relief and a heartache. There was really no other way to describe it. A relief because that feeling of *what if* had abated slightly since there had been no more *what if* left. But also it had just burned sometimes. Knowing he was with someone else. That he'd loved someone else.

But she'd never let herself dwell on it. She hadn't been able to be with him romantically, not when a relationship like that would have required risk and a trust she hadn't been willing to give. But she'd also needed him in her life, and she wasn't about to let something like a marriage come between them.

Now, had Cassandra been a bad wife, Selena wouldn't have been able to stand for it. But Cassandra had always been great. Exactly the kind of woman Selena thought Knox should have been with. So getting all bent out of shape about Cassandra and comparisons now was just pointless.

She twisted her body slightly, frowning as she smoothed her hand over the front of her fitted gold dress. A strange sense of disquiet raced through her as she adjusted herself in the halter top. Her breasts hurt. Like they were bruised.

That was very, very strange.

She knew of only one thing that caused such intense breast tenderness and…no. That was ridiculous. Except her breasts had never been tender before. Her eyes dropped down to her stomach. She looked the same. She couldn't believe…couldn't believe there could be a baby in there.

And the first time…she and Knox had forgotten condoms. That had been in the back of her mind, niggling at her consciousness, ever since. At the time, it had been lost in confessions of her virginity and the deep pain he'd expressed when talking about his daughter.

But the fact remained…the condoms had been forgotten.

The stomach she was currently scrutinizing felt as though it dropped down to her toes.

She could not be pregnant. Well, she could be pregnant—that was the trouble. She really could be. She and Knox had unprotected sex and she was… Well, she was late.

"No," she said to her reflection, bracing her arms on the dresser. "No," she said.

"What's going on?"

She turned around to see Knox standing there wearing a suit and a black tie, and if her stomach hadn't already been down in her toes, it would have done a full free fall.

"Nothing," she said, turning around quickly, still holding on to the dresser. "I just was afraid that I couldn't find my earrings. But I did."

"The ones you're wearing?"

"No," she said, grabbing for another pair on top of the cluttered dresser. "These."

And he kept staring at her, so she had to change into the earrings that she had already decided against. She took out the pair that looked absolutely perfect with her gold dress and sadly discarded them on the top of the dresser. Then she put the others in, smiling. "See?"

"Right," he said, clearly not seeing a distinction between the two. Because he was a man. Which was the only reason that her excuse actually worked. Because otherwise he would know that the other pair was clearly better.

"Are you ready to go?"

"Yes," she said.

"I got us a room at the hotel where the charity event is being held. You know, so that neither of us has to be the designated driver."

He was keeping his tone light, but she definitely sensed the hint of strain beneath it.

"Sounds good," she said.

At the mention of alcohol, she realized that she actually couldn't bring herself to drink a glass of champagne before she knew for sure.

Before she knew for sure if she was pregnant.

Oh, she was going to pass out. She really was. She wasn't sure how she was supposed to get through tonight. She needed to sneak away from him and get a test.

This wasn't happening.

It wasn't fair.

It definitely couldn't crash into the event tonight, because the event was way too important. For the memory of his daughter.

Suddenly, Selena was sure she was going to throw up.

"Are you okay?"

"I guess," she said. "I'm nervous." She opted to be honest about part of her problem so she could leave out the big, scary part. "I haven't seen Cassandra since your divorce. And the two of us are… You know."

"She's engaged," he said.

"It's not her that I'm worried about."

He frowned. "Are you afraid I'm going to see her and want her? Instead of you?"

"I don't know," she said, lifting a shoulder. "Yes."

"I'm not harboring secret feelings for Cassandra," he said. "We'll always be… We're linked. She and I created a life together. And then we both had to go through the experience of losing it. Losing Ellie. So it's not the same as if we were sharing custody or something. But…"

"I'm all right with that. I mean, I get it. I really do. And I am not upset about that at all. I just… She's prettier than me," Selena said finally.

He frowned. "You are the prettiest damned woman, Selena Jacobs," he said. He reached out and brushed his fingertips across her cheek. "I… I haven't felt this good in a long time. And the fact that I still feel pretty good even with all of this Ellie's House stuff looming on the horizon… It's a testament to you. I don't long for my marriage. The man who was married to Cassandra doesn't exist anymore. That's the only real way I can think to explain it. We changed too much and we didn't change together. Nobody's fault. It just is. But the woman she is now has found a different man. The man I am now wants you. Nobody else. I can't even compare the two of you. I don't want to. You're you.

You always have been. You occupy a special place in my life no one else ever has."

Her heart felt swollen, like it might burst through her chest. It wasn't quite a declaration of love, but it almost was. He put his arm around her and started to guide her out of the bedroom, and then they headed to the driveway, where he got into the driver's side of her car and started down the road that would take them to downtown Royal for the event.

This felt right, being with him for this event to celebrate his daughter's memory. She had to wonder what that meant. She had been so convinced that there was no future between herself and him. Had been utterly and completely certain that the two of them could have nothing but sex and friendship.

But they were in some different space where all those pieces had woven together, and her feelings for him were so big. So deep and real. She just didn't know where they were anymore. And she wondered why she was resisting at all. Because when she had decided she wasn't going to have a husband and children, when she had decided that love wasn't for her, that idea had been attached to an abstract man. Some version of her father who might someday betray her.

But this relationship she'd started wasn't with an abstract man. It certainly wasn't with anyone who resembled her father.

It was with *Knox*.

Knox, who had been one of her best friends for all of her adult life. She trusted him, more than she trusted just about anybody. She wasn't afraid of him. She wasn't afraid of loving him. He was a safe place for all those feelings to land.

And if she was having his baby…

She had no idea what to make of that. Had no idea what it would mean to him. She knew he'd said he didn't want to have a relationship again, but what if they were having a child? What would that do to him?

Suddenly, the whole situation seemed a lot more fraught than it had a moment ago. Just one moment of peace, and then it had evaporated.

Surely he would want another child, though—if she was really pregnant. He had been a wonderful father, and it wasn't as if a new baby would replace the little girl he had lost.

Her brain was still tying itself in knots when they arrived at the hotel. Cars and limousines were circling the area in front, valets taking the vehicles away to be parked, doormen ushering people inside. Knox stuck his black cowboy hat on his head and smiled at her, and then the two of them got out of the car and headed into the hotel. She clung to him, mostly because she thought if she let go of him she might collapse completely.

And not just because of those strange feelings of jealousy she'd had earlier. No, not at all. It had very little to do with that. It was just…everything else. Suddenly, what she and Knox were doing, what they were sharing, felt too big.

They made their way into the lobby of the hotel. It was art deco with inlaid geometric designs on the floor reflected in gold on the ceiling panels. There was a banner hung over the main ballroom, welcoming the distinguished attendees to the first annual fundraiser for Ellie's House.

But it was the picture on the stand, right in the entry of the ballroom, that stopped her short and made her breath freeze in her chest. It was a photograph of a lit-tle girl. Beautiful. Blonde.

With the same gray eyes as her daddy.

She was lying in a field with her hands propped be-neath her chin, yellow-and-purple wildflowers bloom-ing all around her.

Selena's heart squeezed tight and she fought to take a breath. She clung even more tightly to Knox, whose posture was rigid. She sneaked a glance at him and saw that he was holding his jaw almost impossibly tense. It hurt her to see that picture. In memoriam of a child who would be here if life was fair. She couldn't imag-ine how it was for him.

He paused for just a moment, and she looked away as he brushed his fingertips lightly over the portrait. It felt wrong to watch that. Like she was intruding on a private moment. On a greeting or a goodbye. She wasn't sure.

He straightened, then began moving forward. She rested her head on his shoulder as they walked, and she had a feeling they were holding each other up now.

The ornate room was filling up, but it didn't take long for her to spot Cassandra, her blond hair pulled back into a bun. She was all pointed shoulders and col-larbones, much thinner than she had been the last time Selena had seen her. But as beautiful as ever. Cassandra had always been a stunning woman, and tonight was no exception. She was wearing an understated black dress, with a ribbon pinned to the top.

She rushed over to greet them, her expression har-ried, her face a bit pale. "I'm so glad you made it," she said. She took a step forward, like she was ready to hug Knox, and then thought better of it. Instead, she reached into her clutch and produced two ribbons, pressing them into Knox's palm. "If you want to wear these."

"Thank you," he said.

"Hi," Cassandra said to Selena.

Selena broke the awkwardness and leaned in, embracing Cassandra in a hug. "Hi," she said. "It's good to see you."

Cassandra looked between them, her expression full of speculation, but she said nothing. Instead, she just twisted the large yellow diamond ring on her left hand.

"Is your fiancé here?" Knox asked.

"He was," Cassandra said. "I sent him out to get me some new nylons because I put a run in mine. He's good like that."

"He sounds it," he said, a slight smile curving his lips.

"Well," Cassandra said. "You know me. If there is a nylon in the vicinity I will cause a run in it."

"I'm glad you have someone to get you a new pair," he said.

"Me, too." After a beat of silence, she said, "I'm sorry—I have to go back to getting everything in order, but I'll find you again later tonight."

"You're gonna make tons of money," he said.

"I hope so," she said. "I hope we do. I hope I am part of making sure that in the future this doesn't happen. Not to anyone." Cassandra's blue eyes filled with tears and she looked away. When she looked back at Knox, her smile was in place. "Sorry. I have to go."

She turned abruptly, brushing her hands over her face, her slim shoulders rising and falling on a long breath. Then she strode forward resolutely, mingling with the other people who were starting to fill up the ballroom.

Selena could only be impressed with the way that Knox handled himself the whole evening. He had pinned the ribbon that Cassandra had given him proudly on his lapel, and Selena had done the same, to the top of her dress. And she did her very best to keep her focus on what was happening around them. Ellie's House—Ellie's memory—was simply too important for Selena to get caught up in her own worries.

There was a buffet, which Selena noticed Knox never went near. And she made a point of acting like she hadn't noticed. But when the band started to play, she asked him to dance.

He surprised her by complying.

He swept her into his arms, and for the first time in hours, she felt like things might be okay between them. "This is a wonderful tribute," she said, softly.

"Yes," he responded, the word clipped.

"I'm sorry." She lowered her head. "I said the wrong thing."

"No. It's just…still hard to accept that my daughter needs tributes. I guess I should be more used to it by now."

"No. Don't do that, Knox. You were caught off guard earlier."

"It was a nice picture," he said, his voice rough. "I remember the day it was taken. Out at the Jackson Hole ranch where we used to take picnics. I don't… I don't even like to remember. Even the good times hurt."

Selena didn't say anything. She just rested her head against his chest and swayed with him on the dance floor. They didn't speak much for the rest of the evening. Knox focused on talking to potential donors, rather than to her. But Selena was used to these types of events and it was easy for her to go off and do the same, to make sure she did her part to bring in money for the charity.

Cassandra gave an amazing speech about the importance of medical research, and the progress that was being made in the effort to treat childhood cancers and other childhood diseases. She talked about the function of the charity, how they donated money to innovative research teams and to housing for the various hospitals, so families could stay near their children while they received treatment and not be buried under the financial burden.

Selena found that she could only be impressed with Knox's ex-wife. She couldn't be jealous. She was just proud. And it seemed…okay then, that Knox would always have a connection with Cassandra. It seemed important even. Selena certainly wanted to be involved in supporting this effort with Ellie's House, and she thought it was amazing what Cassandra had done with her grief.

As the clock drew closer to midnight, Selena hit a wall, so tired that she was barely able to stand. Knox, on the other hand, was still moving dynamically around the room, stumping to have more checks written. It was amazing to watch the way the fire had been lit inside of him since they had arrived. Clearly he had a desire to make all of his family's suffering count for something. To make the loss count for something.

Suddenly she felt so nauseous, she thought she might collapse. Fuzzy-headed. Sleepy. It could just be stress and fatigue. It had been a crazy few weeks and a hard evening. She was just so overly…done.

She walked over to Knox and touched his arm. "I need to go to bed," she said.

He gave her a cursory glance, obviously still focused on the event. Which was fine with her. She imagined he would want to stay till the end. She *wanted* to stay; she was just going to fall over if she tried.

"I'll see you up in the room," he responded.

If he was disappointed about the fact that she would be asleep when he got there, rather than ready for sex, he didn't show it. But then, he was busy. And she could appreciate that. She could more than appreciate that. It was good to see him passionate about something, especially something involving his daughter's memory. Good to see him involved.

Selena slipped out the back of the ballroom and wrapped her arms around her midsection as she walked through the lobby. She felt so awful. So tired she thought she might fall asleep where she stood.

And though it *could* be stress and fatigue.

Or something a lot scarier.

There was only one way to find out whether or not she was carrying Knox's baby.

Maybe the timing sucked, and she should just go to bed. But now that she started thinking about the possibility again, she couldn't wait. Not another minute, and certainly not until tomorrow morning.

She stopped walking, pausing for a moment in front of the concierge desk. Then she took a tentative step forward.

"Is there a pharmacy close by?"

CHAPTER ELEVEN

KNOX FELT GUILTY about letting Selena leave the party without him. But he was engaged in a pretty intense conversation with a local business mogul about donations and ways to raise awareness, and he felt…like he was able to do something. Like he could be something other than helpless.

Tonight, Cassandra made much more sense to him. She had thrown herself into this. At first, her drive had been difficult for him. Because every reminder of Eleanor was a painful one. But now, after participating in the fundraiser, he understood.

Looking around at all of this, he couldn't help but understand. She was doing the only thing she could. Her mother's heart compelled her to let their daughter live on somehow, while Knox had been consumed in the grief.

He hadn't had it in him to take that kind of generous approach. To make sure what had happened to his daughter didn't happen to anyone else. But he had found it tonight. He had found something that he had thought long gone—hope. Like there was a future in this world that was worth being part of.

And that made him feel…like a little piece of himself had been recovered. A piece he had thought he might never access again. A piece that allowed him to be a part of the world, that allowed him to enjoy being alive. To enjoy the taste of food. The touch of a woman. The desire to accomplish something. Anything.

And, yes, the fundraiser had made a difference, but the catalyst for this change was all Selena.

As the night wore on, the crowds began to thin out, and finally, he was left with Cassandra, who sat up on the stage. She looked exhausted, and she looked sad.

"You did a good thing," he said, walking over and taking a spot next to her.

"Thank you," she said, treating him to a tired smile. "But I know."

"Isn't this exhausting?" he asked.

"What?" she asked. "Charity events?"

"Reliving this all the time," he said.

"I do anyway," she said. "So why not make something of it? This charity helps me feel like I'm moving on. Even though it all…stems from her, losing her. I don't know how to explain it, really. Like I'm taking the tragedy and making something positive with it."

He looked across the room and saw Cassandra's fiancé, who was helping with cleanup. He seemed like a good man. A great man. One who had jumped into all of this without having known Ellie at all, but who supported the charity just because it meant so much to Cassandra.

It occurred to Knox then that the truth of the matter was that Cassandra *was* a hell of a lot more moved on than he was.

And he didn't know what to feel about that. He didn't know how to reconcile it. He didn't know if he *wanted* to move on.

And yet moving on was what he had just been thinking about. That experience of beginning to enjoy life again.

Was that what she had now? Could she be thankful to be alive? Was she able to love this man? And not be afraid of loss?

Part of him still wanted to hold on to the past. Wanted to fight against blurry images, fading pain and the normalcy he was starting to feel on some days. Wanted to fight against the past slipping away. He wanted to go back out front and stare at that portrait of his daughter lying in a field of flowers. To memorize her face.

He just didn't want to forget.

He didn't *want* to come out the other side of this grief.

Suddenly, he felt like he was sliding down into a dark pit, and he had no idea what in hell to do about it. If he wanted to do anything about it at all. He had no idea what to do with any of these feelings. Had no idea what had happened to the good feelings from a few moments before, and even less of an idea about why he resented having those good feelings now.

Grief didn't make sense. All of the guides talked about stages and moving on. For him, it wasn't stages. It was waves, coming and going, drowning him. The memory of his child acting like a life raft in his mind.

How the hell could he move on from his own life raft?

Cassandra had said earlier that he was the only person who had been through what she had been through. And that was true. But now he was sitting here alone with these feelings. She had moved on. And there was no one. No one at all.

It scared him.

What would happen if they both went on with their lives like Ellie hadn't existed? If she became only this monument to a greater cause, instead of the child they loved so much.

And suddenly, he needed to get out of there. Suddenly, he needed to find Selena.

He knew she was asleep, but he needed her.

"I'm going up to bed," he said, and if his departure seemed sudden, he didn't much care. He walked out of the ballroom and headed through the lobby, getting into the elevator and checking the key in his wallet to see which room he and Selena were in. Then he pushed the appropriate button and headed up to their floor.

He got to the room and pushed the key card into the door, opening it slowly. When he got inside, Selena was not asleep as he'd expected.

She was sitting on the edge of the bed, her head bent down. She looked up, her face streaked with makeup and tears and a horrific sense of regret.

"What's going on?" he asked. "I thought you were going to sleep."

Then he looked down at her hands. At the white stick she was clutching between her fingers.

THE LOOK ON Knox's face mirrored what she was feeling.

Terror. Sheer, unmitigated terror.

But even through the terror, she knew they could do this. They would get through it as they had every other thing life had thrown at them over the years. They would make it work together.

She trusted him, and that was the mantra she kept repeating to herself, over and over again.

She had given Knox her heart slowly over the past decade. And now he had all of it, along with her trust.

She loved him.

She always had. But sitting there looking at the test results, she knew she was in love with him. The kind of love built to withstand. The kind that could endure.

She loved him.

They could weather this. She was confident they could.

"I'm sorry," she said. "I didn't want you to find out like this."

She had fully intended to talk to him tomorrow, but then she had ended up sitting on the edge of the bed, unable to move. Completely and utterly shell-shocked by what was in front of her in pink and white.

The incontrovertible truth that she was pregnant with Knox McCoy's baby.

She had cried, but she wasn't sad. Not really. It was just so much to take in, especially after spending the evening at the charity event. Especially after seeing the portrait of his daughter by the door and witnessing all the small ways grief affected him. The small ways that loss took chunks out of him over the course of an evening like this.

Now he was finding out about this. It just seemed a bit much.

"You're pregnant," he said.

"Yes. We didn't… We forgot a couple of times," she said, her voice muted.

That first time, down at the camp.

That second night, in her room when they had talked

about Eleanor and graham crackers and her heart had broken for him in ways she hadn't thought she could recover from.

"I can't do this," he said, his voice rough.

"I mean…" She tried to swallow but it was like her throat was lined with the inside of a pincushion. "A baby isn't tea. I can't…not serve it to you. I can't… Maybe this is our sign we have to try something real, Knox."

The words came out weak and she despised herself for them.

"I can't," he said again.

Her heart thundered so hard it hurt. Felt sharp. Like it was cutting its way out of her chest.

"We *can*," she said. "We can do this together, Knox. I know that it's not…ideal."

"Not ideal?" he asked, his words fraying around the edges. "*Not ideal* is a damned parking ticket, Selena. This is not *acceptable*."

Anger washed through her, quick and sharp. At him. At herself. At how unfair the whole world was. They should just be able to have this. To be happy. But they couldn't because life was hard, and it had stolen so much from him. She hurt for him; she did.

But oh, right now she hurt so much for herself.

"I'm sorry that the pregnancy is unacceptable to you, but it's too late. I'm pregnant."

"Selena…"

"I love you," she said. "I didn't want to say that right now either. I didn't want to do it like this, but… Knox, I love you. And I know that I've always said I didn't want a husband and children, but I could do it with you. If we are going to have a baby then I can do it. I *want* to do it."

She straightened her shoulders as she said the words, realizing just then that she was committing to her baby. "I… I want this baby."

He looked at her for a moment, his eyes unreadable.

"Then you're going to have it on your own."

She felt like she had been blasted through with a cannonball, that it had left her completely hollowed out. Nothing at all remaining.

Pain radiated from her chest, outward. Climbing up her throat and making it feel so tight she couldn't breathe.

"You don't want this?"

"I can't."

She felt for him. For his loss. She truly did. But it wasn't just her being wounded. It was their child. A child who was losing a chance at having him for a father.

She had thought…

She had no idea how she could have misjudged this—misjudged him—so completely.

She'd thought…if she knew one person on earth well enough to trust them it should have been him.

This was her nightmare.

But it wasn't just heartbreak over losing the man she loved, over losing the future she'd so briefly imagined for them before he walked into their suite.

No, she was losing her friend.

And bringing a child into the heartache.

"So that's it. You don't want to be a father again." Dread, loss, sadness…it all poured through her in a wave. She felt like she was back in the river with him, but this time, he was pushing her under instead of holding her up. "You don't want me."

"Selena, I already told you. I've had this. I've had it, and I lost it, and I cannot do this again. There is no mystery left in the damned world for me. I know what it's like to bury my child, Selena. I will not... I can never love another child like that. Ever."

She had trusted him.

That was all she could think as she stood there, getting ripped to shreds by his words.

As a young woman, she had been convinced that the hardest thing, the most difficult thing in the world, was enduring being beaten by a man with his fists. Her father had kicked her, punched her while she was down.

But this hurt so much worse. This was a loss so deep she could scarcely fathom it. This was pain, real and unending.

She couldn't process it.

She pressed her hand against her stomach. "Then go," she said, her mouth numb, her tongue thick. "Go. Because I'm not going to expose my child to your indifference. I'm not going to be my mother, Knox. I'm not going to have a man in my child's life who doesn't care about them."

"Selena."

"No. You're the one who said it. Why couldn't my mother love me enough to make sure I was in the best situation possible? Why didn't she protect me? Well, now I'm the mother, the one making choices. I'm going to love this baby enough for both of us. I'm going to give it everything I never had and everything you refuse to give it. Now get the hell away from me."

He was operating from a place of grief, and she

knew it, but he was an adult. She knew full well that her duty was to protect her child, not Knox's emotional state.

She was sick, and she was angry. And she didn't think she would ever recover.

"I just can't," he reiterated, moving toward the door of the hotel room.

"Then don't," she said. "But I don't believe the man who pulled himself up out of poverty, got himself into Harvard, stood by me as a good friend for all those years and came to Will's funeral, even though it was hard—I don't believe that man can't do this. What I believe is that you're very good at shutting people out. You go into yourself when it gets hard, rather than reaching out. Reach out to me, Knox. Let's do this together. I don't need it to be perfect or easy. We have a bunch of broken pieces between us, but let's try to make something new with them."

"I can't." He looked at her one more time with horribly flat, dark eyes, and then he turned and walked out of the hotel room, leaving her standing in a shimmering gold ball gown, ready to dissolve into a puddle of misery on the floor.

There was pain, and then there was this.

Knowing she was having her best friend's baby. And that she would be raising that baby alone.

CHAPTER TWELVE

HE DRANK ALL the way back to Jackson Hole. He drank more in the back of the car as his driver took him back to the ranch. And he kept on drinking all the way until he got back to his house and passed out in bed. When he woke up, he had no idea what time it was, but the sun was shining through the window and his head was pounding like a son of a bitch. He was also still a little bit drunk.

Best of both worlds.

He could hardly believe what had happened earlier. It all seemed like a dream. Like maybe he had never gone to Royal and had never gone to a funeral for Will that hadn't actually happened. Like maybe he had never slept with Selena. He had never gone to that charity event in honor of his daughter. And then Selena certainly hadn't told him she was pregnant with his baby.

Because why the hell would she be pregnant with his baby since certainly they had never really slept together?

And they certainly hadn't been living together like a couple. Playing house, reenacting the life that he had lost. A life he could never have again.

He got up and saw half a tumbler full of scotch sitting on the nightstand. He drained it quickly, relishing the burn as he fumbled for his phone. He checked to see if he had any missed calls and saw that he didn't. But he did see that it was about three in the afternoon.

He frowned down at his phone for a long moment, then scrolled through his contacts. "Hello?"

"Cassandra," he said, the words slurred.

"Knox?"

"Yes," he said. "I am drunk."

"I can tell." She paused, because clearly she wasn't going to help him with this conversation. She wasn't going to tell him why he had called. He wished she would. He sure as hell didn't have a clue. Didn't know why he was reaching out to her now when he hadn't done it during their marriage.

When he hadn't been able to do it when it might have fixed something.

"Are you all right?" she pressed.

"Fuck no," he said. "I am not all right."

"Okay." Again, she gave him nothing.

"How come you're happy?" he asked. "I'm not happy. I don't want to be happy. What happens if both of us are happy and we forget about her? We forget how much it hurt? And how much she mattered?"

He heard her stifle a sob on the other end of the line. "We won't. We won't."

"What if we do?" His heart felt like it was cracking in two. "I don't want to replace her. I can't."

"You won't," she said. "You won't replace her ever. Why would you think that?"

"Selena is pregnant," he said, "and I don't know what to do. Because it's like I traded our life in for a new version. That's not fair to anyone. It's just not."

His words didn't make any sense, but all he knew

was that everything hurt, and he couldn't make sense of any of it.

There were no words for this particular deep well of pain inside of him.

"You're not," she said, her voice cracking. "You're *not*."

"I'm sorry," he said. "I think I called to be mad at you. For being okay. For moving on. But now I'm just sorry. I should've been there for you. Maybe we should have been there better for each other."

"Maybe," she said. "But I didn't want to be."

Silence fell between them. "I didn't either."

"I loved our life," she said. "And it took me a long time to realize that I think I loved our life more than we loved each other. And when we lost Ellie… It wasn't that life anymore. And what we'd had wasn't enough to hold us together."

"Yeah," he agreed, her words making a strange kind of sense in his alcohol-soaked brain. "Yeah, I think so."

"You need to find somebody you love no matter the circumstances. Not just someone you love because she fits a piece in your life. Because she fulfills a role. Not a wife—a partner."

"I'm afraid," he said, the words ripped from somewhere down deep.

Cassandra laughed, soft and sympathetic. "Join the club. Believe me. Nobody is more afraid than me. I mean, maybe you. But it's hard. It's hard to open yourself up again. I think so… I think you already did. I think you're already in love. So don't keep yourself from it. That's not protecting yourself. That's just punishing yourself. And if that's what you're really doing… you need to stop."

"How?" he asked. "How am I supposed to stop punishing myself when I'm here and she's gone? When I couldn't protect her? How am I supposed to move on from that?"

When Cassandra spoke again, her voice was small. "You have to move on from it, Knox, because she isn't here anymore. And as little as either of us could do for her when she was ill, there's nothing we can do for her now. There's nothing you can do by holding on to your grief. She doesn't need you anymore. She doesn't need this from you."

He couldn't speak. His throat was too tight, his chest was too tight and everything hurt.

"Selena *needs* you," Cassandra continued. "The child you're going to have with her needs you. And you're going to have to figure out a way to be there for her, for this child, or you really aren't the man I met all those years ago."

He couldn't speak after that. And Cassandra let him off the hook, saying goodbye and hanging up the phone.

Because he wasn't that man. He wasn't. He didn't know how to be. He didn't want to be. He was changed. Hollowed out and scarred. Like a forest that had been ravaged by wildfire, leaving behind nothing but dead, charred wood.

Selena needed him.

Cassandra's words continued to echo through him. Selena needed him. Not Eleanor. Eleanor was gone, and it was unfair. But there was nothing he could do about it but grieve. And he knew he would do that for all of his life. There was no way to let go of something like that. Not truly. But maybe there was a way to learn to live. To live with the grief inside of you, to allow good memories to come back in and take residence alongside the pain.

To let love be there next to it, too.

Maybe moving on wasn't about being the man he used to be. Maybe it was about doing what Selena had said. Maybe it was about making something new out of the broken pieces.

Selena needed him. Their baby needed him.

He was beginning to suspect he needed Selena, too. That without her he was going to sink into the darkness forever.

The question was whether or not he wanted to let in the light.

SELENA HAD GONE to the doctor to confirm her pregnancy after securing someone else's canceled appointment, and then had gone to Paradise Farms to visit Scarlett and see how baby Carl was doing. While she watched her bright-eyed friend play with her new baby, Selena felt a strange mix of pain and hope.

She had made choices to protect her baby. To protect this little life growing inside of her that she already loved so much.

Watching Scarlett brought it all into full Technicolor. Made impending motherhood feel real.

"Do you like it?"

"What?" Scarlett asked, looking up from Carl's play.

"Being a mother."

"That's a funny question."

Selena lifted a shoulder. "I'm in a funny mood. Indulge me."

"Yes. Although there are periods where I'm so tired

I just want to lie on the floor and sleep." She shifted her hold on the baby and looked down at him, smiling. "And I have done that. Believe me. Sometimes I ask myself why I made this choice. Why I decided to have a baby before I had a life. But... I do like it. Adopting Carl has been the most rewarding thing I've ever done. Even though sometimes it's really hard. But I love him. And adding love to your life is never a bad thing."

Selena tapped the side of her mug of tea, looking out the window. "I like that. It's adding love."

"And a lot of work," Scarlett said. "Are you thinking about adopting?"

Her friend was likely joking, judging by the lightness in her tone. Because Selena had never given any indication she had an interest in adopting a baby. In fact, she was probably the least maternal person Scarlett knew. There was no way to ease her friend into this. No way to broach the subject gently.

So Selena figured it was time to drop the bombshell. "No, I'm not thinking of adopting. I'm pregnant."

Scarlett stared at Selena in shocked silence, opening and closing her mouth like a fish that had been chucked onto dry land. When she finally recovered her ability to speak, it came out as a shocked squeak. *"What?"*

Selena looked down into her teacup. Tea leaves were supposed to tell the future. Her Yorkshire Gold only contained the reflection of her own downtrodden expression. "It happened on the camping trip."

"Damn," Scarlett said. "I guess those tents really are romantic."

"Romance wasn't required," Selena said, grimacing. "It was more than a decade of pent-up lust."

She sighed and leaned back on the couch. "But he's

not ready for this. He doesn't want anything to do with me."

Scarlett frowned. "He doesn't? That's just... I don't know him that well, but everything I do know about him suggests that he's a better man than that."

"He is," Selena said. "He's a good man. But he's also a scared man. He's not doing a very good job of handling his fear. It just got all messed up. I found out I was pregnant the night we were at the gala fundraiser for the charity his ex-wife created in honor of their daughter. He freaked out. And I kind of don't blame him. The night was an emotional marathon."

Her eyes filled with tears, and her throat felt strange, like she had swallowed a sword, making it painful to breathe. "I only just found out I was pregnant and I got it confirmed today. And while I was sitting there waiting for the lab results to come in I just... It already hurt to think that I might lose the baby. That maybe I wasn't really pregnant or something had gone wrong with the first test. I don't even have a little person to hold in my arms yet and my love is so big. Knox lost a child... I'm angry at him for hurting me. But I can't fathom what he's gone through, the grief he feels. And as much as he deserves it, I can't even hate him for walking away."

"You don't need to hate him," Scarlett said. "You might need to punch him in the junk."

"I don't want to do that either. Okay. I want to do it a little bit. But I just... I'll do this parenthood thing by myself. You're doing it, right? I'll raise the baby. I can take care of us. I have plenty of money. My child is never going to want for anything."

Scarlett looked down at Carl and stroked a finger

over his downy cheek. "You're going to be a good mother."

"You say that with a lot of confidence."

"Because I know you. You'll probably be tired, and you'll probably make mistakes. I know I'm making mistakes all the time. But it all comes back to the love. Love covers a whole lot of things, Selena. I truly believe that."

"I just wish love could cover this." Tears she hadn't even been aware of began to slide down her cheeks. "I love Knox so much. I want him. For me. For the baby. But I also just wish he could have had a different life. Even if it meant losing him, I would give him a different life. But there's nothing I can do to ease his grief."

"Sure there is," Scarlett said, looking surprised.

"What?"

"Go after him."

Like it was the most obvious thing. And maybe to her fearless, confident friend, it was. But Selena was different. She didn't think she could survive getting turned down again.

"He doesn't want me to go after him," she said. "He walked away. He said he couldn't be a father to this baby. He said he didn't love me."

Scarlett shook her head. "Because fear makes you stupid. And that's exactly what *he's* letting happen. But you're letting him hide. You're letting him give in to it. Don't let him. Or at least make him tell you no again. Come on, Selena. He can be a coward all he wants, but you're not a coward. Make him look you in the eye in the light of day and say he doesn't want you or the baby. Make him tell you he doesn't love you.

And then make him tell you he's not just saying no because he's afraid."

Selena's heart thundered faster. It hadn't even occurred to her that it might not be over. That there might be something she could do to fix this. "But if he rejects me..."

"Then he rejects you." Scarlett shrugged, looking pragmatic about it.

Selena closed her eyes. "I never wanted to be that woman. That woman who was such a fool over a man. My mother... She stayed with my father even though he was awful. Even after she left him, she missed him. The man who abused her, Scarlett—she said she missed him. I just don't... I don't want to be that person."

Scarlett frowned. "I can understand that. Really. But you know, hopefully, if you go make a fool of yourself for him, he'll make a fool of himself for you at some point, too. If you're going to be together for your whole lives, then there should be a lot of chances for both of you to chase each other down. For both of you to be idiots over love. I guess that's the big difference, right? Your mother was the one doing all of the giving, and your father did all of the taking."

Selena bit her lip. "It would never be like that with Knox."

"Well, there you go," Scarlett said, extending her arm out wide. "It's not the same."

Selena shook her head and sighed deeply. "No. I guess it's not." She put her hand on her stomach. "I don't feel in any way emotionally prepared for this."

"Well, good," Scarlett said, laughing. "Because if you did, I would have to break it to you that you're actually not. It would be up to me to tell you that you are in no way prepared. No matter what you might think."

"It's that different?"

Scarlett nodded. "Harder. Better, too."

Like love in general, Selena supposed.

She stood up, wobbling slightly, her balance off. She blamed the last few days.

"I have to go," Selena said.

"Where to?"

"I have to fly to Wyoming."

CHAPTER THIRTEEN

KNOX HAD SPENT the rest of the day hungover and then
had spent the next day working out on the ranch. Doing
what he could to exhaust himself mentally and emotionally while he got all his thoughts together.

He had been pretty determined about what he
wanted to do regarding Selena, but he had to be sure
he was going to say the right thing. Because when you
told a woman you didn't want her you had to prepare
a pretty epic grovel.

He wasn't going to do anything to cause Selena
more pain than he already had. And he had a lot of
digging to do to find the right words. Through the dark
and dusty places inside of himself.

He'd been restless and edgy in the house, and he'd
decided to go out for a ride on the property. He urged
his horse onward through the field, and he continued
on to the edge of his favorite mountain. One with jagged rocks capped in snow that reached up toward the
sky, like it was trying to touch heaven. Something he
wished he could do often enough.

He wasn't a man who liked graveyards. But then, he
supposed no one did. He just didn't find any peace in
them. No, he found peace out here. With nature. That
was when he felt closest with Ellie.

He looked around at the wildflowers that were

blooming, little pops of purple and yellow against the green. Life. There was life all around him. A life to be lived. A life to enjoy. Maybe even a life to love, in spite of all the pain.

It was like that picture of Ellie. Sitting right here in this field surrounded by flowers.

He knew he wouldn't find her here, and yet he'd needed to come to this place. He'd avoided riding out here for the past two years.

Today had seemed like the day to go again. The last time he'd ridden out to this field, the last time he'd seen this view, he was a different man with a different future.

A man who'd known who he was and where he was going.

Now he was a man alone. Struggling to figure out what came next. If he could heal. If he wanted to heal.

An image of Selena flashed into his mind, of her hurt and heartbreak that night in the hotel room. She needed him. She needed him now.

Selena wasn't gone. Selena was here. And they could be together.

"I've got to figure out how to find some happiness, baby," he said, whispering the words into the silence. Whispering the words like a prayer. "I'm never going to forget you. I'm never going to stop loving you. But I'm going to learn how to love some other people, too. I'm going to take some steps forward. That doesn't mean leaving you behind. I promise."

He closed his eyes and waited, letting the silence close in around him. Letting himself just be still. Not working. Not struggling or fighting. Just existing. In the moment and with all the pain that moment carried.

The breeze swirled around him and he kept his eyes closed, smelling the flowers and the snow, crisp on the air as it blew down from the mountaintop.

That was assurance. Blessed assurance.

Letting go didn't mean forgetting. Moving forward wasn't leaving behind.

And in that moment, as he took a breath of the air that contained both the promise of spring and the bite of winter, he realized it was the same inside of him, too. That he could contain all of it. That he could hold on to that chill. That he could welcome the promise of new life.

There was room for all the love. For the bitter. For the sweet. For everything in between. There was no limit, as long as he didn't set it.

He knew what love could take away. He also knew what it could give. He had despaired of that for so long. That there were no mysteries left available to him. That he knew all about the heights of love and the lows of loss.

But he realized now that he had the most powerful love yet ahead.

The love he chose to give, in spite of the knowledge of the cost.

He just had to be brave enough to take hold of it.

He got down off his horse and bent to pick the brightest, boldest yellow wildflower. He held it between his thumb and forefinger. Ellie's flower. Just like in that picture. He stroked his thumb over one petal and a smile touched his lips.

He put the flower in his shirt pocket, just over his heart, and looked at the view all around him. A view he hadn't allowed himself to enjoy since he'd lost his daughter. A place that was full of good memories. Good memories he'd shut away so they couldn't hurt him.

But they were part of him. Part of his life. Part of her life. And he wanted them. Wanted to be able to think of her and smile sometimes. Wanted to be able to remember the joy loving her had given him, not just the sorrow.

That was what he'd forgotten. How much joy came with love. Of course, you couldn't choose what you got. Couldn't take the good without risking the bad.

But you could choose love. And he was ready to do that.

It was time to walk forward. Into the known and the unknown.

And as long as Selena would have him, he had a feeling it was going to be okay.

He closed his eyes and faced the breeze again, let it kiss his face. Then he mounted the horse and took off at a gallop across the field, heading back toward the homestead.

He got his horse put away and strode out toward the front of the house. He needed to get his private plane fired up, because he had to get back to Texas, and he had to get back fast.

After what he had said to her, a phone call wasn't enough. He needed to go and find her. And he needed to tell her. To tell her he was sorry. To tell her they could do this. They could be together.

To tell her that he was done running.

There was something big, something fierce expanding in his chest. Something he hadn't felt in a long time.

Joy.

Selena.

And almost as if those feelings had brought her out of thin air, he looked up when he reached the front of his house and there she was. Standing in the center of the driveway, looking small and pale and a little bit lost. Selena Jacobs didn't do lost, and he had a feeling he was the cause of that desolate look on her face.

His heart clenched tight, guilt and love pouring through him.

"What are you doing here?" he asked.

She lifted her chin. "I came to get you."

"You can't be here to get me. I was about to get on a plane to go get *you*."

Her bottom lip wobbled. "What?"

"I don't know what you're here for, Selena. But you have to hear me out first. Because I have to tell you. I have to tell you about everything I've realized. It's been a hell of a time."

"Yeah," she said, her tone dry. "You're telling me."

"I'm sorry," he said. "I'm sorry that I hurt both of us, but most especially you. I'm sorry that I did so much damage. I was afraid to move on. Because...because of the guilt. I just... The guilt and the fear. It isn't that I don't want the baby. It isn't that I don't love you. I do. I want you, and our baby, so much I ache with it. I want so much that it scares me, Selena, because I haven't wanted a damn thing in years. I haven't let myself want anything. Not even food. Because wanting, needing, *loving*, in my experience has meant devastation. I can't come up with another excuse. It's just that. I am so afraid that I might lose you someday. That if I love you too much, want to hold you too close, that something will happen, and I'll have to face that dark tunnel again. I couldn't survive it, baby. I couldn't. You've meant everything to me for a long time. And now, wanting you as a lover, loving you as a woman, I know that the loss of you would destroy me. The loss of our life. The loss of our child...

"But I can't live that way. I can't live in fear. I can't live holding on to only bad feelings to try and protect myself."

He walked toward her, took her hands. "I called Cassandra. Drunk off my ass. She said something to me... She was right. She said you have to love the person you find more than you love your life together. What Cassandra and I had felt perfect. But only as long as it *was* perfect. Once that fractured, we couldn't put it back together. We didn't want to. We loved what we had more than we loved each other. But when I fell in love with you, Selena, we had nothing. Nothing but those broken pieces. And what you said... I think it's the way forward. That we put these broken pieces together and we make something new. I can't go back. I can never be who I was. But I can try to be something new. To be something different. I can try to be the man you deserve."

She said nothing. Instead she sobbed as she threw her arms around his neck and clung to him, her tears soaking into his shirt. "Seriously?" she asked, the word watery.

"What seriously?"

"You really want to do this?"

"I need to," he said. "I need you. I realized something today, walking around the property. Winter and spring exist side by side here. It's been winter inside of me for a long time. And there's a part of me that's afraid of what letting go of that means. That it means I don't love Ellie enough. Or that I didn't."

"Of course you loved her enough," Selena said. "Of course you do. I know that in our lives together I want to honor that. This baby, this child, is never going to replace what you lost."

"I know," he said. "That was what I realized. I can make room in my heart for both of them." He reached into his pocket and removed the yellow flower, holding it out for her. "This is us. This spring. New life. A new season. I want to make room inside of me for that. I want less cold. Less fear. More of this."

"Please," she said, smiling and taking the flower from his hand. "Yes, please. More spring. A lot more."

"I love you," he said. "I love you knowing that love is the most powerful thing on earth. That having it makes everything brighter, that losing it can destroy your whole world. I love you knowing what it might cost. And maybe that's a strange declaration, but it's the most powerful one I've got."

He cupped her chin, lifted her face to meet his. "When you're young, you get to dive into things headlong. You get to embrace those big, scary feelings not knowing what might wait for you on the other side. I know. But I want to choose a life with you. More than anything, I want to love you. If you want to love me." He let out a long, slow breath. "You know, if you still can love me."

"I do love you," she said. She held on to his face, met his eyes. "I love you so much, Knox. And the thing is, I could never tumble headlong into it when I was younger because I was scared. But I've grown up. I trust you. And trust has always been the key. I know what kind of man you are. I was afraid of love for a long time, but I was never afraid of you."

"But I hurt you."

"Yes," she said. "You did. But you were hurting, too. You didn't hurt me because you were a bully or because you enjoyed causing me pain. You did it because you were running scared. I get that. But that doesn't mean I'm not going to make you pay for it later."

"Oh, are you?"

"I am." She smiled. "I'm going to make you give my skin-care line preferential shelving in your supermarkets."

"Corporate blackmail."

"Yes," she said, "corporate blackmail. But it could be worse. It could be sexual blackmail."

He wrapped his arm around her waist and drew her up against his body. "Honey," he said, "you couldn't stick to sexual blackmail."

"I sure as hell could," she said, wiggling her hips against him. "And you would suffer."

He leaned forward and nipped her lower lip. "You would suffer."

"Okay," she said, her cheeks turning pink. "Maybe I would."

"Will you marry me, Selena? Marry me and make a new life with me? I'll never be the man that I was. But I hope the man I am now is the one for you."

Her smile turned soft. "He is. Believe me," she said, "he is."

"So that's a yes?"

"Yes," she said. "I never thought I would walk down the aisle for real. But, Knox, if ever I was going to, it had to be with you."

He looked down at Selena, at the woman he had known for so many years, the woman he'd gone on such a long journey to be with.

"Right now," he said, "this moment… It can only ever be you. You're the one worth being brave for. You're the one who made me want to start a new life. And I'm so damned glad that you did."

"Me, too," she said and then squeaked when he picked her up off the ground and held her to his chest.

"I'm also glad that you saved me a flight," he said, heading back toward the house with her in his arms.

"Well, I'm glad to be so convenient."

"You're more than convenient," he said. "You're inconvenient. You made me change. Nobody likes that."

"Oh dear," she said, "however will you punish me?"

He smiled. "I'll think of something."

"You've always been my best friend," she said, hours later when they were lying in bed together, thoroughly sated by the previous hour's activities. "And now you're more. Now you're everything."

"I'm happy to be your everything, Selena Jacobs. I'm damned happy that you're mine."

He kissed her, a kiss full of promise. A kiss full of hope for the future.

And he smiled, so happy that for the first time in an awfully long time he had both of those things.

And more important, he had love.

EPILOGUE

A CHILD'S LAUGHTER floated on the wind, and Selena ran to keep up with the little figure running ahead of her. She had long, dark hair like her mother, and it was currently bouncing with each stride.

She had her father's eyes.

Selena's husband was lingering behind her, his speed slowed by the fact he was holding their new son.

Selena turned to look at them both. Knox was clutching the five-month-old baby to his chest, his large hand cradling the downy head. Knox was such a good father.

He was caring, and he was concerned, and he had a tendency to want to rush to the doctor at the very first sniffle, but she couldn't blame him. And watching the ways in which their children had opened him up…it made her heart expand until she couldn't breathe.

"Carmela!" Selena shouted. "Slow down."

Their daughter stopped and turned to look at them, an impish grin on her three-year-old face. She stopped, in the field of yellow-and-purple flowers, with the snow-covered mountains high and imposing behind her.

Selena turned back and saw that Knox had stopped walking. That he was just standing there, staring at Carmela.

Selena took two steps back toward him and put her hand on his forearm. "Are you okay? Do you need me to take Alejandro?"

"No," he said, his voice rough.

Carmela was turning in a circle, spinning, careless and free out in the open.

Knox couldn't take his eyes off her. He was frozen, his expression full of awe.

"What is it?" Selena asked.

"I just can't believe it," he responded. "That I have this again. This chance to love again. To love her. To love him." He brushed his hand over baby Alejandro's head. And then he turned those gray eyes to her. His desire for her was hot, open. It made her shiver. "To love you."

He leaned in and kissed her, and she shivered down to her toes.

"I remember feeling like I had nothing," he said. "Nothing to hope for. Nothing to hold. And now… I have hope. I have a future. And my arms are full."

Selena wrapped her arms around him and rested her head on his chest. "My best friend knocked me up on accident," she said. "And all I got was…this whole wonderful life."

He kissed her one more time, and when they parted she was breathless. Then the two of them walked on toward their daughter, toward the future. Together.

* * * * *

ONE NIGHT
WITH THE MAVERICK

Melissa Senate

For my mother, with all my love.

CHAPTER ONE

IF THIRTY-FOUR-YEAR-OLD widower Felix Sanchez *were* in the market for a relationship, he wouldn't have to bother with dating apps or pricey matchmakers. Not when his eighty-five-year-old great-uncle Stanley spent his days walking up to women without wedding rings in the grocery store to tell them all about his single nephew. *And did I mention he's a doctor? An animal doctor! Bulls, turtles, puppies, he takes care of them all. Tall, handsome fella, too.*

Santiago "Stanley" Sanchez, who'd moved in with the Sanchez family just a few months ago because of his loneliness after losing his wife, never walked away without a phone number for Felix. Not that Felix ever used any of them. His dresser drawer at home was full of slips of paper and business cards. But tonight, Stanley had Felix roped in. His uncle had promised "a very attractive redhead" that they'd be at Doug's bar tonight at seven if she wanted advice on her Pomeranian who chewed up her running shoes, *So you have to come tonight, Felix.*

Grrr. All Felix wanted to do after having partaken in his mother's great cooking—she'd made tamales tonight and he'd eaten five of them—was watch a game, do a little research on some new medications that would be coming into his veterinary office, and call it a night after a long day of tending those bulls and turtles and puppies. A big animal vet who also had clinic hours at the Bronco Heights Animal Hospital, Felix was zonked. He'd started at five thirty this morning—a sick calf—and finally left the clinic at 6:00 p.m.

"You're wearing that?" Stanley said from the doorway of Felix's bedroom. "Can't you put on a nice button-down?"

"We're going to everyone's favorite Bronco Valley dive bar, Uncle Stanley. My University of Montana sweatshirt, growling grizzly mascot and all, will do just fine."

Stanley gave a slight frown. "Did I mention that lovely redhead who'll be there to talk to you about her little dog is very stylish? A fashion plate."

"Tio. You know I love you. But you've gotta stop with the fix-ups and promises and ruses to put me and single women in the same place at the same time. It's not fair to the women you rope in. I'm not looking for a relationship. It's way too soon."

Stanley waved his hand in the air with a grunt. "It's been three years, Felix. It's time to find love again. And," he added, looking at his watch, which Felix gave him for his birthday last month, "it's almost seven." A big grin split his handsome, lined face. *"Vamos!"*

You go, he wanted to say. But truth be told, he was a little worried about Stanley. Outgoing and warm and funny with his saucy but still G-rated jokes and big laugh, his uncle made friends everywhere he went, yeah. But despite that, Stanley was lonely. He'd lost his dear wife of sixty years just last year, and his grief, the raw pain in his *tio*'s voice when they'd speak by phone, had gotten Felix on a plane a few times to Mexico, where Stanley had still lived, to stay for a few days. Just a few months ago, he'd finally convinced Stanley, with his parents' and siblings' help, to move to the US and start fresh in Montana.

No good deed, he thought, shaking his head with a smile. An hour or two at Doug's, playing a few rounds of darts, nursing a cold beer, didn't sound so bad if it would make his *tio* happy.

"Oh, wait, I forgot something!" Stanley said, hurrying to his room downstairs on the first level. "Meet me by the front door in five."

Felix nodded, grabbed his wallet and keys and was about to head out when his gaze caught on a photo of Victoria. He had just the one now in his bedroom. He'd moved back home soon after he'd lost her to cancer, barely able to slog through a day, let alone take care of the house they'd shared. Had it been three years? Sometimes it felt like *twenty*-three years since he'd been widowed. Sometimes it felt like yesterday.

Downstairs at the door, the smell of his uncle's favorite aftershave overpowered the delicious lingering aroma of the tamales and rice they'd had for dinner.

"Last chance to change your shirt," Stanley said with hope all over his face.

"Nah, I'm good."

"Good-looking!" Stanley said with a laugh and three little punches on Felix's arm.

Felix laughed, too. His uncle's goofy jokes and good-humored kindness were infectious, even when Felix just wanted to brood.

"And no doubt your soon-to-be new girlfriend," Stanley added, "the pretty redhead with the Pomeranian will think so, too."

Felix shook his head and headed for his SUV, till Stanley headed for his own pickup.

Stanley hopped in the driver's seat. "I'll drive tonight. It's one of those gorgeous early fall nights. Sixty-four degrees. Nice breeze. I want to roll the windows down and crank up the mariachi."

Which he did, singing along to an old CD as they drove over to Doug's in Bronco Valley, not far from the Sanchez home in the same part of town.

As they headed in, an '80s-era Bon Jovi song was blaring from the old-timey jukebox. The bar was pretty crowded tonight. An easel by the door had a sign noting that Bronco's resident psychic, Winona Cobbs, would be giving free readings from 6:00 until 7:15 p.m. A few times a year, Winona, who had her own psychic shop in town, held events at Doug's.

Felix had no interest in a psychic reading, even if he'd heard Winona, whose readings were short and sweet, sometimes just one line, *always* got it right. Felix had no interest in what was coming. He'd had his share of bad news coming to fruition.

He and Stanley took two seats at the long bar, and within moments, a redhead, indeed pretty and stylish, had materialized in the open seat beside him. Stanley disappeared with his quarters to the jukebox, naturally. Felix listened to the woman's troubles with her Pomeranian, Peaches, gave her some advice about keeping her sneakers behind closed doors in a closet and giving Peaches toys with a similar texture.

"I hope you make house calls," the woman said in a throaty purr and rested her hand on his arm.

Felix went for honesty. "For emergencies, but I

should add that I'm a recent widower and I'm not ready to date."

The part about being widowed always seemed to let women know his lack of interest wasn't personal, and sometimes he even made a friend out of his uncle's matchmaking ways. The redhead left, and the next time he looked over at her table, she was deep in conversation with a rancher.

The bartender, Doug Moore himself, took his and Stanley's order, plunking down their bottles of beers. Stanley turned around on his barstool until he was facing out, sipping his beer, and keeping his eyes on the dartboard for when it would be free.

"Now there's a woman who knows how to live," Stanley said, sitting up straighter, and—if Felix wasn't mistaken—sucking in his belly. Stanley pointed his beer bottle at white-haired Winona Cobbs, who sat at a round table near the back of the room likely so she could conduct her readings privately and away from the blare of the jukebox. "I like her style. I surely do." Stanley seemed riveted by Winona, his dark brown eyes getting all twinkly.

Felix smiled. Winona Cobbs, wearing a purple cowboy hat, silver fringed pantsuit and purple cowboy boots, was ninety-five years old. An older woman even by eighty-five-year-old Stanley's standards.

"Ooh, that man just left her table," Stanley said, hopping off the barstool. "I'm going over for a reading. You should too, Felix."

"You go ahead," he told his uncle. Felix had always been superstitious—enough to avoid walking under open ladders or crossing the paths of black cats, which also happened to be his secret favorites, and he knocked on wood if he ever proclaimed anything. Plus, he really had heard enough stories about Winona's readings coming true for people to know she did have psychic gifts. But he'd rather his future remain a mystery. It was better not to know.

"I'll need a proper introduction," Stanley said, giving his throat a gentle clear and again sucking in his belly, not that he had much of a beer gut. Stanley Sanchez was six feet tall and robust and liked to wear black leather vests over Western-style shirts, a black cowboy hat and cowboy boots. His look was one of the reasons everyone in town had taken to him so easily and fast. He fit in.

Felix took a slug of his beer, then another, and walked over to Winona's table with his uncle. He knew her only casually from around town.

"Miss Cobbs," Felix began.

Winona's sharp gaze beelined to him. "Oh, my," she said. "Your life is an open book, but I'm afraid there's nothing there for me to read."

Felix frowned. What the heck did that mean?

"But *this* face," she added, staring at Stanley warmly—and with interest—"this face tells a whole story."

Stanley grinned. "I can't wait to hear what's in store for me, Miss Winona." He sat down, never taking his eyes off the nonagenarian. "Felix, bring me my beers, will you?"

"Sure," Felix said, but he doubted his uncle even heard him. He was already chatting up a storm with the white-haired psychic, complimenting her outfit and mentioning that purple was his new favorite color.

Oh, Lord. His uncle was *flirting*.

hair was gorgeous. And the eyeglasses, though maybe not those same ones.

Sarah. Sandra. Stephanie. Selina. Something with an *S*... He could smell her faint perfume, a sandalwood tinge to it that he liked. He sucked down his drink and figured he'd go grab his uncle and they'd head home, but when he turned around, he saw Stanley sitting *beside* Winona now, not across from her like before, and they were both staring into each other's eyes and talking.

Had his uncle picked up a woman in Doug's superdive bar? An older woman? Felix shook his head with a grin. *Hey. More power to you, Tio.*

Felix turned back around, eyeing the plate of buffalo wings and blue cheese dressing Doug had placed down in front of the strawberry blonde. He'd had so many tamales that he wasn't hungry, but man, those wings smelled good.

"Want one, Felix?" the woman offered, pushing the plate a little to the right.

She knew *his* name. Now he felt even worse that he didn't remember hers. He wondered what else she knew about him. That he was a widower? That he was a veterinarian? That he didn't go out much? Or usually drink much?

Yet here was, sucking down his fourth of the night like it was water.

What was wrong with him?

You're alone. In a crowded bar. Realizing that your formerly wonderful life is behind you, not ahead of you.

He sighed and took a wing, swiping it in the blue cheese.

"Thanks," he said. He took a bite. Delicious.

She smiled. The kind of smile that lit up a face that was already *too* pretty.

He felt someone come up behind him, stopping between him and the blonde. It was Everlee Roberts, whom everyone called Evy, a waitress at Doug's. "Hey, Felix. Did you know your uncle just left with Winona Cobbs?"

He stared at Evy. "What? They left?" He glanced at the table. Empty, just like both his uncle's beers.

"No worries," Evy told him as if reading his mind. "They left on foot." He strained his neck to look out the window and saw his uncle's truck still parked in the lot. But no sign of Stanley. Or Winona.

Which meant his uncle had stranded him here since Tio had the keys. Great. Doug's was a quick drive from his house, but still a good four miles away, and two beers and two whiskey shots had made him a little tipsy, he realized. No one wanted to see their veterinarian, big animal or turtle, stumbling home from a dive bar.

He could call his dad, but then remembered his parents had left for the movies not long before he and Stanley had gone out. Darn. He could bother one of his siblings but he'd never hear the end of how he let Uncle Stanley disappear into the night with a woman— a psychic, no less, who clearly had to know the night would end well.

He wasn't sure his uncle wanted any of *that* to be family knowledge, so he ignored his phone. There was always a rideshare, he thought, signaling to Doug for another whiskey. No, make that a draft beer.

Two were set before him.

He drank one, thinking about old times. Thinking

about his old life. And thinking about what the hell the nice-smelling, green-eyed blonde woman's name could possibly be.

Sera. Serena. Sally. Suki. None of those were right. Sensual. That she was.

As she and Evy started chatting, something about a story hour at the library, he started on the second beer. His *second* second beer but his sixth drink. Felix realized he didn't need to know the blonde's name. It wasn't like they'd be flirting up a storm the way his uncle and Winona had. Let alone leaving together, for heaven's sake. He wouldn't be leaving with a woman from a bar for a long, long time. Even if it had been a long, long time since he'd lost Victoria. He was fine on his own.

Just fine. But that didn't stop him from thinking about how they'd so excitedly decided to start a family just days before her diagnosis with cancer. How walking past a playground, how seeing a baby or toddler at the clinic during an appointment for the family pet made his heart clench.

Those times would remind him his heart wasn't numb like he thought. And that he'd never be ready to know the strawberry blonde's name.

SHARI LORMAND MENTALLY shook her head at the gorgeous man sitting next to her, drinking away his sorrows at Doug's bar. She rarely saw Felix Sanchez out, but had been aware of him for years, since high school, when she'd had a secret crush on him. She'd been too shy to start a conversation with him back then. And the morning she'd marched into school determined to at least say hi, he'd been holding hands with a beautiful dark-haired girl named Victoria. So much for Shari and Felix becoming the couple in her dreams.

And now, being single, *very* single at thirty-four, Shari was aware of every eligible bachelor in town, and Felix Sanchez, widower of three years, was *not* eligible. He was clearly not over losing his wife, not that he should be, of course. He just happened to stand out in town since he was so damned good-looking with those intense hazel eyes and dark thick hair that was just slightly long for a veterinarian and made him look a bit like a rebel. Shari always noticed him when she saw him around Bronco.

"Oh, Felix, I have to thank you again," Evy said, collecting empty glasses from the bar, including a few of Felix's. "Archie is doing really well now. Wes and I can't thank you enough for saving our puppy."

Shari glanced at Felix. She remembered how worried Evy had been about her now-fiancé's puppy, Archie, who'd been swatted by a mama bear protecting her cubs back in July. Not only had Felix saved the adorable pup's life, but he'd apparently called a few times to check in on how Wes Abernathy, Evy and Evy's young daughter were doing during the recovery and rehab since they were all so worried about Archie. That Felix was one of the good guys wasn't in doubt. He just wasn't *available.*

"Really glad to hear it," Felix said.

As Evy got called away to take a table's order, Shari thought about making a quick getaway. She'd come for wings and a beer and to drown her own sorrows, but being so close to a guy like Felix—who ticked every box on her list of what she wanted in a man, in a husband, in the father of her future children—made her feel even more alone. She should go home, draw a bath, pour in some of the scented bubbles she'd gotten as a gift, and forget about how lonely she was. She hated that word *lonely*. But between wanting to get married and all the terrible dates and false starts at relationships, Shari Lormand, children's librarian with an otherwise rich and full life, was lonely.

Her mother's call a half hour ago had left her weirdly unsettled, which was really why she'd stopped in at Doug's, needing…something. A little company, a little noise from voices and the jukebox. Her mom lived in Denver, where the Lormand family had moved after Shari graduated from high school because her father had been transferred for work. Shari had gone to college in Denver, loving city life after growing up in a small town like Bronco. She'd dated a little, had a couple of yearlong relationships, and figured she'd meet her Mr. Right soon. She thought she had when she was twenty-six—Paul, a medical intern who was smart and focused and liked to cook for her in his little free time. When he'd used his long hours and stress as the reason why he was putting off proposing—for five years—Shari had believed it all because she'd been unable to bear believing otherwise. That he just didn't want to marry *her*. That became apparent when she gave him something of an ultimatum, a really weak one: *If you're not able to tell me you want to marry me by the end of the year, I'll have to think about moving on.* Paul broke up with her that night.

And he married someone else a few months later. He'd actually sent her a thank-you card for giving him that ultimatum, which had made him realize he just didn't love her in that way and when he'd met his wife, he'd known she was the one right away. *So thank you, Shari, from both of us.*

Shari had been so hurt, so mad at her own inability to see the truth for years, that she'd left Denver and headed back home to warm, sweet, cozy Bronco, Montana. She'd wanted the familiarity of her hometown and all the comforts that went with it. And now, three years later, Bronco *was* comforting. She loved her job at the library. She had really wonderful friends, like Evy. But being strung along like that and then dumped had made her wary and she was probably a little *too* guarded on dates. The few relationships she'd had hadn't gone anywhere. Now here she was, still single—and thirty-four. And now her biological clock was ticktocking and she wanted children, adding to the pressure.

Tonight, her mother had been filling her in on life and gossip in Denver and the family, then casually mentioned seeing Shari's ex with his pregnant wife and toddler daughter. That had put Shari in a mood, to say the least.

And spicy wings, a cheap beer—or two—and a hot but unavailable man right beside her hadn't helped much.

She and Evy had talked endlessly about the state of Shari's love life, her friend assuring her the man of her dreams was right around the corner. Evy was the single mother of a darling four-year-old named Lola and over the summer had unexpectedly found true love with a great guy, Wes Abernathy—a wealthy rancher who was great with kids and loved dogs, as Evy did. Shari was taken by little Lola, who loved coming to the children's library events. The sweet girl made her so wistful about how much she wanted a child of her own.

To the point that she'd stared exploring her options. If she wasn't going to get married and have a baby the traditional way, there were other ways to become a mother. Sperm donor and IVF. Adoption. She'd just started looking into it all, and it was so overwhelming that she hadn't gotten very far.

Because you want what you've dreamed of since you were a teenager. To fall in love. Marry the man you want to grow old and gray with on your porch, sipping sweet tea, an old dog or two beside you. Have three or four kids. Shari loved the idea of a big family, but now she'd be very happy with one child.

Two pretty young women came in and settled on the barstools on the other side of Shari.

"Aren't you a veterinarian?" one of the women asked over her to Felix, a hand twirling her silky blond hair. "I'm thinking of adopting a puppy and would love some tips for a first-timer."

Oh, brother, Shari thought, sure the woman's interest was not in a puppy. She inwardly sighed and pulled a novel out of her tote bag. She'd finish her wings, another chapter of the absorbing romantic suspense, then get the heck out of here. She couldn't help but smile when she noticed Felix was not flirting back. He was polite but so clearly not interested that the women got up and moved to the group of guys playing darts. She heard a "Well, *hello* ladies" from one of them and rolled her eyes. Everyone was having fun but her. And Felix, apparently.

"Last wing is yours, if you want it," she said to Felix. "I've gotta get home. Busy, busy night ahead of me."

"Oh, yeah?" he asked, taking the wing and swiping it in the dressing. "Working on something?"

"Hot bath, Netflix, more of this book," she said, then felt her cheeks turn red. Had she just lied in his face about being busy and then told him the stark truth of her real next few hours? She quickly shoved her book in her bag.

"Sounds like a perfect night to me," he said. "But I'm stranded here." He explained about arriving with his uncle, who had immediately gotten very chatty with Winona Cobbs and left with her.

"Wow!" Shari said, utterly charmed. "That's really sweet." And inspiring. She was pretty sure that Winona was well into her nineties. And now even Winona had a love life.

"Except my uncle has the keys," Felix said. "And his truck is right there," he added, pointing out the window. "Mocking me."

Shari smiled. "Come on. I'll give you a ride home."

"Thanks—" he started, then seemed deep in concentration, as if trying very hard to remember her name.

She scowled as she stood up, careful to not even touch the caution tape around the haunted barstool with her tote bag or elbow lest she add more bad luck to her life. "You don't know my name, do you?" she accused lightheartedly, eyes narrowed. Her voice might be light but *humph*—how dare he not remember her?

"To be very honest," he said, standing up, too, "I've had a few drinks. I can't remember my own middle name. But I'm pretty sure your first name starts with an *S*."

Okay, that was something. "Shari Lormand." She stuck out her hand and he shook it, smiling at her with that killer smile, his dark eyes focused on her. Whoo boy. She felt the effect of his penetrating gaze. She wondered what he was thinking.

Nah, she knew. *Woman in a weird dress, lace-up boots and a book necklace—reading a book at a bar, no less—is not my type.* The problem was that Shari was never anyone's type. Evy always told Shari she was her own woman and one day she'd find her other half, but it was taking annoyingly longer than Shari wanted. Back in high school she'd been the typical plain Jane, but she'd slowly developed her own style, with a bit of bohemian flair, and though it might be different, she liked who she was.

"Shari!" he said, snapping his finger as those hazel eyes lit up. "Yes, Shari, of course. I do remember you."

She nodded. "I was so sorry to hear about your loss."

His lips clamped tight and he gave her something of a nod.

She grabbed her car keys and they headed out of the bar. "What do you think your uncle and Winona are doing right now?" Her cheeks burned again. "Wait, forget I asked."

He laughed. "I have no doubt what they're doing. My great-uncle is a total romantic. He probably asked if Winona would like to go to Lookout Point for the view of the mountains, the valley and the stars. He might have sung her so many old mariachi songs that she got up and ran far, far away a half hour ago."

She grinned and opened her car door, unlocking the passenger side. "I wouldn't be so sure, Felix. I sure wouldn't mind someone crooning mariachi songs in my ear."

"I might just be tipsy enough," he said.

Oh, wouldn't that be nice, she thought, suddenly

imagining him kissing her. Crooning. Kissing her. Crooning.

He directed her to his house and explained that he'd moved into the family home after he was widowed and that Stanley had joined them a few months ago. "It's usually crowded with Sanchezes—my siblings are often around, too—but tonight, everyone's out for the evening."

She was about to turn into the driveway of the modest Bronco Valley house, admiring the flower boxes and well-kept lawn, when she realized it was roped off since it had clearly just been repaved. She pulled up along the curb just past the house. "Well, this is you." *Too soon*, she thought wistfully.

"I could use a cup of coffee or two," he said, taking off his seat belt. "Happy to make you a cup as a thank-you for the ride."

Every nerve ending sizzled. Had Felix Sanchez, all six feet two of muscled hotness and smarts and niceness, just invited her in—supposedly for a cup of coffee? She usually wasn't one to flatter herself, but c'mon. You did not invite someone into your home unless you didn't want your time together to end.

And then what? she asked herself. A one-night stand, which was all it would be, because Felix was hardly interested in dating, let alone a relationship. She knew that just from tonight, from the very attractive women he'd shown no interest in. And he hadn't flirted with her once.

Between that and the fact that she wasn't someone who could handle a one-night stand, she smiled tightly and said that it was getting late.

"Oh, okay," he said, looking a bit glum. "You're just

so easy to talk to. You've made me laugh tonight and I haven't done much of that in a while."

"Yeah, me, either," she said. "Not that I've lost someone very close to me. But I know heartache."

"One cup, then," he said, tilting his head. "My mother makes the most incredible churros and chocolate caramel sauce to dip them into. There are two left from dessert tonight. One for me and one for you. You don't want to miss that."

"I really don't," she said with a smile, almost unable to pull her eyes off his face, his lips, his strong jawline. The man radiated hotness. "Okay, sure, one cup—and a churro." She undid her seat belt.

And just like that, Shari Lormand was walking beside Felix Sanchez into his house. His empty house. Hope chased away any trace of loneliness. Maybe something would happen tonight.

She'd take it one kiss at a time.

CHAPTER TWO

As THEY HEADED inside the house, Felix had nothing more on his mind than the coffee, a churro and talking more to the easygoing Shari. Yes, she was very pretty and he *had* noticed her curves in her dress. And she smelled so good—the slightly spicy perfume was intoxicating. And he was already intoxicated.

Once inside, Felix called out an *hola* to see if anyone was actually home. Silence.

"Just you and me," he said.

Shari smiled, his gaze shooting to her plush pink-red lips. "This is your family, right?" she asked, moving to the wall of framed photographs lining the hallway. There were at least fifty of various sizes, the Sanchezes at various ages. She recognized several of them from around town, his mother and sister, particularly.

He stood beside her, pointing. "My parents, my grandparents, there's my uncle Stanley catching his first fish in Montana this past June. My two brothers, Dylan and Dante, my sister Sofia wearing one of her own fashion designs, and that's my sister Camilla standing in front of the restaurant she owns in Bronco Valley—The Library."

"I work there. The actual library, I mean. I'm the children's librarian."

He winced. Children. When would the word or the

sight of a baby stop making his chest ache? Luckily, Shari hadn't been looking at him just then; she was smiling at the series of photos of Uncle Stanley on a hiking trip the family had taken when he'd first arrived.

"I'm envious of your big family. I'm an only child," she explained. "And so were my parents. No aunts, uncles or cousins. And both sets of grandparents are gone." Her expression seemed wistful, her gaze still on the photos. "You're so lucky to have this big beautiful family and a great-uncle to go to Doug's with. I wish I had a wise great-aunt to talk to about life over wings and two-for-one-draft beers."

"Uncle Stanley *is* plenty wise," he said, smiling at a photo of him and the five Sanchez kids outside a taco stand on a trip to Mexico when they were teenagers. He *was* lucky to have his great family. "How about a dog or cat? Goldfish?"

She shook her head. "Just me. I've thought about adopting a pet, but I work full-time. One of these days, maybe."

He envisioned Shari Lormand coming home from work after a long day at the library in the children's section, toddlers pulling out books into a growing pile on the floor. No one waiting for her at home, no one to greet her or rub her shoulders, hand her a glass of wine. Or a churro. When he'd lost Victoria he'd been unable to bear living alone. It was a reminder of his grief. His family had saved him.

"How about that churro?" he asked.

Once again her smile lit up her face. "Sounds very good."

He led the way into the tidy kitchen. He lifted the lid off the cake plate, but found only crumbs. "Uncle

Stanley!" he said with narrowed eyes. He laughed and shook his head. "The man eats us out of house and home. Why did I think there would actually be leftover dessert? I apologize. If I didn't have, like, five drinks I would have remembered that."

Shari laughed. "No worries. That's the thing about living alone. Every last cookie is mine."

Alone, alone, alone. The word echoed in his head. He'd been alone for three years. The opposite of what Victoria had wanted for him in her final wishes. On her last day, in the morning, when he hadn't known she'd be gone by that evening, she'd said, *I want you to find love again, Felix. I don't want you to be alone. Promise me.*

He promised. Of course, he promised. Only because there was no time component. His promise would be good in ten years or twenty. Maybe when he was eighty-five he'd be ready like Stanley clearly was.

Anytime his family brought up the subject of him dating, which was unfortunately too often, and he said he wasn't ready, one would ask what that meant, what *ready* would feel like. Felix would shrug, but recently Stanley had answered that question for his mother. *He'll feel like his heart is opening like a spring flower instead of closed like a fist.* Felix had asked him if he himself felt that way, and Stanley said sometimes he did and sometimes he didn't. Grief, Felix knew, was complicated—and individual. So was *ready.*

"I'll make us a pot of coffee," Felix said, turning to open the cabinet. "Or," he said, turning to face her, "we could have a glass of my father's incredible sangria."

"I love sangria. Just half a glass, though."

He grabbed the pitcher from the refrigerator, the

sangria topped with sliced oranges, pineapple, pears and peaches. He poured out two glasses then handed one to her and leaned back against the counter.

She took a sip and smiled. "This is great."

"It's why I haven't moved out in three years," he said, taking a long drink. "Between my mother's cooking and my father's drink-making skills and my long days, I'm set."

She took a sip, then another. "I hear ya. I'd love to come home to a delicious dinner and a glass of wine and a kiss. But my romantic prospects haven't worked out."

"You should do what I do," he said. "Just remove yourself from that world. No dates. No expectations."

She seemed to think about that for a moment. "But then there's no home-cooked linguini carbonara and garlic bread and that glass of wine waiting for me after a long day at the library."

"True, but there's no heartache. No loss. No falling to your knees and sobbing in agony and three years later, walking around kind of…removed from the rest of the world." He sucked down the rest of the sangria and poured himself half a glass more. What the hell was he saying? *Why* was he saying it? He didn't know this woman. Even though he kind of felt like he did.

"Is that how you feel?" she asked, reaching over to squeeze his hand for a moment. He liked the contact, but it was gone too soon. So warm, so soft. That intoxicating perfume just a bit closer for those two seconds.

"I'm used to being on my own. While living with my family. Best of both worlds for me right now, so I'm good."

"You must be pretty set on staying single since I noticed women flirting with you at Doug's," she said.

"It drives my family nuts that I never respond to any of that. My parents, siblings and Uncle Stanley all try very hard to turn my single status around. They think I should be finding someone new, starting over. But who the hell wants to go through that again?"

"The dating or the possibilities of heartache?" she asked, her eyes serious on his.

He topped off her glass with more sangria. "Both."

She sipped her drink, his gaze on her lush lips. So pink-red and full. "I wonder what's wrong with me, then. I got really burned by my last relationship and yet here I am, still hoping." She froze and her eyes widened. "I don't mean right here, right now. With you," she added fast. "Just in general."

"So you're looking to get married."

She nodded. "And have a baby. I'm thirty-four and the clock is ticking on me. To be honest, I'm exploring all my options. Just at the starting point." She waved her free hand in the air and took another sip. "Ahh, let's change the subject." She pointed at his sweatshirt. "How about those Montana Grizzlies?"

He smiled gently, full of unexpected tenderness for her. He turned away for a moment and drank more of his sangria. She wanted a husband and a child. A family. Even if he *was* looking to date casually, which he wasn't, she couldn't be a part of his life with those hopes and dreams. His heart, what was left of it, was shuttered closed.

But then why was he noticing the flecks of green and brown in Shari's pretty hazel eyes? The sweep of her lashes? He liked her elegant nose, and her full lips. He liked her dress and the book necklace and the red boots. And her hair…why did he have the urge to run his fingers through that silky mass of strawberry blond, his hand running along the back of her neck?

"I'm glad you were sitting next to me tonight at Doug's," he said, aware of how close they were—the distance between the counters they leaned against in the kitchen. "I haven't spent time with someone who isn't a relative or a patient's human in a long time."

"I'm glad, too," she whispered, setting down her empty glass. "Thank you for the sangria."

"Thank *you*," he said, not quite sure what he was thanking her for. But something. Something big and small.

He set his glass down, too, unable to drag his eyes off her face. He stepped closer, suddenly wondering what it would be like to kiss her. *I'm a little drunk*, he thought. *Of course my inhibitions are lowered. I'm not thinking straight.* Yet he felt in full control of himself. He knew exactly what he was doing as he stepped closer still, reaching a hand to touch a tendril of her hair. "So pretty," he said, his gaze on her hair.

He heard her intake of breath, saw her smile slightly fade as she looked at him, her eyes full of…desire. Yearning.

She stepped a bit closer, too. "I like yours, too. So dark and such contrast with your hazel eyes."

He leaned his face toward hers. Slowly. Looking right at her.

She leaned hers toward his.

And when their lips met—fire. Felix felt those sparks all over his body. Then his arms were suddenly around her, his hands now on either side of her face as he deepened the kiss. *More, more, more*, he thought.

He pulled back for a moment. "I want to kiss you all night. I want more than that. But as I said, I'm not looking…not ready for a…" He trailed off, not wanting to ruin this, not wanting her to leave, not wanting to stop kissing her. But he wasn't a jerk, either. Tipsy or not. He took another step backward and stumbled a bit, and she caught him.

"Mmm," he said. "You smell so good. You *feel* so good."

"How about I help you upstairs to your room and then I'll be going," she said. "When a man tells me he's not ready, I now believe him instead of sticking around for five years and getting my heart smashed."

He tilted his head. The heartache she'd mentioned. He certainly didn't want to add to it.

Suddenly, his head began to spin a little. Then a little more.

He felt her move to his side and take his arm. She led him up the stairs.

"Second door on the right," he said.

She opened the door and his gaze landed on his bed. King-sized. Four-poster. Imported from Mexico. Heavenly down comforter and fluffy pillows. She led him over and he sat down, and she was taking off his boots. Kneeling in front of him. Making him imagine all kinds of things.

"Don't go, Shari Lormand," he said, tilting up her chin. "Maybe we could have just tonight. This unexpected rendezvous."

"Just tonight," she repeated, staring at him. Staring

hard, those hazel eyes working. *She's making a decision*, he realized. *Should I stay or should I go?*

Decision made. Because suddenly she'd whipped her glasses off like a female Clark Kent, set them on the end table and slowly unbuttoned his shirt, her eyes on his the entire time. She flung it to a chair, then unsnapped his jeans. He fell back on the bed, his feet on the rug so that she'd have an easier time shrugging them off him.

"Black boxer briefs. Nothing sexier," she whispered. This close up, she could see them. And the outline of him underneath. He kicked his jeans off, and they landed on top of the lamp on the end table.

"Nothing sexier than *you*," he whispered, pulling her up onto him.

And then they were kissing again. All thought left his head, blessedly, and he just *felt*. Her hands on his skin, in his hair, across his chest, her lips on his, trailing kisses down his chest, a warm soft hand inside those boxer briefs, exploring.

She stepped back and unzipped her boots and took off her socks. Even her feet were incredibly sexy. In the three seconds that she moved to unzip her dress, Felix felt his head spinning again. Then it stopped. His eyes grew so heavy that he couldn't keep them open to see Shari's beautiful form once the dress fell down her body and pooled on the floor. His last conscious thought was that she wore the sexiest white cotton bra he'd ever seen.

And then he felt the pull of sleep overtake him.

FELIX WAS OUT COLD. Fast asleep. And Shari was standing beside his bed, in her bra and underwear, her dress at her feet. She eyed his jeans on top of the lamp.

What the hell had she been thinking?

Until he passed out, he'd been ready for sex, but not ready for a relationship. She'd heard him loud and clear. But in that moment, when she could have left or stayed, she'd thought, *oh, just stay and go for it. Have a new experience. Just don't expect anything in the morning.*

Like she wouldn't have. She was Shari Lormand, *expecter.*

You're damned lucky he fell asleep, she told herself. Because she absolutely would have slept with him. And then she'd have had to slink out after because it wasn't like she could sleep over. And in the morning, he'd remember that he'd spent the night with someone, that woman from the bar, and he'd feel like hell because she knew he was a gentleman. A gentleman told a woman he wasn't ready for a relationship before they went too far. He'd even had the decency to fall asleep before she could get her bra and undies off.

Shari sighed and grabbed her eyeglasses, shoved them on and then got into her dress, contorting her arms backward to zip it. She glanced around for anything of hers. Her necklace was still on. Where did her socks go? Ah, there they were, flung off by the bedside table. She grabbed them, then sat down on the edge of the bed, so aware of the hot sleeping man stretched out on his back, one arm flung up behind his head, and pulled on her boots.

The walk of shame. She got up, smoothed her hair, grabbed her tote bag and headed for the door. But when she opened it, she heard the unmistakable sound of a key turning in a lock downstairs. Then voices. Two voices, a man and a woman. Then the door shutting.

"It's so quiet!" the woman said. "I guess Felix and Stanley are still out."

"I'll bet Stanley is getting Felix into some kind of good trouble," the man's voice said.

Then she heard footsteps. Then: "*Dios Mio!* Who ate the last two churros? I was saving them for us after the movies!"

Shari would have smiled if she were not standing stock-still, hand still on the doorknob, eyes wide. She slowly closed the door, her heart beating way too fast. His parents were home and how was she supposed to leave? Just waltz down the stairs with her mussed hair and clearly kissed lips and flushed cheeks and say, *Oh, hi, I hear ya on the churros, we were hoping to have them, too.*

She leaned against the back of Felix's bedroom door and let out a breath. Now what?

She'd wait for them to come upstairs and go into their bedroom and close the door. Then she'd sneak down the stairs like a cat and hurry out the door. Yes, that was the plan. Okay.

She waited. A few minutes passed. She could hear them chatting downstairs. Laughter. The sound of a song. Spanish, she was pretty sure.

"You devil!" she heard his mother say.

Shari had a feeling they were dancing.

This might be a while. She could pull out her book, but could she really concentrate on one sentence? Probably not.

She sat on the edge of Felix's bed, looking at his beautiful, peaceful face. She sighed again, wishing she could curl up beside him, move his arm over her.

She strained to hear downstairs. Music was still playing. Footsteps. But not coming upstairs.

She lay down as close to the edge of the bed as possible, her booted feet dangling off, her arms folded over her chest. She removed her eyeglasses, setting them on the table again. Any minute now, she'd hear them come upstairs, close their door, and she could flee.

At least she'd have a good story for Evy tomorrow, she thought, closing her eyes with a smile.

But when she opened her eyes, sunshine was coming through the filmy curtains on the window. Disoriented for a moment, Shari sat up, no idea where she was.

And then she looked to the left. She practically jumped. Felix was facing her, still sleeping. The comforter down around his belly button. Oh, my. His chest really was amazing. And the line of dark hair down his stomach…

And then *his* eyes opened.

He stared at her, then bolted up. He glanced at his alarm clock on the bedside table: 6:52 a.m. "Did we…" he prompted. "I hate that I have to ask." He shook his head and scrubbed a hand over his face.

"No," she said, scrambling off the bed, sliding on her glasses and looking for her socks again. Ah—they were stuffed inside her boots. "We might have, but you fell asleep."

"No reflection on you," he said—awkwardly.

She sat at his desk chair and put on her socks and her boots, so aware that he was watching her. "I would have left when you passed out, but when I got to your bedroom door, your parents had just come home. And I waited for them to come upstairs and go into their room, but they never did and I guess I fell asleep."

He shook his head and for a moment she was mesmerized by the sexy tangle of his mussed dark hair. "I don't usually have more than one beer. I don't know what the heck came over me last night."

She could feel her cheeks pinkening. *Awkward*. "Well, I really need to get home and get ready for work." She dashed over to the door. "Well, bye!" she added, then opened the door and peered out, looking both ways. The coast was clear. She didn't hear a sound from downstairs.

"Wait," he whispered. "I—"

She turned and stared at him. *I what?* No—she didn't want to know. She was almost sure of it.

Clutching her tote bag, she hurried out and ran down the stairs. Her eyes widened as she heard a woman's voice upstairs softly singing a song in Spanish. Shari was about to rush for the front door, but froze on the bottom step when she saw two guys, their backs to her, in the kitchen, looking through the refrigerator and cabinets and chatting about their hope that *Mami* would make her incredible chocolate chip pancakes for them. Must be Felix's brothers, stopping over for a home-cooked breakfast. Of all the mornings!

She held her breath and hurriedly tiptoed toward the front door. Clear! She raced out and across the lawn to her car at the curb. Only when she closed the door did she breathe. She drove away, her heart pounding.

Suddenly, she didn't want to share this experience with Evy. Or think about it too much. Because she knew she'd never hear from Felix Sanchez again. Yeah, maybe he'd track her down and apologize for falling asleep on her or her being trapped in his room all night.

Or racing out of his house at just past sunrise to make the drive of shame.

Except as Shari drove home to her condo in Bronco Heights, she didn't feel ashamed in the slightest. She felt slightly exhilarated. The night might not have gone as she expected—and what had she expected, really?—but just when she needed something to happen in her life, just when she needed a little boost of something magical, she'd kissed that gorgeous man senseless to the point that he'd passed out. She'd like to look at it that way.

She grinned, remembering how her hands and mouth had explored his body. She'd had a night to remember, one for her diary.

When she got home and brewed a pot of coffee and then headed into the bathroom for a hot shower, she couldn't stop thinking of Felix Sanchez. All he'd said. The way he'd kissed her. Touched her. Looked at her, up and down, down and up. The way he'd told her the truth. *I'm not ready...*

Yes, one for the diary. Then she'd try her best to forget about Felix, even though she knew that would take a good long while.

CHAPTER THREE

FELIX NEEDED COFFEE and a lot of it. And something for his headache. He stopped in his en suite bathroom for some acetaminophen, the cold water to swallow the tablets soothing his parched throat.

The house was hardly silent; his brothers had clearly come by, which made him wonder if Shari had hustled past them unseen. They were downstairs, talking about pancakes, the rodeo and major league baseball. His parents usually woke up around 7:30 a.m. His mother didn't have to be at the hair salon she owned till ten, and his dad, a postal worker, was off on Fridays. His father and Stanley always spent Fridays together, tinkering on a project in the garage and then going out to lunch at their favorite eatery—the Gemstone Diner for the combo platters with a ton of fries in gravy.

He headed downstairs and found Dante and Dylan in the kitchen, both sipping coffee from mugs and arguing over the post season. Each was so determined to be right about their favorite teams that they barely paused to greet Felix, which let him know they *hadn't* seen Shari. *Phew.* He did not want to be questioned.

He was just pouring his coffee when his parents came downstairs, both in the matching plush white spa robes that his sister Sofia had bought them for Christmas last year. She gave each of her three sons a kiss.

"Where's Tio?" Denise Sanchez asked, her warm, dark eyes peering at Felix closely. She glanced across the hallway at the sliding glass doors to the patio, where Stanley liked to have his morning cafe con leche after his calisthenics. No Stanley out there.

"Wait a minute," his mother added, turning back to him. "Why do you look like you're ill? Are you feeling okay?" She reached up on tiptoe and laid the back of her hand on his forehead. "Hmm, you don't feel warm."

"I'm fine," he said. "Coffee, Dad?" he asked his father to get the focus off him and his clearly hungover state.

"Definitely," Aaron Sanchez said. He leaned his ear up. "Why don't I hear Stanley singing or humming? He's still asleep? At this hour?"

Stanley was a notorious early riser. Six o'clock every morning for exercise on the patio, then after breakfast with the family he'd take a walk around the neighborhood, listening to his podcasts or mariachi music on the AirPods Felix had given him as a welcome gift.

Felix pretended not to hear the question as he poured cream and added a teaspoon of sugar into his coffee. He sipped. Ahh. He needed that. Between the steam and the caffeine, he felt himself coming back to life.

"Felix? Where's Stanley?" his mother asked again, sitting down at the table with her coffee.

"Maybe out for a drive?" Felix said. That wasn't a fib. His uncle *could* be out for a drive—coming back from Winona's place.

"Which one of you ate the last of the churros?" she asked, sitting down and taking a sip of her coffee. She raised an eyebrow and Dante and Dylan.

"Don't look at us," Dylan said.

Dante nodded. "But we would have eaten them if there had been any."

"That was definitely Tio," he said.

There. Maybe his mother would be so mad at Stanley that she wouldn't care where he was. Because Felix wasn't about to reveal that Stanley Sanchez had met a woman and left the bar with her last night. And was still out.

A key could be heard in the lock.

"Ah, that must be him," his father said, taking another sip of his coffee and rooting around in the fridge. "Who wants pancakes? Chocolate chip? Side of bacon?"

"Definitely me," Dante said.

Dylan grinned. "Ditto."

"Make a stack of both for me," Felix said, getting up to pour himself another mug of coffee. He needed more caffeine and lots of carbs—stat. "And thanks."

Stanley was singing a Frank Sinatra song as he appeared in the doorway. "I've Got You Under My Skin." His great-uncle didn't listen to Frank Sinatra. But he clearly had last night.

"How was your walk?" Aaron asked his uncle.

"My walk?" Stanley repeated.

"Weren't you out on your morning walk?" Denise asked.

Stanley grinned a bit sheepishly. "Well, if you must know, no. I was at the home of a new lady friend." He did a little cha-cha dance, then walked over to the coffeepot and poured a mug of coffee. "I met someone special last night. Didn't Felix tell you?"

His parents and brothers all stared at Felix, then at

Stanley as he sat down. "I didn't want to talk behind your back."

"Talk away!" Stanley said. "You might have told your *mami* and *papi* about Winona's lovely white hair, how it glistens in the moonlight."

His parents' eyes widened as they looked at each other, then at Felix then back at Stanley.

"Winona?" his mother repeated. "The only Winona I know in Bronco is Winona Cobbs. The psychic."

"The very lovely lady herself," Stanley said, a smile splitting his face. "A vision in purple. She told me she sees wonderful things for me in my future."

"Oh, did she?" Denise asked with a smile.

Aaron set down a big plate of pancakes and another of bacon. Felix's stomach growled and he grabbed a slice of bacon, then added three pancakes to his plate. His dad brought over the syrup and powdered sugar. He was grateful his father was doing all the work because Felix wasn't quite ready to stand and help with anything.

"Isn't Winona in her nineties?" Aaron asked. "An older woman?" He smiled, wiggling his eyebrows.

"My Celia was two years older," Stanley noted, taking a slice of bacon.

"So when are you seeing your lady friend again?" Dylan asked, also wiggling his eyebrows.

"For dinner tonight," Stanley said, his dark eyes twinkling. "Thank goodness we went out to Doug's last night, eh, Felix? I would have missed out on meeting her."

And I wouldn't have been sitting next to Shari Lormand at the bar, sharing her wings, and then kissing her in this very kitchen last night. Feeling her against me in bed. He would never forget the sight of her in her white bra and undies, her lush curves, that gorgeous strawberry blond hair, which he'd run his hands through all he'd wanted.

Well, until he'd fallen asleep.

And thank God he had. Because if he'd slept with her, he'd feel worse than he already did this morning. There couldn't be anything between them. Felix just wasn't ready for a relationship and wasn't sure when he would be. And because he'd practically seen her naked and her hand had been wrapped around certain hard parts of his body, having a casual friendship would seem...difficult.

But what to do this morning? He wouldn't pretend last night—and this morning—hadn't happened. He'd drop off a note with something from the bakery at the front desk of the library. Just to clear the air and they could both go on with their lives, the scone or pastry taking away any residual awkwardness. The library was right in the middle of downtown Bronco Heights, not far from the animal clinic where he'd be starting off his day, so yes, he'd drop that off during his lunch break.

And try to forget Shari, even though she'd been fully on his mind since he'd woken up.

"CAN YOU HELP me find a book about a hamster that talks?"

Shari looked up from her desk in the Bronco Library's Children's Room at the cute little blond boy standing beside a tall woman. He couldn't be older than four.

"Don't forget to say 'excuse me' first," the woman said to him with a gentle smile.

"Excuse me," the boy said.

"Let's see," she said, typing into her search engine. "Ah, I've got a few picture books that you might like." She stood up and led the way to the shelves, plucking out the three books. *Henry Hamster Goes to Preschool, Harry Hamster Loves Vegetables*, and *I'm a Hamster, Not a Gerbil!* She handed the boy the colorful hardcover books, and he grinned and said, "Thanks!" and then ran over to the couch along the window.

She'd been busy all morning, a good thing. Not much time to think about last night or this morning. Had it just been five hours ago that she'd woken up in Felix Sanchez's bed in her rumpled dress? She'd had a bowl of cereal and two cups of coffee so far, but what she really needed was a nap. With two story hours this morning, plus a bunch of ordering to do from the winter publishing catalogs, Shari wouldn't have a minute to herself until lunch. Again, probably a good thing. The more distance put between her and the memory of Felix, the more it would seem like a dream that couldn't possibly have happened.

Except it had happened. Her friend Evy had texted earlier this morning with a Well??? Anything happen between you Felix after driving him home last night? Shari had glanced around the bar for Evy last night so she could wave goodbye, and Evy had watched her and Felix leave with an excited look on her face. Shari had texted back a quick Let's talk tomorrow. Her friend had texted a few hours later with Sooo? and Shari had sent her a I'll fill you in after story time, which got her back an Oooh, can't wait!

At noon, Shari led the preschool-age story time in the fenced-in garden amid the fresh air and flowers and the interested, curious, happy faces in a semicircle around her, their parents and caregivers sitting on benches just a few feet away. Evy's four-year-old daughter, Lola, was in the group, Evy chatting with two other moms, each sipping from the complimentary coffee the library provided. Shari looked at each and every little face in the semicircle, their rapt attention, their impossibly soft cheeks.

Eye on the prize, she told herself. *Keep focused on what you want, not on what you want and can't have, such as Felix Sanchez. You made that mistake before and it was very painful.* As she'd told him last night when he'd told her he wasn't ready, she would not ignore a man telling her outright that he couldn't give her what she wanted. And what Shari Lormand wanted was marriage and family. If she couldn't have the marriage—at thirty-four and single it was looking less and less likely—she would create her own family.

Since her lunch break began when story time ended, she walked Evy and Lola into the Children's Room, and when Lola sat at a table to color with a friend, Evy grabbed her arm.

"Something happened!" she whispered, her pretty face very excited at the possibility. She whipped her long, dark ponytail behind her shoulder. "Tell me everything."

Shari smiled. "Well, there is actually something to tell."

"I knew it!" Evy said. "I saw that chemistry between you two."

Shari whispered the entire story, start to finish.

"Wow," Evy said. "You two really opened up to each other."

They had, unexpectedly and however briefly—in his kitchen.

"If only it could go somewhere," Shari said. "But he made it clear it can't. And I want what I want, so it can't for me, either."

"*Something* is going to happen next," Evy said. "I know it."

Shari shook her head. "Nope. I will not hear from him again. And I will certainly not chase after someone who told me loud and clear that he's not looking for a relationship."

"I wouldn't give up on the man so fast," Evy said. "As I learned with Wes, what a guy insists and what he feels can be two different things until he's knocked upside the head with how in love he is."

Shari laughed. "Well, I don't think anyone's in love—except you and Wes."

The front desk librarian walked in holding a takeout cup of coffee and a small box from Bronco Java and Juice, one of Shari's favorite places to unwind with a book on her lunch break. "Special delivery for Shari."

"For me?" Shari asked.

"Very good-looking guy dropped it off just a minute ago. Enjoy," she added, setting the coffee and the box on the table and heading back out. There was a little card taped to the box.

Shari's mouth almost dropped open.

"Well, I have one guess who that very good-looking man was," Evy said with a grin. "Open the card!"

Shari grinned back and grabbed the small card with illustrated flowers.

Thank you again for the ride home, Shari. All best, Felix Sanchez.

Shari's heart plummeted.

Even Evy looked deflated. "He did *not* write All Best," she said, shaking her head.

"Yup. And we know what that means. 'Thanks and see you around town if we happen to run into each other, which we won't because you don't have pets and I don't have kids so no chance of that. Have a nice life!'"

"But," Evy said. "But! He *did* think of you this morning. He did go to Bronco Java and Juice and buy you a coffee and whatever is in that box."

Shari opened the box and found three churros inside. Her heart gave a little leap. A wary leap, but still. "Hmm," she said. "Now, if there had been a scone in there or a Danish or a donut, I wouldn't read anything into it. But churros. Java and Juice has them only every Friday morning so Felix clearly went there especially to get them for you."

When she'd whispered the story of last night and this morning to Evy, Shari had not left out the churros as what had gotten her to accept Felix's offer to come into his house for a bit. Or how there had only been crumbs.

"I so agree," Evy said with a grin. "He's making up for something here. You have not seen the last of the guy."

"Wait. Is that a good thing, though? I can't get hung up on a man who's not ready to be in a relationship. I'm thirty-four. I want a child. I want a family." She bit her lip and shook her head. "No, I'm definitely not going to do this—get all wrapped up in a man who can't give me what I want. It's the definition of dopey."

Evy tilted her head. "I'm just saying that I didn't think Wes would come around to opening up that guarded heart of his to a single mother and child. But he did."

Felix's gorgeous face floated into her mind. The sweet stories he'd told her about his family. His furry patients. *No, no, no,* she told herself. *Do not get roped in by that face and how much you like him! Do. Not.*

"Okay, here's how you know if you should stop by the clinic to thank him for the coffee and churros," Evy said.

Shari raised an eyebrow.

"Taste the coffee to see what it is," Evy said. "If it's a latte or an Americano, he's more open to getting involved than he knows since he put thought and a little something extra into it. If it's just a plain old coffee, then maybe he's just being nice."

Shari stared at the coffee. She could detect a hint of sweetness coming from the tiny spout in the lid. She lifted the cup to her lips and took a sip. "Oh, my," she said.

"What is it?" Evy asked, eyes dying to know.

"A mocha latte with whipped cream." She took another sip, the hot, sweet creamy brew going straight to her heart.

Evy gave a little clap. "I have a feeling your nights are gonna get busy, Shari."

The problem was she wanted to hope so, and yet she still told herself she couldn't set herself up for heartbreak again. No, her nights would not get busy.

"Besides, you'll need a plus-one for the grand opening of Cimarron Rose," Evy added.

"I can't wait to see what you've done with the space." Evy was so young, just twenty-five, but she'd had big dreams to open up her own boutique and she had. Cimarron Rose was a boho-meets-cowgirl shop in Bronco Valley and would sell clothing and accessories and some home goods. Shari couldn't wait for the grand opening to buy a few things to support her friend.

She took another sip of her delicious mocha latte. "Well, I'll definitely be there. Solo."

"Even if you don't invite him, he'll be getting an invitation. So you definitely will see him again." Evy wiggled her eyebrows.

Shari gave an inward sigh. "I have to let him go. Not that I ever had him. I have to get him out of my head. I have to remember what I want. A family."

Evy squeezed her hand. "Just be open to everything, then. Including unforeseen possibilities with Felix Sanchez. The mocha latte doesn't lie," she added with a joyful grin.

Shari stared at the cup, the box of churros beside it. She took another sip of the latte. Definitely an order with thought put into it. Nothing quick like regular old coffee and a bagel with cream cheese.

Shari was clearly too hopeful if she was banking on a coffee drink predicting her future.

Maybe what she needed was to make an appointment with the town psychic, Winona Cobbs, who suddenly had a special insight into the name Sanchez.

Yes, Shari thought. *I'll do just that.*

CHAPTER FOUR

AFTER GIVING HIS last patient of the day at the clinic a treat and a good scratch behind his ears, Felix hung up his white lab coat and headed out of the exam room. He was surprised to find his uncle Stanley sitting in the waiting area in front of the huge fish tank. His uncle wore his favorite outfit of jeans, a Western shirt with silver snaps, and a leather vest over it along with a black cowboy hat on his head. His belt buckle had the etching of the Mexican flag.

Felix waved goodbye to the receptionist, who would be closing up in a half hour. "I'm glad you're here, Tio," he said as they walked out into the beautiful mid-September evening, low sixties with a nice breeze. "We didn't get to talk earlier since I had to get to the clinic, but I'd love to hear about your night."

"And I'd love to hear how *you* got home last night," Stanley said with a prompting smile. "Winona and I were at Lookout Point when I realized I'd stranded you without the car keys. Know what she said?"

Ha—so Felix had been right. The senior lovebirds had been at Lookout Point and his uncle probably had been singing Winona mariachi songs. But his date clearly hadn't run for the hills. "What did she say?"

"She said, 'Oh, no worries, Stanley. That lovely gal sitting next to Felix will take care of him tonight.'"

Felix almost gasped. "She said that?"

Stanley grinned, then let out a hoot of laughter. "Yes, she did. And did that lovely gal take care of you last night?"

Felix swallowed. Just how gifted a psychic was Winona?

"She gave me a ride home and came in for a bit," Felix said. A bit *overnight*, but he wasn't going to mention that.

Stanley rubbed his hands together. "Oh, did she, now?"

"Tio, listen. Shari and I will just be friends. I'm not looking to get involved with anyone. I'm just not ready."

"I didn't think I was ready," Stanley said as they reached the parking lot. "I've met so many nice women since I've been in Montana. I mistook *not ready* for the earth not shaking."

Felix raised an eyebrow. "The earth shook last night?"

Stanley smiled. "Did I *leave* Doug's with Winona? Was I out *all night*? The earth shook. And then we made it shake." He laughed, then said, "Actually, we didn't. We did kiss, though. Quite a bit. And danced at Lookout Point and at Winona's house. She lives with her daughter Dorothea and granddaughter, Wanda. I slept on the couch. We're having a repeat tonight."

Felix looked closely at Stanley and could see happiness radiating from the man. "I'm glad, Tio. I really am. But, again, I'm not ready."

The earth did shake for Felix last night, though. Or else he wouldn't have even wanted to *kiss* Shari. Since his loss, he'd never reacted to a woman like that.

"Did you send her flowers for driving you home because of me?" Stanley asked.

"Coffee and churros, actually," he said.

"Ah, so the earth *did* move," Stanley insisted. "Otherwise you would have let it go."

Felix thought about that for a moment. Maybe. But the ride home seemed to warrant a proper thank-you. And given that things got very personal, he'd wanted to make the thank-you a bit more personal. But that was exactly why he'd added *All best, Felix* to the little card attached to the box. And when she'd sent a text not long after he'd dropped off the coffee and churros— just a short and simple Thank you for the treats...delicious!—he wrote back with Glad you enjoyed them. All best, Felix.

He'd specifically jotted All best, Felix both times because he needed that bit of professionalism. Something he'd write to a client.

Something that didn't leave any doors open. In fact, that *shut* any doors. He wasn't open to a relationship, and Shari wanted a serious relationship, leading to a husband and children. He couldn't be that guy.

So he had no business letting their association continue beyond their two short and sweet communications. He'd achieved his goal; the gift had worked, she'd responded just right. He could move on with his evening...and his life.

But once again, he couldn't get her out of his mind. And the yearning to see her was something new. Something scary.

"Felix!" a familiar female voice called out.

He turned around. And there was Shari Lormand running toward him, her strawberry blond hair flying behind her. She wore a multicolored tweed blazer over a long dress and had on a different interesting necklace today and many wooden bracelets.

She was also carrying a small cardboard box with care. "I'm so relieved I caught you!" she said. "I had an evening youth event with the middle schoolers at the library, and we found a tiny kitten all alone in the garden. She was in a recessed area near the wrought-iron fence." She held out the box for him to see.

He peered in. A kitten, no more than three months old, looked up at him with slightly watery eyes. She'd need attention right away.

"I will leave you to care for your new patient," Stanley said, looking at Shari eagerly.

Oh, I'm sure you will, Felix thought. "Stanley Sanchez, this is Shari Lormand. Shari, my uncle Stanley."

Stanley gave her arm a warm pat. "Thank you for rescuing my nephew last night. And now you are rescuing this sweet *gatita*."

"It was my pleasure to do both," Shari said.

Felix smiled. "Well, let's take the kitty in and assess her."

"I'll see you later, Feel," Stanley said and then hurried to his truck.

"I wasn't sure if I should bring him here or to the animal shelter," Shari said, "but your office was closer, so I ran over."

"You did the right thing," he said. He took the box from her, and he could see the relief on her face that the little kitten would be taken care of. Shari Lormand was definitely a woman who cared.

He held open the door to the clinic and went in after her. "New patient," he said to the receptionist,

Allie. "I'll type up the notes, so feel free to head out for the day."

Allie came over to peer in the box. "Aww. Hope the kitty will be okay."

"Might be a stray who got separated from her mama and the litter," Felix said. "She looks sturdy enough."

Felix held open the door to Exam Room 1 and followed Shari in. "Sure is cute," he said, taking out the gray, white and black kitten and examining her in his hands. "No wounds. That's a good thing." He grabbed the padded basket from the table behind him and set the kitten inside to do a more comprehensive exam.

A half hour later, the kitten was resting in the basket after receiving vaccinations and treatment for ear mites, along with some food and water.

"I'll need to find a foster home for her at least tonight since the shelter is closed now," he said, gently petting the kitten's back. "And I'll check the library garden and surrounding areas for the mother cat and any other stray kittens."

"Well, I could foster her for the weekend since I'll be home anyway."

That was kind of her. Kind of her to bring in the kitten and offer the weekend home. "Perfect," he said. "Bring her back here Monday and I'll take her over to the animal shelter. They'll have plenty of foster homes available while she gets in tip-top shape for adoption."

"I've never taken care of a kitten before," she said. "What should I pick up to have at home?"

"I've got a kitten starter pack, actually. The clinic gets a lot of freebies that companies hope will get good reviews and word of mouth. It has food and water dishes, a kitten-sized litter box and fine clay litter. A bag of food and toys. And I can give you a kitten carrier to transport her home in. She'll be feeling so much better within a half hour from just the treatments and food and hydration that she'd probably go leaping out of that little box you brought her in."

"Glad to hear it," she said, giving the kitty a scratch under her chin. The kitten rubbed against Shari's hand. "Should we name her? Or let the shelter do that?"

"You've got naming rights."

Shari tilted her head and regarded the kitten. "I think we have to name her Page since she was found at the library."

He smiled. "A literary kitty. I'll just go get that starter pack and the carrier. Back in a flash."

Anyone who loved animals, who'd rush an ailing kitten to a vet's clinic, was all right in Felix's book. It occurred to him that they could be friends. Who couldn't use a new friend? Someone easy to talk to. He didn't have many women friends or even acquaintances since his and Victoria's former "circle" had slowly distanced himself from him. People got uncomfortable with cancer. With death. With how to include the new widower in the old group. Dynamics had changed and Felix found himself getting fewer and fewer invitations. Of course, that had been fine with him. He wasn't much for dinner parties anyway. But it had felt good to open up to Shari last night. He hadn't done that outside of his family in a long time.

Friends. He nodded to himself as he headed down to the hall to the supplies closet. With a label, he wouldn't even have to think about his attraction to Shari; he simply wouldn't act on it. Because they were friends.

The starter pack bag in one hand and the carrier in

the other, he went back to the exam room. Shari was holding the kitten in her lap on the floor, telling Page that she didn't know anything about kittens or cats, but she'd give her a good weekend home, she promised.

"I see a foster fail in your future," he said with a grin.

"I don't know. I probably will get too attached, but I don't like the idea of leaving a young kitten home alone for eight hours while I'm at work." She picked up Page and held her high, giving her a kiss on the nose. "Though you are seriously cute."

Felix set the carrier on the exam table, put a folded blanket inside, and then took the kitten from Shari and put her inside, zipping up the soft opening. "At three months, she'd be fine on her own and would probably nap a good portion of the day. But there are plenty of people looking to foster or adopt kittens, so no worries either way."

He could tell she was already too smitten with the tiny bundle of fur.

"Ready, Page?" She picked up the carrier and held it up so she could see the kitty and assure her.

Oh, yeah. Foster fail was coming.

"So I'll help you get all this stuff home," Felix said, "and then I'll go look for the mother cat and other kittens."

"I live just two blocks from here. You know the condos on Oak Street?"

He nodded. "My brothers looked at a place there when they were looking to move out. They almost rented in BH247—you know, that swanky complex geared to singles? But they opted to stay in Bronco Valley."

"I looked at that complex when I first moved here, but it seemed a little too 'singles scene' for me," she said. "That was back when I was freshly heartbroken, though. A coworker who lives there met her fiancé at the pool. She keeps telling me to move there and I'd be married within six months. I've been considering it lately, too."

A good reminder that Shari Lormand was looking to get married. And that for him, she was strictly in the friend zone. She wanted a life that he was unwilling to give her.

"Ready to go, *amiga*?" he asked, trying out the word on his tongue. It felt…forced.

"Ready," she said.

Ready to be friends. Ready to let Shari into his life under this new parameter. But could you be friends with a woman you couldn't help noticing little things about? Like the way the light from the setting sun lit up her beautiful hair. Like the way her little tweed blazer highlighted her curves. Like how beautiful she was. Inside and out.

Could you be friends with a woman you wanted to kiss right now?

LAST NIGHT, SHARI was at Felix's place. Tonight, he was at her place. How did this keep happening? He'd helped her home with the kitten and the starter pack, then had left to search for the mother cat in the library garden and vicinity.

"Maybe you're my good luck charm," she said to Page, who was exploring the corner of the living room where Felix had set her padded basket, which would double as her bed. Shari had a few baskets and could put one in each room. She had her food and water dishes on a little mat in the kitchen, and the litter box was in the bathroom, which was thankfully large. A few catnip toys and two plastic hollow balls were on the rug, but right now Page was more interested in the empty shoe box Felix had told her would be kitten heaven. Page kept jumping in, going on her back, kicking at the sides, crouching down, and then catapulting herself out of it, then running back inside. Now she was licking her paw and grooming her face.

Shari had thought a lot about what Evy said, that she shouldn't give up on Felix so fast. As if she could. This was the guy she'd had her first crush on. Instead of guarding her heart, she was hopeful. And she wasn't sure that was a good plan of action.

And her plan of action was important. If she wanted to make her most fervent dream come true, to have a family of her own, she had to work toward that, not against it. And working toward it meant only being attracted to emotionally available men. Not men who straight out told her they weren't looking for a relationship.

A half hour later, Felix knocked on her door.

"No sign of the mother cat or any other kittens. Page must have gotten separated at some point. I'm really glad you found her."

"Me, too," she said. "And thank you for examining her. I like knowing she's on the mend."

"Well, I'll head home, then," he said. "Unless you have any questions about fostering or kitten care. I know it's just the weekend, but better to be in the know."

"Actually, I have a lot of questions, but I didn't want

to keep you. I'm a total newbie at this. I can trade you tips for pesto pasta and garlic bread. The pesto isn't homemade, but it's still scrumptious."

Shari, Shari, Shari, she mentally chastised herself. *What do you think you're doing? How did you go from trying to get Felix Sanchez out of your head to inviting him in for a home-cooked meal?*

"You don't have to go to all that trouble of making dinner," he said. "I'm happy to offer advice."

"No trouble at all," she heard herself say, despite how untrue it was. It was trouble for her as a woman who was going to get hurt again. "And honestly, because I've never had a cat before, let alone a baby cat, I'd feel better having you here to make sure all is well before I officially take over." That part was actually true.

He looked around the living room. "House-proofing wise, just move that pot of African violets from the windowsill to where Page couldn't possibly get to it. Several plants and flowers are poisonous to cats. And avoid giving her people food. The kitten chow is good for right now. And no milk—it can actually cause belly trouble."

Huh. Now she was a little glad she'd invited him to stay for dinner. "Got it," she said. "No saucers of milk even though I always see that in movies." She walked over to the window and grabbed the African violet and set it on the top of the refrigerator for now. She was not only attached to Felix Sanchez, she was attached to that tiny ball of gray, black and white fur running around the living room, knocking around her little catnip mouse.

Get your head on straight, she told herself, hurrying into the kitchen. She rooted around the cupboards and pulled out what she needed.

"Can I help?" he asked, standing in the doorway. More like *filling* the doorway with his broad shoulders. For a moment she couldn't drag her eyes off him.

"Your job can be just keeping an eye on Page," she said. "I've got this."

He smiled and headed into the living room.

As she waited for the pasta to boil and the sauce to heat, she could hear Felix talking to the kitten. "Now, just because you're adorable doesn't mean you get to pee wherever you want, Page. There are rules when you live in a warm, cozy home like this. We showed you where the litter box is, remember? Good. And don't think that super cute face or the black smudge on your nose will get you out of trouble if you use those nails on Shari's nice red sofa. Use your new scratching post only. Got it, furball?"

Shari grinned. She would not be surprised if the kitten meowed a *yes*.

"I appreciate you giving her the house rules," she called out. What she didn't appreciate was how she was liking him more and more every minute.

She sighed as she drained the pasta and poured it into the fragrant pan with the pesto sauce. She gave it a good stir, then took the garlic bread from the oven.

"Something smells amazing," he called back.

"And it's ready, too," she said. She put the pasta in a serving dish and the bread in a lined basket and set everything on the kitchen table. She was itching to light the pretty candlesticks that her coworkers at the library had given her for Christmas last year, but as she well knew, this was not a date.

"Wow," he said as he sat down. "Looks as amazing as it smells." He heaped pasta on his plate and took a piece of garlic bread. "So I've been thinking."

"Oh?" She sat up straight.

That there was something so special between them he wanted to explore dating. Just give it a try. Because he could not stop thinking about her. And their almost evening together.

Yes, say all that, Felix Sanchez, she thought, trying to appear nonchalant as she scooped pasta on her plate.

"I want to be honest with you, Shari. Very honest. I did have a little too much to drink last night and the sangria on top of it, and I guess a part of me deep down wants what it wants. But in the cold light of day, I know I'm not ready to start dating. Or interested in dating. But I sense that you're a special person, Shari Lormand, and I'm so comfortable with you. Around you. I can talk to you." He took a sip of his white wine. "The fact that I'm saying any of this is a testament to that."

She ate a forkful of linguini pesto to seem as if she wasn't hanging on every word, waiting for the finale. She wasn't sure where he was headed with this. But every cell in her body was on alert.

"So I have a proposal for you."

A proposal, a proposal, a proposal. From not ready to date to a proposal. She could hear the sad trombone playing in her head. Surely this wasn't going anywhere good.

He held up his glass of wine. "I'd really like for us to be friends, Shari. And I don't mean acquaintances who run into each other occasionally and maybe have coffee every six months. I mean real friends. You feel down in the dumps, you call me and we go to the movies. I have a long, rough day and need some cheering up? I call you and we go to Bronco Brick Oven Pizza and you tell me some good jokes."

Friends. Real friends. She wondered if he could see how deflated she'd gotten, from sitting up straight, ears perked up to kind of slumped in her chair. Friends.

Who couldn't use a good friend? she thought, twirling the linguini around her fork. Friends were everything. Friends got you through. She'd just have to adjust her mindset about Felix Sanchez, not see him as anything more. But how did you go about doing that? How could you have a great time with your buddy eating pineapple pizza and seeing the new Marvel movie when you were so physically attracted to that buddy that you couldn't stop imaging the two of you in bed. Where you'd briefly been.

Then again, maybe she could handle a friendship with him. She'd just have to take it day by day.

Okay. Friends.

She ate her pasta, trying to think of a joke. Something to start their friendship off. "Do you like book humor?" she asked. "That's all I've got."

"Hit me," he said with a smile—that honestly stole her breath for a second.

"How do books stay warm in the winter?" she asked. "They wear book jackets. Badumpa!"

He had the decency to laugh because he was a great guy. "That's the kind of goofy joke I need after a rough day with a dog fighting for its life or a sick baby goat."

Oh, Felix. Yes, I want to be your friend. Much more. But yes.

"Then I'm the friend for you," she said lightly, but she felt anything but light. Or happy. Could they really be friends? When she wanted to rip his clothes off and feel the weight of him on top of her? When she wanted to kiss him with all the passion pent up inside her?

She really didn't know. The more she'd get to know him, the harder she'd fall for him. And one day she'd be hanging out with him and her heart would ache and she'd know she'd fallen deeply in love with her...buddy.

She tried to remember Evy's advice. *Don't give up on him.* Maybe this was all part of the slow steps toward the two of them being more? Hmm, she thought as she ate another bite of pasta. That was possible. Entirely possible.

"Hit me with another book joke," he said.

She took a piece of bread from the basket and ate a deliciously buttery, garlicky piece. When you didn't have to worry about garlic breath because you would *not* be kissing afterward, you could really enjoy dinner that much more. A plus, she told herself. There was a silver lining to being friends with Felix. "Okay, I've got one," she said. "Why was the math textbook so sad?"

He tilted his head and paused with his linguini-laden fork midair. "Why?"

"Because it had so many problems."

He laughed again, his hazel eyes twinkling and tender, and raised his glass. "To being friends?"

She lifted hers. She hesitated on the clink, though. But she finally did. "To being friends," she repeated.

"Good," he said, his smile lighting up that handsome face that she wanted to kiss so badly.

Here's more library humor, she thought, biting into another piece of supposed silver-lining garlic bread. *Why was the librarian crying? Because she wrote the book on heartache yet chose to be buddies with a man she was in love with.*

Now that was no laughing matter.

He could *fall madly in love with you*, she reminded herself. *He does seem to really like your hair, for one. And your jokes. And you do talk easily. And he wants you. You know he does, even if he's going to suppress the attraction with all his might.*

Patience, she told herself, perking herself up, then felt something on her leg.

She looked down and there was Page, her front paws on Shari's shin.

"No linguini pesto for you," she said to the kitten. "But I'll play catch the catnip mouse with you after dinner." Page let out a pitiful meow. "Okay, fine. You can sit on my lap." She scooped up the sweet bundle of fur and settled her on her lap.

Felix grinned. "Yeah, you won't be giving up that kitten anytime soon."

She did like the idea of having a cute little some-one to come home to. To tell her troubles to. And since she couldn't share her fears about Felix the friend *with* Felix the friend, Page was going to be her new nightly confidante.

CHAPTER FIVE

ANYTIME FELIX WAS due for a haircut, he liked to make an appointment at his mother's salon in Bronco Valley instead of letting her snip away in the bathroom of their house with a towel over his shoulders like she used to do with all the Sanchez kids when they were younger. A home haircut meant an endless barrage of questions about his personal life while he was trapped beneath her scissors, brush and piercing gaze. At the salon, where she was the ultimate professional and surrounded by other stylists and customers, he knew he'd get a great haircut and few personal questions.

Now, after a morning making ranch calls, he'd wolfed down a quick lunch in his SUV, and then headed to his mother's salon. He said several hellos to the other stylists and customers, smiled, answered questions, including two about dogs, then finally settled himself in the big chair, his mother draping a silver smock around him. He was glad he'd been so busy all morning and now was here because it had left no time to check in with Shari on how her first night as a foster kitty mom had gone.

Now that they were friends and had that distancing label between them, he shouldn't have a problem texting or stopping by the library—but he did. He'd been awake for a while last night thinking about her, unable to fall asleep, her pretty face and gorgeous strawberry blond hair, and how she'd looked in her white cotton bra and underwear in his bedroom, and he wasn't so quick to go see her. Maybe a few days of not seeing her would tamp down his attraction. But he doubted it.

"So, Felix," Denise Sanchez began, not catching his eye in the big round mirror in front of him, which told him she was up to no good. "I mentioned to one of my best clients that you were probably looking for a date for your cousin's quinceañera Friday night, and she got very excited about giving me her daughter's number. She's a busy lawyer, smart as can be and very pretty. I've seen a recent photo."

Because she was his mother, she thought nothing of tucking the slip of paper into the back pocket of his pants. "There. Now you have it." She started snipping, suddenly humming a song all innocent-like.

He'd forgotten about his cousin's quinceañera. A traditional celebration for girls turning fifteen, the party would be elaborate, festive and long. His cousins had rented out a venue that generally held weddings and over two hundred people were expected. Many would be loud teenagers.

Snip, snip, snip. "She's expecting your call, Felix. No later than end of business today, okay, *mijo*?" This time she did look at him in the mirror. Snip, snip-snip.

"Mom, first of all, you should have asked me before telling anyone I'd call their daughter for a date. Second, I…" *Think fast, Felix.* A good excuse that would shut her down from the subject. He'd used every one in the book the last couple of years. All he'd gotten from his mother was narrowed eyes, hands on hips, and a *Felix, I just want you to be happy.*

"She's thirty and marriage minded, of course," his mother continued. "And she's allergic to dogs but she's fine with cats."

"Mom, you'll have to tell your client that you were mistaken about me looking for a date."

Denise moved to the other side of the chair and snipped away. "It's just one date, Felix. So unless you already *have* a date, I can't lie to my best client."

There it was. The excuse he hadn't used yet. "I do already have a date, actually."

His mother paused midsnip, her brown eyes lighting up. "You do?"

Shari Lormand's face floated into his mind. "Yes. Her name is Shari. She's a librarian. Children's department. So I can't possibly call your client's daughter."

Denise Sanchez's hand flew to her heart, and she waved at her face with the other. "A children's librarian! She must *love* kids. She sounds wonderful! Oh, I'm so excited to meet her."

His mother sure was predictable. He loved her, but boy, did he have her number.

Hopefully, his newly named buddy was free Friday night.

"You like this Shari?" his mother asked, turning his chair slightly to the left. He wished she hadn't done that because now he realized that both the stylist and customer in the chair just a few feet away were listening to every word and awaiting his answer.

"She's a really good person," he said.

"Pretty?"

"Yes, Mom. She's pretty."

"Marriage minded?"

The stylist to his left began pointing a piece of tin

foil in their direction. Her customer had foils folded all over her head in a pyramid shape. "You can't be too sure these days, so it's a good question. My daughter is twenty-nine and keeps saying she's focusing on herself and her career. Her career is not going to keep her company. Her career is not going to bring her chicken soup when she's sick. Her career is not going to give me grandbabies!"

Denise Sanchez did an exaggerated nod. "Is Shari in her twenties? Or thirties?"

"Mom, Shari's age and how she conducts her life is her concern. Not mine or anyone else's."

"Until you want to start a family and she's busy with her career!" the stylist said. Her customer gave a firm nod.

"Well, if I did get married someday way in the future and my wife and I did have a baby," Felix said, "maybe I would be the one to stay home so that my wife could focus on her career."

"Huh," Denise said. "I suppose so. Things are different than when I got married." Nods from the other stylist and her customer. She waved her hand in the air. "Well, you and Shari will figure all that out."

Whoa. Wait just a minute. In the space of two minutes, Shari went from being his plus-one to a family party to the mother of his children.

"Mom, first of all, let's not get way ahead of ourselves. And second of all, you never stopped working. Yeah, a family of seven needed two paychecks, but your kids are all grown up. You love what you do and that's why you're cutting my hair right now."

"True. If we were rich Bronco Heights types, I'd still cut hair. It's my passion."

He smiled. "Exactly." He was grateful when she swiveled her chair back toward the center. Now it was time to get the focus off *his* love life. "So, Mom," he said, lowering his voice, "what do you think about Tio's new romance?"

"I think it's wonderful. Stanley lost the sparkle in his eye when Celia died, but now, it's back. And it's a good example for you, *mijo.*"

He inwardly sighed.

"Felix, if Stanley could date again after sixty years of marriage to a woman he loved with all his heart and soul, so can you. I know your loss might still feel raw. But three years is a long time."

Why did he think getting his hair cut in the salon would prevent personal conversation? This couldn't get more personal.

He stared at himself in the mirror, avoiding catching his mother's eye. He looked like the same Felix. But three years ago his life had completely changed and no matter how many times his family told him it was okay to get back out there, their voices full of compassion, he just wanted to put his hands over his ears and shut out their well-meaning words.

"I'm so glad you're bringing Shari to a big family party," his mother continued. "For you, that means you're serious. Oh, I can't wait to tell everyone."

Uh-oh.

"Mom, it's a date to a teenager's birthday party. A first step. That's all."

A first step, he saw her mouth with a gleam in her eye to the other stylist.

A first step into assuring him that he and Shari Lormand were meant to be friends and only friends.

"Thank you. See you then," Shari said into her phone, then put it down on the kitchen table—and let out a happy-scared squeal. "Page! Guess what?"

Page did not come running; the kitten was grooming herself on the sofa, not even looking Shari's way, but hey, she was a living, breathing being to share her big news with.

"I made an appointment with a fertility clinic to discuss my options!" Shari announced.

After the "will you be my friend" conversation with Felix last night, Shari had woken up that morning determined to be proactive about her dreams and goals for a family. And she got lucky. It turned out there was a cancellation today at Big Sky Fertility Clinic—about thirty minutes away from Bronco—and Shari grabbed the 4:45 appointment. When she got out of work at four, she'd hurry home, feed and play with Page and then drive out to the clinic.

She'd couldn't put her life and dreams on hold for a man. Did she wish Felix was emotionally available? Yes. Did she wish they could pursue a romantic relationship? Yes. Would she hold her breath on either? No.

Did she now have butterflies flapping away in her belly? Oh, yes. She had so much nervous energy that she decided to just head to work a half hour early.

As the first employee to arrive at the library, she made a pot of coffee, wondering if soon she'd be making decaf for herself. She felt a happy chill run up her spine. Then a scared chill ran down.

As she took her coffee to her desk and turned on her desktop, Shari pictured herself holding a baby. Buying diapers at the grocery store. She wanted to be a mother and today was the start of her dream.

The day went very slowly, of course. That was always the case when she was watching the clock, something she rarely did. With twenty minutes left of her shift, she was looking through the winter catalogs from publishers for new books to order when a woman she recognized as a waitress at the diner and her young daughter came up to her desk. Ariel and her daughter, Mia, had the same pretty fine blond hair and pale brown eyes. Shari had overheard a few conversations between waitresses while having breakfast or lunch at the counter enough to know that Ariel's ex-husband had abandoned her when Mia was just a baby.

"Excuse me, could you point me in the right direction for books for my daughter?" Allison asked. "She's six years old and in the first grade at Bronco Elementary. Mia usually gets books from her classroom or the school library but she accidentally left her book on her desk."

"Why do I have to read at home when I read at school?" Mia asked her mother on a pleading whine. "I hate reading. I'm bad at it."

"Honey, Ms. Templeton said you should spend twenty minutes on reading at home," Allison said with a mixture of exhaustion and impatience in her voice. "Plus, we have to fill out your reading log."

Mia frowned and crossed her arms over her chest.

Shari gave Ariel an "I've got this" nod and leaned toward the girl. "Mia, tell me two things that you like. Really, really like."

Mia tilted her head. "I like French fries. And I like going really fast on the tire swings at recess."

"What if I told you that I could find two fun-to-read

books about French fries and swinging on tire swings?" Shari asked. "Would you like to read those?"

The girl's brown eyes widened with interest—wary interest. "Yes!"

Shari tapped at the search engine. She found two cute books on those very topics with great illustrations that would capture the attention of a reluctant reader. Ariel smiled at Shari and then sank down gratefully on a sofa with an exhausted sigh.

Shari led the way over to the bookcase full of picture books and had the girl help her find the titles.

Mia thanked her and ran over to her mom, plopping down and opening one of the books. Shari watched her move her finger along the few lines of text on each page.

When Mia finished the book, Shari watched her mother almost brace herself to get off the sofa, the fatigue in her eyes and body language visible. But every time her daughter looked at her, her face brightened and she spoke to Mia with energy.

This was what single motherhood would be like, Shari knew. Your heart running around the library, your child sliding a finger under the words she's struggling to read. And you've got everything heaped on your plate. It might be the weekend, but Mia's mother would go home and have to figure out dinner. Then in the morning it would be breakfast and planning the day and making lunch and tidying up the home. Then oversee homework due the next day and sign off on reading logs and go through folders of information. Another dinner to plan and make. More clean up. Then it would be work on Monday.

Sometimes when Shari saw firsthand even just a tidbit of how hard it was to be a single parent, she would put the thought of sperm donors and IVF or foster parenthood and adoption out of her mind, scared to even think more about those options. Parenthood was challenging enough with a loving spouse at your side.

But she was thirty-four and could not be more single. The only man she was interested in had friend zoned her last night.

How did you know when to give up on a dream—marriage with a man she loved, who loved her, and a baby—if time for that baby was ticking away?

As Mia and her mom were leaving, she caught sight of Mia throwing her arms around her mother and hugging her with such love and devotion, Allison scooping her up for a hug and a little duet that must have been a thing they did. And just like that, Shari's heart was soothed and she knew she could do this—face motherhood on her own. Parenthood would be as rewarding as it was challenging.

I want a child, Shari thought again. She knew it with absolute certainty. So yes, she was scared. But she'd always known being a mother would require everything out of her, whether she had a loving, supportive partner or not.

At four, Shari left the library and went home, her bundle of fur yawning in her kitty bed and going right back to sleep. Shari gave her a gentle scratch on her cute head, filled up her dinner bowl and headed out.

The Big Sky Fertility Center looked so inviting. It was housed in a pale peach Victorian at the end of the main street in Wonderstone Ridge, a much bigger town than Bronco about thirty minutes north. Shari went in, taking a deep breath as she pulled open the inside door. The waiting room was crowded with all kinds of people, all kinds of couples.

And now that she was here, she felt so…alone. She tried to perk herself up, to remember how proactive she'd felt this morning when she'd made the appointment.

As she sat down, she realized she should have brought a friend. Someone who'd support her, hold her hand when need be, just be there. Someone like Evy, but Evy had way too much going on for Shari to feel comfortable asking her to take hours from her day to sit at her side, especially when she wasn't even sure this was the right path to motherhood.

And there was no way she could have asked Felix. This was way too personal, too complex, too everything for someone she'd only recently met, no matter how close to him she felt. Besides, if she planned to be a single parent by choice, she'd better get used to being on her own.

On my own. Exactly how I don't want to be.

She couldn't let the chance to have a baby or be a foster parent slip through her fingers.

Suddenly, she wished Felix were here beside her so she could talk all this through. Now that they were friends, maybe she *could* talk to him about this, get his point of view.

Her appointment was running twenty minutes late, so it was a good thing she wasn't expected back at the library. She picked up one of the brochures on the long coffee table and read through it. The information made everything sound less scary.

And the baby on the cover had Shari so wistful that

she knew she was in the right place, that she was gathering facts, feeling things out, exploring her options.

An hour later, Shari had met with a fertility counselor, asked all her questions, had them answered, and put a mental check mark next to the idea of using an anonymous sperm donor. She would be able to choose her donor based on an in-depth profile. As she left, her head full of everything she'd learned, Shari knew she'd feel the same way about all the other options. All the paths to motherhood felt like real options for her. Right now, she was glad she *had* options and was finally starting on her journey.

Just as she stepped into the beautiful September late-afternoon breeze, her phone pinged with a text.

Felix.

Would you like to be my plus-one to a family birthday party Friday night? This is no ordinary teenage girl's party, though—it's a quinceañera and will be like a mini wedding in scale. Good food is guaranteed.

Her heart soared as if a teenaged Felix had asked her to the prom, not that that would have ever happened since he and Victoria had been a couple all four years of high school. But Shari wasn't a teenager with a crush anymore. She knew this wasn't a date. *It's why he very specifically referred to you as his plus one. It's what friends do.*

Still, she liked that he'd invited her.

She wondered if Winona Cobbs would be Stanley's plus-one. Maybe she could ask Winona about a reading at the quinceañera.

No, Shari couldn't wait. She needed answers to her big burning questions now.

She picked up her phone and did a search for Wisdom by Winona.

Winona answered her phone on the first ring.

"Hello, Ms. Cobbs, this is—"

"I know who you are, dear," Winona said.

That was a bit rattling.

"I'm hoping to make an appointment with you for a reading," Shari said.

"Of course you are. I'll see you tomorrow at twelve thirty sharp at my psychic parlor in my great-grandson's ghost tour business. Do you know where that is?"

The last time her parents had come to visit her and the town they'd lived in for decades, the three of them had gone on a ghost tour. Bronco, with its Wild West past, was full of legends and interesting sites. People came from all over to go on one of Evan Cruise's ghost tours.

"I do," Shari said. "And I'll see you there. Twelve thirty sharp. Thank you."

Suddenly Shari wasn't so sure she wanted to know what was coming. What if there was bad news? Sad news?

What will I find out?

CHAPTER SIX

FELIX SAT ON an upside-down bucket beside a sweet brown-and-white calf in the barn at the Kingston Ranch and removed his stethoscope from his ears, letting it drop around his neck. It was six o'clock, and he'd been called in on his way home from the clinic for an emergency check on the poor little guy. The calf had pneumonia and would need to be separated immediately from the other calves and cattle in the main pen. The Double M had a "sick bay barn," so the calf would recuperate there.

"Is Snowball gonna be okay?" a little voice behind him asked. "Daddy? Will he be okay?"

The desperation in little Donovan Marconi's voice made Felix's chest hurt. Ranch kids weren't supposed to get attached to the calves and lambs, but they often couldn't help themselves, naming them when working ranches didn't name their animals or treat them like pets because of the nature of the business.

"Well, let's see what Doc Sanchez says," Hank Marconi said to his son. Donovan was only four years old. Felix had gotten to know the sweet boy these past couple of years, a happy child who loved ranch life and animals.

He turned around to face the boy, remaining seated so he'd be at eye level. "I know this is really hard to hear, but this calf is very sick. I'm going to give him medicine to help him feel better. But tonight, he's going to need company and round-the-clock care. I'll know in the morning if he's going to be okay or not."

Donovan's tearstained face half crumpled and he looked up at his dad. "Can we stay with Snowball tonight, Daddy?"

"Sure we can. You and Mommy and I will camp out."

Donovan's face instantly brightened. "Hear that, Snowball? We're going to have a slumber party with you tonight."

Felix smiled as the boy wrapped his arms around his father's legs, looking up at him with such love and hope. How he managed to smile when his heart felt so shredded was beyond Felix. If he hadn't lost Victoria, they'd have a two-year-old now. Maybe a son like Donovan.

He and Victoria used to talk about children all the time. Even back in high school. They'd both wanted four kids, any combination, though Victoria liked the idea of each child having a brother and a sister. Each kid would be named using the initial of one of their parents. Dylan and Arabella for Felix's parents and Mira and Trevor for Victoria's. As they graduated from high school and then college and further school for their specialties, Felix in veterinary medicine and Victoria in dental school, they'd decided they'd marry young to support each other in their dreams and then would start a family when they were thirty.

It was exactly on Victoria's thirtieth birthday that she went to see her doctor for a physical, just wanting to hear that she was the picture of health before embarking on this huge journey. Two days later, her doctor had asked them both to come in to talk about her lab results. They'd both known immediately that something had to be very wrong. And it was.

One more test and the diagnosis had been confirmed. Ovarian cancer. They'd had just another year together. A year of fighting the cancer. Hoping. Praying. Fighting some more. And then three months of knowing she was dying, that there was nothing that could be done. There were second opinions and third opinions. Everyone was in agreement. But to the end, despite what he knew about cancer, he never lost hope that a miracle would cure her. Or just give them more time. And then time had run out. There would be no children named after their parents. There would be no family and no one. Just Felix.

Love, as even four-year-old Donovan Marconi was learning, was about loss, too. Felix was done with it all. He'd been so numb at his great-aunt's funeral in Mexico, Stanley sobbing beside him, clutching his hand on one side, his sister Camilla's on the other. His siblings, too, had been so shaken by the depth of their dear great-uncle's pain.

Yet despite that harrowing grief, Stanley Sanchez had found it in himself to fall for someone again. Felix couldn't understand how it was possible.

For Felix, the key to never hurt like that again was to not love again. It was that simple.

Yeah, he'd invited Shari to be his plus-one at the family birthday party this weekend. That didn't mean they were a couple—they weren't.

He was on his own, as he had been for the past three years. As he'd be for the next three years. And beyond.

Felix wanted nothing more to do with love. Love just led to loss. Sure, he had family he loved. But he didn't have to *add* anyone to the list of those it would destroy him to lose.

THE NEXT DAY, Shari parked in the small lot at Bronco Ghost Tours and walked into the main building. Evan Cruise stood in the lobby, surrounded by around eight people, welcoming them to the tour. She gave him a little wave and headed down the hall, looking for a door with Winona's name. The moment she saw the purple door with the crescent moons and stars she knew she'd arrived. She tried the doorknob, but it was locked. Her heart sank at the thought that Winona wasn't available to do a reading, after all. Shari needed to know something. Anything.

Anything that would direct her one way or the other.

To giving up on love and going full speed ahead on her plans to be a mother.

Or to giving Felix a little more time to get to know her, to fall hard for her.

She'd thought she was settled on the idea of pursuing single motherhood. But another fitful night, unable to stop thinking about Felix Sanchez, about what *could* be, had her all confused again.

It was possible that the more they got to know each other, the closer they'd become. It was possible that he could fall for her. Entirely possible. And Shari always ran with *possible*. If something could happen, she'd help it along until it did. Glass half-full and all that.

He'd been in touch only once since his text about the family party he'd invited her to this Friday night. To ask about the kitten and if she felt comfortable fostering

Page until at least the end of the week. He'd called the animal shelter and since their foster families were all spoken for at the moment, keeping the kitten with her would provide a good continuity while she got stronger.

She'd texted back her agreement and got back a smiley face emoji and one of a cat.

What she wanted was a row of heart emojis.

Gathering herself, Shari knocked on the door, and within seconds, Winona opened it. She had a completely neutral expression. Flanking her were two heavy purple drapes tied on each side. Winona wore a purple sweater with silver beads all over it, purple jeans, purple cowboy boots and a purple headband with a pin on it in the shape of a crescent moon.

"Welcome," Winona said. "Right this way."

Shari followed the elderly woman through the drapes and into a dimly lit small room. Antique floor lamps cast a glow. A small round table was in the center of the room, with a purple high-backed chair with velvet padding, and a pink one.

"Please sit," Winona said, gesturing at the pink chair.

Shari sat—and swallowed.

Winona was studying her. Her sharp dark eyes traveled all over Shari's face, even lingering at her right ear where her earring—a tiny green ceramic turtle—dangled. Now Winona was looking directly into her eyes. "You're here because you're unsure what path to take."

Shari gasped. "Yes. That's exactly it. That's exactly why I'm here." She leaned forward.

"For you, I simply have a question."

"A question?" Shari repeated. "But I already have a lot of questions. And no answers."

Winona raised a finger. "Ah. Yes. Maybe because you're not focusing on the *right* question."

Shari swallowed again. What was the right question?

"What do you want most of all, Shari?" Winona asked, leaning back in her chair.

"I—" Shari began, then clamped her lips shut. "I…"

"I'm waiting, dear. I *am* ninety-five."

Shari sat up straight. "Um, yes, of course. I don't mean to take up your time. It's just that I want a *few* things."

"Which is why I asked you what you want *most of all*. What is the answer?" Winona was staring at her hard now.

"I want Felix Sanchez to feel about me the way I feel about him," she blurted out—and promptly burst into tears.

"There you go," Winona said with a firm nod. She reached under the table and handed Shari a box of tissues. "The truth often brings tears. And clarity. Now that you know what you want most of all, you can go for it."

Shari took a tissue and dabbed under her eyes. "But it's not up to me. If he's not ready or willing to have a relationship, what can I do?"

"You can do a lot, Shari Lormand."

Shari was about to ask, *Like what*, but Winona was already standing up and walking toward the door.

"But I'll tell you the only thing you need to do," Winona said.

Shari's eyes widened. She wanted to either pull out her phone to record this or her little notepad and pen to jot down every word the woman said.

"Let that man see who you are."

Shari tilted her head. Disappointment socked her in the stomach. That was the equivalent of *Be yourself.* Sigh. "Right," she said with a nod, trying not to sound dejected. "Be myself."

Winona shook her head. "Dear girl, thinking you know what's what is why you've been stuck. I'm not telling you to be yourself, though of course you shouldn't fake anything. I'm telling you to let Felix see who you are."

Shari took in a breath. "But I don't know what you mean by that."

Winona reached out and patted Shari's hand, her white hair glinting in the low lighting. "Well, don't think on it. Just *do.*"

"Do?" Shari repeated.

"Do," Winona said. "Listen, dear. That man is as lovely as his great-uncle, so I get it." Then she turned and walked away.

Shari smiled at the sweet comment, but found that instead of giving her a clear path, Winona's reading left her as confused as ever.

CHAPTER SEVEN

"LET HIM SEE who you are," Evy repeated slowly a half hour later on her break at Doug's, enunciating every word as though that would help her and Shari figure out what Winona had meant. The two were sitting at a table far from the jukebox and the dartboard and the noise of the lunchtime crowd. She'd needed her friend's advice—and a plate of nachos piled high.

Shari scooped up a tortilla chip laden with black beans, cheese, guacamole and sour cream. "I've been thinking about what she meant by that ever since I left her parlor. And I'm drawing a blank. I've been pretty open with Felix. I told him a little about getting my heart broken and dreams crushed. And I've told him what I'm looking for, so isn't that showing him who I am?"

"I think so," Evy said, popping a nacho into her mouth.

"And what did she mean by 'don't think, do'? Do what?"

"That Winona is very mysterious," Evy said. "But she's never wrong."

Did Winona actually *say* anything, though? Shari wondered.

Evy glanced up at the door and waved hello to someone. Shari turned to see Audrey Hawkins and her fiancé, Jack Burris, entering and heading for the bar. Shari waved, too. Audrey and Jack were famous—Audrey was one of the four Hawkins Sisters, rodeo competitors, and Jack was the younger brother of celebrity rodeo champ Geoff Burris and a star in his own right.

Evy sipped her soda, then sat up straight and snapped her fingers. "I've got it, Shari! Like with the kitten. You found a poor little kitty by herself in the library garden, rushed her over to Felix's clinic and then took her in to foster. That's showing him who you are for sure."

Shari was ninety-nine percent sure she was going to adopt Page, too. Hmm. Evy might be onto something there. Or not. "Remind me to ask you about kitten care later," Shari said, thinking of adorable Tina, the kitty Evy had adopted from Happy Hearts, Daphne Cruise's animal sanctuary. "But isn't my saving Page just being a decent human being? Being myself? She said she didn't mean that."

"But what else could she mean? That's showing him who you are. Isn't it?"

"I was kind of hoping for a more straightforward reading," Shari said.

"I think maybe Winona is just telling you that as you and Felix spend time together, to not be afraid to be vulnerable. To talk to him from the heart. Share what's going on in your life. I mean, your appointment at the fertility clinic was a big deal, Shari."

"It was just a first step to talk about how it all works."

"Yeah, and a big deal. Maybe Winona means that since you and Felix are friends now, you should take that to heart—as a friend, open up to him."

"But he's not even ready to date, Evy. The last thing he wants to hear about is my ticking biological clock at age thirty-four and what I plan to do about it."

"Winona didn't say anything about keeping your feelings to yourself. On any subject."

Shari ate another nacho, extra guacamole this time. "I think you're right, Evy. Maybe she was telling me not to hold back who I am."

Evy nodded. "Definitely."

Raised voices could be heard over at the bar on the far left. Evy turned around and Shari strained her neck to see what was going on.

"I'm not afraid of some dumb barstool," a big guy in his twenties was saying. "Let me at it."

"If you go near that Death Seat, we're through!" the woman standing next to him snapped.

Shari shook her head as the blond guy in a cowboy hat moved closer and closer to the haunted barstool. Didn't he realize it was cordoned off for a reason? She wouldn't sit on that thing for a million dollars. Because the moment she did and got her million, she'd somehow lose it. That was how the legend went.

The entire bar let out "oohs" and shrieks of laughter and various opinions were called out.

"So you believe in legends?" the guy said to his girlfriend. "Come on. If I sit on the Death Seat, I'm gonna get fired the next day or get food poisoning? Please."

Doug was drying beer steins behind the bar. "I could give you a list of the bad stuff that happened to anyone who sat on that stool. Take Bobby Stone. A few years ago, he sat on that stool—just like you want to. And know what happened to him?"

The tough guy raised an eyebrow. "What?"

"He died. While on a hike. Dead. Just like that. But go ahead, sit on the barstool. Break your mother's heart. Lose your gal. Sure. No skin off my back."

The bar was dead silent.

"He died?" the blond guy repeated.

"Sure did," Doug said.

The guy backed away. "Well, I feel like standing anyway."

"You bet you do," his girlfriend said with a relieved smile, socking him in the arm.

He pulled her in for a kiss, which got cheers and wolf whistles from the crowd.

Evy rolled her eyes. "I love this place, but I'm really looking forward to my boutique's grand opening and working there full-time." She glanced around. "I will miss good old Doug's, though. Cowboys and all." Evy was very close with Doug and his family and would always help him out any time he needed an emergency waitress like today, but otherwise, she'd be hanging up her apron and order pad in a couple weeks.

"I can't wait for Cimarron Rose to open," Shari said. "Talk about going for what you want and getting it. I'm so proud of you. You're such a great role model. For me *and* Lola."

"Aww, thanks." Evy popped up and gave Shari a bear hug. "My break's over too soon. Go get your man, Shari."

Shari grinned. "I'll try."

She would try. Felix wasn't her string-Shari-along ex, who'd known exactly what he was doing. Felix Sanchez was protecting his heart—his big, lovable heart. It was up to Shari to show him he didn't need to.

By showing him who she was.

Shari let out a shriek, but because she was at Doug's, no one even looked her way.

That's it! she thought. *That's what Winona meant. Now I understand!*

She happily finished her nachos and her soda, then got up to head home to Page for some cuddle-time and list-making. A Friday night date at Felix's big family party called for a new dress. Something colorful for a quinceañera. Maybe some super high heels.

Oh, yes, Shari was looking forward to this more than she should.

USUALLY WHEN SHARI got home, Page would come shyly explore over near the door, then rub against her leg, and Shari would scoop her up to cuddle her. A little ear-mite meds, a gentle brushing, dinner and then more petting. While Page would then play with her favorite toys, sending her little plastic ball with the bells and her catnip mouse flying, Shari would tell the kitten everything.

What she'd found these past couple of days was that sharing her every thought aloud let her really hear what she was saying. Who knew that bringing a tiny bundle of fur into her home would bring so much joy and reward?

But when she unlocked her apartment door, there was no pitter-patter of little claws on the hardwood floor.

"Page? Where is my little cutie?" she called out.

No Page.

No tiny mewing, no slight noise indicating Page was batting around a toy or scratching at her post. Her

worry let her know she was now one hundred percent
on adopting Page. As if there were any question.

"Page?" she called again, looking in all the rooms,
not that there were many. Kitchen, no. Living room, no,
including under the couch. Bedrooms, no. She wasn't
under the bed or behind the drapes. She wasn't in the
bathroom.

A chill ran up Shari's spine. Where was the kitten? She couldn't have gotten out this morning when
Shari left, not without her noticing. She opened the
door again, hoping it would lure Page out. It didn't.

She grabbed her phone and texted Felix.

I can't find Page anywhere. I don't know where she
could be!

Be there in ten, he texted back immediately.

Relief flooded her. She spent the next ten minutes
searching the apartment, the closets, under the beds
and sofa again. Where *was* this little creature?

By the time Felix buzzed downstairs, Shari was
in something of a panic. She pressed the button to let
him in and paced by the door. When he knocked, she
opened the door and ran right into his arms, tears in
her eyes.

"I don't understand what could have happened," she
said, her voice muffled against his jacket.

"Hey," he said gently, giving her a hug before stepping back. "She's in here somewhere. Kittens can get
in crazy tight spaces. Don't imagine the worst. She
might be fast asleep."

"But where? I looked behind the toilet. In the cabinets under sinks. In my closets." She bit her lip, her chest aching.

"Hmm," he said. "Let me think like a kitten." He walked in the living room and slowly turned around. "Kitty condo would be a draw, but she's not in the two little caves. Let's try your room." She trailed him into her bedroom, glad she'd tidied up this morning before leaving for work. His gaze beelined to the small shag rug on the side of her bed. Her fuzzy orange-and-white slippers were there, where they always were when they weren't on her feet. He walked over to the rug and kneeled down, then swiveled around the slippers.

Shari saw the whiskers poking out of a slipper. "Page!"

The kitten sleepily opened an eye, then both. Then closed her eyes and curled herself up into an even tighter ball and went right back to sleep.

Shari burst out laughing. "I'm so embarrassed. I didn't even think to check in my slippers!"

"Warm and fuzzy and smells like you," he said. "A kitten's happy spot."

"Smells like *feet*," Shari said, smiling and shaking her head. "I'm sorry I dragged you out here. Next time this happens I'll look in the slippers first."

"That's what friends are for," he said. "No trouble at all."

She heard the message loud and clear. Friends.

How can I show you who I am when you only see me as a friend? It's all the other stuff I want you to see. All the elements that make up a romantic relationship. Not just the core friendship.

"Cup of hot cocoa as a thank-you?" she asked.

"I'd love some."

She was so aware of him following her into the kitchen. She wanted to turn and slink her arms around him, pull him close against her, kiss him…

Instead, she heated up milk and poured it into two mugs full of the fancy cocoa her mother had sent her from Denver.

They sat down at the table. Felix wrapped his hands around the mug and breathed in the scent. "Mmm. Reminds me of the best of my childhood. My parents always made cocoa when it rained or snowed or if I was feeling sad about something."

"Pure comfort," she said, taking a sip. "Were you close with your siblings growing up?"

"Definitely. Dylan's just two years younger at thirty-two, so we were close from the get-go, and I always felt protective of Dante, who's thirty. Camilla and Sofia are still in their twenties and fierce, so I always knew they could take care of themselves, even if we're still protective of them. They'll always be our younger sisters. Now with Camila married and Sofia engaged, Uncle Stanley is working on my brothers' love lives, too. They're both relieved he has a girlfriend now so he won't have much time to hand out their cell phone numbers and astrological signs in the supermarket to women who seem single."

She laughed. "Is that what he does?"

"Constantly. The night we…met at Doug's, he'd arranged for me to give veterinary advice to a single woman he met in the produce aisle. His eyes go straight to the left hand. No ring makes him move right in with the 'have I got a guy for you.'"

"Will he bring Winona to the quinceañera?" she asked.

"No doubt. My mother tried to set me up with a client's daughter, but that's where having a good friend as a plus-one comes in handy."

Clunk. Her heart dropped straight into her lap. So *that's* why he invited her—to get out of a blind date. Sigh.

"I'm glad you think of me as a good friend," she said, which was true. Having a friend was nice, but a good friend—someone you could really talk to, someone you could count on, was golden. She knew she was lucky to have hit it off with Felix Sanchez—finder of lost kittens. But she wanted much more.

"My mother won't rest till I'm remarried," he added, drinking more of his cocoa. "And because I'm the oldest, she's focused on me and not my brothers. She may slyly interrogate you at the party. This will be the first time I've brought someone to a family function since—"

She gave him a few seconds to finish or not and when he drained his mug, she reached over and squeezed his hand. "I'm looking forward to meeting your whole family."

He looked at her and smiled, and she could tell he was grateful she'd let that go. He stood up. "Well, I'd better be getting back. Early-morning ranch call at seven."

"That *is* early," she said. "Thanks again for finding Page."

"And thank you for the hot chocolate."

All too soon he was at the door, smiling that dazzling smile that made her knees weak and her stomach fill with butterflies. But underneath she could see he was still mired in the sentence he hadn't finished. He was bringing a woman to a family function. Friend or not, it was a first since his loss. And he was clearly heavyhearted about it.

The moment she closed the door behind him, she missed him. The object of her secret teenaged crush would always have a little piece of her heart—no matter what.

But then she felt a furry warmth at her ankle and looked down and there was the sleepyhead, rubbing against her leg. She picked up Page and cuddled her.

"What's gonna happen, huh?" she asked the kitten.

Page didn't answer, but she was as comforting to hold as the hot chocolate had been to drink.

CHAPTER EIGHT

THE NEXT AFTERNOON, an overcast Monday, Felix was writing up his report for his last patient at the Bronco Heights Animal Clinic, a beagle named Josie who needed to lose a good ten pounds. He had two more dogs to see, then two cats, and then he was going suit shopping with his brothers since Dante had sat on something on a park bench that had never come out of his one pair of dress pants and Dylan had said all his ties were boring. Felix had a few suits and ties to choose from for the quinceañera, but he hadn't seen much of his brothers lately and wanted to catch up.

He also liked filling his time. Keeping a little too busy. So he'd have less time to think about Shari and invite her places, like friends do. Coffee. Or a bite after work. The entire time he'd been in her apartment last night, he'd wanted to kiss her.

So what did this mean? He knew he wasn't ready for a relationship. Nowhere near it. He supposed being attracted to someone—very attracted, to the point that he dreamed about her last night—had nothing to do with whether he was ready to date. Attraction had a life of its own.

Then again, this powerful hold that Shari had on his thoughts and libido was new. He'd found women attractive in the past three years, but that hadn't messed with him.

And it wasn't just the pretty face and strawberry blond mass of curls and her interesting outfits and sexy body that had him all turned around. He really liked her. He could have sat at her kitchen table for hours, enjoying the view of her face, listening to her talk, appreciating that she'd taken in the stray kitten, but then that stark reminder about the quinceañera had sent chills up his spine.

In three years, there had been a lot of family functions. Big ones. Camilla's wedding, for one. Sofia's engagement party. Birthdays. Work promotions. Personal goal celebrations. Thanksgivings. Christmases. His father's thirty years at the post office. His mother had even thrown a party to mark being debt free on the salon. He'd never brought a date—even a friend for a plus-one.

So why now? Just to get his mother off his back about inviting her client's daughter? Maybe. Denise Sanchez had been getting as pushy as Stanley these past few months, his great-uncle egging her on.

Truth be told, he wanted to bring Shari to the party. Wanted to have his own person there as a haven of sorts. The Sanchezes and their various branches could get overwhelming fast with their big hugs and "*Tell me everything*," and though it had been three years since he'd been widowed, some of his aunts or friends of the family still went overboard. *"Oh, you poor baby, losing your high school sweetheart to that terrible disease,"* they'd say, hand to the heart, tears in the eyes. He'd needed to escape and take deep cleansing breaths outside, wondering if he could slip away unnoticed.

Now, though, he'd have Shari beside him. He'd introduce her as his friend, Shari Lormand, the children's librarian at Bronco Library. And then the busybodies would go pester his mother and sisters about what the "friend" label really meant and leave him be.

He was half-comfortable with the thought of taking her. Half not. He'd see how it felt to walk into an event with another woman. All dressed up. Clinking wineglasses. Dancing. He'd see.

"Wes Abernathy and Archie awaiting you in Exam Room Five," one of the vet techs said, handing him Archie's file.

Enough thinking. Time to get back to work. He was looking forward to seeing the cute pup again.

Felix tapped on the door and went inside and there were Wes and Archie, Wes sitting on the padded bench, and Archie, white and furry with brown spots, on the floor gnawing on a toy, an orange chewy dolphin with a squeaker in the fin.

"Good to see you, Wes," Felix said. "And this gorgeous dude looks great. No struggle as he went from prone to sitting. No wincing."

"He's a trooper," Wes agreed, his blue eyes tender on the puppy.

Felix scooped him up and placed him on the exam table. Archie was a calm pup, easy to handle.

Weston stood on the other side of the table, giving Archie a pat. "Sometimes I'm still amazed when I realize I not only have a dog, but a fiancée and that I'm gonna be someone's dad. Whodathunk?"

Felix glanced at Weston Abernathy, then resumed his examination of Archie, checking his legs and back. Wes was part of one of the richest families in Bronco.

He was a good guy, but he'd been long used to getting whatever he wanted without lifting a finger—his looks, name and money just made things happen. But when he'd met Evy Roberts, a young single mom and a waitress at Doug's determined to fulfill her dream to open her own boutique, Wes had probably heard the word *no* for the first time in his life. Evy worked for what she wanted, and if Wes wanted her, he'd have to show her he was serious. About commitment. About being a father to her four-year-old daughter, Lola. And he had.

When Lola had fallen madly in love with the adorable furry puppy and Evy had been unable to imagine one more thing on her plate, Wes had adopted the pup so that Lola could have access to Archie anytime she wanted. Felix had known then that Wes had it bad for Evy and that his life was about to change.

"Big changes," Felix said, looking inside Archie's ear with his otoscope. "But I guess when you're ready, you're ready."

Wes looked at him like he'd grown an extra nose. "Did you say something about being *ready*?" He chuckled. "More like everything I didn't know I wanted and needed was suddenly right in front of me."

"So how did you know?" Felix asked. "I mean, what made you realize that was what you actually wanted?"

Maybe he'd learn something about himself here. Answer some of these questions plaguing him the past couple of days.

"Well, I think you know when you meet someone who's…everything. You can't stop thinking about her. She's got you tied in knots. She makes you think. Makes you laugh. Makes you wonder about things you normally don't think about. She makes you more *you*.

And so you just *know*, even if you try to ignore it at first like I did. Like that ever works."

Felix smiled. "I might be doing a little of that myself," he admitted. "I'm not ready to get back out there. I'm not sure I'll ever be. But there's something about this woman that's got me all... everything you just said." He'd just said it aloud, admitted it. How was it possible to feel a weight lifted off one shoulder, but a heavier one dropped on the other?

He was grateful that Wes didn't ask who he was talking about. He was opening up but wasn't ready to divulge everything. "Damn, Felix. I'm really glad to hear that. Not that it's easy when you're in *No, I'm not and No, I don't* mode. But they just become part of you when you aren't even looking. The way I started feeling about Evy and Lola felt huge. And scary as hell. But then nothing felt more right."

Felix was in the very beginning stage, he figured. At the point when Shari Lormand was sneaking inside his heart and soul when he didn't even know it. Lodging in there good. He was beginning to realize he had feelings for her. But he wasn't at the scary stage yet because he and Shari were just friends. That kept her in a safe spot mentally because she was technically off-limits, even if he'd wanted to slowly remove her dress last night and kiss her shoulders, her collarbones, along her neck until he got to her mouth.

A sudden lick from Archie on his wrist brought his attention back to the dog on the table. He finished his examination and gave the pup a good scratch behind his ears. "Archie is one hundred percent recovered. Just keep him away from mama bears from now on."

"Can't wait to tell Lola," Wes said, picking up Archie and putting him down on the floor and attaching his leash. "She's crazy about this pup."

If the Heartbreaker of Bronco Heights had fallen for a single mom and her little girl and just like that had become a family man—with a dog—anything was possible. *Even for you, Felix*, he told himself. But it was hard to keep an open mind with a closed heart.

He knew he wouldn't change overnight. So he'd just do what he'd been thinking ever since he invited Shari to the quinceañera. He'd see how it felt. To walk into an event with a woman. *Be* with a woman. Dance with a woman. Have family and friends assume they were a couple.

It wasn't going to feel right, that much Felix knew. And then maybe he could go back to thinking of her solely as a friend and move on from this whole sneak attack.

And if he was so sure it wasn't going to feel right, then why did having Shari by his side feel so necessary?

"NOTHING BUT DEAD ENDS!" a voice grumbled.

Shari glanced over at the woman using one of the communal computers on the first floor of the library as she crossed the reception area Monday afternoon carrying a stack of children's returns. She recognized Sadie Chamberlin; she owned a popular gift shop in Bronco Valley, right near Evy's soon-to-open shop. Cimmaron Rose.

Sadie flung her long, wavy blond hair behind her shoulders and let out a huff before leaning back in her chair.

"Can I help with anything?" Shari asked her, shifting the books in her arms.

"Sorry for being loud," Sadie said. "I'm just so frustrated. I'm trying to find information and I guess I don't even know what I'm looking for."

"Well, I'm not a reference librarian, but I could try to help," Shari told her. She set the books down on the desk next to Sadie's.

"Did you know Bobby Stone?" Sadie asked.

Bobby Stone—the man whose name had come up at Doug's when that show-off had wanted to sit on the haunted barstool to prove nothing bad would happen to him.

Bobby Stone. A few years ago he sat on that stool. Know what happened to him? He died. Dead. Just like that.

"No, but I know *of* him," Shari said. "I did hear that he died a few years ago."

Sadie took a breath and nodded. "He fell off a cliff while hiking in the mountains just outside Bronco. He'd told some folks he was going on the hike, and his belongings were found on the cliff. It was a pretty treacherous drop into desolate, heavy forest. His body was never found, but everyone thinks he took a bad fall—that he'd been drinking. The rescue operations just couldn't see through the dense brush down there."

Shari shook her head. "So awful. Did you know Bobby? Were you a close friend?"

Sadie looked down for a moment. "He was my sister's ex-husband," she said, her brown eyes sad. Dana and Bobby got divorced six months before he died.

"Oh, I'm very sorry."

Sadie was quiet for a moment. "I lost my sister, too.

She died because of a drunk driver last year. Both she and Bobby are gone. But the past couple of months, weird stuff has been happening."

"Like what?" Shari asked, sitting down in the chair beside Sadie.

Sadie glanced around, then leaned close to Shari. "Did you hear about the incident at Doug's back in July? Someone threw a big rock through the window. There was a note wrapped around it: *A Stone You Won't Forget* was written on it. No one had any idea why someone would vandalize Doug's like that—everyone loves that place. And whoever threw it was gone when everyone ran outside to try to find the culprit. The police came, but nothing ever came of it. I didn't think anything about it either until last month."

"Last month?" Shari repeated.

"There were flyers posted all over the rodeo at the Bronco Convention Center: *Remember Bobby Stone*."

"Oh, gosh, that's right," Shari said. "I did hear about that. No one knew what to think of it."

"Well, when I saw those flyers, I remembered the note on the stone thrown through the window at Doug's. I think the two are related."

"I wonder why someone would be stirring up his memory now, though," Shari said. "Three years later."

Sadie nodded. "Exactly. Why? And who's behind it? I feel like there's more to come."

Shari felt a chill run up her spine.

Sadie stood up. "I'd better get back to my shop. Thanks for listening. I really appreciate it."

"Of course," Shari said. "It's unsettling. I completely understand."

Sadie nodded and then hurried out.

Shari had just moved back to Bronco when she'd heard about Bobby's death. The haunted barstool had taken on even greater legendary status because Bobby had sat on that stool just a few days prior to his death. A little shiver ran along her neck.

Shari was set to go on a half-hour break in five minutes. And boy, did she need it. She stared at her phone and tapped on Felix's contact info. She bit her lip. *Don't think, just do*, she reminded herself, Winona's words coming back to her.

Text him, she told herself. *Do it now. Before you lose your nerve. Friends text each other about meeting up for coffee. You're not asking the man on a date.*

Could use a cup of coffee. Double espresso. Just got chills over something.

You okay?

Yeah. Just...unsettled.

Meet you at Java and Juice in five minutes. I have a patient at the clinic in 45 minutes, but coffee and something decadent and an ear even for a bit might help.

You're the best, she typed and hit Send before she could delete it.

But he *was* the best.

COULD HE BE better-looking? Shari thought as she walked into Bronco Java and Juice and saw Felix sitting at a round table. She wasn't the only one who thought so because he was surrounded by three women standing around him, holding iced drinks and tossing their hair and laughing at whatever he'd just said. As she slowly approached, she heard him say something about tiny Chihuahuas thinking they were the boss, and that they were, but a good training class or private trainer would go a long way in helping the relationship. The redhead in the center let out an exaggerated "Phew, I will definitely call this trainer you recommended."

Shari walked up to the chair across from Felix and smiled.

Felix stood. "Ah, my lovely date has arrived."

It was amazing how one line could give a gal hope and thoroughly deflate her at the same time. He'd referred to Shari as his *date*. But she knew he was using the term very loosely—as in coffee date—and to send the flirty trio on the way.

The women eyed Shari and gave her tight smiles, then thanked Felix again for his "so helpful info!" and left.

"Does any of them even *have* a Chihuahua is what I want to know," Shari said. Meanly. Jealously.

She usually wasn't a snarky person, but…she was a little jealous. When Felix Sanchez decided he was ready to date, he'd have a long line of attractive women to fill his dance card.

Felix laughed. "Actually, last month Stanley was talking me up at the supermarket to a woman he met in the frozen food aisle. She told him all about her sick cat and he assured her I'd meet her at my sister's restaurant that night to discuss the situation."

"Wow," Shari said.

"Wow is right. He had no way to contact her to cancel, so I felt like I had to go and somehow get through it and explain my uncle's habit of unsolicited matchmaking. Turns out, it was the woman's grandmother's cat that was sick—and twenty-one years old. Stanley hoodwinked me into a date. And trust me, I was not happy when I realized I'd been played—by both of them."

"Yikes. What happened?" Shari asked.

"I ate quickly, kept it professional, paid the check and then I told her I wished her and her grandmother's cat well and gave her my colleague's card at the clinic should she need emergency veterinary care."

Shari liked that. "Did you give your uncle a talking-to when you got home?"

"I sure did. He pulled out all the stops. 'I just want you to be happy. I just want you to find love. I just want to see you smile.' And let me tell you, Uncle Stanley can pour on the theatrics and waterworks like no one."

Shari smiled. "Hence why he got you to go to Doug's the night we met—the woman with the sneaker-chewing Pomeranian."

"Exactly. Let's go order before we run out of time. I spied something very chocolatey with my name on it."

Shari grinned. "Ooh, my name is on half of it if you want to split it."

"Deal," he said.

She practically floated up to the counter at his side, all the anxiety that had gripped her after talking to Sadie dissipating.

They chatted with Cassidy Ware Taylor, the owner of Bronco Java and Juice, who'd recently married rancher Brandon Taylor, about the amazing renovations she'd recently made to the place. The spacious coffee and juice bar was now even bigger, with more seating and a big kiddie section with a train set and

little tables and chairs for kids to color on. The Taylors had a four-month-old baby girl whom Brandon's
stepmother, Jessica, watched during the working day.
One of the wealthiest women in town, Jessica had surprised everyone by not only offering to babysit, but by
being a doting caregiver and not minding if her pricey
silk dresses were spit up on.

They ordered an iced mocha latte for Shari and a
cappuccino for Felix, plus the Mississippi mud pie slice
with two forks. Once they were back at the table, Felix
cut the slice in two and they dug in.

"So what happened earlier?" he asked, taking a sip
of his cappuccino. "Is everything okay?"

She told him about the run-in with Sadie Chamberlin. Shari sure hoped there would either be answers
soon about the strange happenings or that they'd stop.

"Huh," he said. "That *is* strange. And I agree that
the stone with the note and the flyers going up at the
rodeo have to be connected. Someone doesn't like that
Bobby Stone seems forgotten."

"She mentioned he was married to her sister, but
that she died in a car accident last year," Shari said.

Felix's expression changed in an instant. His jaw
went tight, his eyes troubled. "Yeah. Her name was
Dana. She was young like Bobby. I remember thinking how damned unfair life is when I heard about her
death. I mean, what the hell lasts?"

She flinched as she looked at him.

"I mean, my wife gone at thirty-one years old. Dana
gone. Bobby gone. And then there are the breakups.
The receptionist at the animal clinic was left at the
altar, Shari. Stood up in front of two hundred of their
friends and family. Because the bastard met someone

else the week before and wanted to 'explore his feelings.'" He hung air quotes around the phrase. "And there's you."

"Me?" she repeated, hearing the choke in her voice.

"You got blindsided. It's why you moved back here, right? You were with a guy for five years and he strings you along and then you ask for what you want and need, and he says, 'Oh, this isn't what I want,' and he marries someone else a few months later? Love is—" He stopped talking, his jaw still tight, his eyes stony now. He shook his head and let out a breath, then picked up his cappuccino and took a long drink.

Whoa. In the space of a minute, everything had changed. From lighthearted quips about their Mississippi mud pie to…this. Had she ever seen him look this way, heard that hard edge in his voice?

She thought she was unsettled from talking to Sadie Chamberlin at the library? Now she just wanted to inhale the dessert and go home and cuddle Page.

"Sorry," he said, glancing at her. He let out a breath and dropped his head down for a moment, then leaned back in his chair.

"Love is everything," she said suddenly. Out of nowhere. "It's *everything*."

"It's the *end* of everything."

Oh, Felix. It's not. It's the beginning of everything.

Suddenly she wanted to order three more lattes and another treat and just sit with him for hours, letting him talk, letting him get it out. Maybe that was what he needed to do. And friends listened. Yes, love was everything and it was right of her to say so. Yes, she'd had her heart broken bad. But she hadn't lost a spouse. Of course Felix was down on love.

She needed to not forget what Winona Cobbs had told her. *Show Felix who you are.* She'd figured out what the nonagenarian psychic meant; now she had to remember that.

Felix wasn't her string-Shari-along ex, who'd known exactly what he'd been doing.

He stood up, taking his cappuccino. "I've actually got to get back for my next patient." He looked at her, his hazel eyes contrite now. "You asked me here because you needed a friend and now you probably need a drink. Maybe two. At least there's one last bite of the Mississippi mud pie." He gave her something of an awkward, sweet smile, and she just wanted to wrap her arms around him.

She stood up too and took his hand. "You can be yourself with me, Felix. And you just were."

He squeezed her hand, then let go. "I appreciate that more than you know," he said.

And then he walked out.

CHAPTER NINE

WHEN HE ARRIVED home the night after their coffee date, Felix had called Shari to apologize for getting so intense, and the moment he heard her voice, he'd calmed down, felt soothed. Now, a few days later on a beautiful Friday night, he knew it was because she'd been right. He stood before the mirror on the back of his closet door and adjusted his tie. He *could* be himself with her. That was the hallmark of a true friend. That also had him feeling better. No matter how attracted he was, Shari was simply his friend.

He glanced at his reflection. Charcoal suit in pristine condition. Tie, not crooked. Black leather shoes shiny. He was ready. He grabbed the birthday card he'd gotten for his cousin Alejandra, in which he'd inserted a hefty check, and slid the envelope in his inside jacket pocket.

Downstairs was quiet, which normally would not be the case with a family of four getting ready for a big family event, but his parents had left a half hour ago to go "help" Dante and Dylan at their apartment, which meant making sure they were dressed to the nines. Now that Felix had a plus-one, Denise Sanchez had turned her attention to her younger sons and their love lives, and each unknowingly had a list of five women his mother thought would be just perfect for them, depending on the personal chemistry.

Felix was about to knock on his great-uncle's door, which was slightly ajar, to see if he was ready to head out, when he heard Stanley talking. He could see Stanley sitting on his bed, facing away from him toward the window. On Stanley's bureau was a photo of Celia taken just last year, with her trademark big smile.

"I know you're watching over me, *mi amor*," Stanley continued. "So I know you know that I am taking a date to the quinceañera."

Felix stood stock-still, holding even his breath.

"You would approve, Celia. Winona is a strong, smart, kind woman who doesn't take guff from anyone, just like you didn't. I'll tell you, she's been through a lot. *A lot.* I had tears in my eyes as she told me the story of being separated from her young love. They were still just teenagers. Not much younger than we were when we met."

Felix's chest constricted.

"Winona became pregnant and her family sent her away to some kind of home," Stanley continued. "They told her the baby died and she was so distraught that they institutionalized her. But her teenaged love, Josiah Abernathy, he found out that the baby *didn't* die and he vowed to find her—a daughter—before it was too late. Josiah was in his nineties and his memories were fading fast because of dementia, but he finally achieved his dream. Thanks to friends and family, Winona was reunited with her long-lost daughter, Daisy. They even share a home now. A whole family opened to Winona."

Felix loved that the story had had a happy ending. Last year, many were trying to figure out the mystery of who the long-lost "baby" Beatrix was, what had become of her. Felix had been amazed at how some important people in both Winona's and Josiah's lives had pulled together to find her—all for elderly Josiah Abernathy, who at that point was in a care home, and Winona, who'd lived in Rust Creek Falls, then. But Josiah had done it. He'd made it happen. Josiah had passed not long ago but the family had been reunited in spirit.

"Winona has a gift," Stanley said, still facing Celia's framed photo. "She knows things. When I'm with her, I feel like a combination of a teenager and the eighty-five-year-old I am. But I want you to know, *amor*, that no one will ever replace you in my heart. What I have discovered is that there is room in this old thing," he said, and Felix heard a thump, which meant he'd probably patted his chest. "The heart expands. But you always knew that."

The heart expands? Not Felix's.

Maybe that was the difference between him and his great-uncle. The reason why Stanley was able to date someone and Felix couldn't.

Felix's heart had shrunk. Not expanded.

He relaxed enough to actually move, though his muscles felt tight, especially in his shoulders. He went into the kitchen and slugged down a glass of ice water.

"I'm ready to dance the day away!" came Uncle Stanley's voice as he exited his room.

Felix left the kitchen to find his uncle looking especially dapper, his tie purple, likely to match his date's outfit, he figured. He glanced at Stanley's face; you would never know, unless you'd been eavesdropping, as Felix had had no business doing, that the man had just had a poignant talk with his late wife. His heart went out to his dear, sweet great-uncle Stanley. He loved the man so much. He had such an urge to pull

Stanley into a bear hug, but his *tio* would know Felix had been listening.

"Ah, almost forgot," Stanley said, slipping past Felix into the kitchen. He opened the refrigerator and pulled out two square white boxes. "For the ladies," he said, handing one to Felix.

Felix opened the box. It was a corsage, blush- colored tiny roses. Stanley showed Felix's his—purple, of course, with silver bows.

"I wasn't sure what color to get for you to give to Shari, so the florist told me blush would go with everything."

"I wasn't planning on giving Shari a corsage. It's not part of the tradition anyway." He frowned at it, shutting the box.

"Oh, shush," Stanley said. "Since you're just friends, you can put it on her wrist."

Felix inwardly sighed.

"You look good, Felix."

"You, too, Tio."

Stanley clapped him on the back and pulled open the door. "Off to pick up my lovely date. See you there," he said, and practically skipped to his truck.

Felix got into his own car, the corsage resting on the console, and drove to Bronco Heights to pick up Shari. He pulled up in front of her building. But it took him a good half minute to get out of the car. Another minute to press the buzzer. His collar felt tight.

He and Victoria had dressed up for a lot of occasions in their time. The junior and senior prom at Bronco High. Various family functions. New Year's celebrations. Their engagement party. Their wedding.

Now he was in his suit and tie and shiny shoes—and about to escort another woman to a family party.

Shake it off, man. You're taking your friend Shari to a teenager's birthday party. Calm the hell down.

Shari buzzed him in and he slowly walked up the flight of stairs to the second floor. She opened the door before he reached the landing and he stopped in his tracks. Whoa.

She wore a slinky red dress that skimmed her curves and swirled around her knees. Silver high heels. Her strawberry blond hair was loose past her shoulders. Every cell in his body went on red alert.

He swallowed his reaction and walked up the rest of the way. "You look nice."

She smiled. "You, too."

"This might be the first time I'm seeing you without your glasses," he said. "When I think of you, I picture the strawberry blond curls, the round tortoiseshell glasses and interesting necklaces. Like the night I had the good fortune to be sitting next to you at Doug's."

"I wear my glasses to work every day, most places, really, so putting in my contacts makes me feel more party-mode."

"I get it. I feel that way about not wearing my white lab coat."

She seemed about to say something but a little sound made them both look down.

"Mew. Mew-mew."

Page was swishing around Shari's ankles. "Sorry you can't join us, kitty."

Shari picked her up and gave her a nuzzle, then put her down on her scratching box, where she immediately turned upside down and began clawing the sides. "I'm all set."

He swallowed again, watching as she grabbed her little purse with its long silver chain from the hallway counter.

Friends, friend, friends, he reminded himself. But he was still unable to stop looking at her glossy pink-red lips. The fullness of her breasts in the slinky dress and how the material moved with her.

But the biggest problem was that his intense attraction to Shari Lormand wasn't just about how sexy she looked in that dress.

SHARI DIDN'T KNOW Felix Sanchez that well, but she knew this: the man could not take his eyes off her. Every time he looked at her, his gaze was smoldering. She wasn't one to flatter herself or see what wasn't there, either.

He wanted her. Bad.

Even if he'd told her she looked "nice." What he meant was smokin'. Which was exactly the word Evy had used when she'd texted her friend a selfie of herself in the dress she'd bought in a fancy boutique three years ago, the very first week she'd arrived back in Bronco. A promise to herself that someday, she'd feel okay again. Someday her heart wouldn't hurt. Someday, she'd wear it for the man who'd make her forget there had ever been anyone else but him in her heart.

That someday had finally come.

And did the man not say *Every time I think of you, I picture...* and then describe her trademark accessories?

He thought of her.

He pictured her.

He noticed.

She couldn't wait to get Felix Sanchez on the dance floor. For a slow dance.

But the moment they walked inside the festively decorated space, the band playing a popular song on the stage, they were surrounded by Sanchezes. Their debut on the dance floor would have to wait through quite a few introductions.

"You must be Shari," a woman with auburn shoulder-length hair, warm brown eyes and a big smile said, pulling her into a hug. "I'm so happy to meet you. I'm Denise Sanchez, Felix's mother."

Shari grinned. "Shari Lormand. It's so nice to meet you."

Before Felix could get a word in, Denise added, "Felix has only told me a little bit about you, but I'd love to know more." She glanced over by the buffet tables. "Ooh, there's no line at the buffet. Let's go load up before the teens stop dancing to this loud song and take all the mini empanadas." She took Shari's hand and led her over.

Shari loved how vivacious and friendly Felix's mom was. Her mother was polite but slow to warm up to people, which was fine, of course, but made for very awkward introductions.

"Mmm, everything looks and smells so good," Shari said. Her eyes widened at the end of the buffet table where a salad bar and range of Mexican and American dishes was set up, including an enchiladas station with mole sauce. "I can't resist enchiladas ever." She took one, then forked a bite. "Delicious. Yum." Two more bites quickly followed.

"No doubt," Denise said with a smile. "My daughter

Camilla is catering the party." She craned her neck to try to spot her. "Ah, there she is, in the yellow dress," she added, nodding toward a beautiful woman chatting with a group. Shari had had contact at some point or another with all of Felix's relatives at the Bronco Library, just as she had with most of the town. But she'd never been formally introduced to any of the Sanchezes besides Stanley. Denise turned back to Shari. "Camilla owns The Library right here in Bronco Valley. And I understand that you work in the actual library in the Heights. I think I've passed you in there a time or two. It's been a long time since I've had a *niño* or *niña* young enough for the Children's Room."

Just like that, Shari and Felix's mother were deep in conversation between bites of the delicious food and the sangria Denise got them from the bar, chatting about everything and anything so easily. Every few minutes, someone would come to say hi to Denise, and she'd introduce Shari as Felix's date—with a smile. There was nothing sly in the smile, nothing but warmth. But from the smiles she'd get back it was clear that being his *date* was big and everyone at this party knew it.

Denise had been telling Shari a funny story about the time she'd tried hair extensions on herself when the woman was grabbed away and Shari was quickly ensconced in another group. On the dance floor she could see Stanley and Winona dancing with old-school formality. Camilla and her husband, Jordan Taylor, and Sofia and her fiancé Boone Dalton, were chest to chest, looking up at each other with moony eyes. She glanced around for her handsome date, her heart speeding up when she found him chatting with two guys who looked a lot like him. Probably his brothers. She hadn't met them yet.

"Remember the tortoise," a voice suddenly said. "Like the eyeglasses you usually wear."

Shari turned to find Winona Cobbs standing behind her, picking up a mini taco and taking a bite. She looked spectacular in a purple dress with fringe at the hem, a silver scarf around her neck. Shari almost instinctively reached up to touch her glasses, then remembered she'd put in her contacts for the party.

"The tortoise?" Shari repeated.

"The tortoise." Winona took another bite of her taco. "There are a few hares all over this party. Sometimes that works, too. In it to win it and all. But you know what they say about slow and steady."

"Winona, are you trying to tell me something positive about the super slow pace of my relationship with Felix?" Shari whispered.

"Yes, dear."

"Well," Shari said, telling herself not to blurt out what was on the tip of her tongue. "I don't know if I'm relieved or not because I've barely seen him since we arrived. Granted, that's been all of twenty minutes, but…" She wanted him at her side, introducing her to all these people who were special in his life. Instead, he was…not.

Winona fixed her with her piercing eyes, then turned to gaze around. "He's avoiding the dance floor."

Shari almost gasped. Of course, he was. Why hadn't she thought of that? This was his first date since he lost his wife. His first dance floor with another woman. "Winona, I don't know if I should go hug him or just stand here and admit defeat and eat ten more mini tacos." She sighed. "I know I want to be a mother," she added. "I've been exploring my options. But I'm so torn about giving Felix a chance or just going ahead with my plans."

Winona put down her empty plate, adjusted her scarf and nodded. "I understand. But slow and steady is always the best course. And if you were defeated you wouldn't be here."

Winona had walked away by the time Shari had processed the strange conversation.

"I'm sorry we got separated," came the voice Shari had been dying to hear in her ear.

She whirled around, her dress fluttering around her knees.

Felix had two glasses of champagne in his hands and gave her one. "Every time I excused myself to go find you, another relative grabbed me into a hug. I hope my mother and other family members didn't give you the third degree."

"Not at all," she said, holding up her flute.

They clinked glasses and they both took a long sip.

The band began playing a ballad that Shari loved. She almost asked Felix to dance but then remembered what Winona had said. *He's avoiding the dance floor.*

How could her heart not go out to him?

It's a good enough start to be here. He asked you to come. You're his date, as far as his family and friends are concerned. That's big enough.

"This is the most dumbest, stupidest, boringest party ever," a young voice said.

Shari exchanged a glance with Felix, both their eyebrows going up as they turned their heads slightly to the right.

Diagonally across from them, near the dessert buffet, were three boys, around eight or nine years old, in polo shirts and khakis. Looking very bored despite the cookies and treats heaped on their plates.

One of the boys crammed a cookie in his mouth, chewing around his words. "Yeah, and my mom said speeches are starting soon and if I burp on purpose I'm grounded for a week. I was planning to."

"You still should!" the third boy said. "I'll pay you five bucks."

"Ten," the burper insisted.

They giggled and high-fived.

"I would have been among them, no doubt," Felix said with a smile, then took a sip of champagne.

"Not me. I love speeches," Shari said. "Even the long ones that lose the train of thought. There's just something about someone standing up and saying how they feel—onstage, with a microphone. It always seems special to me."

More evil giggles erupted from the huddle of boys. "I know," one said. "Let's take turns bumping into the table with the ice sculpture. Whoever makes it fall over wins."

"Wins what?" the second one asked.

"Bragging rights."

"I'm in," the third said.

Felix grimaced. "This doesn't sound good. That ice sculpture is actually an ice bust of the birthday girl."

Shari eyed the boys. "I know what to do."

"You do? Are they about to get the librarian lecture in your sternest voice?"

"Nope." She walked over to the group, Felix coming up behind her. "Hey, guys. You might recognize me from the Bronco Library. I'm the children's librarian. I could use your help, if you're not busy."

"Our help?" the one who came up with the bumping-the-ice-sculpture idea asked, his dark eyes curious.

"I'm putting on a Halloween Spooktacular Reading Party next month," Shari said, "and I want to tell only the scariest stories. *Really* scary. Could I get your opinions on the stories? They're short, just a few minutes each. And for listening and giving your thoughts, you'll each get a Spooktacular gift kit at the library on Monday—but participating means you can't try to knock over the ice sculpture. Or do anything that would make the birthday girl or her mother sad."

The boys stared at her with wide eyes. "Okay," the ringleader said. The other boys nodded.

She turned to Felix. "Works every time," she whispered.

"You amaze me, Shari," Felix said, tucking an errant curl behind her ear.

Making her knees all shaky.

"Right this way, guys," she said, leading them to the back of the room.

She was sure Felix would disappear into the crowd again, but as the boys assembled their chairs in a semicircle around her, Felix took a chair too and smiled at her with so much in his expression that her knees felt wobbly again. Good thing she was sitting.

"Let me get your scare meters," Shari said to the boys. "Do you want medium scary or super scary?"

"Super scary!" they said in unison.

She nodded. "I thought so. Bronco is a town with a lot of legends. Scary legends."

The boys scooted their chairs in closer. So did Felix.

"Even the library has a legend attached to it," Shari said. "The basement mummy."

"Mummies are so cool!" a boy said.

"Well, the library basement mummy wasn't having a good day," Shari went on. "Someone did him wrong— a bully. And the basement mummy wanted revenge."

Three sets of wide eyes were glued to her.

"Wait, is the bully a mummy, too?" the ringleader asked.

"That's the thing," Shari said. "The mummy doesn't know. The bully could be a thousand-year-old bully. Or a kid from town around nine years old. No one is sure. Not all mummies are wrapped in gauze once they get out of their…resting places."

Shari had their complete attention, the demise of the ice sculpture forgotten as she continued the story. But when a statuesque blonde in a hot dress and killer heels kneeled down beside Felix and whispered something in his ear, Shari almost lost her train of thought.

When Felix stood and mouthed a *Sorry* to Shari— whatever that meant—she did lose her place. She watched the pair leave, the woman wrapping her arm around Felix's.

She frowned and leaned back in her chair.

"Wait," one of the boys said. "What happened to the library bully?"

"Yeah, does the mummy get him?" another boy asked.

Shari snapped back to attention and took a breath. She owed the boys better.

"Well," Shari continued, her heart feeling as if it was filled with water balloons, "the mummy was chasing him up and down the stairs from the second to the third floor…"

Three faces, waiting on her every word, stared at her. A flick of long blond hair caught her attention for a moment.

Felix was being led away and out the door.

Maybe the blonde was another cousin, she told herself.

Sure. That was about as possible as her *ever* having a romantic relationship with Felix Sanchez.

CHAPTER TEN

"HOW DOES THIS not go to your head?" Felix's sister Sofia asked him as she shook her head with a roll of her eyes. Sofia had watched him try to disentangle himself from the slinky blonde with a few pointed shakes of her head. His sister wore an emerald-green dress—one of her own designs—that complemented her long auburn hair, the late-afternoon sun glinting off her bare shoulders.

Felix and Sofia stood on the patio where the tall blonde had led him—on a ruse—to find a stray little dog she'd supposedly seen limping in the bushes separating the start of the property from the parking lot. *Oh, the poor thing must have run off*, the woman had said when they'd gotten on the patio and Felix had spent a good ten minutes looking for him, crouching down to peer under cars. No sign of a dog. *I'm Eleanor*, the blonde had practically purred.

Felix had shaken her hand and informed her he was going to go through the lot row by row to try to find the dog. It would involve a lot of crouching and might get her dress dirty. That was when the woman confessed it was all a flirty ruse to get him out here where they could chat. Would he ever forgive her? she asked, with a wink and a faux-sorry face despite the smoldering look in her eyes.

Felix had had it. He'd fallen for it—again. He'd been pulled away from Shari for the second time that night. And just when he'd finally pulled himself away from friends and family he hadn't seen for a while. A lot of those conversations had been about how sorry everyone was about Victoria, so maybe it was better that Shari hadn't been by his side for that. A few too many of those he'd spoken to had also lost loved ones.

"Wait, I know why it doesn't go to your head," Sofia said, leaning against the gray stone railing of the patio. "Because you've never been interested in dating the past three years, so you don't care that women are literally lying to get you alone."

"Well, I do care about that—it bothers the hell out of me. Why would anyone think I'd find that a positive trait?"

"Boone's single brothers Shep and Dale get the same," she said, her rock of an engagement ring, as their sister Camilla had called it, shining on her left hand. Boone Dalton, Sofia's fiancé, came from a wealthy ranching family relatively new to Bronco Heights. Shep and Boone were the remaining single siblings out of five. "Though not ruses about stray limping animals. They get everything from sudden interest in the care of cattle to horseback riding lessons at the Dalton Grange. But I think they like it."

"Why are people so focused on other people's love lives?" he asked. "If I wanted to date, I'd be dating, you know?"

"Love is the one thing that brings the world together. People like it. They want it for themselves and for others." She eyed him. "And besides, aren't you dating now? I mean, this is the first time in three years you've brought a date to a major family function."

A waiter passed by with a tray of mini chicken taquitos. Felix took two plates while Sofia snagged them two glasses of white wine from another tray.

"To be honest, I don't know what I'm doing, Sof. My head says I'm not ready. But I can't stop thinking about Shari. We're just friends, and I mostly asked her as my plus-one to get Mom off my case about bringing the daughter of her best client. But it's more than that, too."

Sofia nodded. "No doubt. I've seen her in that dress. Shari got it at BH Couture, you know. The year she first moved back to Bronco. I was working in the boutique that day and I'll never forget her telling me she was buying it for the future, that she had absolutely nowhere to wear such an amazing dress and wouldn't be dating for, like, ten years after getting over her last relationship. But she wanted that sexy dress in her closet to always remind her that she knew the day would come when she'd put it on and know she was back."

Huh. He'd been so focused on himself that he didn't stop to think about Shari's own loss. She'd had dreams, too. And they'd been crushed, just like his.

Now she was here in that dress of…hope.

"Part of me wants to go with what I'm feeling," he said. "And part of me feels like it's wrong. That's where I keep getting tripped up."

"So take it slowly. We all can't be Uncle Stanley," she added with a smile.

Through the glass-paned double doors to the event room, he could just see Stanley and Winona dancing to a popular rap song that all the teenagers loved. In fact, they were surrounded by teens on the dance floor and only had eyes for each other.

He craned his neck around the crowd for a glimpse of that sexy red dress and strawberry blond curls. Ah, there Shari was, talking to Camilla and her husband, Jordan. Shari threw her head back and laughed, and even though he couldn't hear the sound, he knew it, could imagine it filling his ears. He watched as those three young would-be quinceañera-destroyers approached her. She kneeled down to be at their level and seemed to be listening intently. Whatever they were talking about, there were big smiles around. She high-fived each one of them.

A crack, a sliver, really, opened in his heart. Instead of the tiny space feeling drafty or outright cold, it felt...warm.

And as his gaze traveled down her curvy body in that dress, that sliver of space felt hot.

Shari. What have you done to me?

"Yup, you've got it bad for this woman," Sofia said, following his gaze with her own.

He couldn't deny that.

Sofia's eyes got misty, and he stared at her for a second as he realized why.

He squeezed his sister's hand. Sometimes he forgot how deeply his parents and siblings had shared his pain when Victoria had gotten sick, how devastated they'd been when she'd died. Uncle Stanley and Aunt Celia had flown in from Mexico and stayed for six weeks, Stanley barely leaving his side. For Felix to be interested in another woman was a big deal, and now the positivity, the possibility for happiness was getting him hugs and teary eyes from all his siblings, even Dylan and Dante, who hid that kind of thing well.

"I'm just so overjoyed for you, Felix," Sofia said. "Shari must be that special, you know? If she got in there," Sofia added, patting the spot where that sliver had cracked open.

"So maybe instead of standing out here, I should be in there."

She nodded. "Asking her to dance. But wait till this song ends."

He smiled. "I'll do that."

Dancing with Shari would either remind him of every scintillating moment during their one brief night together where they'd come very close to having sex— or it would remind him of everything he'd lost three years ago. He was rooting for the former.

But scared spitless of the latter.

THE PAST HALF HOUR had been a whirlwind of telling scary stories and chatting with so many guests, including all of Felix's siblings. Then she'd been incredibly touched when the three boys asked her to tell scary stories at the library for their age group. She'd promised to add it to the roster and they'd happily run off to the dessert buffet.

Despite it all, she found herself glancing around the crowded space looking for Felix, but she didn't see him. Because she *did* know him, even just a little, she knew he wasn't in a coat closet having wild sex standing up with the hot blonde.

Because he was a good guy, a stand-up guy, and her date, just friends or not.

She looked around again, but didn't spot Felix. She

did see Maddox John, a local rancher, all decked out in a suit instead of his usual jeans and Western shirts, standing by the buffet. Alone too. Shari knew Maddox from around town and, of course, because she'd seen him every now and then at Doug's. And she also knew from gossip that his wealthy parents were none-too-pleased that Maddox's older brother Jameson and his fiancée, Vanessa Cruise, were planning on a small homespun wedding instead of the huge event the Johns wanted. Shari couldn't help but notice a few women checking out the attractive blond rancher; given his reputation as a relentless flirt and serial dater, if he was here alone, it was because he wanted to be, for sure.

Maybe Felix wanted to be alone, too.

She brought her wrist corsage to her nose and gave it a sniff, the fragrance of the roses lifting her spirits.

"May I have this dance?"

Shari almost gasped as she turned around. There he was, gorgeous with his sexy dark hair and hazel eyes, in his charcoal suit.

Whatever had led to this dream of a moment, he certainly wasn't avoiding her or the dance floor right now.

The rap song had just ended and now the band was playing an old Celine Dion ballad that Shari had always loved, even if it cleared away the teenagers. As Felix led her by the hand to the dance floor, she could see his uncle Stanley and Winona Cobbs dancing with her cheek against the lapel of his suit.

The moment she was in Felix's arms, all thought faded from her head. All she could think about was how good this felt, how good he felt, his arms around her, her head against his chest, her arms around his neck.

"I'm sorry I left the mummy story," he said. "I was

as captivated as those boys were. It was a false alarm, too."

"Oh?" she asked. She pictured the blonde and mentally narrowed her eyes at her.

He nodded. "Never mind. I'm just glad I'm back. I've…been thinking about doing just this for days."

She looked up at him. "Have you?" She almost squeaked the words. *Please be talking about slow dancing with me to a romantic Celine Dion song.*

"I might not be ready to date, but I can't stop thinking about you, Shari. Or wanting to kiss you again. So where does that leave me?"

Her legs did shake this time.

"I guess you might be a little bit ready," she said. "Just a tiny bit."

He lifted her chin with his hand. "Maybe so."

A surge of hope fluttered in her heart. She almost wished she had a hand free to pinch herself with, to make sure this wasn't a dream, that it was actually happening, but no way was she disengaging even a finger from around Felix Sanchez's neck.

"Did I mention how beautiful you look?" he whispered.

"You did tell me I look nice."

"Yeah. I meant incredibly hot."

She gasped, and he smiled, then leaned down and kissed her. And kissed her. And kissed her.

"I think they're more than just friends," she heard someone nearby say.

FELIX HAD HELD Shari in his arms for the next hour, whether the song was fast or slow—and even through a line dance involving all the teens. They'd disengaged only for more of the delicious buffet and more chatting with his relatives. Luckily, outside of Felix's immediate family, Uncle Stanley's romance with his older woman was the real talk of the party more so than Felix's first date in three years. And then finally, the event had wound down and Felix was driving Shari home.

And *not* planning to peck her on the cheek at the front door and then leave.

Once inside her apartment, Shari slipped off her high heels, Felix's gaze going straight to her long legs. She picked up Page, who was rubbing her shin, and gave her a nuzzle and a kiss on the head, then set her down in her kitty bed.

"I love how much you love that kitten," he said.

"Who knew I was a cat person? I almost can't remember ever *not* having her."

"Yup, that's the way it works. They get you with those adorable little furry faces." He stepped closer to Shari and pulled at his tie. "I've been dying to loosen this tie all night."

"Let me help." She reached up and undid the tie, using both ends to gently tug him closer.

He looked right at her, the playfulness between them turning to smoldering, and then he kissed her. The only illumination came from a lamp and the glow of moonlight spilling in from the sheer curtains on the living-room windows. He pulled off the tie and tossed it on the sofa. Then leaned in for another kiss, very aware that Shari was undoing the buttons on his shirt, yanking the ends from his pants. When his shirt joined the tie, he pulled her against him, kissing her so passionately he heard her gasp and felt her almost droop against him.

He picked her up, her arms shooting around his

neck, and she breathed, "Oh, Felix," in his ear as he walked toward her bedroom.

He set her down in front of the bed and whispered for her to turn around, which she did.

He slid down the zipper of her dress to the middle of her back, his hands going inside to move aside the slinky red fabric, and then the dress dropped, pooling at her bare feet.

"I thought white cotton was sexy the last time I saw you, but this..." He admired the delicate black lace bra and matching barely-there panties before he kissed the side of her neck, his hands up in her luscious hair. "And that's just from the back," he added on a whisper.

She slowly turned around. Her plunging bra left little to the imagination, which was fine with him. But before he could even reach a hand up to touch her creamy skin, her hands were on the button and hook of his pants, the zipper going down before the pants dropped at his feet. He stepped out of them.

"Nothing is sexier than those black boxer briefs," she whispered, her gaze down, down, down.

"Except you in these tiny black scraps of lace." He let his eyes feast on her breasts, her cleavage, her light perfume intoxicating him again. He reached up both hands to cup her face. "You're so beautiful, Shari." He could hardly believe it, but all he could think about was Shari Lormand. How she looked, how soft her skin was.

He was with a woman for the first time in three years. The only other woman he'd been with in his entire life.

"You, too," she whispered, closing her eyes.

They opened when he took off her bra and threw it

to the chair by the bedside table. She licked her lips, and he inched her closer to the bed with his body. They gently fell onto the bed, him on top of her, and he slid down the length of her, stopping at her breasts to let his hands and mouth explore every bit. Then he moved farther along, kissing his way past her stomach and using his teeth to pull her little black panties down her legs.

"Felix," she said on a moan, arching her back.

He shrugged off his own underwear and then was back on top of her, but she shimmied her way out and straddled him, giving him a hell of a view of her gorgeous body, her full breasts and the curve of her hips. He sucked in a breath, barely able to contain himself as it was, and then he felt her cool hand gripping him. Hard. He dropped his head back and groaned, and a delighted giggle erupted from her.

"Oh, yeah?" he whispered, his hands discovering every hidden inch of her, his mouth and tongue following as best as they could from the angle. The giggle had long since been replaced by moaning that was driving him wild. "Shari," he whispered.

She reached over to the bedside table and opened the drawer. He saw a box of condoms. Unopened.

"Every time I leave the house, I find out that my uncle put a condom in my wallet," he said on a chuckle. "More than three make things crowded so I move them to my drawer. I have no doubt there's a new one in my wallet right now."

"But is that one 'ribbed for her pleasure' and does it faintly smell of cherries?" she asked, opening the box and taking out a foil-wrapped condom.

"I really don't want to know the kind my *tio* has."

Shari laughed. "Allow me," she said.

"Oh, I will."

She inched down a bit to get to work, his head on her soft pillows, his eyes closed as he fought for control when her hands unrolled the condom along the very hard length of him. He actually could just slightly smell cherries.

And before he could open his eyes, she was poised over him, the sensation so powerful he had to grip the sheet at his sides.

She leaned down and whispered in his ear, "Are you ready?"

Dimly, he was aware that she was giving him a chance to get back in his head. But he was there already. And he wanted this.

"I'm ready," he whispered back and then set a hand on either side of her hips and guided her onto him.

He could barely hear her moan over his own groans. There was no way he'd last unless he was fully in control so he turned them over, Shari scooting up on the bed. He suckled on one of her luscious nipples, then the other, as his hand found the hot, wet core of her. And then with one last look at her beautiful face, he slowly let himself fill her, pressing down against her, his face buried in her neck, kissing her collarbone, then her mouth.

"Shari, Shari," he whispered as he thrust and thrust, fighting to control himself as her long legs wrapped around his hips.

He could feel her hands in his hair, tightening, then her nails on his shoulders, digging in.

And then he lost all conscious thought as sensation after sensation rocked his body, her lips on his neck, her soft breath in his ear, followed by flicks of her tongue.

The nails dug in harder as he thrust harder, her back arched, her neck exposed, his name on her ragged breath.

And then his world exploded in the best way and all he could think was *Shari*.

SHARI WOKE UP in the dark to the sound of Page trying to claw her way up onto the bed, even though she had her own kitty ladder.

Which was how she'd become aware that Felix was actually standing by the window, wearing only his super-sexy black boxer briefs, his profile just visible as he stared out into the inky night—along with the hard set of his jaw.

Uh-oh, she thought. She glanced at her alarm clock: 1:24 a.m. This could go either of two ways. Either he was simply—not so simply, really—coming to terms with the fact that they'd made love and would come back to bed and spoon her with his face buried in her neck to give himself some privacy with his thoughts, or he'd say he had to go.

Don't leave, she thought. Prayed, actually. *Give this a chance, Felix. Give us a chance.*

If he did leave, she'd have to remember what Winona said. Slow and steady and all that. What had happened between them during the second half of the party and then continued just hours ago in her bed was fast. Inevitable, if you asked her. But fast.

Maybe now he needed to slow things down a little. Not sleep over. Not wake up with her. Take time to process that they'd had sex. And that it was a big deal.

Because it wasn't just sex. And they both knew it.

"It's okay if you need to go," she blurted out, pulling the quilt higher up on her chest. Then she mentally kicked herself. What if he wasn't thinking that? What if she was now putting ideas in his head?

He turned, his expression holding more emotions than she could sort out. She could see tenderness. But also tentativeness. He looked...off guard.

Maybe that was a good thing.

"You've got to see what Page is up to," he said, shaking his head on a chuckle.

She scooted over to the edge of the bed on her stomach and looked down. And there was her kitten, all four claws stuck in the bed skirt and looking up at her with determined gold-green eyes. The poor thing hadn't gotten very far in her big climb. Shari disentangled her and scooted back to the headboard, sitting up against it, the kitten snuggled against her chest.

Oh, Page, what would I do without you right now? You're all that's standing between me and this man about to walk out the door and tell me he can't, he's sorry, but he can't.

She kept her eyes on Page, who was purring like a jackhammer. Shari couldn't bear even the thought of watching him walk around the room, picking up his clothes. Or sliding that pale gray shirt over his rockhard torso.

But he didn't move from the window. She glanced over at him, and he was looking at her, and this time, all she saw in his expression was that tenderness. The tentativeness was gone.

Because he's about to say buh-bye. And feels really bad about it.

She held her breath.

"How about if I want to stay?" he asked, coming over to the bed and sitting down on the edge.

Her heart did all kinds of leaps in her chest. "That's good, too," she whispered because she could barely find her voice.

He slipped under the quilt, Page jumping out of her arms and onto his chest. "How does something that weighs all of three pounds pack such a punch of a landing?" He gave her a scratch on her head, and she crawled up one perfect pec to his shoulder and curled up at the top of his pillow between his head and the headboard and closed her eyes. "As long as *you're* comfortable," he said.

Shari laughed. Then she sobered up very fast. He was back beside her. He was staying. And suddenly *she* was the scared one. Her heart felt like it was pounding out of her chest and she turned away, onto her side, ridiculously happy and very nervous.

And then he turned too, molding his long, muscular body to hers, his arm around her. Felix Sanchez was spooning her.

If she had him, she could lose him. She hadn't thought of that before; she'd been too busy wanting him. Should she even be here? she wondered just as a tiny human combination of her and Felix came to mind, a baby boy with her strawberry blond curls. A baby girl with his dark hair. She knew she should be focusing on her dream to be a mother, but every time she looked at Felix Sanchez, thought about him, he was becoming more and more a part of that dream. Was she too hopeful about him opening his heart to her?

Slow and steady, she thought, closing her eyes as

she felt Felix drop a kiss on her shoulder. Even if there was nothing slow or steady about how her feelings had snowballed. What began as a high school crush was now full-blown love. And Shari was here for it.

CHAPTER ELEVEN

SOMETHING WAS PUSHING on his head. Felix opened his eyes, aiming them at his phone on the bedside table: 6:22 a.m. He rolled his head back up on the pillow to see two furry paws kneading into his hair, the occasional claw making it feel like anything but a head massage.

He felt himself go very still. Because he suddenly remembered where he was. Shari's apartment. Shari's bed. He quietly sucked in a breath and glanced over to his right. She was facing him, eyes closed, a hank of strawberry blond hair over half her face.

He looked up at the ceiling. Were the four walls of Shari's bedroom pushing in toward the bed? He sat up, the kitten scrambling from the pillow to his lap.

What had he said last night—exactly? Had he made any promises?

I might not be ready to date, but I can't stop thinking about you...

Okay. That was pure truth. He was okay here.

I guess you might be a little bit ready, Shari had said.

Maybe so, he'd said.

He didn't feel "a little bit ready" to be in bed with Shari right now under these circumstances. He certainly wasn't ready to cook breakfast together and read the morning paper, sharing sections while munching on bacon the way couples did.

He'd never been so glad that he had an eight-thirty ranch call. He would have to leave now. There would be no breakfast. He could process all that had happened. All that was happening now. That he was here in her bed the morning after.

All he'd do was overthink.

The kitten leaped onto Shari's ribs, and her eyes popped open.

"Oh, that felt good," she said. "Not." She looked at Felix. "Morning."

"Morning. I've got a house call at eight thirty," he said more abruptly than he meant to.

She picked up Page and sat up against the headboard. "You're like me—Saturday hours."

"You're working today, too?" he asked, relief flooding him. That meant they'd both be busy. No time for… anything. Like cuddling in bed. Or breakfast. Or making any kind of plans.

"Ten to five today," she said.

He got out of bed and reached for his pants, stepping into them. He was doing this wrong, he knew. He was *supposed* to stay in bed a little while. Kiss her. Chat. Not do anything to make her feel unsure.

Which was exactly what he was doing. And he couldn't stop himself. Because *he* was unsure and uncomfortable. When he woke up at 1:30 a.m. beside her and had gone to the window, he'd felt at peace— strange, not entirely himself, but at peace. Maybe it was the time of night or the dark room with the glow of moonlight. Maybe it was how comfortable he was with Shari. All he'd known last night was that the pull to get back in bed with her, to hold her, to let himself feel what he was feeling—which was a lot—was stronger than any urges to leave, that he didn't belong there, that he'd done something wrong by letting loose last night.

"I make a great Western omelet," she said. "But next time."

She looked so beautiful, her hair kind of wild, her tortoiseshell glasses on now. He wanted to tell her, but he just reached for his shirt and slid it on, quickly buttoning the buttons that she undid last night. A flash of memory got him, of her hands and lips on him, and he paused for a second.

Part of him wanted to stay a bit longer. He'd love that omelet and a lot of coffee. But a bigger part had no appetite and that feeling was back, that the walls were closing in, that he needed air. "Next time," he repeated, but he wasn't even sure if there would be a next time.

He crammed his tie into his pocket and sat in the chair by the window to put on his shoes and socks. "Well," he said, standing up.

"Know what Page thinks?" she asked, sliding her glasses up on her nose.

He looked at that gray, white and black ball of fur, her white whiskers glinting. "What does she think?"

"She thinks everything is just fine," Shari said. "This doesn't have to be called something or even mean something. We had a great time last night. A big first for you."

This woman is special. He walked to the edge of the bed and sat down, reaching out a hand to cup the side of her face. "You are absolutely lovely in every way, Shari."

He squeezed her hand and then he headed out, something in his head, in his chest, closing down, like a steel gate over the windows and door of a shop, as he left.

He didn't want to know what Page thought of *that*.

"OH, NO," HALEY BUTTERMAN SAID, shaking her head, her precisely cut dark bob swishing against her chin. Shari and two of her coworkers, adult librarian Jemma Garcia and library assistant Haley, were at the coffee station in the break room. "That makes you the rebound sex, Shari. Rebound sex happens maybe three times, then you never hear from the guy again. Sorry."

Shari frowned and almost dropped her coffee mug.

"Um, first of all, Haley," Jemma said, glaring at the young woman, "you shouldn't make pronouncements about other people's relationships. And second, a little sensitivity, please. Especially when you overhear something and then barge into the conversation."

Haley shrugged and poured two packets of sugar into her coffee. "It's not my fault you were talking in the break room. And I'm honest. If you want sugarcoating, go somewhere else. If you want the truth, come to Haley."

No, thanks, Shari thought, taking a bracing sip of her coffee. Jemma was a good friend and they'd shared their triumphs and troubles from the get-go. But maybe she shouldn't have shared what was going on with Felix. It was his business, too. And he did seem like a private person. Then again, it was just as much her business. Her life. And of course she needed to talk to her friends.

But having Haley eavesdrop from the doorway before coming fully in—ugh.

"Just sayin'," Haley added before leaving with her

mug and one of the scones from the box that Shari had brought in from Bronco Java and Juice.

"Ignore her," Jemma said, taking one of the mixed berry scones and standing up. "I've gotta get upstairs. I think everything is going to be just fine, Shari. I really do. You two took a major step forward last night. There's no taking back sex."

Shari smiled. "I guess there isn't. But there might not be more." That Felix had been uncomfortable this morning was obvious. She'd done her best to help, to let him off the hook, whatever the hook was to him, because dammit, that was who she was. A caring, compassionate person who knew when to put someone else first. This morning, Felix was that person. And she'd set aside everything twisting and turning in her heart, her gut.

At least she was following Winona's advice. Even to her own needs, her own detriment, her own impending broken heart.

"I think there'll be plenty more, hon," Jemma said with a warm touch on Shari's shoulder before leaving.

Shari wasn't so sure about that. In fact, she'd say there was a ten percent chance there would be more.

After Felix left this morning, she'd tried talking out her thoughts and feelings to Page, but the one-sided conversation didn't help. And then she'd shared it all with Jemma, who thought Shari should keep what Winona said at the quinceañera in mind—to a point. Slow and steady until it became too slow and made her feel unsteady. That was when she'd bow out. And return to her plan to make her dreams come true herself. The options for having a family and being a single mother.

Listen to Jemma and not Haley, Shari told herself.

She and Felix had taken a major step last night. He *had* stayed over. There *was* no taking back sex. But there were endings. And that could be coming.

Shari bit her lip, then picked up her chocolate coconut scone and took a bite. Maybe Haley was right, though—and Shari couldn't really think of this as a major step for her and Felix. It was more a major step for Felix himself.

No, that was wrong. That took Shari out of the equation and made this about Felix. He hadn't been alone in that bed last night. She hadn't kissed herself at the quinceañera.

Sometimes love and romance was about the right place and the right time. If Shari had been sitting next to Felix Sanchez at Doug's a year ago, he probably wouldn't even have accepted her offer to drop him home, let alone invited her in for churros. Then again, maybe he would have. Maybe the chemistry between them, even if friendship was as far as he'd go, would have had the same effect. Maybe it wasn't about time and place so much as the people involved. Take her ex-boyfriend. He'd strung Shari along for five years because he recognized, at some level, maybe even not consciously, that she wasn't really *it* for him. Then he met someone who was and he knew it. Which was why he'd married her three months later.

Huh. She hadn't really thought about it like that before.

Still once again, Shari's future was a big question mark.

What she needed was another session with Winona.

She's not going to tell you what you need to hear, Shari. You know that.

But Winona was wise. Her business was called Wisdom by Winona, not 100% Psychic Glimpses into Your Future. *So call her.*

She got up and poked her head out of the break room to make sure that Haley wasn't around, then sat back down with her phone and pressed in Winona's number.

"Hello, Shari."

"I hope I'm not interrupting you, Winona, but—"

"Actually, I've got five minutes before Stanley is picking me up for apple picking. My favorite are Honeycrisps. Costly but delicious."

Shari hesitated. Was Winona trying to tell her something? That her relationship with Felix was going to be delicious—obviously, à la last night—but costly as in to her heart and well-being?

She shook her head at herself. Haley had gotten in her head and that was all. Winona was talking about apples and only apples!

"Did you have a question for me, dear?" Winona asked.

"Not so much a question but a… but…well—" She let out a breath. "I'm just a little unsure of myself."

"I can plainly hear that."

"Any advice? Wisdom?" Shari asked, realizing she was waiting on Winona's every word, banking too much on hope.

That wasn't right. *This* wasn't right.

She was going to let her feelings for a man who was only half-available shake her up like this? When she might end up brokenhearted for another three years? Or forever?

She scoffed at her own words. Half-available. As

if there were such a thing. A person was either available or not.

But there would never be another Felix Sanchez.
There might be a perfectly fine guy in the wings. But
Felix was…special.

"Listen, Shari. Life, every bit of it, is full of ups
and downs. From the happiest of days to heartbreak so
painful I thought I wouldn't survive it. In my ninety-
five years, I've felt it all."

Shari had no doubt that was true. She sucked in a
breath.

"All I can tell you is that you can't control other
people," Winona said. "You can only control yourself. You know what's right for you. You know what
to do. Do that."

Shari's shoulders slumped. "I'd really rather you just
tell me what to do." And think. And feel.

"But you already know, dear," Winona said. Shari
could hear a doorbell. "There's my Stanley. Bye, now."

Did she know what to do when it came to Felix?

Her phone pinged with a text a few minutes later,
from Winona. I forgot to say something. Don't think
on it too much. Just do.

Actually, that made Shari feel better because she'd
been sitting there, wracking her brain for what she supposedly knew. *Just do.*

But do what?

*MAYBE NO ONE noticed that I didn't come home last
night,* Felix thought as he unlocked the front door of
the Sanchez family home later that afternoon. He'd
had a long day—three ranch calls this morning—one
to the Double J, the John family ranch, where Mad-

dox John had assisted him in saving a very ill foal—
and then he'd been the doctor on call for the past four
hours at the clinic. He hadn't gotten much sleep last
night and just wanted to fall into bed and hopefully
take a good hour's nap.

Anything not to process his evening with Shari.
He'd been thankfully distracted all day. Not that he
hadn't thought of her or hadn't had very vivid flashes
of memory. The only thing he knew for sure when it
came to Shari Lormand was that he didn't want to hurt
her. *Couldn't* hurt her.

So did he move forward with seeing her as more
than friends? They'd crossed that line—*he'd* crossed
that line. And he wanted to be with her again. But Shari
wasn't looking for something casual and he wasn't
looking to jump in to anything serious. He didn't know
what he was doing.

But being with Shari had felt good and felt right
last night. This morning, in the cold light of day, he'd
been out of sorts, his skin had felt tight, and he'd just
wanted to leave. But that seemed like part of the process. He wondered what she was doing right now. What
she was thinking. Had he made her feel bad when he'd
left? Uncertain? She'd been so kind last night, this
morning again, by telling him it was okay to leave if
he needed to, by telling him they didn't have to label
what was going on between them. Why couldn't he be
more like that and just let himself explore this? Why
was it so damned hard for him?

As Felix opened the door to the house, he glanced
at the driveway for Stanley's truck, and there it was.
He sighed. His *tio* would be full of questions and sly
smiles about his big date last night. Felix had kissed

Shari right in the middle of the dance floor too, so if Stanley hadn't seen that with his own eyes, family gossip would have made sure he knew about it. At least his parents' cars were gone. He'd chat with his uncle for a minute, then disappear upstairs to take that nap, make a pre-dinner snack of delicious leftovers his parents had likely brought home from the quinceañera, and then he'd be more ready to face the barrage of questions he'd get hit with.

When he stepped inside, he could see his uncle Stanley sitting on the sofa in the living room, an old photo album open on his lap. And unless Felix was mistaken, Stanley Sanchez was wiping under his eyes. As though he was crying.

Felix frowned and peered closely at Stanley as he closed the door and headed into the living room. "Tio? Everything okay?"

Stanley quickly shut the album and put it behind him, as if hiding it. He quickly swiped under his eyes again with his knuckles.

"Looking at old family pictures?" Felix asked, not wanting to let this go. His great-uncle was a dramatic, emotional person, but if Stanley was crying and not wanting Felix to know he was looking at photos, something was wrong.

Stanley took a breath and pulled the album back out and onto his lap. "After the quinceañera, I went to Winona's like I have every night since we met." He bit his lip and clamped his lips shut.

"Did you have an argument or something?" Felix asked.

Stanley shook his head. He picked up his drink from the coffee table and took a sip. "We were standing on the back deck, enjoying the night, and all of a sudden I saw a shooting star." He covered his face with his hands and then wiped under his eyes.

Felix went over to the couch and sat down, putting his hand on his uncle's arm. Stanley took in a breath, his mouth down-turned, his shoulders slumped.

"The night I proposed to Celia, sixty years ago," Stanley continued, "I'd seen a shooting star. I saw it and I knew it was a sign from the heavens that I had to ask her to marry me that minute. I ran to her house even though it was close to midnight and woke up her parents. I asked for permission to marry the most wonderful woman in the world. I told them a shooting star had blessed our union. Her parents said yes. And so did my Celia. We got married the next day."

"I've always loved that story," Felix said gently, knowing there was more to come, the part that had made Stanley feel so awful.

"Seeing a shooting star is a once-in-a-lifetime thing," his uncle went on. "But there it was again, right in the sky last night, just when I was looking up. I saw that star and I told Winona I wasn't feeling well and that I had to leave."

Felix was bursting to ask why, but he held it back. He had to let his uncle talk at his own pace.

Stanley shook his head and swiped under his eyes again. "I think that star was Celia. She must have been so hurt, Felix." His uncle hung his head and covered his eyes with his hands. "She must have felt so hurt and betrayed that I was with another woman—that I have a girlfriend."

Oh, Tío. Felix felt his own eyes tear up, his throat clogging. "Uncle Stanley," he said, leaning closer and pulling the man into his arms. His great-uncle sagged against him, sobbing.

"Do you want to know a secret?" Felix said, pulling away a bit so that his uncle could see his face.

Stanley sat back and leaned his head against the cushion. He nodded.

"The morning that Victoria died, she told me she wanted me to find love again, that I shouldn't be alone."

Stanley tilted his head. "Really?"

Felix nodded. "When she fell asleep a few minutes later, I went into the bathroom and broke down crying. I thought, *never*. I'll never love another woman. I was hurting bad—but I was angry, too. Not at Victoria. At the world. At everything. But until right now, I never stopped to think that my vow of *never* meant I wasn't honoring what she wanted for me for the future."

He honestly hadn't considered that until the words came out of his mouth. But now he saw how true they were. He might not be ready for a relationship, but he'd finally taken *never* off the table. Last night, in fact.

"What are you saying?" Stanley asked.

"That I think Aunt Celia would also want you to find love again. To be happy. To not be alone."

Stanley looked at him, his dark eyes so heavy with emotion. "You think the shooting star was your great-aunt Celia giving her permission like her parents did all those years ago?"

Felix was so choked up he couldn't find his voice for a minute. He nodded. "That's exactly what I think."

"We had a date to go apple picking today," he said. "But I canceled. I told her in person, at least. Not that I told her anything. I just stood there, and no words would come. Winona took my hands and kissed both of them and said it was okay. And then I came back home. Maybe I should go try to explain."

Felix had a feeling that Winona already knew exactly what was going on with her new beau. "I think that's a great idea."

Stanley brightened and stood. "I'll see you later, Felix. And then I want to hear all about your night." A bit of the twinkle was back in his eyes.

As his uncle left, Felix headed upstairs, but he had a feeling he wouldn't be able to nap for a second. His head was a jumble. And tomorrow night was the weekly Sanchez family dinner, tradition for decades. His love life would be a big topic.

He did want his uncle to have love in his life again. Someone special to share in all the big and small moments. Just like his family wanted for him. But he also knew why Stanley was struggling over that shooting star.

Felix went into his room and changed into a T-shirt and sweatpants and then slid under the comforter and closed his eyes for that nap. But thinking about Shari kept him wide-awake.

CHAPTER TWELVE

AT SIX O'CLOCK, Shari had settled on her sofa with Netflix, a bowl of popcorn for dinner and a chenille throw over her, when her phone rang. She paused *The Great British Baking Show* and hoped it was Felix with a sweet sentiment. Something. Anything.

She hadn't heard from him today. No mocha latte. No churros. No note. Not even an *All best*. That was probably a good thing, though. The first time they'd spent the night together, even if they hadn't had sex, he'd felt compelled to send her something that showed he was a gentleman—the coffee and treat—but that he had regrets, hence the professional sign-off from hell. Today, though, he wasn't trying to say anything or put any distance between them; he'd likely spent the day processing how he was feeling.

You can't take back sex, she recalled Jemma saying.

But you could say goodbye. And every time her phone rang or pinged and it wasn't Felix, she actually felt *relieved*.

She slowly slid the phone closer on the coffee table.

Not Felix. Evy.

"Hi, Evy," Shari said.

"Hi, and I have a huge favor to ask. My dad is out for the evening, and our sitter just canceled on us at the last second and we're expected at a rancher's association fundraiser in a half hour. Lola's very hopeful that you might be available? She's dying to play with Page."

Shari glanced around at her empty house—well, empty except for Page. Evy had a full house with her dad and Lola and Tina the kitten and all their toys, and soon Evy and Lola would be moving to the Flying A ranch when she married Wes Abernathy.

Shari smiled and said, "Sure thing. We'll make cookies instead of watching people make cookies. Page is looking forward to the extra attention."

"You're the best," Evy said, sighing with relief.

Shari adored four-year-old Lola. Plus, babysitting meant experience around children in a home setting. The one time Shari had babysat and put the little girl to bed, reading her a story and giving her a kiss on the forehead, her heart had felt close to bursting with how much she wanted to be a mother herself. Tonight, she'd really focus on all that was involved in taking care of a child, even for just a few hours. Evy and Wes would no doubt pick up Lola way past her bedtime, but apparently she transferred easily from bed to car to bed.

Which had her imagining herself and Felix picking up *their* child from the sitter's—maybe "Auntie" Evy and "Uncle" Wes—Felix carefully carrying her to their car and then Shari laying her down in her cozy bed with her favorite stuffed animal, Page curled at her side. The two of them watching their child sleep, the rise and fall of the little chest, and they'd be overcome with emotion, wrapping their arms around each other before tiptoeing out.

Love. Family.

The fantasy had her so wistful that she had to suck in a breath and bring the chenille throw up to her neck to comfort her. Everything in her life was a big maybe right now.

Her phone pinged again. And this time it *was* Felix. She closed her eyes, not wanting to look.

Not that Felix would say much in a text. If he had regrets, they sure wouldn't come that way.

She opened her eyes and grabbed her phone.

Thought I'd bring by a pizza and we could talk.

She swallowed. Talk about…what? That he was very sorry, but he just wanted to be friends? That he had the time of his life last night and wanted more of that?

I'm babysitting for Evy and Wes tonight. Lola's coming to my place to play with Page.

Three little dots appeared. And stopped. Then started. Then stopped. Then started.

In that case, I'll get two pizzas. One plain and one pepperoni.

Interesting. She expected him to say: *Another time, then.*

I don't think we'll be able to talk with a four-year-old around, she texted back.

Maybe that's better, he wrote.

Huh. Maybe it was.

CRAZY THING WAS, Felix didn't even know what he'd planned to talk about when he'd sent that text. He only knew he wanted to be with Shari, see her, be in talking range if subjects came up that should be discussed. He didn't want to *not* call her, not see her just because he was unsure of what the hell he was doing. Or feeling.

And Lola would be a buffer. Her being there was probably a plus. He could spend time with Shari yet the evening would be kept light out of necessity for little ears.

As he parked in front of Shari's building, he sent his uncle a quick text.

How are things? He added the emoji of the smiley face wearing a cowboy hat. His uncle used that in every text, no matter the content.

Bueno, Stanley texted back. Winona says honesty is everything. We just made popcorn and are planning a Hitchcock marathon, starting with *Rear Window*.

He smiled at the notion of Stanley and Winona cuddled on the couch watching old thrillers. But he was hoping for a little more elaboration. Felix knew honesty was always the best policy. And sharing how seeing that shooting star had made Stanley feel had very likely brought him and Winona even closer.

But how honest could he be with Shari when he wasn't all that sure what he was feeling? No one wanted to hear *I don't know, I can't say, can't we just*.

Especially not Shari, who'd dealt with that for five years and then got badly hurt.

He wouldn't mind having a reading with Winona. Maybe he should set that up. Get some clarity, a little guidance. And now that Winona and Stanley were a couple, maybe the psychic would have some extra insight for her paramour's grand-nephew. Hey, he'd take what he could get.

He got the delicious-smelling pizzas from the passenger seat and headed into Shari's building. When he got up to the landing, he could see Shari and Lola, holding the kitten, waiting for him in the doorway.

"Doc Felix, does Page like pizza?" Lola asked, her long dark hair in a ponytail and her green eyes bright.

Felix was amazed at how sweet and docile the kitten was, allowing Lola to hold her. The little girl had some great training in baby pet care when Wes had adopted the puppy she'd fallen in love with and Evy had adopted Tina the kitty. Evy and Wes had both taught her how to approach Archie and Tina, how to hold them, how to treat them. She'd clearly shown that same care with Page under Shari's supervision.

"Even though pizza is so good, it's not good for kittens," he said. "And that was a really smart question to ask me."

"Page likes me," Lola said, giving the kitten's head a nuzzle.

"She sure does," Felix agreed, smiling at the girl and up at Shari.

Even with the aroma of the pizza, he still got hints of Shari's sexy perfume, that slight sandalwood scent. She wore a V-neck hunter-green sweater and skinny jeans that hugged her curves and he had to drag his eyes off her body—the body he'd explored every inch of last night.

He focused on her socks—with little books all over them—no shocker there. Lola was wearing a similar outfit but her socks had little puppies on them.

"Well, let's head into the kitchen and attack that pizza," Shari said, clearly aware that his gaze had lingered on her body. There was nothing *All best, Felix* about the way he'd looked at her. He was getting to know her well, and there were questions in her eyes. What did he mean by *We should talk?* What did *Maybe it's better that we can't* mean? What was going to happen?

"Yay!" Lola said. "Sorry you can't have any, Page," she told the kitten solemnly as she set her down. "Maybe when you're four years old like me."

As Felix opened the two boxes on the round table and they all helped themselves, Lola's excited chatter about the cheese being the cheesiest and the crust being the crustiest had him suddenly flashing back to those conversation with Victoria about starting a family. Hopes, dreams, plans. Gone in a second in a doctor's office.

When would he look at a child and not think about what he'd lost?

"Mmm, this is so good," Lola said, a stretchy piece of mozzarella extending from her mouth to the slice in her hand.

Shari laughed. "Agreed. Bronco Brick Oven Pizza is my favorite ever."

Lola finished her big bite. "Doc Felix, are you and Shari married?"

Felix froze for a second. He shook his head. "We're friends. Like you and Page."

"One of you is a kitten?" Lola asked, looking from Felix to Shari. "You don't have whiskers, Doc Felix. But Shari doesn't, either."

"Yeah, Felix, which one of us is the kitten in this friendship?" Shari asked playfully.

He quickly took a big bite of his slice of pepperoni and then pointed to it, making an exaggerated facial expression for why he couldn't respond to either of them.

How this conversation went from potentially awkward to funny did a lot of good for how heavyhearted he'd been feeling a couple of minutes ago.

After they finished eating, they went into the living room to play Lola's favorite board game, Candy Land. Sitting on the floor on the soft area rug, they explored the Peppermint Stick Forest and Peanut Brittle House and Gumdrop Mountain. Three times. Lola won the first game, Shari the second, Felix the third, and now Lola was trying for her second victory.

"Uh-oh, Doc Felix," Lola said, lying on her tummy. "You landed on a licorice, so you lose a turn! Are you sad?" She peered at him closely.

"Nope. Not sad at all. Know why?"

She tilted her head. "Because you don't like licorice?"

"Actually, I do. Red *and* black. But I'm not sad because I'm having such a good time playing this game with you and Shari."

"And Page," Lola added.

"And Page," Felix agreed.

He glanced over at Shari and the look on her face sent a chill up his spine. Everything about her expression was wistful, yearning. He knew she wanted a family, a husband and a child, but that she was worried time might be running out so she was exploring her options.

That expression told him he couldn't screw around here. Whatever was going on between him and Shari wasn't just about him—and he kept forgetting that.

He was grateful when Lola won the game and turned her attention to Page and trying to count how many toes were on each paw. Because he was kind of worried about the expression that had to be on his face, and Lola missed nothing.

Neither did Shari.

Lola let out a giant yawn. Then another. "I'm not tired," she said.

Shari smiled at her. "I have a great idea. Lola, why don't you help me put the pieces back in the game box, and then you'll pick out a book from my collection for my most special visitors."

"Yay!" Lola said, clapping her hands. She quickly helped pack up the game and then bolted up and slipped her hands into Shari's. "Can I pick the book now?"

Shari nodded, and they headed toward the book-shelf, where it looked like Shari kept a row of chil-dren's books.

Lola took out a few and slid them back and then took out another, her face lighting up. "It's about a kitten! Doc Felix, will you read it to me?" Lola asked.

Felix felt a pinch in the region of his heart. *Let it all go*, he told himself. *This is not your and Victoria's almost child. This is not your and Shari's would-be future. This is just a sweet little girl, the daughter of mutual friends, asking you to read her a bedtime story.*

"I'd love to," he told her, and she handed him the book.

"Let's go wash up while Doc Felix gets the story reader chair all set up beside your bed," Shari said.

Felix took the book into the guest room. He hadn't been in here before. He moved the rocking chair from the window over to the bed, where Lola had already set her favorite stuffed animals. Her little backpack with flowers on it was on the dresser.

He sucked in a breath, unsure why he couldn't stop

his head from going there. From the almost and the what-ifs and the losses.

He tried to shake himself out of it before Shari and Lola came in, and by the time they did, he was sitting down, the book called *A Friend for Fluffers* open on his lap.

Lola slid into bed, turning on her side to face him, Page trying to claw her way up. Shari laughed and put the kitten on the bed and she curled up on the covers beside Lola and closed her eyes.

Nothing's ever easy, he thought. *Even the easiest thing in the world.*

He only got two pages in when he looked over at Lola and realized she was sleeping.

"Am I a bad bedtime storyteller or was she zonked?" he whispered to Shari.

"Definitely zonked. Evy mentioned she'd had an active day in the park."

Shari turned off the lamp and they quietly left, leaving the door ajar.

"You're so good with kids," she said. "I spend all day with children and parents and caregivers, and trust me, you have a special touch."

"Once I thought I'd be a really great dad," he said. "But that's done with." He felt his face burn as he realized he'd said that aloud. What the hell was wrong with him?

Then again, maybe it was a good thing he had said it. Even when Felix wasn't sure how he felt, if he blurted it out, there it was.

He should get going. The pizza was gone, the little charge was asleep. And this had gotten awkward as hell because of him.

Shari was looking anywhere but at him. What he'd said was too charged—for him to elaborate, for her to ask any questions. To respond at all.

Luckily, her phone pinged and took her attention off him. She went into the living room and picked it up off the coffee table. "Oh," she said, her voice a bit squeaky. "Your great-uncle just invited me to Sunday dinner with the Sanchezes. He says it's family tradition and that he'd love for me to join tomorrow night."

Oh, man.

He glanced at her, then down at his feet. What was Stanley doing? Without asking him first? "That sounds like Uncle Stanley. He's an inviter. He said he loved talking to you at the quinceañera and was excited that you're going to order more Spanish language books for the library."

She tilted her head. "So you're okay with me going?"

I don't know, he thought. *No, maybe I'm not. Maybe it's just too much. Too, too much.*

"Let me ask you this, Felix. Would *you* have asked me to go?"

Honesty, he remembered. Best policy.

"Probably not," he said. "Because that implies something I'm not ready to imply."

That was honest. Maybe too much.

"That we're a couple," she said.

"Right."

"I know we're not, Felix. And even if we were, you just said you're done with the idea of having children when it's something I want more than anything."

He stared at her—hard. She was handing him his out right there. Both their outs. But…

But what? Why was everything in his head, in his heart a damned *but*?

"So I guess we're back to being friends," she said—stiffly.

But that's not what I want, either.

"Look," he said. "Whatever we are, I would like you to join us for dinner. You *are* my friend, no matter what. And now the entire Sanchez clan adores you." Trying to uninvite her would get even more awkward than the last ten minutes had gotten.

"Who knew pizza and bedtime stories could get so fraught?" she asked, her voice heavy, her expression sad.

Dammit. This definitely wasn't what he wanted. To hurt her.

"I'll see you tomorrow night," he said. "I'll pick you up. Six okay?"

"Six would be great."

So now they were kind of back to being friends but she was attending his weekly family dinner.

And no matter how causal the Sanchez Sunday dinners were, that he was bringing someone was a big deal. And everyone would know it.

Including Felix.

CHAPTER THIRTEEN

AT FOUR O'CLOCK on Sunday, Felix had an appointment with Winona Cobbs at Wisdom by Winona, which operated out of her great-grandson's Bronco Ghost Tours business. Sundays were always popular for tours, and a big group was just leaving as Felix arrived.

Follow the moon and stars, Winona had said.

Felix went down the hall. A purple door stenciled with moon and stars had to be the one.

He knocked. He'd purposely made the meeting time close enough to the family dinner so that he'd be anxious enough to ask real questions. Hard questions. But still give him enough time to decompress before he had to pick up Shari.

The door opened and there was Winona, not smiling or frowning, wearing a purple turban on her head, and a purple velvet dress.

"Right this way," she said, directing him into the room and to a table with two chairs, one purple, one pink. She gestured at the pink one, and he sat down.

He got right to it. "My wife died three years ago. Cancer," he said. "The first year, I was a grieving mess. The second year, just kind of going through the motions. This year, I've felt a little more like myself, but aware of this heaviness inside me. Like a stone right here," he added, tapping his chest.

Winona nodded. She didn't say anything and continued to stare at him with that same completely neutral expression.

"I haven't dated. Haven't been interested. But then I ran into someone I knew back in high school and we got to talking. The night you and my great-uncle—the night you gave Stanley a reading at Doug's."

She nodded again and still said nothing.

"Shari's the first woman I've been interested in. The first woman I've been attracted to. And there's something really there between us. But—"

More staring. The expression didn't budge.

"But..." *I can't go through that again*, he thought. That was really it. That was the *but*.

"I loved Victoria so much. I was so excited for our future—for the baby we were planning on. And then just like that, a diagnosis. And she's gone. Our plans are gone. I'm gone. I guess I don't see the point in letting myself love someone again."

This time, Winona's expression did change, just a bit, but Felix caught it. A flash of fire in her dark eyes. It made him stop to think about what Winona had been through. A teenager in love. Sent away when she got pregnant. Lied to by her parents that the baby was stillborn when actually, she had been adopted out to another family. And left in so much pain that she was institutionalized for a time. Not until a couple years ago had Winona been reunited with her child because of Josiah Abernathy, who'd never given up on finding their baby who he'd known was alive and out there somewhere.

If after all that betrayal, heartache, separation and hope, Winona saw the point in falling for Stanley Sanchez, then why couldn't Felix see it for himself with Shari?

"What if you already love someone?" Winona asked.

He narrowed his eyes. "I didn't say anything about loving Shari. We're just…" Something.

"You know what they say, Felix. You can't stop progress."

He frowned. He'd just poured out his soul to her and that was what she had to say? The oldest cliché in the book?

Winona continued to stare at him. "There will come a point when you'll know which way to go."

"Which way is that?" he asked.

"You'll know."

This was just too frustrating. "Can you at least tell me what the ways are?"

"I'll be honest, Felix. I don't tell people that they're going to meet a tall, dark stranger. Or that their next girlfriend's name will start with *B*. Teenaged girls like hearing stuff like that. What I know I *feel*. So I'll tell you this. There are two ways for you to go. One way is to Shari. The other is to nothing."

He frowned again. "Nothing? It's either Shari or nothing?"

Winona reached up her thin arms to adjust her turban. "If you let Shari go, you're choosing nothing over her. That's what I mean."

No. Winona wasn't right. Psychically gifted or not. "*Or* I'm choosing to wait until I'm ready. Completely ready. I mean, is it fair to hold back in a relationship? Is it fair to not give all of myself? Is it fair to take a step forward then two back? That's not how I want to treat Shari. She deserves—" He let out a heavy sigh and clamped his lips shut.

She deserved much better than that.

"You're very conflicted, Felix Sanchez, so I'll add this—as I said, you can't stop progress. Progress is what you feel for Shari. Even if you don't know what that is exactly. Or what you want. The opposite of progress is stagnancy. Nothing."

Felix didn't like this reading. At all.

"Can you give me the teenaged girl's reading?" he asked.

That got a smile from Winona's beautiful, lined face. "I guess your burning question needs to be *why* stagnancy—and I know you've had years and years of education, but I do suggest you look up that word in the dictionary and a thesaurus—is even an option in this particular scenario."

This was *not* the teenaged girl's reading. He frowned and let out a breath. "So my burning question is why I might choose stagnancy over Shari Lormand?"

She nodded and stood. "I'll see you at dinner," she added, leading the way to the door.

Well, if Winona had conspired with her beau to invite Shari to the family dinner and then push him into Shari's arms with this beyond frustrating psychic reading, mission accomplished. Because right now, Felix really needed a damned hug.

YOU'D THINK FELIX's sister Camilla would want to take a break from the kitchen when she owned a restaurant, but nope, there she was at the stove, insisting their mom and dad, who loved making their big Sunday dinners, relax in the living room with the family while she took care of making the enchiladas. It was just after five o'clock, so only Camilla was here so far. The rest of the group would arrive at six.

"Put me to work," he told his sister. Her long dark hair was in a ponytail, and she wore their mom's apron, which was hot pink with Chez Sanchez imprinted in silver, a stocking stuffer from the five kids years ago.

"Wait, *you* want to help cook?" she asked, turning her big brown eyes on him. She'd already made what looked like fifty enchiladas, the sauce, both red and mole, simmering on the stove. A big pot of fragrant rice was also cooking.

"Sure," he said. "I can pour tortilla chips in a bowl or something."

Camilla laughed. "That you can. And you can tell me what's on your mind. Because I know something is."

He sighed. "Let me ask you a question," he said, reaching into the cabinet for five bags of tortilla chips. His great-uncle had made his incredible salsas this morning so at least Felix didn't have to start chopping green chiles. "How would you define the word *stagnancy*? And what would you say are synonyms?"

Camilla eyed him for a second, then reached for the pan of red sauce and poured it onto the enchiladas in the two baking dishes. "Stagnancy. I guess at its core, it means stuck. Not moving—and certainly not forward.

Felix thought about her definition as he poured the mole sauce over the next two baking dishes of enchiladas as his sister had done with the red sauce. Camilla opened the oven and he slid them in.

"But can't stagnancy be a good thing?" he asked. "Don't people meditate to be still?"

Camilla reached into the high-tiered basket of vegetables and fruits and pulled out several avocados. Even in his jumbled state of mind, he was already anticipating Camilla's homemade guacamole. "Well, meditation is forward-moving. It's not about stagnancy at all. It's about letting your mind clear, to be in touch with yourself and your mind and your emotions and your body."

Oh.

"Felix, if you want to know what I think…"

"I do."

"After you lost Victoria, you weren't stagnant," she said. "Think about it. You were actively grieving. Then you were finding your way back to your life in a world without the woman you thought you'd spend forever with. You moved back home and have been a big help to Mom and Dad, you got back to work, you added volunteer hours at Happy Hearts Animal Sanctuary. But until recently…"

He watched his sister slice the avocados in half and scoop out the pits. "Until recently?"

"For a while there, yeah, I'd say you were stuck, Felix. Not because of inability, but because of unwillingness, and there is a difference. But not lately. I'd call making out with Shari Lormand at the quinceañera moving forward, brother dear. I'd call not coming home that night moving forward."

He narrowed his eyes. "How'd you hear about that?"

She only laughed and began mashing the avocado in a big orange bowl.

"I still don't feel ready, though," he said.

"For?" she asked.

"Giving in to what I'm feeling for her. Yes, I have

strong feelings for Shari. But seventy-five percent of me doesn't want to act on them."

"The ole head versus heart."

He nodded. "Winona says I'd be choosing stagnancy over Shari. That I should be asking myself why."

"Do you know why?"

He shook his head. "Do you?"

She gave him a gentle smile. "Maybe because it's really scary to put yourself and your heart out there again. To love someone again. After what you've been through. The three quarters of you that doesn't want to act on your feelings is probably about that."

He knew she was right. He'd always known that.

The front door opened and closed and Felix was pretty sure he heard his soon-to-be brother-in-law Boone Dalton's voice.

"Mmm, something smells amazing!"

Yup, that was Boone.

"Do not eat all the guacamole this time," his sister Sofia said on a laugh as they both came into the kitchen.

Perfect timing, too. Because this conversation was making his head spin.

SHARI KNEW JUST about everyone at the Sanchez family dinner because she'd met them at the quinceañera, but she'd seen them in town or at the library at some point or another over the past three years. There were Denise and Aaron, Felix's parents, and Stanley and Winona, who once again was decked out in purple, this time a pantsuit. Felix's sister Camilla and her husband, Jordan Taylor, were at the far end of the long rectangular dining table. Shari knew that Jordan's family, one of the wealthiest in Bronco Heights, owned Taylor Beef. In fact, it was the Taylor family who'd donated the beautiful, grand building that housed the town library.

Felix's other sister, Sofia, and her fiancé, Boone Dalton, were across from the Taylors. Boone was also from a wealthy ranching family, but the Daltons were relatively new to town. Next to Sofia and Boone were Felix's two younger brothers, Dante and Dylan, and at this moment, Denise was telling both that she had a double date in mind for them, the twin daughters of her newest client. These two Sanchez brothers were as good-looking as their older brother. Both hadn't hit it off with any of the women Denise had had in mind for them at the quinceañera, much to their mother's dismay. Still, she'd never give up.

"We can find our own dates," Dylan said, heaping yellow rice onto his plate next to four enchiladas. "But thanks."

"I saw a photo," Denise singsonged. "Both lovely."

"Fix-ups rarely work out," Dante said. "And what if the date is a disaster? Then your client is pissed and never comes back to the salon."

"I'd rather you and Dylan were happily settled down than I keep a client, even if she does spent a fortune on lowlighting and extensions."

"All in good time," Winona said suddenly, and all eyes swung to her.

"Yeah, all in good time," Dylan said, giving his mother a pointed look.

Shari took a bite of the enchilada with mole sauce and almost sighed with how delicious it was. "Wow, this is beyond delicious, Camilla."

"Thank you. Your date helped me cook."

Shari smiled at Felix. "Scrumptious. I've never had rice this soft or flavorful."

"That's Camilla," Felix said. "All I did was put the pans in the oven. She wouldn't even let me slice an avocado."

As the family laughed and talked and ate and told stories, Shari so aware of her gorgeous date beside her, an unexpected wistfulness to be part of this family came over her. She'd love to attend the mandatory dinner every Sunday. She imagined herself pregnant, Felix rushing her to the hospital at the tail end of a Sunday dinner, the entire family crowding in the waiting room to find out if it's a boy or a girl.

The feeling that she was being watched shook her out of her little fantasy, and when she glanced up, Winona was staring at her.

That sharp dark-eyed gaze, all the life and experience in that lovely ninety-five-year-old face, made Shari face facts.

Once I thought I'd be a really great dad. But that's done with.

Just the thought of what Felix had said triggered the same sharp ache in her chest now as when he'd said it. And how he'd said he wouldn't have asked her to go with him to this very dinner because of what it implied.

That we're a couple, Shari had said.

Right.

I know we're not. And even if we were, you just said you're done with the idea of having children when it's something I want more than anything.

So I guess we're back to being friends.

And because they'd slept together and he was a good

guy, he'd wanted to come over with pizza the next night and clear the air, which they had.

They were friends.

There wasn't going to be a serious relationship with Felix Sanchez. She wasn't going to be rushed to the hospital with her extended family of in-laws awaiting the birth of their child. She was once again waiting for something that wasn't going to happen. Putting someone else's needs and wants before her own.

Shari was here not because Felix had invited her, but because his great-uncle had.

Oh, Shari, wake up, girl. Face facts. Don't be stupid.

When she got home tonight, she'd take a long, hot soak in a bubble bath, focus her mind on what she wanted that she *could* have, and go from there.

And she couldn't have Felix Sanchez so it was time to let this dream go.

As Winona had said: *just do.*

By the time the last enchilada was gone and the five different desserts gobbled up, Shari's heart couldn't take much more of this. Stanley and Winona had left to attend one of Evan Cruise's ghost tours. Sofia and Boone were on their way out, and Denise and Aaron resisted all Shari's offers to help clean up.

"You two go enjoy a walk around the neighborhood or have a drink at Doug's," Aaron said.

"Actually," she whispered as they headed out after goodbyes and hugs with the Sanchezes, "I'm ready to get home."

He tilted his head. "Oh. Okay. Are you feeling all right?"

"Not really," she said. "Here," she added, tapping her heart.

His face fell. "Ah. My fault."

"Not your fault. You were always honest. I've been hoping for a different outcome, but I need to accept that you can't make promises."

"Shari, I—" He turned away for a moment, then looked back at her.

"Well, you can't. And I have big dreams, Felix. I want a family. I want a child. I started looking into my options and then we… And I thought *maybe*. But you can't even commit to dating me, Felix."

He was quiet for a long moment. "I wish I could give you everything you want. But I'm not…"

"Ready."

He just wasn't there. He might like her a lot. He might be very attracted. But he wasn't available. And she had to let herself go.

"Can we be friends?" he asked. "And I mean that. Real friends."

Because it's that easy to spend time with someone you're in love with when they just want to be buddies. She'd thought she could handle it because she cared about him and they were already friends. But this back-and-forth, trying to be okay with "going with the flow" when they were kissing on dance floors or having sex in her bed and then trying to be okay with just being friends… Well, she couldn't really be okay with either. The former would lead her only to the broken heart of all broken hearts. And the latter would be painful even when they were at their most playful and happiest, naming a new litter of stray puppies or something.

Either way, she was doomed.

And now she kind of understood how he was feeling. Unsure and unsettled.

"Of course," she said. Because she did care about Felix.

"Good."

And then he drove her home and instead of wondering if he might kiss her as she would have before their awful conversation, she smiled, thanked him for the nice evening, which killed her to say, and then got out of his truck and ran inside.

To a waiting Page. Thank God for cats.

As she stripped off her clothes and drew a bath, she sat on the edge of the tub with her iPad and searched for "foster parent" and "Montana" and "Bronco County." She hadn't explored that route to motherhood yet. Tonight, she would.

By the time she got out of the tub, she'd put the idea of becoming a foster mother and adopting through that channel at the top of the list. There were so many children who needed loving homes.

She couldn't have what she wanted most of all, she thought—the man she loved. But she could have a family. She could create what she wanted.

As she slid on her terry robe, Page sniffing her lavender-scented ankles, Shari was well aware that when she pictured a little boy or girl in the living room, building a block tower or doing a little dance, Felix was there, too.

Now it was Winona's words that came back to her. *You know what to do. Do that.*

She didn't anymore. Because she didn't want a family without Felix Sanchez beside her. And he didn't want a family at all. Or a relationship.

No, Shari didn't know what to do at all.

CHAPTER FOURTEEN

MONDAY: FELIX TEXTED a comment about the weather and a rain cloud emoji. And that was it.

Tuesday: Felix texted that he was at the diner, trying to decide between a meatball parm sub or the Thanksgiving club—including stuffing and cranberry sauce—and had she ever tried the club? She reported back that she had, twice, actually, and it was pure comfort, leaving out that it reminded of her last Thanksgiving, a real bust. She hadn't flown to Denver to spend the holiday with her parents because her father had had the flu. So she'd been alone but embarrassed to say anything. Evy and Lola had spent the day with Doug's family, Jemma had gone to Las Vegas to meet her three sisters for their annual family tradition, and so Shari had had cereal for dinner and gone to bed early. Sometimes, being single was great. And sometimes it was the worst. P.S. He didn't ask if he could pick her up lunch and drop it by the library.

Wednesday: Felix texted that a calf, Snowball, he'd been worried about pulled through and would be fine. Champagne emoji. For a minute she'd thought he was inviting her to celebrate with him and stared at her phone like an idiot for the next hour, awaiting the ping. But that had been the only text from him.

Thursday: Felix texted that one of his furry patients

from the shelter had a litter of kittens and maybe once Page was medically cleared and the kittens weaned and ready for adoption, they could pair Page up with a buddy. Shari sent back a Definitely! Everyone can use a buddy!

Because she was who she was, she'd fretted about that last part for the next few hours. Would he think she was being sarcastic? Was she? But because Felix was who he was, and she was getting to know him pretty well, she doubted he'd read anything at all into the text.

Friday: Felix texted to ask how that night's grand opening of Evy's new boutique, Cimarron Rose, was. He hadn't been able to go due to an emergency at a local ranch. Shari reported back the night had been a smash success and that the Hawkins Sisters, the four rodeo competitors, were there with their mother, Josie, and practically bought out the place. Shari added that she'd spent a lot of money herself for a good cause— her good friend's cash register—and absolutely loved everything she got, including a multi-chain-link belt with dangling little green cactuses, a scented candle called Cowgirl Grit, which she hoped would fill the air of her apartment with determination, and some very interesting bracelets. She didn't add that she'd gotten him the matching candle to hers: Cowboy Grit, which smelled like sandalwood and a little vanilla. She'd give it to him the next time he did her a favor, like when he'd come over to help find Page.

This was good. He was respecting what she'd said about not being able to deal with the one-step-forward two-steps-back approach to their relationship and was keeping his distance, yet still checking in.

Every day. Because dammit, she was special to him and she knew it.

She missed him. Everything about him. Two days ago when she hadn't been able to find Page after two hours of searching, she'd almost texted him for help, but having him in her apartment, especially when she was anxious about her beloved little pet, would have made her even more aware of how much she wanted him in her life. Needed him in her life. She'd learned last time Page had gone missing that the kitten was very likely fast asleep somewhere Shari would never have expected. Fifteen minutes later, when Shari had pulled out a book on the bottom shelf of the bookcase, there she was, her tail curled around a mystery novel.

Felix had basically taught her the same principles during their time together. She'd been able to predict some things, such as his kindness, that he'd be there for her. But otherwise, she'd had no idea what to expect.

So it was better this way. Really, it was, she told herself for the hundredth time that week as she now reshelved books on Saturday afternoon in the Children's Room.

"Ooh, your super hot rebound sex guy is here," Haley Butterman whispered, jerking her thumb toward the doorway.

Haley was leaving the library in a week to attend pastry school and Shari couldn't wait until her last day.

"I'll put the rest of these away," Haley added. "Remember to channel Beyoncé," she added on a whisper. "If he likes it he should put a ring on it. Even metaphorically speaking."

Maybe the library could give Haley an early send-off. Or at least stick her in the archives on the third floor for her final week. She'd conspire with Jemma about that.

Shari turned and walked over to meet Felix. He looked so good. It was slightly chilly today, and he wore a black leather jacket and jeans and work boots.

"I have a favor to ask," he said. His expression gave nothing away about seeing her again. He simply seemed…pleasant. As if she were Jemma or any other librarian and not the woman whose heart he broke. Which meant he was working hard for that pleasant expression. She sighed inwardly. "My uncle Stanley says that Winona's feeling under the weather and he'd like to bring her a couple of books. He says she likes to read everything."

"That's thoughtful of him. Hmm, maybe a biography and a mystery."

He nodded. "Sounds good. Could you help me choose?"

She should direct him to Jemma. Before she burst into tears, which she might do at any moment. This was just too much, too hard. But she lifted her chin and composed herself from the inside out. "Well, let's see. There's a recent biography of Amelia Earhart that's gotten great reviews. And a new cozy mystery series has a female detective named Winona."

"How'd you do that in two seconds?" he asked.

"Trick of the trade. I'll lead the way." The sooner he checked out his books, the sooner she could hurry into the women's restroom to cry in private. But of course she didn't want him to leave at all.

Because she was deeply in love with the guy.

Five minutes later, as they headed to the checkout

desk with both books, where Jemma was sitting on her stool, his phone pinged.

"Animal control officer is asking for my help," he said, reading the text. "Hikers spotted a stray skinny white dog up near the base of the mountain but the dog was too skittish to go to them, and he can't search for him now. He's on another call."

"I'm off in five minutes," Shari said without thinking. As if thinking would have elicited a different answer. "I'll help."

"Yeah? That would be great."

She felt like he was saying, *Look at us, starting our friendship again after all that...awkwardness, isn't this nice?* Or maybe Felix Sanchez was as hurt and confused and sad inside about where they were as she was. *You know that's the case, Shari*, she told herself.

Jemma checked them out and then said, "I'll run these books to Winona's house on my way home. I live close by. You two go find that poor pup."

Felix smiled. "I appreciate that. I'll let my uncle know."

Jemma took the books, Felix texted his uncle and then they were off. They stopped at the clinic to pick up some treats to lure the dog with, a light blanket just in case he needed to wrap up the dog to carry him, a leash with built-in collar, and a kennel for the cargo area.

Of course, she was too aware of Felix beside her in his SUV. As they drove the fifteen minutes to the mountain and the woods, she veered between being happy to be with him, near him, helping him on this mission, and heart-wrecked about their status as just friends. She had no idea why she'd thought she could be friends with Felix. Was she supposed to yearn and wish and hope every time they were together that he'd feel more for her? Enough to break through the barriers he'd erected?

He parked at the base of the mountain where a well-marked trail led through the woods and to the famed cavern that had served as a hook-up spot for Bronco's teens for generations. The dog might have gone to seek shelter in one of the many nooks and crannies. The farther you went in, the easier it was to hide from anyone.

Shari walked alongside Felix on the two-person trail, breathing in the beautiful scent of pine and fresh air off the September breeze. She heard a twig snap and turned her head.

"There! I saw a swish of a white tail!" she said.

Felix turned and pointed. "I see it. Let's follow him laterally and when he realizes that we're not chasing him, he may rest. And then hopefully we'll get close enough to lure him with the treats and I can get the leash over his head."

"Got it," she said.

They walked slowly, once or twice brushing against each other.

Shari saw a flash of white again, but it seemed to be heading away from them, not parallel. A wet drop pinged off Shari's forehead. "Uh-oh. Was rain forecasted? I thought it was just supposed to be overcast."

The sky opened up in one of those downpours with very little warning.

"Cavern opening right there," he said. "Let's run for it. I think the dog took off in the opposite direction, but he'll find shelter in these caves, I'm sure. I'll come back in the morning and look for him."

They dashed into the cavern on the side of the moun-

tain. Decades of canoodling in these caves had left
thousands of initials carved into the rock walls. Shari
could smell the remnants of a fire, but she didn't hear
anything or see anyone.

"Could we actually have this place to ourselves?"
Felix asked, shaking the rain from his hair. He draped
the blanket around her shoulders. "Warm enough?"

"It's a gorgeous evening even with the rain," she
said. This couldn't be a more romantic setting, she
thought with another inward sigh.

As they walked a bit farther in, searching for the recently stamped-out fire, they found it down a winding
path with a nook that hid it from the walkway. Maybe
the dog would find it a good place to feel safe and they
could get him to the clinic tonight.

Felix grabbed a book of matches from his backpack
and relit the pile of partially burnt wood, and in moments, their nook was warm and cozy.

"We'll wait out the rain here," he said. "We might
even get lucky and the dog will come right to us because of the warmth."

Shari took off the blanket and laid it down on the
ground at a reasonable distance from the fire. "Just
what I was thinking," she said.

"Liver snap?" he asked, holding out the baggie with
the treats.

She laughed. "Uh, no."

"Kidding. But I do have granola bars and water. And
a box of raisins. I actually love raisins."

"Me, too."

They munched the raisins and drank the water, the
fire casting the most beautiful glow on Felix's face.
Here they were, chatting like…friends.

This might be the last time you see Felix, she thought suddenly. Because this hurt too much. *So just get through it. The bittersweet pain. Be his friend. Let him be yours. For tonight. Then you're going to have to let go.*

"That was so sweet of your uncle to want to bring Winona books when she's not feeling well," she said. "Warms my heart."

"Mine, too."

"Do they see each other often?" she asked.

"Every day. I heard my mother ask him if he thought he was rushing into this new *amor*, but Stanley said at their ages they don't have all the time in the world left. So taking it slow doesn't make a lot of sense to them."

"Aww, I'm so glad they found each other. Every time I catch them around town, they look so happy. You can see the sparkle in their eyes from across the street."

He nodded. "I love seeing my *tio* like this again."

He must want that for you, she wanted to scream, but held back. Felix was who he was, wanted what he wanted, and that was it. The only one who could change his mindset was the man himself. And he wasn't budging.

What maybe hurt most of all was that he'd tried. With her. And had gone back to friends. Yes, she'd told him she couldn't handle the back-and-forth, but he'd chosen friendship over exploring what was between them, taking it slow.

"Ever been to these caves?" he asked.

"Nope. I always wanted to have my first kiss here," she said. "Most of my high school friends did." She looked at him. "Was yours here?"

"My first kiss?" He shook his head. "Stairwell between the first and second floor at Bronco High. On the landing by the window."

She gasped. "Mine, too. With Eric Fieldwalker."

"I remember his bright red hair, but that's about it."

She chuckled. "He constantly chewed peppermint gum. He almost burned my lips once."

Now he was staring at her lips.

And she was staring at his.

Her own thoughts just a few moments ago came rushing back to her.

"I have a proposition for you," she said before she could change her mind.

He waited, looking at her with a mixture of wariness and tenderness.

"I know that being friends with you is just too much for me. I want more and I can't have it, and it's impossible to hang out with you as if there's nothing wrong. Here," she added, patting her chest.

"Shari, I—"

She held up her hand. "Look, we're here, in a cave with a fire burning, no one around, rain pouring outside, and neither of us has ever kissed in the famed kissing cavern of Bronco, Montana. I think we should. As a final goodbye to all that stuff that had been brewing between us. We'll kiss, walk out into the washed air and forest, and we'll go our separate ways."

"Separate ways," he said. "I don't like the sound of that. But I understand."

She nodded.

They were both sitting with their legs crossed. Crisscross applesauce, as they called it at story time at the library. And they both leaned forward. Maybe they should have discussed the details of the kiss. The last kiss they would have. Because when their lips touched, she felt the singe of his mouth, soft and warm and hungry. They both got up on their knees, one of his hands in her hair, hers around his neck.

"Mmm," she whispered. "Now we're part of Bronco tradition."

"I think a lot more goes on in these caves than just kissing," he said, staring at her with smoldering hazel eyes.

She put a hand on his chest and just that touch sent chills all over her body. "Maybe we should extend our final hurrah to include more than just kissing, then."

"A final hurrah," he repeated, very slowly nodding. "I think I would like that, Shari."

"Me, too. Even if it feels sad."

He reached out a hand to the side of her face.

I love you so damned much, she thought.

They would make love again. For the last time. And then, as they'd said, they would go their separate ways.

The fire crackled then, which she took as a sign that she could absolutely do this. She was wearing a sweater dress, easy to smush up around her hips, easy to pull down just in case a bunch of teens came wandering through. Felix came closer on his knees, then gently laid her down on the blanket and kissed her, one hand in her hair again, the other pulling up her dress—and pulling down her underwear. She unsnapped and unzipped his pants and pulled them down. There was something *un*romantic enough about this that made it easier to bear.

"Luckily I still have the condom that Stanley put in my wallet," he said, producing it in his hand.

She took it and rolled it on, loving his groan. A

groan that helped her focus on what they were doing, not what she was feeling in her chest. *Let yourself go, Shari*, she told herself. *Just give yourself this. One night. One last night with the man you'll always love.*

"A last hurrah," he whispered, his eyes serious on hers.

"A last hurrah," she whispered back and kept her eyes open, wanting to remember everything.

Because they *were* in a cave in late summer on a warm mid-September evening, the rain could still send people inside seeking shelter. She wished she could be naked. She wished they could stay for hours. Take their time. But that wasn't what this was about anyway.

This couldn't be slow and tender. It had to be fast and hot. And that was exactly what it was. He was on top of her, the glow of the fire casting shadows on his gorgeous face, and the moment he thrust inside her, she closed her eyes despite wanting to see everything, to remember the look on his face. But the sensations were just too much, too great, too explosive. They rocked together, both trying to keep their moans to a minimum, Shari biting her fist at one point so she wouldn't scream in ecstasy and bring other cave-lovers running to her aid.

She'd need aid later. Not right now.

She opened her eyes to find Felix's beautiful hazel eyes looking at her. And then it was over all too soon, both of them spent and sated, breathing hard. He held her hand for a moment, then let go.

Just like she'd let him go.

Shari would never forget tonight. It was a good send-off. Painful, but good.

As she wiggled her dress down and he wiggled his pants up, he glanced at the rock walls full of initials.

"I have a pocketknife," he said, reaching into his backpack.

What would he carve into the wall? she wondered, watching as he scooted over on his knees and put the knife into the rock. When he was done and moved to the side so she could see, she grinned.

FS & SL were here.

"I love it," she said. "Old school."

He nodded, his eyes focused on her. She could tell he was searching for the right thing to say.

"You don't have to say anything, Felix. This was perfect. Not perfect in the big-picture sense, but for right now, for us."

"You're an amazing person, Shari Lormand."

"You mean SL," she said, trying so hard not to cry. She stood up, and Felix put everything in the backpack and then tamped out the fire with sand and his boots.

The downpour let up and they waited by the cavern entrance for the drizzle to stop completely. There was no sign of the stray dog. But like Felix said, he'd come back tomorrow morning.

"This was magical," she said. "I'll always remember it and you."

"I wish we could be friends, Shari. But I understand—clearly."

Yes, she knew he understood. "Look, if you need me, I mean *really* need me, I'm there. I'll always be your friend, just from afar. But if you need me, call me."

"Same," he whispered.

How she held in the flood of tears she had no idea.

But when he dropped her off at her building, refusing his three offers to walk her up, she ran inside and upstairs into her apartment, then slid down the back of the door and sobbed.

THERE WAS ANOTHER hour of sunlight, even if overcast, and Felix couldn't bear the thought of going home with his heavy heart or leaving that stray dog out there, probably soaked from the downpour, for a chilly night, so he went back to the woods.

As he walked along the path, keeping watch on both sides for any flashes of white fur, he couldn't stop picturing Shari's face. And how she'd looked at him just an hour ago when they'd been in the cave. With *everything* in her eyes. Feeling, yearning, desire, lust... maybe even love. It was that last one that had kept him from saying or doing anything beyond what he had, which hadn't been much. Just saying yes to her proposition for their final hurrah.

That look—the love, if that's what it was—had locked him up and all he'd been able to think was that her idea was a good one. One more time and then goodbye. Go their separate ways. It had to be for the best right now.

It just hurt like hell. Finding the dog would help. It'd give him an immediate purpose and soothe his aching chest.

"Hey, pooch," he called softly into the low brush on both sides of the trail. "I have liver snaps. No dog can resist, not even one who's scared and alone."

He stopped and listened. Was that a whisper of rustling to his right? He reached into his pocket for the baggie of treats and took one out so the dog could smell it.

He heard the rustling sound again.

"It's me, actually," a familiar voice called.

He whirled around, shocked to see Shari, in jeans and a black wool sweater and hiking boots, holding a bag of treats in one hand and a leash with a collar in the other.

"I couldn't bear the thought of him being out here alone and hungry and scared and soaked," she said.

Oh, Shari. He was speechless for a moment. Of course she was here.

"Same," he said. "You're a very good person, Shari Lormand."

"Just an animal devotee," she said. "Like you."

Another rustling sound could be heard to the left. He turned that way. And saw the flash of white. Yes!

"We're friendly," he called out in a singsong voice. "And have treats. And a warm clinic to take to you so we can get you checked out and then into a foster home and registered with the shelter. Doesn't a soft cozy memory foam bed sound good to you? Regular meals? Belly rubs?"

"Lots of belly rubs," Shari added.

He strained his neck to peer into the brush and around trees and there was the face. Long snout, tall ears. Between small and medium, not more than twenty pounds. And dirty. But a beauty.

"I see him," she whispered. "Aww, what a pretty dog."

"Here, good boy," Felix said, tossing the treat. He turned to Shari. "Let's sit down to appear less of a potential threat."

They sat. The dog sniffed and tentatively came forward. Then a bit more.

He stopped about ten feet away.

Felix threw another treat so that it would land closer to the dog. The pooch walked to it and sniffed it and then gobbled it up. Then went for the first one Felix had thrown.

"There's more where those two came from," Shari said, tossing another treat at the halfway mark between them.

As the dog took a couple more steps, Felix assessed his demeanor and body posture best he could. Tail was half up, half down, which meant he was wary. His eyes weren't showing slivers of white, which often indicated fear, but neither did he see aggression in the face or stance.

"I have a good feeling about his demeanor," Felix said to Shari. "One more?" he called out and threw another a foot away from himself.

The dog came over and ate it, then just stayed there.

"One more treat," Felix said, "and then we'll see if we can get the leash on you, okay?" He took it from the backpack and set it down beside him so the dog could see it. He threw one more treat just a couple feet from the leash, and the pooch ran to get it.

"Well, hello," Felix said, holding out his hand palm down for the dog to sniff. Again, he didn't see aggression or fear. This dog had likely been someone's pet who'd gotten lost.

Shari held out her hand just as Felix had. The dog sniffed hers too, his tail slightly wagging.

Felix let him sniff him some more and then gave him a scratch-rub under his chin. The dog instantly relaxed. "Yup, just as I thought. A good boy. Let's get the leash on you and we'll go to the clinic and get you checked out and see if you're chipped. And we'll get you a better meal. Sound good?" Still seated, he slipped the rope part of the leash around the dog's neck, which the sweet guy accepted, and he tightened it just the right amount. Relief washed over him.

"Well, this wasn't my favorite day, but it sure has a nice ending," Shari said.

He looked at her and nodded. "Agreed." He wanted to say more. He wanted to do more. Like take her in his arms and just hold her. But he'd just apologize again and that wasn't what she wanted from him.

Felix and Shari gave the pup one more pat each and then they both stood. He slung on his backpack and held firmly to the leash, but as he started walking, the dog walked easily beside him, Shari on the other side.

At the parking area, Shari got down on one knee and petted the dog. "I know you're gonna find a really great home," she said. "You were a trouper up there. You were scared and alone and now look at you. About to get a full belly and a fun toy, too."

With that she gave Felix something of a lopsided, sad smile and ran to her car.

"That woman is something special," he told the dog. "But you already know that. Dogs just know."

The dog looked up at him, head tilted as if to say, *And what are you going to do about it?*

Nothing. Just like Winona said. Nothing, nothing, nothing. The word echoed in his head, and he frowned, trying to shake it off. Not that he could.

But I'm not going to think of it as stagnancy. It's just calm. Easy. No risk.

Nothing was just the absence of something, he told himself. That didn't sound dire.

His head and heart a bit more settled, Felix got the dog in the back of his SUV and into the kennel.

A half hour later, because sometimes things *did* work out like in the movies, a family, including eight-year-old sobbing twin boys, came rushing into the clinic to pick up their beloved Scampy, who'd been missing for a week and a half. Felix had found the microchip and had looked up the information in the registry and called the owners. Scampy was in good condition, no injuries, and once back on a good diet, would bounce back very quickly.

Felix headed home feeling a lot better than he had when he'd started up that path to find the stray. He texted Shari that the dog was microchipped and his family had already picked him up, and she sent back a smiley face. There. That was it. The end of their friendship.

As he parked in the driveway, the Sanchez house was dark, which was strange, since Stanley was usually home at this hour, making his prized salsa that he'd put into individual little containers for Denise and Aaron and Felix to take with their lunches, along with a side of tortilla chips that he always special ordered from Mexico.

Felix turned on the light, but then realized one lamp was on in the living room. And Stanley was again sitting on the sofa, a stack of old photo albums on the coffee table. He didn't look happy. Felix walked into the living room and sat next to his uncle. "Tio, are you feeling heavyhearted again?"

Stanley wiped under his eyes and nodded. "I ran into Shari in the supermarket about an hour ago."

"Oh?" Felix said, tilting his head. Must have been right before she'd decided to head back to the woods.

"She was buying a lot of cat food. I was right behind her in line with my basket of green chiles and tomatoes and that coffee I like."

Somewhere between that and home, Stanley had gotten very upset. What could have happened?

"I invited Shari over for dinner tomorrow night. Told her I was making my award-winning salsa and that I'd also make black bean and cheese quesadillas with whatever her favorite filling was. And, Felix, her eyes filled with tears and she said she appreciated the invitation, but that you two had gone your separate ways."

He glanced away, trying not to think of Shari in line at the grocery store with tears in her eyes.

"I told her I was very sorry to hear that. And on the drive home, all I could think about was Celia and how wrong it is that I'm seeing someone else now. It's just wrong. If it's wrong for you after three years, it's wrong for me after just one. So I pulled over on the side of the road and I called up Winona and I told her I was very sorry, but I just couldn't do this."

Oh, Tio. No.

"Stanley," Felix said, "just because I'm not ready for a relationship doesn't mean you're not. I mean, clearly you are."

Stanley shook his head. "It's not right. Winona is so wonderful. So funny and smart and full of sass. So many stories. I could listen to her talk all day and night. And when we kiss, it's like fireworks are going off over our heads. But I had my great love and that was enough for one lifetime."

"But you have such strong feelings for Winona and you enjoy her company," Felix said. "There's no reason to stop dating her."

Stanley shook his head. "After Shari left the grocery store, I realized why you're choosing to be alone over a relationship with that lovely woman who you clearly have deep feelings for. And all of a sudden, I started to shake. I realized you're absolutely right."

Felix swallowed. "I'm right? What do you mean?"

"I can't go through another loss. I just can't. Winona means too much to me. I need to just be on my own. I have my family and my salsa and my mariachi music and Doug's once a week—that's enough for me. I'll be on my own, just like you."

With that, his uncle stood up, his eyes red-rimmed and teary. He straightened his leather vest and practically ran into his room down the hall.

Oh, no, Felix thought, his head dropping down. Wasn't he just thinking earlier when he was looking for the stray dog that some things worked out like in the movies?

How the hell am I going to fix this?

CHAPTER FIFTEEN

MONDAY MORNING, SHARI was at the library, giving a young patron his very first library card, which always called for celebration. The boy not only got his card but two stickers. Little moments like this at work helped her forget her personal life, which had her so heavy-hearted she was surprised she wasn't tipping over constantly. Ten times last night she'd picked up her phone to text Felix to ask more about the dog's owners, what his name was, if there were kids in the family. But she'd put the phone down. His text about finding the owners was short and sweet, just to let her know the dog's story had a happy ending. Unlike theirs. She had to let it go at that.

She looked at the proud little boy holding his library card and smiling up at his dad, and that warmed her heart to the point that even she could smile as the pair left.

Then the smile faded.

Sadie Chamberlin, the woman who'd been in a couple of weeks ago to look up information about her late brother-in-law, Bobby Stone, came in, looking pale and nervous. She was carrying two books, which she set on the counter. "Hi, Shari. Just returning these."

"You okay, Sadie? Honestly, you look like you've seen a ghost."

"That's a perfect description," Sadie said, tossing her long blond ponytail behind her shoulder. "But it wasn't me who saw a ghost—it was one of my neighbors. She said she could swear she saw Bobby carrying a bunch of papers in the park while she was walking her dog last night. Then this morning, when she took her dog to the park again, she told me she found a couple of flyers about Bobby Stone blowing around." She frowned. "Could Bobby still be alive?"

Shari didn't know every detail about what happened to Bobby Stone, but it seemed clear to everyone that he'd died. He'd sat on the haunted barstool at Doug's and then had fallen to his death off that mountain ledge three years ago. It was a tragic accident. A man in good health in his thirties. But rumor said he'd been drinking and lost his footing. Shari felt terrible for him, especially anytime she was in Doug's and saw that awful cordoned-off Death Seat.

"Wouldn't he just let people know?"

Sadie bit her lip. "I don't know. I don't know what to think anymore."

"Your neighbor must have been mistaken, that's all. It was dark, right? Maybe it was just someone who reminded her of Bobby."

"Maybe," Sadie said. She sighed and glanced up at the clock on the wall. "I'd better get going. Thanks for listening, again."

As Sadie left, Shari checked in the books she was returning. *Are Ghosts Real?* And *True Tales of Haunted Places.* In a town that had a booming ghost tours business, the idea of ghosts and haunted places being real wasn't all that far-fetched.

Shari recalled the stone being thrown through the

window at Doug's back in July with the note on it: *A Stone You Won't Forget*. And the flyers saying *Remember Bobby Stone* going up all over the rodeo last month. Now, someone thought they actually saw the man in the park.

Shari didn't know what was going on but she hoped Sadie would find some peace.

She set the books on the return cart and was very glad Haley Butterman wasn't around to take the cart up to the adult floor because Felix Sanchez had just walked in the library—and Haley would definitely have something to say.

Shari's heart fluttered at the sight of him. He wore a light gray button-down shirt and charcoal pants and his black leather jacket. What was he doing here, though?

"Remember you said that if I really needed you, I could call you?" he asked, his expression grim.

"You must *really* need me if you're here in person, then," she said. What could be going on?

"Can we talk?" he asked.

"Of course." She led him over to the wing chairs in a recessed area by the stairs. They sat down and Felix dropped his head in his hands.

"Oh, boy. What happened?" she asked.

"It's my uncle. He broke up with Winona. And it's my fault. He's following my lead."

She felt her eyes widen. "Oh, no. Did I have something to do with that?" She frowned, a pang hitting her hard in the chest. "I ran into him in the grocery store before I headed out to the woods to look for the stray. Stanley so kindly invited me to dinner and I was in a…mood, so I guess I blurted out that we're not in each other's lives anymore. Ugh, I'm so sorry, Felix."

"No, no, Shari. It's not your fault. He told me last night that he realized I'm right—that he's too afraid of ever going through the hell he went through when he lost my great-aunt Celia. That he understands why I'm on my own and that he should be, too."

"But he shouldn't be." *And neither should you.*

He leaned his head back. "I know. What can I do to fix this? Stanley wouldn't talk to me anymore last night. He just stayed in his room. I knocked, but he wouldn't answer. And this morning, he didn't come down to breakfast and then when I came knocking on his door again, he told me he would be okay eventually and to please give him some space. Stanley never wants space."

Shari wracked her brain for an idea, but kept coming up empty. "I'm trying to think, but beyond flat-out lying and pretending we're a couple, I don't know how to get them back together."

Felix leaned back against the chair. "But maybe the four of us can get together? Have dinner at your place?"

"For what purpose, though?" she asked.

He let out a breath. "I don't know. Just to talk it out?"

"I'm not sure there's anything to talk out, Felix. You said Stanley was following your lead. You're afraid to put your heart on the line again. So why shouldn't Stanley be?"

"But he can't give up the woman he loves because he's afraid of losing her."

She was about to say *You are.* But Felix had never said anything about loving her.

"All that matters is how he feels about Winona, not

what I'm doing or not doing!" he said, exasperation in his voice and expression.

"Hmm," she said, sliding her glasses up on her nose. "Okay. I'll invite them. I'll tell them both that we'd like to apologize for our relationship getting in the way of their relationship. Which is true." Maybe it would help somehow. It was worth a try. "We'd be getting them together in the same room, talking openly and honestly. Maybe it'll make a difference in Stanley's mindset."

He looked so relieved. "Thank you, Shari."

She pulled her phone from her pocket. She pressed in Winona's number.

"Hello, dear," came Winona's voice.

"Winona, I'd like to invite you over to dinner at my apartment tomorrow night to talk things over. Felix is calling Stanley to invite him right now."

"What time, dear?"

Shari's shoulders slumped with relief. No questions, no nothing. Perfect. "Six o'clock?"

"I'll be there," Winona said. "But only because I know exactly what's going to happen. So nothing will be too big a surprise."

Shari swallowed.

What was going to happen?

"Winona, could you give me an idea of what to expect?" Shari asked.

"See you tomorrow at six, dear," Winona said and then disconnected the call.

Shari bit her lip and told Felix what Winona had said.

His hazel eyes widened. "What's going to happen?"

"I don't know. And now I'm kind of nervous."

"Me, too," he said. He took out his phone, called his

uncle and invited him to Shari's place. "She's invited Winona and it's a yes from her." He stared at Shari and crossed his fingers. Shari could just faintly hear Stanley's reply, peppered with Spanish, coming from the phone. Felix was listening and listening. "I know… Yes…No…Yes, I know. But will you come?" More Spanish. More listening. "Yes, but will you come, Tio? Tomorrow at six?" More listening, then Felix flashed her a thumbs-up and something of a smile. "Oh, good. No, you don't need to bring anything." He rattled off Shari's address. "See you at six."

"Phew," he said. "At least we've got them in the same place at the same time. I feel sort of good about this."

She gave him a commiserating smile. "Me, too. Hopeful."

She wished she could say as much about them.

"What should I make for dinner?" she asked.

"I don't want to put you to any trouble. I'll bring takeout from the Italian restaurant Pastabilities. I know they love that place."

A night when Shari wouldn't have to make herself dinner for one along with Page's little bowl of Fancy Feast? Oh, yeah—she was in.

"Shall I order you your favorite entrée? Linguini carbonara with a side of garlic bread, right?"

She inwardly sighed that he remembered from the one conversation they'd had about favorites—and at the thought of once again being able to eat all the garlic bread she wanted without worry about kissing afterward. There would be no more kisses with Felix Sanchez. "Exactly that."

"Done," he said. "I already know Winona's favorites because Stanley has talked nonstop about her the past couple of weeks. I know her favorite kind of soda, cocktail, color, songs—you name it."

"Aww, we definitely have to get those two back together. We *have* to, Felix."

He nodded. "We do. But no matter what, thank you, Shari. I don't know what I would do without you."

You're going to find out, though, aren't you? And you're okay with that.

She turned away before her eyes could get as misty as they felt. And when he left, she watched him go and really did think the heaviness of her heart would tip her over any second.

AT 5:30 P.M. THE next night, Shari set the table in her dining nook, opting for pretty candlesticks that wouldn't obstruct anyone's view of the other guests. Felix was bringing the food, Uncle Stanley insisted on bringing his favorite dessert, tres leches cake, and Winona was bringing a bottle of both red and white wines. That left Shari to be a very free hostess who could concentrate on the room—the emotions, the expressions, the conversation.

At five forty-five, she went into the bedroom to check herself out in the full-length mirror in the corner. She wore one of her favorite dresses—the one with the circles and squares that had accompanied her to Felix's house that night she'd spent in his bedroom. That seemed very long ago. This time she didn't pair it with the book necklace that Felix had liked so much. Instead, she went with her horseshoe pendant since horseshoes were all about good luck. She pushed her glasses up on her nose, smoothed back an errant curl, and sent up a silent prayer for the best for tonight.

For the happiness of a very dear elderly couple.

The buzzer rang. It was Felix. She opened the door and almost gasped at how good he looked. He always did, but something about him tonight, in a dark green sweater and dark pants, black leather shoes, and the black leather jacket she found so sexy, had her absolutely rapt for a moment. In one hand he held a bouquet of roses, white, pink and red, and in the other a huge bag containing their meal. Page came over to rub against his pants leg and he reached down to pet her.

Unless she was imagining it, his gaze lingered on her dress. "You wore that the night we sat next to each other at Doug's," he said.

She nodded, but didn't respond. She'd rooted around in her closet for what to wear tonight, this important occasion, and the moment her eyes hit the dress, she knew it was the one. That night had been magical in its own way. The dress would always be special to her, always remind her of Felix. To the point that she probably wouldn't wear it again after tonight.

"The flowers are so beautiful, thank you," she said, taking the bouquet into the kitchen to put them in a vase. She knew they weren't for her, but for the dinner itself.

He followed her inside and put the bag from the Italian restaurant on the counter, then started removing containers. "They're for you," he said as if he could read her mind. "The flowers. Just my way to say an extra thank-you for doing this. Helping me out. Helping out Stanley. And Winona."

"Of course," she said. "Love is everything."

Did he wince? Or had she imagined that?

"How did Stanley seem today?" she hurried to ask as she took out plates and bowls and a basket for the Italian bread.

"Down in the dumps." Felix's shoulders slumped. "I called him a couple times to check in, but he didn't say more than two words."

"Poor Stanley. I can't bear to even imagine that sweet, vibrant man sad for one second. We've got to get him and Winona back together."

He nodded. "I'm just not sure how."

By taking a risk yourself, Felix Sanchez. That's how. By showing Stanley that the great-nephew he loves so much is willing to give someone his heart. "Let's see where the conversation goes."

When the buzzer rang again, Felix went to the door while Shari ladled out the food onto plates and bowls and brought out the dishes to the table. The redolent food was still steaming.

"Stairs can't best me," Winona said, stepping onto the landing. She wore a purple coat with silver trim and silver Mary Janes, her white shoulder-length hair gleaming. Stanley was behind her, looking dapper in his leather vest and Western shirt, black pants and cowboy boots, a black Stetson on his head.

Shari grinned. "They get me when I have to run back up when I forget something I need, which is always when I'm already blocks away." She held open the door for the two to come in, then took Winona's coat and Stanley's hat, hanging both in the closet. "Welcome. Please have a seat. You and Winona are here and here," she added, pointing to the two chairs on one side of the table.

Felix sat across from his uncle and Shari took the seat across from Winona.

Winona glanced down at her plate. "Oh, goodie. I just love spaghetti Bolognese." She twirled a forkful. "Mmm, just delicious. Did you know that Stanley took me to the Italian restaurant for our first date?" She put her fork down and looked at Stanley. "I sure do miss you, Stanley."

Stanley pushed his chicken piccata around on his plate and sheepishly glanced up at Winona, his expression so sad.

Shari glanced at Felix. He seemed to be searching for just the right thing to say.

"I know that my uncle misses you too, Winona," Felix said. "This whole thing is my fault."

Stanley sat like a rock, eyes downcast, his expression glum.

"What do you mean, dear?" Winona asked.

"I tried to explain to Stanley that just because I'm not ready for a relationship doesn't mean *he's* not ready," Felix said. "Clearly, he is ready." He tried for a smile, looking between Winona and Felix.

Stanley shook his head. "Oh, it's not about being ready."

"Isn't it?" Felix asked.

"It's about being unwilling to go through the heartache again," Stanley said. "Who can handle that more than once? Not me. Not you, Felix—and now I understand. I'm sorry I tried to fix you up with all those women I ran into in the supermarket. What a fool I was. No one needs to go through what we both went through twice."

"Are you saying I should never date again?" Felix

asked, staring intensely at his uncle. "That doesn't sound like you."

"It doesn't sound like the old me," Stanley explained. "The new me knows better now. Better to be like you. You always say you have your work and your family. I have my family and my salsa. And my mariachi and the weekly true crime podcast I like." He looked up at Winona. "I'm so sorry. You're such an amazing woman. But this is what I need to do. I admire my grand-nephew and how he lives his life. I'm going to follow his lead. And be alone."

"But, Tio," Felix said.

All eyes swung to him.

"But what?" Stanley asked.

Felix sat up straighter and looked pointedly at Stanley. "You don't want me to ever have another relationship? Ever? Because that's what you're saying."

Stanley shrugged. "Well, maybe just with women you're not really interested in. No one you'd fall for. Like Shari. I mean, that's why you're not a couple, right? You like her too much."

Felix glanced at Shari. "I do like her. Very much."

"I know," Stanley said, cutting a piece of his chicken piccata. "That's why you decided you can't have a romantic relationship with her. It's too much. The potential heartache."

Felix tilted his head. "*Potential* is the key word there, though. Potential means maybe, not definitely."

"But then why aren't you and Shari a serious couple?" Stanley asked.

Now it was Felix who was staring at his plate. "Because... I'm not ready."

"For?" Winona asked, her dark gaze on his.

"A relationship," Felix finally said.

Winona took a piece of Italian bread from the basket. "May I ask why?"

"Because…" Felix stammered a bit, clamped his lips shut, then responded. "Because of what Stanley just said. Who needs to go through that heartache again?"

"So you *are* ready for a relationship," Winona said. "You just don't ever want to feel the way you did when you lost your wife. Is that right?"

Felix looked at Winona, then at Stanley, then back to Winona. "I don't want to feel that way. No. And to avoid feeling that way ever again, I don't date."

"Except you kind of dated Shari," Winona said.

"Kind of," Shari added—unnecessarily.

Felix gave something of a nod. "But we realized a romantic relationship wasn't right for either of us. I'm not…in the market. And Shari has hopes for her future that I can't give her."

She felt the weight of sadness in his words and wanted to cover his hand with hers, show him some support, but she took a sip of wine instead.

"Ah, but you just told Stanley he shouldn't hang his hat on the word *potential*," Winona put in. "You don't know you'd feel that same heartache. Nothing is guaranteed—we all know that. I mean, I suppose Stanley knows that I won't be around forever. I plan to live until I'm one hundred and twelve, by the way."

Stanley brightened.

"At Doug's," Winona said, staring at Felix, "when you and Stanley came to my table for a reading, I said your life was an open book, but there was nothing there for me to read. That's not the case anymore."

Now Shari felt herself brighten. Not that she under-

stood what Winona meant exactly. But it sounded like
back then, everyone knew Felix Sanchez was a widower who didn't date—*open book, nothing to read
here, folks.* But now, he'd opened up his life a bit to
include Shari, even if it was just pieces, false starts.
They'd made love twice. That was big for Felix. He'd
let her inside and then needed to shut her out. Except
for the safety of friendship. And Shari had been the
one unable to handle that. Felix's life had changed. He
was changing. And change did not come easy.

"You can?" Felix asked—warily. "What do you
see?"

Winona narrowed her gaze on him. She nodded
slowly. Then nodded again. "Oh my."

"Oh my what?" Felix asked.

But Winona returned her attention to her food and
didn't look up at Felix even though he kept trying to
catch her eye.

"What does she mean?" Felix leaned close to Shari
and whispered. "'Oh my'?"

"I'm not sure," Shari whispered back. *Oh my* could
mean anything.

Once everyone had pushed their plates up a bit, just
crumbs left, Stanley stood up. "This was a mistake.
I'm sorry, Winona. But Felix is right. I adore you, but
I can't see you anymore. I just can't risk it. I can't lose
again. I'm so sorry," he added, tears misting in his dark
brown eyes. He turned to Felix and Shari. "Please see
Winona home. It's just too painful for me to be around
her anymore." Then he rushed out the door, forgetting his hat.

Winona's eyes filled up with tears. She stood. "I'd
like to go home."

Shari glanced at Felix, about to burst into tears herself. "We'll take you right now."

Felix stood. "I feel so bad. Just terrible. This isn't what I wanted. This wasn't how it was supposed to go."

"Like I said, nothing comes with a guarantee," Winona said to Felix. "Tonight proved that. But at least you tried. Trying is all we can do."

"Can I wrap up the cake for you?" Shari asked Winona.

"Oh, yes, please," Winona said. "My heart is broken and the cake will make me think of Stanley and tonight, but I like reminders of my deepest feelings. It means I feel. That I care. That I love. And that's everything. Even after all I've been through."

Shari glanced at Felix, hoping Winona's beautiful pronouncement would get through. But he just looked upset, stony, his hazel eyes downcast.

Now what?

CHAPTER SIXTEEN

SHARI AND FELIX walked Winona to the home she shared with her daughter and granddaughter and she hurried inside and practically closed the door in their faces. Felix let out a groan. That wasn't a good sign. Not that anything tonight had been, but he'd been hoping she'd have some wisdom to impart. That she knew something they didn't.

Shari sighed as a lock clicked from inside. "She's had enough of us, for sure."

"Yeah," he said. "We didn't exactly fix anything." He leaned his head back and stared up at the dusky sky. "I wish I knew how to get through to Stanley."

"You could always take your own advice," she said as they walked toward his SUV.

"That advice applies to Stanley, not to me."

Shari put her hands on her hips. "So you really think it's better for you and only you to be on your own than with someone you have strong feelings for because you know you could lose that person at any minute?"

"Why risk it, Shari? And it's not like *I'm* deciding this."

She stopped walking. "What? Who is, then?"

"I mean," he said, "that it doesn't feel like a choice I'm making. It's just the way I feel. Here," he said, slamming his palm against his chest.

"Fight for me," she said, lifting her chin, her eyes blazing. "Fight for me and fight for Stanley's happiness."

"What?" he asked.

"That's right. Fight for me, Felix. If you have strong feelings for me, if you want me in your life, if I'm special to you, if for the first time since your loss you feel something big, then fight for me. For us. And in doing so, you'll be giving your uncle a gift. Love. Winona. And the peace that comes from knowing that his beloved grand-nephew is happy."

He turned away, looking out toward the stand of trees across the street. "Maybe a few days away from his love will make Stanley realize he can't bear to be apart from Winona. He has to come to that himself."

"It hasn't worked for you," she said, her voice heavy. "And that's how I know it *is* a choice you're making. You're deliberately shutting me out of your life to protect yourself. And I do understand why, Felix. You went through absolute hell. But we found each other. You might not have been looking for me, but there I was, there *we* were, and what's between us has a life of its own."

The neckline of his sweater felt like it was squeezing him. His ears were clogged. His chest was tight, the muscles of his shoulders bunching. He looked at Shari, this beautiful, wonderful woman who did have him all turned around, but he...couldn't. "I'm sorry, Shari. I know I keep saying that. But I am sorry."

"No, I'm the one who's sorry. And Stanley and Winona. You're just...stuck. And you want to stay stuck."

With that, she turned and walked with slumped shoulders to his SUV, getting in the passenger side.

He got in too and started the engine. "Shari—"

"Unless you're going to tell me that you've had enough of being stuck, of turning away the most fundamental thing in the world, I don't want to hear it. You heard what Winona said. There are no guarantees in life. But can you tell me you would rather not have loved and lost than never have loved at all?"

He didn't say anything. He started the car and pulled away, driving in silence.

He'd hurt Shari. He'd hurt his uncle and Winona.

He'd hurt himself.

And there was nothing he could do about it.

AFTER A TERRIBLE night's sleep, Felix threw off the blanket at the crack of dawn, the sky still a hazy pink-yellow, and figured he'd make a cup of coffee, then go ask his uncle the question that had been bothering him all night. When he entered the kitchen, he found Stanley working on his salsa. But there was no pep in his step as there usually was when he made salsa. No mariachi music. His shoulders seemed slumped, his face more lined. Or maybe it was just the unusual sight of his uncle's heavy frown. Stanley Sanchez was a smiler. Except lately.

Thanks to Felix.

Stanley didn't even have the energy to say good morning. He just gave Felix a nod and pointed at the coffeemaker, which was full.

Felix got out a mug and poured a cup, adding cream and sugar. "Uncle Stanley, let me ask you something," he said, leaning against the counter on the other side of the chopping board where Tio was hard at work on tomatoes.

"Okay." Chop, chop, chop.

"Do you believe it's better to have loved and lost than never to have loved at all?" Felix asked.

Stanley turned to him and put down his knife. "What kind of question is that? Of course I do."

Felix slugged down half the mug of coffee. "I'm not sure I can say the same."

Stanley Sanchez let out a string of curses in Spanish, waving his hands in the air. To the point that Felix's parents had come rushing out of the rooms in their bathrobes and were halfway down the stairs, stopping when they saw Felix was with Stanley. They stayed put, clearly wanting to eavesdrop on whatever Felix had said to make his uncle so upset.

He was doing that a lot these days.

"Let me ask *you* something, Felix," his uncle said angrily. "Given what you went through—starting with Victoria's diagnosis. The loss of your dreams to start a family. The knowing that she was going to die. The year of hell while she fought. And then the night you had to say goodbye to the woman you'd spent half your life with. Your wife. Your heart and soul. Given all that, would you rather have never known Victoria? Never loved her?"

"Of course not!" Felix ground out. "What kind of question is that?"

"What do you think you just asked me?" Stanley said. "What do you think we're talking about?"

Felix froze. He stared at his uncle, something inside Felix clicking—as if he suddenly understood.

He wouldn't have given up his life with Victoria to have avoided the pain of losing her. Of course he wouldn't have.

And he shouldn't give up his chance for happiness with Shari out of fear—which had had a death-grip on him—that he could lose her, too.

He would rather *love*.

He *did* love. He loved Shari Lormand. With everything he was. With all his heart.

"Oh, my God, Tio," he said. "I didn't understand. I've always known that phrase. Everyone knows that phrase. But I never really thought about it until just now. I didn't even think about it last night when Shari threw it at me."

"Threw it?" Stanley said, shaking his head. "She asked you the right question, but you didn't have the answer. Now you do."

He remembered going silent right afterward, turning away. Starting the car and dropping her off. Everything in him stagnant. Nothing.

"I would rather have loved and lost than never have loved at all," Felix said, grabbing his uncle into a fierce hug. *I would*, he thought.

Stanley hugged him back hard. Felix could hear his mother crying—her happy tears—and his father whispering that everything was going to be okay now.

Maybe everything was.

"I get it now, Uncle Stanley. I finally get it."

"I'll believe it when I see you and Shari together. I'll know it by your faces if you said what that woman needs to hear you say."

Felix smiled. "I'm going, I'm going."

He just hoped that Shari would listen. That he wasn't too late.

"Wait," Stanley said with a wistful gleam in his eye. "Come with me first." Stanley turned and headed toward his room. "There's something I want you to have. Just in case it's the right time."

Felix glanced at his parents still on the stairs, and they hurried down, wiping their tears, and following him, their curiosity clear on their faces.

And thirty seconds later, peering into Stanley's room as he handed Felix something very special, they both gasped, their hands over their hearts.

"WHAT DO YOU THINK, PAGE?" Shari asked, holding up her black sweater dress and her tweed pantsuit.

Page walked onto Shari's foot and sat down, half on her toes and half on the rug in front of her closet. How Shari managed to laugh, given how utterly awful she felt, was something. But that was a pet for you. Pure joy. She scooped up the kitten and snuggled her.

"The black sweater dress, it is. I am mourning something, so it's fitting, right? Right." She slid the dress over her head, the medium-weight soft wool instantly comforting. She'd add her book necklace to liven it up. Maybe her black suede knee-length boots since the forecast didn't call for rain and it was getting cool enough for boots finally.

She put on the necklace, which instantly reminded her of Felix. She'd worn it the night she'd sat down beside him in Doug's. The night he'd switched places so he'd be closer to the haunted barstool. The night he'd been ditched by his wily great-uncle who'd left with a date. The night he'd had a little too much to drink and she'd driven him home. The night they'd kissed and fooled around to the point that she'd been down to her bra and underwear—and he'd been in those incredibly sexy boxer briefs. The night she'd been trapped in his room till morning.

The night that had started it all.

He'd told her how much he liked her book necklace.

And now that it was around her neck, the colorful little ceramic books against the black wool, Felix's face flashed into her mind, and she felt a pang in her chest so sharp she staggered backward and had to find the edge of the bed to sit down. And breathe.

She could so vividly picture Winona taking the tres leches cake home with her the night that her own love had turned his back on their love. What had she said? *My heart is broken...but I like reminders of my deepest feelings. It means I feel. That I care. That I love. And that's everything.*

Oh, Winona. You are so right. You've been right all along. I did show Felix who I was and that was all I could do. Same for you.

Today she would call Winona and invite her to lunch. Two gals with heavy hearts. Broken hearts. Getting through.

Her phone pinged.

Shari's eyes widened when she saw it was Winona Cobbs.

The diner has my favorite kind of quiche on special today. Lunch at 1. If you're free.

Shari stared at the text, then looked at Page and held out the phone to the kitten. "Do you see this? I'm not imagining it, right? The woman really is psychic."

She texted back that she loved all quiche and would see her there at one.

Oh, goodie, Winona typed back with a smiley face emoji.

The front door buzzed, and Shari practically jumped. She didn't get many visitors at barely eight in the morning.

"Maybe it's Winona," she told Page. "She definitely is gifted so she knows I'm really sad and she's come to give me a hug. Not that Winona seems the hugging type."

She went to the door and pressed the intercom. "Hello?"

"It's Felix."

Felix. Here. Very early. If he was bringing her coffee and a scone, she'd throw it at him. The scone, not the coffee. If he was going to apologize, she'd... She'd interrupt him and tell him she knew he was sorry, so was she, and they should start going their separate ways immediately because if they didn't, she'd burst into tears and she'd just put on her makeup for work. She'd cry on and off all day, no doubt, but now she didn't want Felix Sanchez's last memory of her to be her looking like a raccoon.

Shari opened the front door and he was right there, as if he'd jogged up. He looked...energized. Not like a man here to apologize. He also didn't have coffee or a bag from Bronco Java and Juice.

"You're the literary one here," he said, "So I did have to look up the quote you asked me last night— about whether I think it's better to have loved and lost than never to have loved at all. Turns out Alfred, Lord Tennyson, nineteenth-century English poet, says it is. And I do, too. My answer is yes, Shari."

She felt her mouth slightly open in surprise.

"I'm not the same guy I was last night. My uncle had to knock some sense into me. You should hear that man curse in Spanish."

She smiled, but it didn't last long because her heart was still hovering between *please be here to say you love me* and *what if he's here to say he gets it now, but he's still not ready*? He'd be ready for the next woman—like her ex had been.

"I knew you were special that first night at Doug's. That there was something so big between us. But I couldn't get out of my head, out of my own way. I got used to my life being one way. But then how I feel about you blew that out of the water."

"How do you feel?" she asked.

"I love you. I love you so much, Shari."

She couldn't help the gasp that slipped between her lips. Everything she'd longed to hear, to believe, had just come out of his mouth.

"I can't live my life being afraid of risk and loss," he said. "Thank you for showing me that." He took her hand and held it, an electric current zapping up her arm.

This was real. This was happening.

"I want to give you everything you dream of, Shari. I want us to have that dream together. I *am* ready. I was ready the minute we sat down on those stools and shared those chicken wings. I just didn't know it."

"I'm pretty sure Winona did," Shari said with a smile."

Felix laughed. "Yes, both of them. And someone else. My great-uncle Stanley. He knew."

"He definitely knew," Shari agreed with a smile.

"I love you," he said. "And if I'm not too late, if

I haven't driven you away, I'd like to show you how much." He got down on one knee, Page instantly jumping on that knee. "Excuse me, Page, if you don't mind, I'm trying to do something here."

Shari was too much in shock to speak or move. She kept her gaze on Felix's face, which was equally serious and tender.

He reached into the pocket of his black leather jacket and pulled out a small black velvet box. When he opened it, Shari's hand flew to her mouth.

"My uncle gave me this ring. It was the diamond ring he proposed to Celia with sixty years ago."

Shari's eyes filled with tears. "It's so beautiful. And so symbolic of everything love is."

"Will you marry me, Shari?"

"Yes!" she whispered and then dropped to her knees and threw her arms around him, knocking them—and the kitten—over. "I love you too, Felix. So much."

"And it turns out that this is the way to get my uncle and Winona back together. He wants proof that I've seen the light. This ring on your finger and the happiness on our faces will do the job."

She held up her left hand, the exquisite diamond ring twinkling on her finger. This might feel like a dream for days to come. Shari knew she'd be floating around Bronco, floating around the library.

She leaned close and kissed him and he kissed her back with all the pent-up love and passion that had been brewing for weeks.

"Let's go to your house right now," she said. "As another famous saying goes, I want forever to start right away."

"Me, too," he said, pulling her into an embrace. He

pulled back to look at her. "Including starting a family. A baby."

Shari gasped. "I love you so much, Felix Sanchez."

"I love you, too," he said and kissed her all the way up to the bedroom.

WHEN FELIX AND SHARI arrived at the Sanchez home, the house was quiet. His parents had both left for work, and Felix didn't see Stanley or hear him humming or singing. His great-uncle had helped change his entire world, and Felix couldn't wait to show him his ring on Shari's finger. The shooting star was in that ring—both of them. Love was in the ring. The future was in the ring.

Felix understood now.

"Maybe he's out back," Felix said as they moved through the living room.

It was a beautiful late September morning. Bright blue skies, seventy degrees and just a hint of humidity to remind them all of summer. He held Shari's hand as they headed toward the sliding glass doors, open to let the warm breezy air flow though the screens. He glanced at the ring again—the ring that symbolized everything he felt for Shari Lormand.

As they were about to turn the corner, Felix could hear Stanley's voice. He was outside on the deck with Winona. They were seated on chaises, facing toward the yard, a carafe of coffee and a plate of crumb cake between them.

"My sneaky plan worked on that stubborn nephew of mine," Stanley was saying. "If you hadn't been so sure, I wouldn't have been able to go through with it.

I didn't want to even pretend that I had said goodbye to you, Winona."

Felix gasped, something he rarely did.

Two lined faced turned toward the sound.

"Busted," Winona said, her expression ever neutral.

Stanley stood up and put out his hand for Winona; she stood up, too. "Okay, you caught us, you two. But Felix, I wasn't pretending when I told you about the shooting star. I was conflicted and worried that day. Talking to you about that, being honest with Winona about it, helped me understand what I was feeling. But if you think I'd follow your lead to be alone when I have this amazing woman in my life, you're *loco*!"

They all burst into laughter, Winona reaching up on tiptoe to kiss Stanley on his cheek.

"I had to help you understand, Felix," Stanley added. "Forgive me?"

Felix pulled his uncle into a hug. "Forgive you? I *owe* you," he said. "Both of you," he added, smiling at Winona.

"Well, Felix," Shari said with a grin, "we were played, but *well* played."

He laughed and shook his head. "I should have known."

"I did," Winona said, dry as can be. "Oh, and by the way, your ring is beautiful, Shari. Congratulations."

Shari's eyes misted with happy tears. She held up her left hand. Stanley wrapped his arms around her and welcomed her to the family.

"Well, we're finally going apple picking," Winona said. "You two have the house to yourself this morning." Hand in hand, the two left, all smiles at their hard work.

Felix picked up his fiancée and carried her upstairs to his room.

"We never finished what we started here that very first night," he said, laying her down on his bed and touching the little red book on her necklace.

One night that had changed his entire life and given him everything.

* * * * *